THE REVERSE COMMUTE

by

Sheila Blanchette

Cover Design by Steve Davidson

Photo by Sheila Blanchette

Book Shepherd Publishing, LLC.

ACKOWLEDGEMENTS

I have so many friends and family to thank.

First and foremost, I would like to thank my book shepherd and dear friend Sandy Staines. She was there every step of the way, from the time I told her my idea and she said I had a home run to the actual publication of the book. I could never have done this without her. Also, thanks to her very patient and understanding husband Michael.

My sister, Maureen Stabile, for reading the very early drafts and giving me sage advice on dreams and flying turkeys. My nephew, Nick Stabile, for devoting an evening of editing and tequila to straightening me out on my prepositional phrase problem and telling me to crush that beach chair.

My good friend, Liz McConnell, who also read the early drafts. You have always been a shoulder to lean on.

Mary Jane Doughty, thanks for the title advice, Mardi Gras and more stories to come.

Liza Jones, my editor, for getting the ball rolling and all the great input. To Freddie Templeton for being on call in Vermont. And to all my beta-readers who gave me positive input and encouragement. You kept me going even when I thought this was an impossible dream.

To Rich, there is a light at the end of tunnel.

Kathy, you are my guardian angel and you are always with me.

And special mention to Jason Matthews, author, and his book, "How to Make, Market and Sell Ebooks All for Free". He is the guru for Indie Authors, and without his advice, we wouldn't be here.

"You come to love not by finding the perfect person, but by learning to see an imperfect person perfectly." —Sam Keen

ROSE: "Do you love him, Loretta?"
LORETTA CASTORINI: "Aw, ma, I love him awful."
ROSE: "Oh, God, that's too bad."

—from the movie Moon Struck

THE REVERSE COMMUTE

She met the Best Boy on the train heading home from work one evening, having almost missed the five fifteen train that day. She worked on the North Shore and lived in Boston with her college boyfriend. A reverse commute.

It had been a particularly slow and tedious day in her cubicle. When it had finally reached its long awaited conclusion, she had not completed the daily requirement of editing five articles. Rushing through the last piece, she realized it was sloppy work. She was sure she would hear about it tomorrow after her boss then edited her work.

As she came out of the office building, it was dark and snow was falling, starting to pile up quickly. White mushroom caps were growing on the roofs of the cars in the parking lot. Several people were sweeping snow off their windshields as they waited for the windows to defrost, their headlights sparkling on the freshly fallen snow.

Dan came running up behind her. He was thirty years old, handsome with golden brown hair, blue eyes and a scruffy beard neatly trimmed to look like stubble. He was engaged to be married. He and his fiancé were planning a destination wedding at a resort in the Bahamas in June, sixteen months from now. She thought this very odd, to plan a wedding so far in advance. Who knew what could happen between now and then? There was an awful lot of wiggle room in such a long engagement. But she thought, maybe that's just me. Engagement was a commitment after all, right?

Dan grabbed her arm and shouted "Come on we've got to catch that train. Otherwise we'll be waiting in the pub for an hour."

"Did you know it was going to be snowing like this?" she asked him.

"Yeah, I watched the weather last night. Six to twelve inches by tomorrow morning."

"I guess I heard that too. I forgot about the snow after spending the day on cubicle alley. It was so busy today. I ate my peanut butter sandwich at my desk and never once looked out a window. But if you asked me what it was I did for eight hours, I couldn't tell you. Certainly not anything of value. Besides the fact I've been nursing a hangover all day."

"I know, it sucks doesn't it?"

They ran through the snow, occasionally slipping and holding onto each other. This wasn't that easy, as Dan had a laptop on his shoulder and she was carrying her purse and a canvas bag over a heavy winter coat, which caused the bag to keep slipping off her shoulder and getting caught up with her purse and Dan's laptop.

As they raced across another parking lot the traffic lights at the railroad crossing started flashing red and the bells were ringing. They could see the red and white gate lowering to stop traffic and the train's headlights off in the distance. The platform was about a football field away.

Dan grabbed her hand, laughing. "Come on, we're gonna make it. Holy shit! Look at all those people waiting. Have you ever seen this many people waiting for the five fifteen?"

"No, never. Where are they all going?" she wondered.

"Must be the snow. Everyone wants to get home," Dan replied.

They ran up the steps to the platform as the train came to a stop. They were both winded. Dan bent over and put his hands on his knees, taking deep breaths. As he exhaled out he coughed and made a cloud like he'd just taken too big of a hit off a joint.

She leaned her head back and let the snowflakes fall on her face as she tried to steady her breathing. Her long brown hair was wet. Small stray curls framed her face and her cheeks were flushed and rosy. She was pretty in a pleasantly attractive way. Friends would often describe her as the cute best friend or younger sister type of girl. Her parents would describe her as the girl next door. She was approachable, guys always flirted with her at work and in bars.

"You've gotta stop smoking those cigs Dan."

"I know. Next week I'm back off them. Just had to finish month end. Too much stress in the accounting department at month end to try quitting right now."

After just making it to the train, they got onto the first car that pulled up in front of them. Most of the seats were taken. As they passed the first empty one, Dan told her to take it.

"I'll see you tomorrow."

"Oh yeah. Same time, same place. See ya Dan."

She took the seat next to a heavy-set girl with a baby in her lap. The baby was sleeping against the girl's large, swollen breasts. The young mother seemed to be roughly the same age as her, twenty four. Chewing gum and occasionally snapping it loudly, she stared sullenly at the businessman across from her who was working on his laptop.

As she squeezed into her seat she bumped legs with the boy directly across from her. He looked up and she caught her breath. He was exceptionally good looking in a Seattle grunge sort of way. Definitely her type. He had long wavy brown hair to his shoulders topped with a knitted green, yellow and black cap and a scruffy beard similar to Dan's just not as neatly trimmed. He was wearing an open, untucked flannel shirt over a Blazed and Confused Summer Tour T-shirt, faded jeans and well-worn work boots. His eyes were a beautiful shade of light blue. As he looked up and smiled at her, they seemed to twinkle like the first star in the night sky.

He was listening to his IPod just loud enough for her to make out the music. It was a reggae song and he was nodding his head and drumming his hands on his thighs to the beat. Occasionally he sang along softly to the music, oblivious to the fact that anyone might hear him.

The train blew its horn and pulled out of the station. She reached over, tapped his knee and when he looked up again, she mouthed the words, "I love that song." He pulled his ear-phones out and smiled the biggest, most charming smile that had ever been directed at her.

HOME FROM THE PICNIC

It was a warm beautiful evening in late summer. A silver Hyundai with a dent on the front bumper pulled into the long driveway of an old house. On the back bumper was an Obama for NH sticker and the Dave Matthews silver fire dancer, a headless woman dancing with her arms in the air and one knee bent. At the end of the driveway, there was a barn to the right and to the left a dilapidated garage with no door. Between the barn and the garage were piles of fire-wood, an axe stuck in a chopping block, ladders stacked up in two neat rows and a rusted wheelbarrow. An army of sumac soldiers marched out of the pine trees as if planning an attack on the yard.

The Hyundai pulled into the two car garage fighting for space with workbenches piled high with tools, paint cans and dirty rags. Drop cloths were neatly folded on the floor. There was a table saw with mounds of sawdust beneath. An old dresser was to the left of the car with a beach chair resting against it.

Sophie was only five feet tall and in her late forties. She had tousled blonde hair and wore no makeup, which some-how worked for her, and was fairly attractive for her age but in a very harried and distracted sort of way. As she opened the car door, she bumped into the dresser and knocked over the beach chair. She shouted out loud. "Shit!"

She leaned over to the passenger seat, grabbed her laptop, pocketbook, the mail and a half full cup of coffee from the center console. The coffee had a skim of curdled cream float-ing on the top. She struggled to get out of the car juggling all these things, spilled some coffee on herself and shouted out loud again. "Shit! Shit! Damn it!"

As she stood up, she kicked the door closed and squeezed by the dresser. At the door into the house, she rested some of her things on an antique milk box. Turning the doorknob, she kicked the door open and walked into her house.

Shoes clogged the doorway and a long farmers table sat in the middle of the room, piled with mail. Sophie dropped the mail she was carrying on the table, adding to the collection. She walked into the kitchen past a stone hearth with a wood burning stove. There were happy family photos on a blue slate sill beneath a bow window looking out onto the backyard.

Pausing for a moment, she gazed wistfully at pictures of her family at the Grand Canyon, on a Caribbean beach and making snowmen in the backyard. Lifting her gaze, she stared off into the distance at another log splitting area set amongst apple trees planted from an old Yankee line but the apples were now full of worms. Weeds and climbing roses grew up the bottom of the trees and tangled their way through the branches. Sumac soldiers were also marching their way into the yard back here and were turning a deeper shade of red as summer would soon be turning into fall.

There was a sitting area grouped around the wood stove. Sophie put the rest of her things on a faded blue recliner and called out "Ray?"

Walking into the living room, she passed the fireplace mantel where another wood stove was tucked into the hearth and high school graduation pictures of her twin boys were displayed. The furniture was homey but well worn. Two large French doors opened onto a deck, which was in desperate need of a drink. The stain was worn and fading. Beyond the deck and at the end of the long yard was the river, the best feature of their property. It was the reason they bought the house in the first place. They both loved the changing view as the seasons passed. The sun was glinting on the water and Sophie could hear the crew coach calling instructions from a bullhorn as two long skulls glided by. In winter, this river would freeze and during a really cold year there could be close to one hundred ice fishing shacks out there. The river was tidal causing the shacks to rise and fall with the tides.

She stepped out onto the deck and called "Ray?"

No one answered so she walked back into the house. In the kitchen, just past the sitting area, the answering machine was blinking. Sophie hit the play button and leaned against the kitchen counter, listening to the message.

"Hello Mrs. Ryan. This is Helen at Central Health. We're calling about a past due balance..."

Sophie sighed and hit the delete button. She walked to the fridge and looked inside for something to make for dinner. There was a bottle of wine on the top shelf, so she grabbed it and poured herself a glass. She walked out to the deck, sat down on a chair sipping her wine and gazed off at the river.

Ray was never around when she needed him. She desperately wanted to talk to someone about what had happened today. She could not fathom going about her daily routine right now. How could she even begin to make dinner and fold the clothes she knew were waiting for her in the dryer?

Despite her glass of wine and the soft light of the sinking sun, she couldn't forget the disaster in the kitchen. Dirty dishes were in the sink and crumbs were scattered across the counter. It looked like the handiwork of Jesse, one of her twin boys. After graduating from college over a year ago, he moved back home while he continued to look for a job. He promised it was only a temporary situation. Now, finally, after fifteen months of searching for a job, he would be moving to Providence next week to work as a baker at a coffee shop. She audibly breathed a sigh of relief.

She took another big sip of wine then leaning her head back, she closed her eyes and felt the warm sun on her face. She imagined herself kayaking down the river through tall river grass and cat o'nine tails, the sun setting in the distance. The sky was ablaze in shades of red and orange.

A heron flew out of its nest and passed by. The only sound was paddles quietly slicing through the water, birds chirping their evening song and the croaking peepers.

* * *

Ray was in his recliner by the doors to the deck. His hair had turned all white but he was very fit thanks to a life of manual labor. His biceps bulged against the tight white T-shirt he was wearing. He was a self-employed house painter and carpenter, a jack-of-all-trades really. He could do electrical work, plumbing, lay tile and fix oil burners and automobiles. A very handy guy to have around an old house like the one they lived in.

Ray had just gotten home, gone straight to the shower and was now eating the sandwich Sophie brought him. She sat down on the couch and started to tell him about her day and the awful accident that happened at her company picnic.

Suddenly Jesse came flying through the room. He had a backpack on his shoulder and was holding car keys dangling from a long strap. He was tall and athletic with long blond hair he had pulled back in a ponytail. He was wearing a Bob Marley T-shirt, long baggie gym shorts past his knees and flip-flops.

He turned to his parents as he rushed by and told them "I'm going out."

Ray had finished his sandwich and had just started to drift off to sleep but opened his eyes and sat up straighter. "Who's driving?"

"I am," Jesse said defiantly.

"I thought I told you no car for the rest of the summer. Every time I get in that car, it reeks of marijuana."

"Yeah well that's stupid Dad. I'm moving out next weekend. There is no rest of the summer. Labor Day is this weekend, so summer's over. It's a ridiculous punishment. Besides

I'm twenty three, you can't punish me anymore. You smoke too man. Oops, I forgot my IPod." He turned and ran back upstairs.

Sophie shot an exasperated look Ray's way. "I told you that would come back to bite you Ray. You think you're all set smoking in the barn, but you reek as much as the car does when you get back in the house. You don't realize the smell clings to you."

"That's not the point."

"No?" She arched her eyebrow at him and shook her head. "It's really funny, he's all grown up at twenty three and thinks he can't be punished, but he also can't clean up the kitchen after making a sandwich. I got home to a huge mess in that kitchen. Are you gonna stop him Ray? It's my car he's planning to take."

Sophie rested her head back on the couch, closed her eyes and thought about her boys. Jesse's twin brother Sean graduated from college last year too, but with honors. He now had a job in Providence with an Internet startup company and lived on the East Side with some college friends.

On the other hand, Jesse barely got through college and had to take Internet summer courses just to graduate on time. He moved back home after graduation and got a job at the bakery he had worked at in high school. He had graduated from working the cash register to learning how to bake. This had led to the job in Providence where, thankfully, he would be living with his brother.

Baking meant he woke up at four in the morning, showered and for some unknown reason ran up and down the stairs numerous times before he left the house. Therefore, Sophie and Ray also woke up at four in the morning. Finishing work at two in the afternoon, he went to bed then woke up at ten P.M. right around the time Sophie and Ray were collapsing into bed after a long day at work. He would bang around the kitchen making food then spend the evenings getting high with friends, hanging at the beach or in the winter just lounging around the house, playing video games and watching TV.

In high school, Jesse was always getting into trouble. He was never a good student and struggled in all his classes. He always hung around with the wrong crowd, drinking and smoking pot. Sophie couldn't help but think his friends' parents also thought Jesse was the wrong crowd. Often defiant, he loved starting arguments with his parents and never wanted to be the first one to back down. 'I'm sorry' was not a part of his vocabulary.

Sophie looked over at her husband, eyes wide open and overwhelmed. "Quick Ray. He's got the keys. Pull the spark plugs or something." Ray was visibly angry but seemed immobilized in the recliner. "Come on Ray, you've got to stop him. Disable the car, for Christ's sake."

They heard Jesse stomping down the stairs. He ran by them. "See ya. I won't be too late.

Thanks!"

Jesse turned the corner, breezed past the farmers table, knocking some mail onto the floor and headed out the door to the garage. Sophie got up and followed him.

"You better not be getting high and driving. What about the bong I found on the deck? That is not your car, by the way."

Meanwhile, Ray was moving slowly out of the recliner. Jesse had already hopped in the car and was backing out of the garage as Ray caught up to Sophie. They both stood there watching their son pull out of the driveway on to the road. Feeling helpless, they watched the taillights disappear into the warm summer night. A fingernail moon left the night dark despite the hundreds of stars blanketing the sky.

Sophie turned to Ray, extremely annoyed. "What on earth were you doing? How could you move so slowly? The nuns in the Sound Of Music moved faster than you for God's sake."

"I'm tired OK? I couldn't think fast enough. It was a back-breaking day and it's been a long summer. He's gone next weekend. I can't take much more of this. Thank God he finally found a job and a place to live. It's been torture having him back here. He graduated from college a year ago for Christ's sake. Grown children aren't meant to live with their parents, OK? I'm tired. Exhausted."

Sophie rolled her eyes in despair. "You have no idea the kind of day I just had."

It was too late to talk about it then, she'd just try to put it out of her mind. If she brought it up now, Ray would just say some trite words of comfort to make her feel better. He often dismissed her fears, swept them under the rug and tried to cheer her up instead of really exploring the root of her worries and anxieties. She was too exhausted to get into it right now and the argument with Jesse had distracted her. She couldn't wrap her mind around the idea that she had witnessed a random, senseless loss of life but when she got home her life and her own problems just picked up where they left off. The kitchen was dirty and needed cleaning. Jesse was willfully acting out and taking the car although he wasn't supposed to. Ray was too tired from a hard day at work to respond to the situation adequately.

Ray had already turned around and walked back into the house. He got a beer from the fridge, went out to the deck and down to the river.

Sophie was still in the driveway looking up at the star strewn sky. She wanted to make a wish but she knew the wish needed to be made on the first star she saw and there were too many in the sky to say which one she saw first. She decided to just skip the first line of the childhood ditty.

"I wish I may, I wish I might, have the wish I wish tonight. Please let Jesse get home safe and sound tonight and every night." She blew a kiss to the whole night sky, thinking that had to work.

Ray was walking through some pine trees near a creek, which ran along the back of the house and into the river. A hammock hung between two tall pines. Tall river grass and cat o' nine tails gently swayed in the warm breeze.

Ray hoisted himself onto the hammock, opened his beer, pitched the cap into the woods and took a long cold swallow.

Reaching into his pocket, he pulled out a small wooden homemade pipe and a Ziploc baggie. With his beer bottle between his legs he loaded the pipe, found a lighter in his other pocket and lit it. He sat there quietly drinking his beer, smoking and listening to the gurgling of the creek and the peeping and chirping of frogs and insects.

Back in the house, Sophie slowly climbed upstairs to bed, first stopping in the bathroom. An addition was being built off the back of the house. A drop cloth was covering the opening from the old bathroom to the new part of the house. There was an old crank out style window where the house used to end but it now looked into the addition. Looking out the old window, she could see rolls of insulation and pallets of sheet rock cluttered amongst a claw foot tub and other bathroom fixtures. Sophie brushed her teeth and took out her contact lenses, placing them on a shelf that was a jumbled mess of lotions, hair accessories, makeup, and earrings hanging on an old window screen.

She stood for a minute looking through the window into the addition and sighed, then turned and headed to her room. Dropping into bed exhausted, she thought she'd fall asleep in an instant but sleep eluded her. She tossed and turned trying to get comfortable, flipping her pillow several times. Finally giving up, she reached for the remote by the side of the bed and turned on the TV. On one of the cable news shows, several pundits were discussing the impending debt ceiling fight. Sophie groaned and shut the TV off.

Thinking about her company picnic that afternoon, she wondered how she would ever get to sleep tonight. She hoped she wouldn't have nightmares. She wished she'd told Ray right when he got home. She picked up a book and started to read.

Ray came in the bedroom an hour later and saw Sophie sleeping with the light still on. A book was open on her chest. "The Grownups' Guide to Running Away From Home". He picked up the book, put it on the night table, shut off the light and got into bed without waking her.

Later that night at around three A.M., Sophie was awakened by the sound of the train blowing its whistle in the distance as it approached the tracks across the river from her house. She lay there for a moment then remembered Jesse had gone out that night. She got up and headed down the hall, walking through the bathroom into the addition where Jesse's bedroom was. She could hear the fan blowing behind his closed door. Ever since he was a little boy, he needed the fan on, even in the dead of winter. The white noise helped him sleep. Although she knew he must be in there, she quietly opened the door and peeked in to make sure he was home.

THE COLLEGE BOYFRIEND

She worked in the suburbs but lived in Boston, just outside of Cleveland Circle, with her college boyfriend Nick. She met Nick at a Halloween party her freshman year. The theme of the party was dead celebrities and she came as Marilyn Monroe. She wore a low cut, sexy white dress with a padded pushup bra, fake diamond necklace and a blonde wig. He was wearing a suit.

He was a little too conservative looking, wearing a suit at a frat party. His hair was close cropped and parted on the side. She thought this haircut was called a 'Boy's Regular'. His face was clean-shaven. However, his brown eyes looked soulful, like a Saint Bernard's. Those eyes made him look very kind. On the other hand, he was much taller than her, which could be awkward. She knew he was not her type but for some reason she was drawn to him. Maybe it was the eyes and his shy smile. Maybe she just needed a new type. "And who are you supposed to be?" she asked.

"Jimmy Stewart in "It's a Wonderful Life."

"Hum. So, George, you're not really good at coming up with costume ideas. Is that what you're saying? You just grabbed a suit and called it a costume?"

He looked puzzled. "My name is Nick not George. Do I look like a George to you?"

"But you're George Bailey tonight, right?" She threw her head back and laughed loudly. "Have you ever actually watched 'It's a Wonderful Life', George? Come on, what's your favorite scene?"

"I've watched it, but it was a long time ago. And you're right. I'm not very good at costumes. I hate Halloween. So I threw on this suit and my roommate came up with the idea of... who is it? George Something or other?"

"George Bailey. My family watches the movie every Christmas. For some reason I have always loved this tiny scene, it actually happens a few times in the movie. George is at the staircase and the knob at the top of the banister keeps coming off in his hands. You know, they live in an old house? There's something very touching about that scene. I find myself drawn to imperfect things. And the fact that they never fix it. I grew up in an old house. And believe it or not, the knob on our newel post was loose too. My Dad was not very handy, so he never fixed it either."

"Vaguely. I remember the scene vaguely. Why wouldn't you want to fix something like that?"

"Hmm. Interesting question. My Dad was a firm believer that we learn more from our mistakes than our successes. I like to think that he left it like that to remind us that no one is perfect. That's what makes us human and realizing that gives you the capacity for empathy. Don't you think?"

"I really don't know. I would have fixed it."

She purred and spoke in her best whispery Monroe like voice while fiddling with his tie. "I know this is going to be hard for you because I don't think you really saw the movie but stay in character George."

She grabbed his hand and dragged him to the living room floor. "Come on, dance with me. Then maybe later tonight I'll tell you the plot of my latest movie. 'Some Like It Hot'? Have you seen that one?"

Later that night they went back to his dorm room. She thought she noticed a look of disappointment when she took off her costume to reveal long brown hair and much smaller breasts. Despite their differences, they quickly became an item and dated the rest of their college years. He seemed, at least for the time being, to be Mr. Right. She had a tendency to live in the moment and wasn't really thinking beyond right then.

He was much more cautious and conventional than her. This was sometimes the source of numerous arguments but most of the time they had a lot of fun. He seemed to like the fact that she was a little unconventional. Dating her was his one act of rebellion.

He had a car and they would go into Boston to Red Sox games and concerts. On Sundays, they would sometimes drive up to Cape Ann with a cooler of beers and a picnic. They would walk the beach and make love behind the sand dunes.

He was majoring in accounting. She was a creative writing major. He quite often asked why she had chosen that major. "What kind of job are you going to get when you graduate?"

"Do you think college is all about getting a job? Shouldn't it be about getting a well-rounded education? Becoming an informed, thoughtful, knowledgeable person?"

"Hey you're the one with school loans. I would think you would be concerned about getting a job and being able to pay them."

"I have more scholarships than loans. I'll only owe about twenty thousand when I graduate which isn't that bad considering other kids' loans. Not everyone's as rich and fortunate as you or did you forget about that?"

"Oh right. I'm dating the smart girl." Then he would kiss her and they would drop the subject.

But before they knew it, four years had flown by and they were soon to be the Class of 2008, whether they were ready or not. Before he had even graduated Nick had landed a job as an auditor for a bank. He credited this to planning ahead and doing an internship his junior year. She, on the other hand, had chosen to study abroad in Paris her junior year and had not been seriously looking for work.

"I am intentionally not planning ahead," she told him. "College is one of the greatest times in our lives so I am living in the moment and enjoying it. Life is short and we will never be here in this time and place again."

He rolled his eyes at her. "Well I'd like us to move into Boston together this summer but you'll need to pay your half of the rent. I can help you rework your resume, give it more of a business angle. And how about I talk to a friend of mine in HR at the bank?"

"I'm a creative writing major, what would I do at a bank?"

"Maybe advertising, promotional writing. The HR department sends out a company newsletter and targeted reading on motivational stuff like 'Becoming a Better Manager' or one I just read, 'Employee Work Passion'. Someone must be writing this stuff, right? What? Why are you looking at me like I have two heads?"

"Do you honestly think that is what I want to write? You haven't even started the job yet and you're already reading their corporate propaganda? Work passion? In a bank? Who are you?"

"Hey I'm just trying to help. You're the one with school loans coming due a few months after we graduate. And it's not propaganda, it's team building."

"Will you stop with the school loans! I think I can come up with two hundred dollars a month even if I'm waitressing. And where did you ever get the idea I would want to play on a team? Have I ever mentioned playing team sports? I was on the school newspaper, remember?"

"Waitressing? Is that your plan? Four years of college and you're going to waitress?"

"No! I am going to write the great American novel. Or the next big Indie screenplay. Maybe work for a newspaper. I'd only be waitressing to pay the bills until I get my first big break. And with this attitude you are not coming to Sundance with me."

They continued to fight and argue the last month of school. Nick was eager to start his illustrious career. His goal was to become the CFO, Chief Financial Officer, of a large corporation. What Nick refused to see was that she wasn't ready for any of that. She had another plan. Her best friend from grade school was moving to Oregon to go to graduate school. Katie wanted her to come along for the drive out West. They would have most of the summer to travel and sightsee. They planned to hike the Grand Canyon, Bryce Canyon and any other canyon between Boston and Portland while also visiting the big cities along the way like Chicago, Denver and Las Vegas.

They would zig zag their way to Oregon and 'see the U.S.A. in their Chevrolet' because Katie was getting a Prius from her parents as a graduation gift. Think of the gas they'd save! They'd camp and cook most of their meals to save money too. They planned to travel the entire summer for about a thousand dollars. It was the opportunity of a lifetime!

She finally told him about her plans the week before graduation. Nick was pissed and not very keen on the idea at all. "Wasn't junior year in Paris the opportunity of a lifetime?"

"Yes, but if you're lucky you get many opportunities in life and you need to pursue them."

"You should be pursuing a job not a camping trip."

"Who are you? My father? I need experiences to write about."

Nick scoffed. "Your crazy father would tell you to go to Oregon with Katie. Listen, I can't promise you I will want you to move in when you get back."

"That's fine. I'm not sure I want to settle down into that kind of relationship anyway. I'm not ready for all of that commitment. Maybe I'll want to stay in Oregon for a while. Or head south to L.A. It is the place to be if you're trying to write a screenplay. And by the way, my father is not crazy."

"I think you're making a big mistake."

"Haven't we talked about this? If it is a mistake I will learn from it."

"Why would you purposely set out to make a mistake?"

"I said IF it's a mistake. Right now I don't think it is and I won't know until I try."

"You're just wasting time. You're avoiding responsibility."

"I absolutely don't see it as a waste of time. It's something I need to do. Hey! Steve Jobs quit college and backpacked through India, didn't he? Tripping on acid no less! And look where he is now. Stay hungry. Stay foolish. Right?" She left for Oregon the week after graduation.

SQUIRRELS IN THE BATHROOM

It was six in the morning, mid-September, several weeks after the picnic and the alarm went off in Sophie and Ray's bedroom. Sophie moaned, lay there a few minutes then got up and walked down the hall to the bathroom. Turning on the shower, she sat on the toilet waiting for the water to warm up. They had a well and it usually took a few minutes. She looked through the window into the addition and saw three squirrels running across the rafters.

"Holy shit! God damn it!"

She jumped off the toilet, pulled the drop cloth a little tighter at the opening to the addition and hopped in the shower. She washed quickly, every once in awhile peeking out from behind the shower curtain. As she quickly rinsed the shampoo from her hair she closed her eyes and whispered breathlessly, "I love my life. I love my life. If a squirrel runs in here I will definitely have a heart attack. Life is good. Life is good. That's what the T-shirt says, right?"

Ray was downstairs in the kitchen making coffee. After her quick shower, Sophie was back in the bedroom, making the bed while watching TV. The news was still about the debt ceiling crisis. Congress would not approve raising the debt ceiling and the government might shut down again. How nice would that be she thought, to simply say 'I don't like how things are going here so I'm shutting work down.' As a matter of fact, she'd like to shut down work today and stay home. She had a million other things she needed to take care of, not the least of which was squirrels in her house. She turned off the TV and ran downstairs.

In the kitchen, Sophie poured herself a cup of coffee and started making lunches. Ray was sitting at the table eating a bowl of cereal with bananas and drinking coffee. "Hey Ray? There are three squirrels in the addition."

"There are what?"

"I saw three squirrels running across the rafters in what should be the master bathroom."

"Damn. I thought I'd heard something in there the past few nights. It's probably that bastard who kept climbing up the bay window here. I think they're entering under the soffit at the back of the house."

"You know these squirrels? You saw these guys crawling up the back of the house?"

"Well I didn't see them entering the house. I suspected they were but I didn't know for sure. I did try getting them with the pellet gun the other day." He paused. "I've been watching them."

Sophie rolled her eyes, put her hand on her hip and copped an attitude. "Hmmm, okay. Did ya ever think about closing up the hole below the soffit? I mean you just said that's where you suspect they're getting in."

"Calm down, I've got an idea. A guy I worked with had squirrels in his attic and he's got this strobe light thing that scares them away. It gets them out and after a few days they stop coming back. I'll stop by and get it from him on my way home. I'll take care of it. There are probably babies in there somewhere. We've gotta get them out too. Then I'll fix the soffit once I get them out of there."

"Great! Just great. Oh and by the way, some collection agency has been bugging me about a copay for Central Health that I know I already paid. I am so sick of dealing with these idiots. I do this all day at work, Ray. People who don't know why I sent them a check, people who don't cash their checks, the check was in my pocket and I washed it in the laundry, I lost my check, the dog ate my check blah, blah, blah. Who are these people? I get a check and I run to the bank because nine times out of ten the money's been spent before I get it there.

Then I have to come home and deal with Central Health who received my check and cashed my check but have turned me over to a collection agency for not paying the bill. But I paid the bill. They just didn't do their job, which would be recording my check that they received. So I have to do their job. I have to find the canceled check, print a copy of the check and send it to them. Maybe I should stop by their office and record it for them. But Ray, you know what the real kicker is? When I was unemployed those fourteen months, I sent them my resume." Pausing to take a deep breath, she began to shout. "Looks like they hired the wrong person! I could be working ten minutes from home, God dammit! Instead I'm doing their job and I'm not on the payroll."

Getting all worked up, she wielded the bread knife in her hand and slapped mayo on the sandwich. She dramatically sliced the sandwich in half, angrily tore a piece of plastic wrap off the roll, wrapped the sandwich and dropped it in the small cooler Ray used as a lunch box. She continued her rant while grabbing a yogurt, a bottled iced tea and an apple from a bowl on the table in front of Ray. As she approached the table to get the apple, Ray ducked and covered his head with his hands, laughing and pretending he was afraid of her. Still chuckling, he got up from the table, brought his bowl to the sink and then poured himself some more coffee.

"When are you getting a check this week? The mortgage is due and the cell phone company has been calling and texting me about a payment that's only two days late. Calling me at work, because they can, they have my number, they're the cell phone company!!!"

"I'll have a check tomorrow. I'm finishing the MacKinnon job today. Why do we have to start every day like this?"

" Because every morning just seems to get better and better. And you know full well this isn't the first time. Remember the squirrel who was running across the beam over there?" She pointed to the wall in the sitting area near the wood stove. "The beam you exposed while you were working on the addition down here? And what about the mother raccoon and her babies in the fireplace? And how many times have we had bats in here? Remember the time you thought you had chased the bat out and closed the bedroom door so I wouldn't know what you were doing? I was laying there in the dark and heard something. When I turned the light on, I saw the bat and screamed bloody murder. Sometimes I think I'm living in a barn."

"Come on, admit it. That was kind of funny. I thought the bat flew back downstairs. I didn't know he was in there."

She sighed. "Oh Ray. Remember you used to live in a barn when we met? The renovated barn in the suburbs with those five other guys? I guess I should've been paying attention to those subtle hints. Foreshadowing, right?"

Sophie sighed loudly, poured another cup of coffee and headed to the door. Ray grabbed her arm as she passed by him. He tried to kiss her cheek but she ducked her head and his lips grazed the top of her head. She pulled away from him and headed out the door. As she got in the car, she pulled the sun visor down. While looking in the mirror on the back of the visor, she ran her fingers through her hair. "Shit! I still have soap in my hair. Fucking squirrels in the bathroom."

She slammed the visor back up and saw Ray standing just outside the doorway. Waving with a sarcastic smile on her face, she backed out of the garage. She heard a crunching sound but kept backing out into the circular driveway and as she shifted the car into forward she noticed the mangled beach chair she had just driven over. Ray watched her leave, shaking his head at the broken chair and looking over-whelmed. As she pulled out of the driveway, she looked at the dashboard panel. It registered forty-five miles to empty. The clock said 7:45.

She thought to herself, "Shit! I'm gonna be late again, sup-posed to be at work in fifteen minutes. That ain't happenin'. I've got a forty-five minute drive ahead of me and I need gas. Well Sophie, you commute forty five minutes to work, you always need gas."

Sophie drove down the road and pulled into the gas station at the end of her street. At the pump, she saw regular gas was up to $3.35 per gallon. Again she had a running dialogue go-ing on in her head. "When did it become okay for gas to be so expensive? For people to just accept this and not fight for lower prices? Where are the patriots who threw tea in Boston Harbor now that we need them again? Oh right, they're the Tea Party." She scoffed out loud. "We'd still be part of England if people behaved like they do now. What did that guy I saw on TV say about Americans? Something like, in the U.S. people are afraid of their government but in France the government is afraid of the people? Someone needs to remind me why Americans hate the French." She rummaged through her pocketbook on the passenger seat. "Damn, no cash."

Pulling out a credit card, she looked at it in distress and seemed to hesitate. Then she shrugged her shoulders and got out of the car. She slid the card through the machine and started to pump the gas. The wind was blowing. Staring off into the distance at the shopping center across the street, she gazed at the stream of cars, trucks and school buses driving down the road. Then holding the pump with one hand, she squatted down to look in the side rearview mirror and tried to fluff her hair with her other hand.

* * *

Sophie was driving down the highway with the radio blaring. She passed a sign that read NH State Liquor Store/Lottery Tickets. She laughed out loud while thinking "Lottery tickets. Yeah, that's what I need. One chance in a billion of solving life's problems. Better off just buying a case of wine." She passed another sign that said 'Entering Massachusetts'. Driving another fifteen minutes, always in the far left lane and going eighty, she sang along to the radio. The clock on the dashboard now said 8:15.

She finally got off the highway at her exit but still had a way to go. She drove through several green lights but then had to stop behind a school bus. Looking at the clock, she drummed her fingers on the steering wheel. One of her favorite songs came on the radio. Turning up the volume, she started to sing. The sun was sparkling behind a white barn at the farm on the hill up ahead. There was a large field of sun-flowers along the road, their happy yellow faces bobbing in the wind.

Sophie was singing really loudly now as she approached the office and the parking lot. There was construction ahead and a large DETOUR sign. Traffic was being directed around the street she usually took and being rerouted through a neighborhood up the hill. Kids with backpacks were standing on corners waiting for the school bus. The clock said 8:25.

As she approached the intersection at the train crossing, the red stoplights started blinking and the bell was clanging. The red and white gate began to lower and she waited, still singing. A few minutes later, the bells clanged again and the gate started to rise. She finally pulled into the parking lot of the office building where she worked. She shut off the car but didn't get out right away. She was singing at the top of her lungs. "Aaaah, aaah."

She imagined herself at a place like Bryce Canyon on top of a large red rock with her arms up in the air, spinning around, singing.

* * *

Walking into her office, she cheerily said hello to several co-workers then entered a large room with no windows and several cubicles as her smile turned to a frown. There was a constant hum from the HVAC system and the ever present clicking sound of people typing on their keyboards. It was now 8:35. She passed the cube next to hers. The computer was on but no one was in there.

She walked into her cubicle and turned on her computer. There were two computer screens on her desk angled strategi-cally in a V so the one on the left was facing the back of the cubicle. The screen couldn't be seen by anyone entering the cubicle or walking by. When she passed other cubicles with the screens set up like this, she couldn't help but wonder what they were reading or watching on the screen facing the back wall.

There were piles of papers all over the desk and on the floor. A corkboard on the wall had photos of Sophie, her family and friends. Sophie and Ray on a Caribbean island, drinks in hand. Prom pictures of her sons and their dates. Friends and her in New York City. The whole family at the Golden Gate Bridge. There was a vase of wilted flowers on her desk.

Sophie pulled up email on the right screen and the New York Times on the left screen. She started answering emails.

And so the day begins, the day begins.... Susan, I am losing it on this one. This wire has bounced twice now. Can we get this guy to actually give us the correct information? Does he want his money or does he work because he loves his job? If so, lucky, lucky him. Do we have to start every day like this? I think I am going to get a few nips of Baileys and keep them in my bottom drawer. Put them in my coffee. When do the liquor stores open around here? Thanks, Boca Baby."

She hit send and turned to the NY Times on the other screen, opening an Op-Ed piece by Paul Krugman. He was warning that austerity was not the solution to the recession. She could see at the bottom of her screen an email reply had come in from Susan.

Okay you are seriously making me laugh out loud. I have to stop laughing to check on this one. I'll get back to you.

It was only nine o'clock. She had heard Dan come back to the cubicle next to hers so she got up and went over to talk to him. "Hey Dan. Where's Tina?" Dan was thirty years old and Sophie thought he was handsome, the kind of guy she would be attracted to back in the day. He had golden brown hair, blue eyes and a scruffy but neatly trimmed beard.

Dan looked up, took his head phones off and smiled. He was slouched down in his chair, with his legs sprawled out underneath his desk and his head so low in the seat it was almost resting on the back of his chair. "Hey! She's gonna be late, had to bring one of her kids to the dentist or something."

"Phew! I was late this morning."

"Me too. I missed the train by two minutes and had to drive in."

"How about all that construction in town? It's killing me."

"Sucks. I'm glad I take the train most days."

"So what's going on?"

"Big news. Broke off my engagement this weekend."

"NO!"

"Yeah! It's been a long time coming. I think I got cornered into the whole thing. Tracy wants the house, the kids, the whole package and I just started asking myself, what the hell am I doing?"

"What about the wedding in the Bahamas? Didn't you have all that stuff booked?"

"We were holding a date for this June and put a small deposit down but we can get it back."

"That's good. Ya know, I think you're doing the right thing Dan. I hear you talking about your friends and the things you want to do and I just get the impression you're not ready to settle down. And trust me, marriage is tough. If you have any doubts, don't do it until you're ready. If ever. Because really, it's not all it's cracked up to be."

Dan laughed. "I hear ya. Nah, I feel good about it. I know I made the right move."

"But hey, don't you guys live together? What's gonna happen with that?"

"We're still gonna live together. I'm just not ready for the final commitment."

"Hmmm." She contemplated this for a few seconds. "Well, good for you. See what happens. Anyway, I better get back to work before Tina gets here and I haven't done a thing."

Sophie went back in her cubicle. She had another email from Susan.

Here's the correct bank info. He said he had the wrong info the last time. Can we try resending?

Sure, why not? Did he say anything about the first time he sent the info? Because that was wrong too. Oh well, maybe the third times a charm. But 3 strikes and he's out. Then I take the money and put it towards my B&B in the islands.

You're not going anywhere. Running a B&B is too much work.

As compared to what?

Time passed slowly. Sophie worked on some spreadsheets and continued to answer emails. When she looked up at the clock again it was one o'clock, her usual lunchtime. She stretched and got ready to go outside. She stopped by Dan's cubicle. "Hey Dan, is it raining out?"

"No man, it's sunny and really nice. Why do you think it's raining? It was sunny when we got here."

"I know but once we're in here it always feels like it's raining."

"Yeah, I know what you mean. Lack of natural light I guess. But I just got back from lunch and I can attest to the fact that it is a beautiful day. Too bad I'm stuck here for the rest of the afternoon."

"I hear ya. Be back in half an hour."

"Peace."

She took a short walk around town but as she passed the parking lot she headed to her car. She meant to get some exercise and take a much longer walk but she was feeling down and just not up for it. She got in her car, rolled down the window and closed her eyes. The clock on the bank across the street said 1:10.

It was warm in the car even with the windows down. She closed her eyes and dozed off. Suddenly the commuter train came by and woke her. The clock on the bank now said 1:25. She'd been sleeping for fifteen minutes. A snappy nap as one of her friends would call it. The train was just pulling out of the station. The smiling conductor had his arm out the window. One of the ticket takers was standing at an open door, surveying the passing scenery.

Sophie closed her eyes again and imagined herself on a train in a uniform, walking down the aisle, punching people's tickets, chitchatting and laughing with the passengers. She passed between cars, reached the end of a car and leaned against the door. The breeze blew through her hair as she smiled and watched the scenery pass by. Suddenly she opened her eyes, quickly hopped out of the car and headed back to her cubicle.

Later that afternoon, at three o'clock, Sophie was reading an article in the New York Times travel section on Costa Rica while still handling emails.

Yes I am sorry about that. I gave you the wrong bank code. Here's the correct one.

She slit her eyes and stared at the computer screen, thinking to herself "Another one? Really? Can I bitch this guy out or will I lose my job? Like why did you give me the wrong bank code? An honest mistake? You're just a lazy ass? You're stupid? What? Why?"

She replied *Thanks so much. I will resend that wire tomorrow after I correct your banking information. Once it's sent you can expect it in 3-5 business days. Please let me know if you don't receive it. Respectfully yours, Sophie Ryan.*

Another email came in from London. *The first account number was duff information. Here's the correct account number.*

Sophie was really losing it now and muttered under her breath "Duff? What the hell is that? Bullshit in England I guess, that's what it must mean. Crap? God there are even stupid assholes in England."

She replied *Duff, well there's a new one on me. No problem, I will correct your banking information and resend that wire tomorrow. Once it's sent you can expect it in 3-5 business days. Please let me know if you don't receive it. Respectfully yours, Sophie Ryan.*

Time passed slowly. She started another project, coding a stack of invoices. Another email came in. After reading it she put her head in her hands for a minute and tried to compose herself.

She called loudly over her shoulder to the cubicle next to her. "Hey Dan, listen to this. I just got this email and it says *we put the checks in a drawer and just found them now. Could you please reissue them as they are now stale?"*

Dan shouted back incredulously, "Stale? Checks get stale?"

"Apparently. And, get this. It was fifteen checks we sent them over 7 years! And they just found them now? Do they know where their bank is? More importantly, do they know they have to bring the checks to the bank? Do they know what a bank is? Do they know what a check is?"

"This uncashed check thing you have to deal with is really insane."

"No. I'll tell you what is insane. Me! That's who's insane."

"I hear ya."

A few minutes later Dan peeked in her cubicle. "Time to go. See ya tomorrow. Hang in there."

"I can't make any promises."

* * *

Sophie pulled into her garage. It was just starting to get dark out. She had groceries in the back seat. A strobe light was flashing from the window in the addition. She stayed in the car for a while listening to the radio and looked up at the flashing strobe light. The radio was playing a bittersweet song, Springsteen's 'Tunnel of Love'. Listening to the lyrics, she thought they might be an omen. This house was haunted.

Sophie got out of the car and grabbed the grocery bags on the back seat. Before she entered the house, she stopped in the yard and looked up at the sky. There was a bright star near the crescent shaped moon. "Star light, star bright, first star I see tonight. That's probably Venus though, right? Or Mars, I don't know. I always forget. Oh well. I wish I may, I wish I might, have the wish I wish tonight."

She turned around searching the sky for another star. She saw a bright spot in the distance. "I wish I could learn to rise above all this bullshit. And live my life the way I dreamed I would, at that B&B in the Caribbean." She blew a kiss towards the second star but it had moved closer.

"Oh God that's a plane." She went to the door and struggled to open it with the grocery bags in her hands.

THE SAD SOUND OF AN OBOE

She and Katie arrived in Oregon the week before Labor Day, just in time for Katie to move into the graduate dorms. It was really nice in Portland and she loved the relaxed vibe so she decided to stay. She tried finding a job on a magazine or newspaper. Portland had the largest number of independent publishers in the country. After a few weeks of chasing that dream she took a waitressing job at a vegan restaurant near the college and rented a bedroom in a rundown house on the outskirts of town with six other recent grads. They were all working as waitresses and bartenders while they looked for work that might have anything to do with what they had studied in college.

Everyone worked late hours and got home and stayed up even later. They drank craft beers they couldn't really afford, smoked ganja and discussed their favorite topics such as getting off the grid and avoiding corporate work. Or was there really such a thing as true love and, if there was, could it really last a lifetime? So many of their parents were divorced, so it was hard to imagine it lasting a decade never mind a lifetime. They dreamed of becoming entrepreneurs, writers, artists or musicians.

Their favorite thing to complain about was the ridiculous cost of college and the school loans they owed. And how the greedy bastards on Wall Street were destroying the economy just in time for them to graduate with their two hundred thousand dollar degrees in hand. They all shared the fear that if they didn't get decent work soon they might have to move back in with their parents. Would it be better to do what they loved for little money while living at home? Or should they break down and take a job they didn't want so they could afford to continue to live on their own? No one knew the right answer and it was not on their radar that a global recession was only weeks away.

She rarely heard from Nick. He had ignored her the first year, only sending brief birthday and Christmas wishes. That was OK, she didn't think about him very often. At first, she was having too much fun on the road. She sometimes sent him postcards from quirky places she visited like the Corn Palace in South Dakota, the Paul Bunyan statue in Minnesota and the Elvis wedding chapel in Vegas. Later, she regretted that last one. She thought she might be sending the wrong message.

When she got to Portland, she was still having a lot of fun. She loved her new friends. The waitressing was OK. It left time for writing during the mornings. She sent a few stories to literary journals but hadn't gotten anything published yet.

Nick sent his first text message in early September 2009, almost exactly a year after she arrived in Oregon. He wanted her to come back to Boston. He missed her. He had sublet the extra room in his apartment to a guy he met at work who had recently transferred from Australia. But that was temporary and he had now moved out. Would she please consider coming back and giving him another chance?

He didn't say he loved her. But she knew on her part this also wasn't love. What she was hoping was if she moved back to Boston she might find a job in publishing or something. Possibly a newspaper? He had gotten a raise. Already! He'd only been at the bank a little over a year and he was moving up the corporate ladder, just as he had planned. He offered to pay two thirds of the rent. This could be better than waitressing or moving back home. She told herself she was just being practical. After all, Lehman Brothers had filed Chapter 11, the Dow Jones had collapsed and everyone was scared. She didn't really understand all of this but she was running out of money and struggling to pay her bills. And who knew, maybe they could repair their relationship and fall in love all over again? That sometimes happens, doesn't it?

They continued to talk this over for a couple of months. She was hesitant about the whole idea. But in the end she packed up shortly before Thanksgiving and flew back to Boston. She'd been living with Nick for over a year now. Thousands of people were still out of work but somehow she had found a job on the North Shore after being back for only two weeks. She worked in the editorial department of a large company. The commuter train brought her right to the office. Her reverse commute.

She worked in a windowless room in a cubicle on a computer all day. It was a really large room with rows and rows of cubicles, over eighty people clicking and clacking on keyboards all day. The building was a renovated old warehouse and all the offices with windows were along the walls. She was in the big, dingy middle of the room where the light was always dim and dreary. Even worse than the noise of the eighty keyboards was the HVAC system with its constant hum of blowing air. One of the pipes must have had a leak because there was also a steady high-pitched sound like a teakettle whistling.

Her job was to convert printed material into a web-ready format. She edited everything from literary works to medical and scientific journals. She had read very few articles that interested her in the fourteen months she had been here.

She was required to keep a minute by minute timesheet of how long it took her to edit each article. She was expected to do five articles a day. When she became proficient at meeting this requirement, she would be expected to improve on it. She started at four and that was hard enough. She wondered where it would ever end, if ever. If she did too good a job too soon, she might end up reaching a plateau where the bar was finally set too high and then what would happen?

These were not her expectations when she graduated from college. This was so far from creative writing she felt she had lost her energy and spark. She started to write a story about her cross-country trip shortly after she got back to Boston. She was also working on a screenplay about a group of college grads living in an old house in Portland. But she hadn't worked on either project in four months. She complained bitterly about this to Nick.

"It's work. What do you expect? You're lucky to have a job in this economy," he said.

"I expect to be fulfilled. I expect to be mentally, creatively and spiritually challenged."

"Spiritually? Seriously? You're always so dramatic. Work is not a spiritual experience. Join a church or something."

She stared at him with a look of disgust. "Do you know me at all? Hey, you're the one who was studying up on work passion, weren't you?" She paused for a second, furrowing her brow. "You know something? That reverse commute of mine is a double entendre. I just realized that."

"A double what?"

"A double entendre. A phrase that can be understood two ways. Most people commute into Boston for work but I do the reverse, commuting to the suburbs for work. And it could also mean that I had all these expectations when I graduated from college and here I am moving backwards, not moving towards my dreams but further away from them."

"I don't get it."

"That's because you majored in accounting and didn't get that well rounded education."

"Very funny. You know what you're problem is? You over think things. People have to work. It's a fact of life. Get over it. Just do your job well and maybe you'll get a promotion. You might even get an office with a window. Maybe your problem is the lack of sunlight. I've heard that can cause depression. So set a goal and go for it. Soon you'll be working in an office with a view! Why do you always give me that look? What?"

"This is what I have to look forward to? An office with a window? That's not working for me Nick. Life is too short to not be doing what you love."

"Well I tried to help. I've got to pack for a business trip to Chicago tomorrow."

"Okay. I'm going for a walk."

"If I'm asleep when you get back don't wake me up. My flight is really early."

She put on her flannel, fleece lined parka and headed out the door into the crisp, cold January night. Gazing at the dirty snow banks lining the sidewalk, she thought about how the snow only looked nice in the city while it was coming down. Then the plows came by, creating hard packed black mounds speckled with chunks of tar that didn't even look like snow.

She walked over to a small city park with a playground and sat on one of the swings. She reached in her pocket and found a bud. She rummaged around in the other pocket and found a lighter and a small wooden pipe. She sparked up and took a few long drags then slowly exhaled, leaning her head back and watching the smoke drift up into the starry night. It was quiet here although she could still hear the noises of the city. Cars honking, a siren from a police car or ambulance, a few people walking by talking quietly. But the sounds were muffled and off in the distance. She started to swing, pumping her legs, swinging higher and higher.

She realized she was going to have to do something about her situation. Moving back to Boston with Nick was not working out. Her job was not working out. She knew she had to move on but she couldn't figure out how to do that quite yet. The logistics overwhelmed her.

Rents were really high in Boston. Nick had originally wanted to live in Back Bay but couldn't afford it. So he settled for a two family apartment near Cleveland Circle. But it was still expensive there. She was having a hard time paying just her one third of the rent on the small salary she made. And she had that two hundred dollar a month school loan to pay. If she moved out on her own, she definitely couldn't quit her job.

It dawned on her that she was really not much better off than she had been waitressing in Portland. Yes, she had what some would consider a good job but it was certainly not what she imagined it would be. She did have health insurance and two weeks paid vacation but she had little time to write between working forty hours and commuting. Maybe she should bring her laptop and start writing on the train?

She sighed and hopped off the swing. She'd just have to figure it all out. She could get on Facebook when she got back to the apartment. Check and see if any of her college friends were looking for roommates.

Arriving in front of her apartment, she stopped on the sidewalk and looked up at the second floor. There was only a dim light glowing in the left front window from the night light they had in the living room. The rest of the apartment looked dark. Yes! Nick must be asleep. She walked up the steps slowly, holding onto the ornate, black wrought iron railing. As she stepped into the hallway, she could hear the tenant downstairs playing his oboe. It was a sad, mournful sound.

The couple downstairs was gay. They had been together for twenty years and recently got married when Massachusetts passed the gay marriage bill. They used their spare bedroom as their TV room because their living room was set up as a Japanese tearoom.

They had made a little house in this room with screens made out of paper on wooden frames. There were straw mats on the floor and a teak table in the middle of the teahouse. A few traditional Japanese scrolls hung on the walls and beautiful vases were on the floor in the four corners of the house. It was very simple and peaceful.

They invited her downstairs for a formal tea ceremony quite often but only when Nick was out of town. They had invited Nick once but he wasn't really comfortable. From the minute he had to take his shoes off entering the apartment, she could tell he was uptight. She wasn't sure if it was the ceremony or something else he didn't like but either way this pissed her off.

She loved the peacefulness of the whole ceremony. The ritual of making and pouring the tea. The quiet Japanese music, the trickling water fountain they had.

Bruce worked as a fundraiser at a women's shelter in Roxbury. Bill played the oboe for the Boston symphony. They were happy in their work and after twenty years of being together, they took the wildly romantic step of getting married. This amazed her and she loved thinking about what this said regarding the possibility of finding happiness.

Upstairs in her apartment she only heard the oboe when she was in the bathroom. If she was feeling sad, which was quite often these days, she went in there. She put the toilet seat cover down, piled a few towels on top to make it comfortable and sat there listening to Bill practice. If sound had a color the sound of the oboe would be blue. Sometimes she liked to think Bill sensed her sadness through the floorboards and was playing just for her.

When she got into the apartment she took off her coat, brushed her teeth and headed to the bedroom. She quietly took off her clothes, dropped them on the floor and crawled into bed without waking Nick. She dreamt of making a bed out of fluffy towels in the bathtub and drifting off to sleep listening to the sad sound of the oboe.

A B&B IN THE ISLANDS

It was early October at the Ryan house. In the backyard the leaves on the trees were turning orange, red and yellow. The sun was rising later now and the light that filtered through the bedroom windows where Sophie and Ray were sleeping was not as bright and warm as it was in the summer time.

It was six A.M. and the alarm went off as usual. Ray rolled over and shut it off. He got up and put his slippers and bathrobe on. He went downstairs to make coffee.

Sophie walked down the hall to the bathroom, turned on the shower and brushed her teeth while waiting for the water to warm up. The strobe light was still blinking in the addition although it was harder to see it in the early morning light. She hadn't seen the squirrels in a few weeks. Ray hunted around for babies in the attic rafters, which were accessible from the addition but didn't find any. She needed to remind him to shut that thing off. She hadn't checked the electric bill this month but knew it had to be higher than usual.

Sophie walked back to her bedroom, got dressed and made the bed while watching TV. Rick Perry was talking about keeping the birth certificate thing alive for the fun of it. Sophie turned off the TV while muttering to herself. "Another stupid jerk from Texas. Obama's as American as you are dummy. God help us all. Why do they waste our time with this shit? This is news?"

Downstairs she made lunches in the kitchen then went into the living room and folded clothes while sitting on the couch. Ray was sitting in the recliner dressed in his paint clothes, watching a John Wayne western.

"So Ray, Jesse has been launched. Finally. We are officially empty nesters. Do you think you could finish the bedroom up there by Thanksgiving? You'll have two months and although the twins never really got to enjoy it while they lived here, it would be nice to have it ready when they come back for the holidays. And if we're really selling the house in the spring, it's got to be done. There's still the bathrooms to finish you know." She looked up at the TV. "Hey can we get some news on here?"

Ray pointed the remote at the TV and put the Today show on. They were interviewing the family with nineteen kids. "Ray, this isn't news."

"Nineteen kids? I would say that's news. Insane. Imagine raising nineteen teenagers. I'd be dead by now." He turned back to the Western he was watching. "Yeah, I'll start working on that bedroom."

"So you'll finish the closet and put in the floor?"

"Well we have to decide what kind of floor we want. Hardwood, wall to wall carpeting, linoleum."

Sophie looked at him incredulously. "Linoleum? Are you serious? I thought we discussed this and said we would go with what's in the dining room. Yeah linoleum, that's what I want. That's really nice in a bedroom. Easy to clean. Here you go with the passive aggressive shit again. You know what? I don't care, you pick. If you want linoleum, fine! I just want the floor done."

"I didn't really mean linoleum. I just meant we have to decide."

"We did decide. You're just pulling my chain. Avoiding what you have to do. Throwing up roadblocks like you always do. I think you're leading me on about running a B&B in the islands too. You have no intention of really doing it, do you? You want to stay here in this house forever. Die here and be buried in the backyard."

"I'd rather have my ashes scattered in the river."

"See!"

"I'm joking Sophie. Not about the cremated part though. You know I want to be cremated, right?"

"Ray, you know I'm thinking about you too. Do you really want to be climbing ladders at sixty five, struggling to pay the bills and battling with that stupid old snow blower of yours every winter?"

"Maybe I'll be able to afford a new snow blower one of these winters."

"Oh my God, I can't tell when you're teasing me or telling the truth anymore. I don't know, I just don't know. Maybe I'm crazy but it makes sense to me to go somewhere and run a B&B. You've got the handyman skills. You do plumbing, electricity, carpentry, yard work."

"And painting. My specialty. And, yes, you are slightly crazy. Why are you always so difficult?"

"I could handle the reservations, the accounting, the website. We both love to travel and we cook. We'll make banana bread for the guests and have happy hour in the evenings with one free drink and an appetizer of the day."

"It sounds great, Sophie. And hopefully it will be in the islands because we love it there."

"Yes and hopefully a French or British island because they have healthcare. I think the islands fall under those countries' universal healthcare. I'll Google that at work today." Sophie carried the basket of folded clothes to the bottom of the stairs then grabbed her things. Heading to the door, she suddenly stopped and turned to Ray. "Oh right, you're leaving for the golf weekend after work, right?" She walked over to the recliner, leaned over and kissed Ray on the cheek.

"I'm sorry I'm so bitchy honey. It just overwhelms me sometimes. You know we have no retirement, right? I cashed out that 401K when I lost my job, to pay for health insurance. Then got slammed with taxes and penalties for early withdrawal. And we haven't contributed to your IRA in years. The last ten years to be exact. So we're working to the bitter end. Hey, that's the name of a resort in the BVI. I wonder if they did the same thing we're thinking about?" She shook her head as if she were waking herself up, trying to focus. "Anyway, if we're working forever, let's make sure we're doing something we love. Right?"

"Right. I'm with you. Believe me. I'm back in the addition next weekend. I love you too. Relax this weekend. Do something fun for yourself."

ABOUT THE WEEKENDS

She thought she was much too young for this life she was living. Working in the suburbs at a nine to five job. Living with her boyfriend in what was turning out to be a loveless relationship. She was way too young for a loveless relationship. She should be having mad, passionate sex. She wondered if they stayed together out of habit. Or maybe insecurity? He said he loved her but when she asked him why, he didn't really have a good answer. Not the answer she was looking for. Just the other day she asked him, "What is it you love about me?"

"Ummm. Everything."

"Everything, like what? Give me something specific."

"Your smile. You can be very funny. I like your sense of humor although you could lay off on the sarcasm once in awhile."

"That is my sense of humor. Sarcasm and irony are two of my favorite things."

"I don't really get the irony." She arched her eyebrow at him and dropped the subject.

Nick thought they should be saving money to buy a condominium. He had set up a savings plan for them and it included splurging for dinner once a month at a restaurant on the last Friday of each month. He said it would be something to look forward to.

"Who gets to pick where we eat?" she asked.

"We'll take turns."

"Can't we do this every week? Once a month seems kind of harsh."

He always picked the Italian restaurant around the corner from their apartment. He liked the fact that it was close to home. "I'm tired at the end of the week. I don't want to have to go far just to eat out," he said.

"That's why I thought Saturday was a good idea."

"But don't you think it's nice not to have to cook when you get home from work on a Friday?"

"Yes and that is why I also thought every Friday would be a good idea."

"We'll never get a condo doing that." Nick was getting exasperated with her.

"Why do we want a condo? The housing market sucks. Some economists say it's better to rent right now."

"Are you reading Krugman again? I told you the Wall Street Journal has a better editorial page than the Times."

"Hey Krugman was right about the housing bubble."

He always ordered the veal marsala or the chicken saltimbocca, alternating each month. She tried something different every time but was worried if she stayed with him long enough she would end up having to order the Roman style tripe in red sauce. She was an adventurous eater and liked most things but she drew the line at cow stomach.

When it was her turn to pick the restaurant, she chose something different each month. Thai, Sushi, Lebanese. This past month she chose an Ethiopian restaurant in the South End. "The South End? What time are we having dinner?" he whined.

"It's not that far. Just the Green Line into town. I actually think it's closer to the theatre district so it's not far from the Copley Square station. I don't know. I'll look up the directions at work today."

"What kind of food is this? Isn't there a famine in Ethiopia?"

Needless to say, the evening didn't go well. It was a snowy Friday night in late January. When she checked the website that morning, she saw it was a little further from the T-stop than she thought it was. She suggested they drive because she knew he would complain about the walk, especially in the snow. Instead he complained about the parking. It took them twenty minutes of driving around to find a parking space.

She loved the restaurant the minute they stepped in the door. The room was filled with colorful rugs and wicker baskets. They were seated on low footstools at a short round wicker table. The top of the table was actually a round basket with low sides and the food was served in the basket, family style.

"We don't get plates?" He sounded like a little boy fussing and complaining.

"You use this bread as your plate." She held up a piece of soft bread with little holes in it.

Disgustedly, he said, "It looks like a sea sponge you'd find at the bottom of the ocean. How do we get the food onto the bread?"

"You use your hands." She picked up some chicken with her hand and rolled it up in the bread. "This is really delicious." The chicken was spicy with sweet hints of cardamom and nutmeg. She braced herself for his response, knowing he wasn't going to like this at all.

Later that evening he made himself a peanut butter sandwich and watched the Celtics game. He had barely eaten the food at the restaurant and sat there most of the evening like a sullen child waiting for her to finish. All night he talked about an audit he had coming up in Dallas. It would require him to be gone every week in February and most likely through March. He might even have to stay some weekends.

She didn't tell him she had been to the restaurant before. She didn't tell him she ate out quite often when he was traveling on business. She met friends from college or people she worked with who lived in the city too. Sometimes she stayed on the North Shore after work and went out with her friend Dan from accounting and the guys in the IT department. She justified it by telling herself he got to eat out when he was traveling for business all week. But she knew he would point out that his dinners were on the company's expense account and she was spending money she should be saving for the all important condominium.

She also went to concerts in small clubs in Cambridge and Kenmore Square. Last week she saw a great reggae band at the Middle East in Central Square. He would never want to do something like that although they used to go to concerts when they were in college.

"It's the bars I don't like. Standing all night in a crowded room, elbow to elbow with a mob of people."

"Hey at least you're tall. If I can't work my way to the front, I'm lost in a sea of people spending the night looking at someone's back. But I always manage to worm my way to the front." She laughed nervously, not wanting to reveal too much.

"Concerts are so expensive. We can't really afford that."

"That's why we should see new bands at small clubs. Tickets can be as little as fifteen bucks. There's such great new music out there. And when they become famous you can say I saw them at the Middle East and was just this far away." She reached out and poked him in the chest.

"I don't know. I like the old stuff. The music we grew up with."

"Music we grew up with? How old are you? Speak for yourself. I for one am not done growing up. Although there are times you certainly act like a pouty little boy. Like when you don't get your way."

She didn't tell him she was very much looking forward to February and March.

* * *

Nick was spending his first weekend in Dallas. Katie called and said she was home from Oregon for the weekend. Her grandmother passed away and she had flown back for the funeral. They made plans to get together Sunday night before she went back to school. She'd sleep over and catch a cab to Logan airport in the morning. She wanted to come over and see the apartment anyway.

"Sure you can do that. And there's a great little bistro not far from here. We'll go out for dinner. My treat. After all, I'm the working girl and you're still the struggling student."

Katie loved what she and Nick had done with the apartment. The Pottery Barn sofa mixed with the hand me down pieces they got from her parents when they decided to leave Vermont and move to Florida. "You guys have made such a cozy little home here."

"Yeah. I guess."

"What's with the sigh? What's wrong?"

"Oh Katie. I'm just not ready for this. I'm not looking for a husband. I don't want the ring and the house and the babies. Not yet. I want experiences. I want to travel and have adventures. I can't be a writer if I just settle down and get married."

"Why can't you write about that? Settling down and getting married?"

She rolled her eyes. "Boring! Hey, let's go. You've seen the place. My little love nest. Not!" She paused, bit her lip and looked around the room then clapped her hands. "So let's get out of here. We can catch up over drinks at the bar. Enough of this boring domesticity."

"You are still the same old girl I knew in fourth grade. Do you remember we used to love playing with Barbie dolls back then? But we only each had our Barbies and some old army guy your dad had in a box in the attic."

"Right, GI Joe."

"Yeah Joe. He wore army fatigues and had that jeep. Why did your Dad keep his old toys in the attic?"

"Because my Dad kept everything, remember? The nutty old professor."

"Yeah, that's right. Well, anyway, then Vanessa Morretti moved into the neighborhood and she had everything Barbie. She had the penthouse, the convertible, tons of clothes and Ken. She always wanted to play Barbie's. So we would make up all these games. Barbie living single in the city, Barbie going on vacation with her friends."

"Right and the friends were our Barbies so we had to re-name them because Vanessa's Barbie got to be THE Barbie. They all lived in the penthouse, drove to the beach in the convertible and dated Ken and Joe. That was so much fun."

"But do you remember the wedding dress? Vanessa had the wedding dress and a tux for Ken so the games were always working towards the big wedding. We'd have the whole ceremony, our Barbies were the bridesmaids and Joe was the best man and then what would you say?"

"I don't remember Katie."

"Yes you do."

"All right, all right. I'd say let's go back to the beginning because I thought that after Barbie got married the game would be really boring. I wanted to start the game over. Admit it, the beginning of a romance is always much more exciting than the middle or the end."

"Do you also remember how Vanessa really got into the honeymoon? She would have them humping like crazy. I don't think you thought that was boring! You'd think you would've liked the marriage part better because Vanessa started banging those dolls together! God! Was Barbie even anatomically correct for sex?"

"Well Ken certainly wasn't!" They both started laughing. She turned to her best friend with a wistful look in her eyes. "Oh Katie, how quaint we were. Saving the sex for after the wedding. Anyway, I should have known I was doomed. I'll never find true love because I don't believe it exists."

"You think it's boring."

"Maybe that too. But it's because I don't think I've experienced it yet. It won't be boring if I truly find it, will it?"

"How the hell would I know? I haven't had a decent relationship since I started grad school. You're right, let's get out of here and hit a bar."

They walked several blocks to a tavern in Washington Square. The room was loud and full of young, successful looking people laughing and having a good time. It was all dark wood and low lighting, a warm and welcoming spot on a winter night.

"Can we grab those seats at the bar? I love sitting at the bar. It's much more social. Nick never wants to sit at the bar." They grabbed the last two barstools and ordered drinks. Katie ordered a cabernet.

"I'll have a vodka in a rocks glass with a splash of club soda." She held up her thumb and pointer finger indicating a small amount. "Just a splash of the soda. And a lemon peel. Thanks. Oh and a chaser of Captain Morgan too. In a shot glass." She turned to Katie. "I have been dying to try this place but Nick didn't like the menu when he checked out their website."

Katie looked concerned. "A chaser of Captain Morgan? What's the matter sweetie? You don't seem very happy."

"I am so not happy. I hate my job. It is so mind numbingly boring. And Nick. Oh God, Nick. I don't know what's happened to Nick but he is not the guy I knew in college. I came back from Oregon and he was all grown up. Mr. Bank Auditor. He's got all these big plans. And he's always telling me what to do. Like you should be putting more money in your 401K. Why aren't you more aggressive at work? You need to focus on getting a promotion. It's about time you changed your wardrobe. Enough of this casual hippie chick look. You need a more polished look. And a more sophisticated haircut, like a bob or something. How about I get you a gift certificate to Talbots for your birthday in March. Talbots? Is he serious? No one our age shops at Talbots. Some corporate type lady at the bank probably recommended it to him."

"Wow, he wants you to shop at Talbots? He called you a hippie chick? And I'm sorry but I can't see you with a bob although it is a cute look on you. Remember you had one all through middle school."

She looked at Katie and rolled her eyes as their drinks arrived. She took a few sips of the vodka and then knocked back the shot of rum.

Katie smiled sympathetically. "Anyway, that does sound a little bit overwhelming. But we always knew he was going to have the big career. He's a great breadwinner type of guy, you know? Marriage material."

"But I don't want to get married. I want to travel, have wild adventures and meet interesting people. Experiences I can write about. If I had known it was going to turn out like this, I would have broken up with him long ago. I regret spending all of college with just one guy. What was I thinking?" She looked across the bar wistfully. "I regret coming back too."

She saw two women sitting across from them. One was a tall, very attractive blond with a graduated bob like the Spice girl who was married to the soccer player. She was wearing a sleeveless, linen black dress with pearls.

She nudged Katie. "Look. Over there across the bar." Katie looked across the bar and she hit her on the shoulder. "Don't be so obvious." Katie laughed and pretended she was waving to someone past the blond.

"Don't you think she's the perfect wife for Nick? I bet she has some job in an art gallery on Newbury Street or something. Maybe even a trust fund. He should get past the menu here and just come for drinks some night. Find himself the perfect little soul mate."

"Looks like she's already spoken for. Do you see that humungous rock on her left hand? Guess she got the memo."

"What memo is that?"

"The memo that college is really about getting your M.R.S. degree."

"M.R.S?"

"Missus. You know, find a husband at college? A boy with good prospects. Sometimes I think it could be the way to go. Some girls I go to school with got married and then were able to stop working to get a graduate degree. Their husbands have good jobs and cover their living expenses while they go back to school. Unlike me, going to grad school and working. It's taking me two years instead of one."

"How come I never got this memo? I have thought about that though. Like once Nick really starts making the big bucks, I could quit work and write. But Nick would never agree to me doing that. He wants the double income. But really, why go to college in the first place if you're just going to get married?"

"Because that's where the boys with good prospects are. My nanny always used to say, remember two things. First find a man who likes to work. Second.... hmm, I can't remember the second thing. But I guess the point is if he likes to work the rest of it all falls into place. You get to stay home with the kids or you can join the country club and play tennis. If you want to work and use that college degree, you start a little business but work part time. Hire someone to manage the day to day."

"I can't believe you had a nanny."

"I know. But she wasn't really a nanny. She was an older woman whose kids were grown up and she helped out because my mom worked. We just called her our nanny. I think we had been watching too much Mary Poppins around that time." They both started laughing and ordered another round of drinks including the Captain Morgan.

"We better eat something before we get too drunk. Let's order the mussels in wine sauce. I bet the food is great here and I love mussels."

"Oh and let me guess. Nick doesn't like shellfish?"

"That's right. Should we get something else?"

"You decide. Poor baby doesn't get out much and when she does get out she has to eat what her boyfriend likes." Katie leaned over and gave her a big kiss on the cheek. "I miss you so much."

* * *

As they walked back home, it started to snow. She was feeling a little tipsy so she held onto Katie's arm. Small flakes were drifting aimlessly, nothing heavy enough to start accumulating. Not yet anyway. The real storm was due late tomorrow afternoon. The weathermen were calling for a possible six to twelve inches.

"I hope my flight doesn't get canceled. I have a huge paper due this week."

"Your flight's at seven, right? I think you'll get out of here in time."

"I wish we lived closer. I could be your shoulder to lean on. You really seem to need one right now. So what are you gonna do about Nick?"

"I've been trying to contact people. No one's looking for a roommate right now. I put an ad on the employee message board we have at work. I'll figure it out. Hopefully by the end of March when this gig of his in Dallas ends."

"Gig in Dallas. Makes him sound like a rock star." They both started laughing and held onto each other on the sidewalk, which was getting a little slippery. She leaned her head back, with her arm around Katie's waist and shouted "He is so NOT a rock star."

Sighing, she looked up at the stars and paused for a moment, seemingly lost in her thoughts. "But seriously Katie, we're laughing about all this MRS shit and finding the boy with good prospects. But where's the love? Is it all just a business proposition? It sounds so mercenary. I want to fall madly in love and have lots of mad, passionate sex and live happily ever after. And when I die, it will be in my true love's arms." She blew a kiss towards the night sky.

Katie smacked herself on the forehead. "That's the second thing my nanny said! It's just as easy to fall in love with a boy with money as it is a poor boy." Katie stopped and hugged her. "Well, you have to keep me posted. You know you can call any time you need to talk. And do not shop at Talbots. Ever." They squeezed each other tight. "Oh honey, you're my best friend."

THE WINE EMERGENCY

Later that Friday before the golf weekend, Ray was in the bathroom of an old house in Portsmouth. He and his coworker were demolishing the room, ripping down the old fixtures with crowbars. Ray was trying to detach the shower unit from the wall. Suddenly the crowbar snapped in his hand and his fist banged against the wall with a loud thud.

"OWWW! SSSHIT!" He shook his hand madly and then stuck his thumb in his mouth.

His coworker looked over and chuckled. "Watch what you're doing there Ray, don't want to lose a finger. That's not gonna help your golf game this weekend."

At the same time, Sophie was in her cubicle leaning way back in her rolling office chair, staring at the clock on the wall. It was three o'clock. She suddenly snapped out of her funk, sat up and rolled closer to her desk. She started working on a pile of checks, entering numbers on an Excel spreadsheet and flipping to the next check as she went. Opening email on her other screen, she started to compose a message to Susan.

Hey Susan. I know you're a Mad Men fan. Just wanted to share something. Do you remember the episode when Ida Blankenship died in her chair at her desk in the office?

Of course I do. That was hysterical. Loved that episode.

OK, well. I was just sitting here in my cubicle thinking what if that happened to me. Because as you know Ida sat in a big room with lots of other secretaries and all they had to do was look up once in awhile and see she wasn't moving. Her head was on the desk and it had been like that for a while. So then I started thinking, what if that happens to me? What if I die at my desk?

Sophie you're not going to die at your desk.

You don't know that. I have high blood pressure.

You're on medication.

So? Anyway, I was thinking. I'm not in the middle of some big secretarial pool. I am in a cubicle. By the time someone finds me, riga mortis could set in!!!!

That's not going to happen. People walk by your cubicle. Emails will go unanswered. Dan will eventually notice. TGIF. Enjoy yourself this weekend. Relax!

Dan will eventually notice? How long is eventually? Relax? That's funny. That's what my husband said this morning.

Well he's right.

Right before they leave the office, Susan sent an email.

Sophie I just remembered something. You know Karen in marketing? Her mother used to work here. One day she had a stroke in her cubicle. She knew something was wrong when she couldn't lift her hand to dial 911. She ended up surviving the stroke but had some minor paralysis. She later told people although she couldn't lift her hand she was able to roll her desk chair enough to get to the cubicle's opening and when she fell out of the chair she fell into the walkway and someone passing by shortly afterwards noticed her. That saved her life. Make sure you don't forget to take those blood pressure meds.

Susan, why are telling me this at four fifteen on Friday when I'm home alone for the weekend? See I told you it's not good to work in a cubicle.

Later that evening, Sophie was driving home in her car. She fished for her cell phone in her pocketbook on the passenger seat while steering with her other hand and keeping her eyes on the road. When she finally found it, she hit speed dial.

"Hey Lynn. I need a wine emergency. What are you doing tonight?"

Sophie got off at her exit and took a left instead of a right like she usually did. She drove less than two miles and pulled into a well-to-do neighborhood with large houses and well landscaped yards.

She pulled up in front of Lynn's house. Grabbing the bottle of wine she purchased at the state liquor store on her way home, she got out of the car and walked up to the large front door passing beautifully kept perennial beds. She knocked quickly, opening the door while knocking. The house was decorated with beautiful but quirky furnishings. Sophie walked straight to the back of the house where the kitchen was. It was a large open room with granite countertops and an island where three women were gathered, drinking wine and talking.

Lynn was an attractive brunette. People often told her she looked like a famous movie star. She was the only one not sitting at the countertop. Instead she was busy cooking dinner, wiping down the counters and stove top and washing dishes. She was always in constant motion.

Kelly was a distracted blond who was half listening to the conversation around her while texting her twenty four year old daughter and checking Facebook on her Blackberry.

Linda was the red head of the group. She was a no non-sense person, very direct to the point of being blunt.

Sophie took off her jacket and threw it on a chair. "Hey, everybody made it and on such short notice."

Kelly looked up from her Blackberry. "Well Marc's still in Texas on business. He won't be home until after midnight. Ashley's in New York with her boyfriend Connor and Tyler is sleeping over a friend's house. So I'm free for the night."

Linda chimed in, "Well free as you can be while checking in with Ashley every few minutes. So Sophie, how are you doing? Why the wine emergency? You called it?"

"It's Friday and I'm home alone tonight. Ray's on his annual fall golf trip. Jesse finally, finally got a job, has gone to Providence and moved in with Sean. I thought we were going to be having a failure to launch problem on our hands but he's off. God it was so easy with his brother. Anyway, empty nest. Loving it!"

She helped herself to the bottle of wine on the counter and poured herself a glass. "God, work is so boring! I was in desperate need of a glass of wine."

Lynn turned around from the stove where she was stirring spaghetti sauce, picked up her glass on the counter beside her and raised it towards the group. "Aren't we all? There is not enough wine in the world."

"Oh and listen to this. Did I tell you there were three squirrels in my house? Running around the addition?"

Kelly stopped texting and shouted. "Oh. My. God. Well that's all Ray's fault. When is he ever going to finish that addition? When was the last time he worked on it? I don't know how you put up with this Sophie. He started it ten years ago, right?"

Kelly's ring tone went off and she answered a text message, half listening to Sophie's reply.

"Well in his defense, it was a really busy summer. Thank God he had a lot of work because the winter was so slow and we needed the money. God knows I can't support us on my salary alone. And you know the summer, it rains half the time around here and the lawn keeps growing and growing. He works all week, plans to get into the addition on the weekend and then has to mow the two acres because the grass is up to our ankles. That takes up a lot of the day. Before you know it, the weekend's over and nothing gets finished."

Linda chimed in. "But it's been ten years."

"Eleven but who's counting. As you know, we started the addition when he had steady work with that builder and we had money. Then the builder overextended himself, the housing market crashed and the builder went bankrupt. We ran out of money to buy materials. I mean I'm not making excuses for him but there have been circumstances beyond our control."

Lynn stopped cooking for a while and sat down next to Sophie. "Is he working on it now?"

"Yeah. He's golfing this weekend but he's promised when he gets back he will finish the bedroom in there then move on to the bathrooms."

Kelly looked up from her phone and shouted, "He's golfing this weekend?"

Lynn looked really concerned. "The bedroom isn't done? Wasn't Jesse sleeping in there this year?"

'It's mostly done. Just the floor and closet need to be finished. Ray painted the floor and we put a rug down." She decided to change the subject. "I got the rug at IKEA. Have you guys ever been to an IKEA? It's awesome, there's one on the way to the Cape."

Lynn hopped up and drained the pasta. "Okay everyone, the spaghetti and meatballs are ready. Can someone grab the garlic bread from the oven and there's salad in the fridge."

Everyone got up to help and then moved to the kitchen table, carrying food and bottles of wine. The conversation continued, everyone speaking at once about kids, work and the IKEA store. Linda was telling a story about an irate parent who came into the school she worked at as a receptionist and insisted she hand deliver a sandwich to her son in his history class.

"I told her it's against the rules. We cannot interrupt a class of thirty kids for one student who forgot his lunch."

The wine had been flowing. Three bottles were empty on the island counter and they carried two more to the table, one white and one red. Sophie poured another glass of red. "So Linda, how is John's business going?"

"Slow. If the economy were better he'd be doing great but everyone is hesitant to sign on, they don't want to make the financial commitment. He's working really hard, doing all the right things but they just can't get the big contract they need to jump start things. It's not the best time to get involved in a startup. Meanwhile, we have no health insurance."

Sophie rolled her eyes. "Health insurance. Don't get me started."

Lynn laughed. "Yes please don't get her started."

"Well Linda brought it up. To think I used to run my own bookkeeping business when the boys were little. I worked from home in the nineties. I was an entrepreneur. A small business person politicians on both sides of the aisle, as they like to say, are fighting for. But they never do anything for us that actually helps. Like health insurance. Someone had to get the job with the benefits. Guess who that was? The guy who paints houses for a living or his wife with the accounting degree? So much for her small bookkeeping business. I am no longer an entrepreneur."

Kelly looked up from her Blackberry. "But didn't Hillary set this whole health care crisis in motion when Bill was president?"

"Only because she was sabotaged by the insurance companies and they ended up writing the bill. Don't you remember those Harry and Louise commercials? Anyway, I'm not talking about politics here. I'm talking about health insurance."

Lynn raised her hand. "I just have to point out, health insurance is about politics."

"Yes you're right but anyway, I got the job with insurance. Then I lost that job due to layoffs and cutbacks. Got another job then got laid off due to a corporate buyout. So, I was unemployed for fourteen months and then finally got my current job in a cubicle forty-five minutes from home. I went from being my own boss to working in a cubicle. So much for climbing the corporate ladder. And that's my story. The working title is 'Life in the first Decade of the New Century'. Did I tell you guys I am thinking of writing a screenplay?"

Lynn passed the salad bowl to her left and the garlic bread to her right. "Doug won't stop nagging me about getting a job. Every day he's on me about it. Complaining we're not saving enough and what if he loses his job again, on and on."

Kelly looked up from her phone. "Okay everyone. Ashley just texted me."

Linda laughed. "She's been texting you all night. Sophie, did you say you were writing a screenplay?"

"She's in New York with Connor. I told you his Dad works for a big computer company right?" Kelly was talking and texting at the same time, she had barely touched her food.

Linda rolled her eyes. "Yes we all know that."

"So they're at this big event for Facebook. Connor's dad knows people who work at Facebook and somehow they all got invited to this promotional thing. He's trying to set Connor up with a job. Anyway, Ashley just saw Mark Zuckerberg. I've got to call her." Kelly got up and went in the other room.

Linda rolled her eyes. "So Connor's dad is going to get him some awesome job with Facebook? What are we doing wrong ladies?"

Sophie poured another glass of wine and also filled Linda's glass. Lynn was at the sink washing dishes. "Hey Lynn, get back here. We'll clean up." She filled Lynn's glass too. "Come on Lynn. I poured you some more wine."

Lynn walked back to the table, wiping her hands on a dishtowel tucked into her jeans.

She shook her head. "Like my mother always said, it's not what you know, it's who you know. Unfortunately my parents didn't know anyone."

Sophie sighed. "Where did I go wrong? But I'm not giving up. This is just a detour. I am going to own that bed and breakfast in the islands."

Linda scoffed and put down her wine glass. "Sophie that is going to be hard too you know. And do you honestly think Ray will finish the work there or will you just be nagging him about something different? And what is this screenplay you are now writing?"

Sophie ignored the screenplay question. She didn't mean to reveal that information. "Sure it will be hard work. But it'll be a hell of a lot more interesting than crunching numbers in a cubicle. Anyway, sounds like Ashley may have hit the jackpot with this guy Connor. His dad's loaded and he's setting Connor up with a job?"

Linda laughed. "Well she got the memo. Kelly made sure of that."

Now it was Lynn's turn to laugh. "Yes THE MEMO. Go to college, get your MRS and marry well."

Sophie shook her head. "Does everyone know about this memo? Because I never got the memo."

Linda nodded. "Neither did I. But it's out there. I think our mothers were supposed to tell us about it. Lynn, your mother must have told you. I mean Doug makes good money and look at this house you live in."

"Well yes my mother did send me the memo. But there are no guarantees. Doug has lost his job twice over the years and we've had our ups and downs. Sometimes you just have this overwhelming feeling you have no control over the course of your life. You do everything right-graduate from college, get a job, buy a house, pay your bills on time, and contribute to your 401K. Everything they tell you to do. Then they lay you off and pull the rug right out from under you."

They could hear Kelly laughing and screaming in the other room.

'You're right Lynn," Sophie agreed. "There are no guarantees. Ashley will get married, she'll buy a house, she'll have kids, and those kids will become teenagers. Her young, handsome, exciting husband never did get that job at Facebook or maybe he did but it's now ten years later and Zuckerberg sold out Facebook to someone else. Her handsome husband's been laid off. He's ten pounds heavier and balding. They've got bills to pay, dinner to make, car repairs, college and the economy is tanking. They're always fighting about money. Where's the romance now? Where are the dreams and aspirations?"

Linda grimaced. "Listen to Debbie Downer. Ha! I love that. Aspirations. Who at our age has aspirations?"

"Do you remember Ellen, that woman I worked with at the foundation?" Lynn asked.

Sophie nodded. "Wasn't she at your Cinco de Mayo party?"

"Yes she was. She asked her husband for a divorce. You know what was the first thing the bastard did? Quit his job. She has a really good job as director of a foundation so now she has to pay him child support. Alimony too, I think."

Linda poured a little more wine in her glass. "Do people still get alimony?"

Lynn shrugged her shoulders. "I guess if they're unemployed they do."

Banging her hand on the table, Sophie shouted, "Well that's not fair. He can do that, just quit his job and get alimony?"

"I don't think people get alimony anymore unless it's a hardship case. And life isn't fair Sophie. Who ever told you it was?" Linda said.

"Trust me I already know that. You might be right about the alimony Linda."

Kelly walked back in the room. "What did I miss? What are you guys talking about?"

Linda tried once again. "We are talking about Sophie's screenplay."

"Oh my God. You have a screenplay? We should tell Connor's dad about this. He knows people in Hollywood. What is it about?"

Sophie smiled at her. "Life and love. How do you make love last? How do you go back to the beginning? When you first met and the passion was there?"

Lynn sighed, "Oh wouldn't we all love the thrill of falling in love again?"

Linda laughed again. "Is that what it's about? Well I agree there's nothing like the excitement of meeting someone and falling in love. The period before your first fight."

Kelly scoffed. "I don't know about that. I can certainly live without the sex."

"You can? Not me but anyway I haven't written anything down yet. It's all just in my head but I think about it constantly while I'm driving to and from work."

Lynn clapped her hands. "You've got to start writing it down. Will the wine emergencies be in it?"

THE BEST BOY

The train blew its horn and pulled out of the station. She reached over, tapped his knee and when he looked up again, she mouthed the words "I love that song." He pulled his earphones out and smiled the biggest, most charming smile that had ever been directed at her. She smiled back at him.

"Yeah I love this too. It's got a really positive message. Chill, ya know?" His voice was very deep and pleasant sounding. She thought he could be a disc jockey.

"What other music do you like?" She definitely wanted to keep this conversation going.

"Bob Marley, Phish, Sublime, Dispatch, older stuff too like Led Zeppelin, The Dead. A lot of different things. How 'bout you?"

"All of the above. Plus I really still do love the Dave Matthews Band. Mostly their older stuff from Under the Table and Crash. Jack Johnson. His music really makes me happy. It's a guaranteed pick-me-up when I'm feeling blue."

He smiled that smile again and leaned towards her, resting his arms on his knees and folding his hands in front of him. His gaze was really steady and although she was feeling a little shy and nervous, she looked right back at him. "Well I hope you're not feeling blue very often. I can play some Jack Johnson songs. Not very well but his chords are pretty easy to learn. I definitely don't sing as well as him."

He laughed at himself. "You heard me singing just then, didn't you?" She smiled and nodded yes. She imagined laying in bed with him, hearing that deep, sexy laugh and rolling over into his arms. She hoped her cheeks were still rosy from the cold run to the train because she felt herself blushing. A young mother was leaning against the window and watched them through slit eyes. "So, you play guitar?" she asked.

"I try. Do you work at that last stop?"

"Yes. How 'bout you?"

"I live in Newburyport but I'm headed to a show at the Paradise. Are you going into town tonight too?"

"I live in town, out near Cleveland Circle."

"Sweet. So you commute out here to work?"

"Yeah. Kind of backwards, huh? It's called a reverse commute."

"Do you like your job?"

"No."

He waved his hand flat in front of him like a blackjack player who doesn't want another card. "That's a definitive no? Not a maybe? Sorta? A little bit? Just absolutely no?" He crinkled his nose. "What do you do?"

She sighed. "It's really boring and hard to explain."

"Go ahead. Try and explain."

"You know when you're reading something on the Internet and some of the words or phrases are highlighted? If you click on them it brings you to another article or more information?"

"Uhhuh." He seemed to be really paying attention. He was concentrating on what she was saying.

"Well those are called tags, the highlighted words. I get the finished article with the tags and then I click on the tag and make sure it directs you to the correct information."

"Are the articles interesting?"

"No." She smiled.

He waved his hand like before. He had beautiful hands, strong with long fingers. "Again with the flat out no? Bummer." He leaned back in his seat and rubbed the stubble on his chin, smiling at her and shaking his head. "How do you get a job like that?"

"You major in creative writing in college and want to be a writer but that doesn't pay the rent. Not yet."

"Not yet. That's good. Ya gotta believe. So you write?"

"Well, yes, I try to but most days my brain is fried from working eight hours at a computer and I don't want to get back on the computer when I get home. I haven't sat down and written seriously in months. I had such big plans when I graduated from college but now I feel like I'm treading water or even worse swimming backwards. Drowning. Watch out for the undertoad!" She shook her head.

He laughed. "World According to Garp. I love that book."

"You do?" She gazed at him with what felt like such a look of longing she knew she was blushing again. She really hoped he hadn't noticed how wistful she had sounded but he was looking directly at her, focused on her every word.

"Geez, sounds like you're always going backwards. You're commuting backwards to work and your big plans for the future aren't going in the right direction either." He snapped his fingers. "What is that? The reverse commute. Hold on. I know it." He rubbed the stubble on his chin for a second. "Double entendre, right?"

She jumped a little in her seat, clapped her hands and very excitedly and loudly said, "I can't believe you just said that. Yes. You get it. I used that exact same phrase a while ago. But my...um the person I was talking to, he so did not get it." She shook her head and smiled. The young mother sat up in her seat and shifted the sleeping baby to her other shoulder.

"Oh I'm so sorry. Did I wake her?" she whispered.

The young mom shook her head no. The businessman was closing his laptop, sliding it in its case and getting up to leave as the train came to a stop. The train conductor could be heard saying loudly "Swampscott, this stop."

The baby started to whimper and the young mom shot her a look like it was her fault instead of the train conductor's. As the businessman stood up he said, "Excuse me" and the Best Boy hopped up and moved into the aisle. While he was standing there she checked out his lean body. He was about five ten. All four people across the aisle also got up to leave the train. He tapped her on the shoulder, nodded his head towards the empty seats across from them and whispered, "Let's bounce."

She grabbed her bags, he picked up his backpack and they moved across the aisle. They took window seats across from each other, placing their things on the seats next to them. He was smiling and winked at her mischievously.

"So do you work? Go to school?" she asked.

"Which one should I start with? Umm let's see. I graduated from high school and went into an electrician's apprenticeship with the IBEW. Do you know what that is?"

"The union, right?"

"Yup, my uncle helped me. That took four years. Now I work with my uncle. But I'm saving money to move to L.A. I've got a buddy out there who works on films. He's a Best Boy. And that's what I'm hoping to do too. On my way to being head electrician on academy award winning movies."

"I always see the Best Boy in the credits. So that's what a Best Boy is? An electrician?"

"Well there are two kinds of best boys, the electrician and the grip. The grip stages the rigging and moves the cameras. A best boy is just another name for head assistant. I should have enough money to move out there by the fall. That's what I'm planning anyway, mid-September is my goal."

"That's awesome. Maybe if I ever write a screenplay I can send it to you and you can give it to some director or something."

He rubbed his chin again and looked out the window then he turned to her with a smile. She thought he seemed to be one very happy guy. He was always smiling and it was a killer smile. The kind of smile that made your heart skip a beat.

"Hey are you doing anything tonight?"

Nick popped into her mind but she remembered he was out of town and thought to herself 'Thank you Dallas audit department'.

"No plans," she said nonchalantly, aiming for a casual demeanor although her heart was racing.

"I have an extra ticket to this show at the Paradise. My buddy was supposed to come with me but he got sick. I was just going to sell his ticket outside the show but you could come with me instead. It's a reggae show. Four really great bands. You interested?"

"Sure. That sounds fun. Why not?"

"Exactly, why not?" He nodded his head in agreement. "Cool."

The train pulled into North Station and as they got up to exit, he put his hand on her back and guided her through the train station towards the subway. When it got really crowded on the stairs to the Green line, he grabbed her hand. "Yo. Follow me" and they slipped through the crowds down the side of the stairs. When they stopped by the tracks to wait for the next train, he didn't let go of her hand. He pulled her closer. "Are you hungry?"

"I'm starving. I only had a peanut butter sandwich for lunch."

"I know a Mexican place on the way to the Paradise. You like spicy food?"

She nodded her head yes and laughed. "Do they have margaritas?"

"Of course they do. Hey have you ever tried peanut butter with nutella?"

When they got to the restaurant he asked her if she minded sitting at the bar. "I really prefer it." He took his hat off, bent over and shook his shoulder length hair. He stood back up laughing and pushed his hair off his face. His curly bangs kept tumbling onto his forehead and he finally gave up trying to push them back. "Hat hair, " he laughed. His hair was really thick and wavy, very luxurious, not like some guys with ratty, stringy long hair. It looked very clean and soft. She was sure some girls were very envious of that head of hair. She really wanted to touch it and run her fingers through it. She was pretty sure it smelled good too. The evening was turning out really well. "I prefer the bar too, much more social."

"Word."

She shook her head. He talked in surfer dude lingo but knew what a double entendre was. They ordered nachos and chili rellenos to share and a pitcher of margaritas. She told him about college and her trip cross-country with Katie. She mentioned how she really liked Oregon and was not sure why she moved back. She didn't mention Nick.

He told her after he finished his apprenticeship, he went to Australia and New Zealand. He did some surfing. He loved to surf, which is why he wanted to move to L.A. and to be a Best Boy. When he was getting ready to leave New Zealand, he got the opportunity to go to Vietnam. He surfed there for two months.

"That is so awesome. Did you like it there?"

"It was bonus. This guy I met just invited me at the last minute. The surfin' is gnarly and it's so cheap to stay there. You gotta go."

"I would love to. Hey how do you get back to Newbury-port tonight? Don't the trains stop early?"

"Yeah it's a bummer. The last train out leaves at midnight, which means I would have to leave the show early to catch the train. But I have a friend in Cleveland Circle who told me to give him a call anytime I need a place to stay. He usually hides a key for me if I'm gonna be late. I asked him to take my buddy's ticket and join me but he has a hot date tonight. Hey, he probably lives near you."

The bartender brought their food. "So what are you writing about?" He was serving up food from the platters for the two of them and passed a plate to her.

"Well I started a screenplay about a group of underemployed college grads living in Portland. It was based on my roommates and me. I thought it was pretty funny. But then that show came out. Portlandia?"

"Oh yeah. Well just move the characters to a different city, like Boston."

"That's true. But then it would be like Cheers and if I move it to New York it's Friends."

"Those shows are old. And you know what they say. There are only so many stories in the world. It's all in the telling of the story. Your version of the story."

"You're right. I got so bummed out, like the writers of Portlandia stole my idea by osmosis. One of my roommates was even doing standup comedy like that character that bombs out in his one man stage performance? The whole thing got me so bummed out I got writers block."

"This happened to me too. I wrote a song and Jack Johnson stole it. Seriously. It was that song Flake, about maybe really meaning no." He softly sang a few lines.

"You really do have a nice voice."

"No, I don't but thanks. Anyway. My Mom always used to say that. She'd ask me to do something or tell me I should take advanced math, stuff like that, trying to get me to push myself and I'd always say maybe."

He cleared his throat and then tried to sound like his mother, using a bossy Mom kind of voice. "She'd say 'I know that maybe really means no you know, you can't fool me'. So I wrote a song about it and then whatta ya know, Jack Johnson writes a song about it. Unreal. How does this happen? You might be right. It could be osmosis." The evening just kept going like this. He was so funny and relaxed. He seemed to understand or anticipate everything she said. It was like she'd known him all her life.

After the restaurant, while they were walking to the club, she was lost in thoughts about how the evening was going to end. She definitely didn't want it to end. They'd be taking the same train to Cleveland Circle. Should she ask him to come over for one more drink? She did a quick inventory of her apartment. Were there any photos of Nick in the living room? She didn't think so. They didn't have any personal photos displayed around the place. What about the bathroom? Nick usually kept his things in his shaving kit because he'd been traveling a lot lately so he would have that with him in Dallas. She used the guest room as her writing room where they also had a double bed. It would be really bad to stay in the master bedroom she shared with Nick. What was she thinking? She knew this whole train of thought was really bad. She was planning to bring another guy back to the apartment where she lived with her boyfriend. But she also knew she didn't care. She felt his elbow nudge her arm and she smiled up at him, "I'm sorry, what did you say?"

"Do you blaze?" He passed her a joint. She took a big hit and tried to relax and not get ahead of herself, just let the evening take its course.

* * *

The club was packed and the music was loud. Everyone was dancing. They were standing in the middle of the crowded room. She was craning her neck around a tall guy in front of her. The Best Boy leaned over and shouted in her ear, "Can you see anything down there?"

"Not really but I can get closer. Stay right with me. I'm good at this." She grabbed his hand and pulled him close behind her. She nudged the tall guy and he turned to look down at her. When she smiled up at him, he smiled back and moved a little to his left. They slipped into the open space next to him and continued doing this until she worked herself to the stage, pulling him along right behind her.

"You really are good at that. I'm stickin' with you babe." He wrapped his arms around her waist. She turned her head to look back at him and as she did, he kissed her. Whispering in her ear, he murmured in that deep sexy voice of his, "I've been waiting to do that since the train pulled out of the station." A lock of his wavy hair fell across his face and she reached up to push it back. It was as soft as it looked.

The last song of the evening was a cover of one of her favorite Bob Marley tunes, 'Mellow Mood'. They were at the back of the room now where it was cooler and not so crowded. He took her beer glass and put it down on a nearby table. He reached out his arm, grabbed her hand, twirled her around and swung her under his arm then pulled her close and put his other arm around her waist. They danced to the mellow love song.

I HAD A DREAM LAST NIGHT

Later that night, after the wine emergency, Sophie was sitting in Ray's recliner. She was watching the movie 'Blue Valentine' and drinking another glass of wine, the bottle of cabernet on the end table next to her chair. Once in awhile she spoke out loud to herself.

"Oh my God, look at his hands. They have paint on them. He paints houses for a living."

"Why am I watching this?"

"This is my life."

"This is so sad. My life is so sad."

"My marriage is falling apart."

When Ryan Gosling played the ukulele in the storefront doorway she rewound the DVD and watched it again. "This guy is so cute. Is this the guy from the Notebook?" She also rewound the oral sex scene, twice.

She was getting weepy and poured another glass of wine. The movie ended with her quietly sobbing as she shut off the TV. She wiped her eyes with the back of her hand, got a glass of water and went up to bed alone.

* * *

Sophie was asleep, stretched corner to corner in the queen size bed, wearing a T-shirt and undies. It was early dawn, still a little dark in the room. She was dreaming.

She was in a nightclub, dancing with friends. She was young, about twenty. A boy was watching her from over at the bar and he looked an awful lot like the actor in the movie she just watched. He was wearing a black leather jacket, white T-shirt and jeans. He caught her eye, smiled and joined her on the crowded dance floor. There was a sense she knew him, that he was her boyfriend. He walked up to her very confi-

dently, smiled and grabbed her by the waist. They began to dance erotically, holding onto each other and kissing, laughing, flirting. She had one leg bent and was wrapping it around him. As he put his hands on her butt, she hopped up and wrapped both legs around him. Holding her and rocking to the rhythm, he slid one hand under her shirt, stroking her back.

Suddenly the dream jumped to the interior of a jeep in the parking lot of the nightclub. In that weird world of dreaming they were somehow making it from the front seat to the back of the jeep without encountering any obstacles. The actor was undressing her, pulling her jeans down and lifting her T-shirt over her head as they inched their way back. He moved his hand along her bare leg, kissing her stomach. They began to make passionate love.

Sleeping Sophie was in her bed, tossing around, apparently aroused. Sunlight was beginning to stream into the bedroom through the lace curtains. Her eyes drifted open then shut as she moaned and rolled over, trying to go back to sleep and recapture the dream. She felt herself bouncing and floating around the room. As she rolled onto her back, her eyes popped wide open and she stared up at the ceiling.

Later that morning, she was trying to do housework. She was vacuuming, picking things up and dusting. She looked out at the deck towards the river, as leaves blew across the yard, and noticed the furniture on the deck with no cushions. She knew they were stacked up behind the couch on which there was a pile of folded clothes. She got some large black garbage bags from the kitchen, put the cushions in them and carried them out to a shed past the deck. Returning to the deck, she brought three chairs, one at a time, to the shed. The wind was blowing harder and her hair kept flying across her face. She came back in the house and shivered as the wind blew leaves from the deck into the house and onto the floor she had just finished vacuuming. She put the folded clothes in a laundry basket and carried it upstairs. Lying on her bed, she closed her eyes, drifting off between wakefulness and dreaming.

* * *

Young Sophie entered a subway car in Boston, listening to her IPod. She had long brown hair and her silver bracelets and hoop earrings caught the light from the harsh overhead lighting of the subway car. She was wearing faded jeans, a Che Quevera T-shirt and a flannel jacket with a soft fleece lining. The Actor was sitting across from the door as she entered. He was in jeans, a black hoodie, jean jacket and boots.

He looked up at her, was instantly attracted and smiled. She didn't notice him because she was looking down at her IPod, selecting music and walking down the aisle to a seat running along the side of the subway car. The Actor got up and followed her, taking a seat perpendicular to her, his legs bumping hers. She looked up and he said "Sorry." He smiled. She smiled back and took a map out of her backpack, studying it. The Actor tapped her on the knee and asked, "Where are you headed?" She looked up again. "Government Center."

"Me too. Are you going to the rally?"

"Yes, I am."

"You can walk with me if you like. I know where it is."

"Ok, that'll make it easy." She laughed then folded her map. She looked him over, assessing him. He was very attractive and had a really nice smile and a twinkle in his eyes.

Her dream drifted to them talking on the subway, leaning towards each other. At one point he put his hand on her arm and pointed to a sign above the seats across from them. It had graffiti all over it and the people in the advertisement were made up with funny faces, mustaches and large glasses. He looked at her, widening his eyes in a very inquisitive, endearing way. Almost like he was asking "What's up with that?" They laughed.

The subway car stopped at Government Center. He took her hand, pulled her up from the seat and said "Come on."

They wove their way through the large crowd of people, some wearing Obama '08 buttons or carrying signs. He took her hand. "This way, it's less crowded." She bumped up close to him and also grabbed his arm with her other hand.

Sophie rolled over in her sleep. She moaned.

She was in a studio apartment in a small galley kitchen with the Actor. He was cooking spaghetti and meatballs while she drank a beer, leaning against the counter. They were flirting with each other. He was waving a wooden spoon in the air while he talked and laughed. She was clearly fascinated with whatever it was he was talking about.

She heard a song coming from her IPod, which was setup on a docking station in the other room. She grabbed his hand and pulled him into the other room where they started to dance.

A HAT TRICK

They were riding above ground on the Green line down Commonwealth Avenue towards Cleveland Circle. Her stop was the next one. They had already exchanged cell phone numbers. He asked her if she was on Facebook and she said no. She needed to get on the computer ASAP and close her account. She didn't want him to see she was in a relationship with Nick. And if she removed her relationship status, Nick would see it. She thought it must have been easier to have an affair before the Internet.

Was that what she was doing? Planning to have an affair? She never pictured herself as That Girl.

"Is your place right on Comm Ave?"

She snapped out of her reverie. "Huh? Oh no, it's about five blocks up that way." She pointed out the window. The snow was still coming down steadily. It had been like this since she left work. "Then two blocks to the right. I'm closer to Beacon Street, I usually take that line home but we were on Comm Ave and I can get there from here."

He frowned and looked concerned. It was after one and the streets were empty. "That's a long way. I'm gonna walk you home."

"You don't really have to do that. There won't be any more trains at this time of night and it's a long walk from my place to the Circle. This is a safe neighborhood and I've done it by myself plenty of times."

"Hey, I'm not taking no for an answer." He made his blackjack player's signal from earlier in the evening and then placed his hand on hers. "You shouldn't be walking around alone like that late at night." He squeezed her hand. She didn't protest. She wanted him to walk her home. She had already decided she was going to invite him in when they got to her apartment.

* * *

Once inside the apartment, she gave a quick look around in case there were some photos she forgot about. He let out a long, slow whistle, pointing to the bay windows with the seat looking out at a park across the street and the beautiful woodwork.

"This is a nice place."

"Thanks, my roommate found it and she pays two thirds of the rent because her parents help her." Lying didn't seem like it was going to be a problem for her. Where was this coming from?

He whispered and pointed to the master bedroom door, which was thankfully closed. "Is she here?"

"No, she's away on business. Would you like a beer?"

"Thanks. I'm all set. What does she do?" He looked around curiously, checking out the Pottery Barn sofa and the giant flat screen TV that Nick splurged on with his first bonus check.

"Accounting. She does pretty well. Most of this stuff is hers. The old stuff is from my parents house in Vermont before they moved to Florida."

"You're from Vermont? Do you board?" He seemed nervous. He was rocking on his feet.

"I ski. I learned when I was little and got pretty good so I never wanted to go back to being a beginner on a board. I beat most boarders down the mountain."

He laughed. "Yeah I could see that." He looked down for a minute. "Hey I'm not really good at this. I had a girlfriend for three years. About a year ago she got a job in New York and bounced. She told me it was time to move on. I haven't really been dating much since getting burned, just hanging with my buddies and working a lot. Saving money 'til it's my turn to bounce to L.A."

"That's OK. I had a really nice time tonight. A really, really nice..."

He leaned in, cupped her face with his right hand while putting his left hand on the side of her head, running it through her hair. He started kissing her, long and deep. She put her arms around his neck, running her hands through that really soft hair of his, responding with equal intensity. She moved her left leg around his right one and he reached down with both hands to grab her ass while she hopped up and wrapped her legs around him. His voice was deeper and husky sounding. "Where are we going?"

She nodded towards the guest bedroom.

* * *

The alarm went off at six in the morning. It was still dark outside. She moaned and as she came to, she realized she was in the arms of the boy she met last night. She rolled away from him and groped for her cell phone on the night table. "That's annoying," she mumbled as she shut it off.

"Hmm. Hey, get back here." He rolled on his side and reached for her, but she hopped out of bed.

"I have to go to the bathroom."

"Hurry back. I need you."

When she got back to the bed, she was wearing a silk bathrobe. He was lying there with his arms behind his head eyes wide open. He pulled himself up on his elbows. "Where you going?" His voice was groggy. He had some seriously sexy bed head going on and she wanted to jump back in and pounce on him.

"I have to get ready for work. The snow is slowing down but it looks like we got eight inches out there." She leaned over and kissed him. He grabbed her around the waist and pulled her onto the bed.

"Ahha! I gotcha ya." He kissed her. "Hey no fair, you brushed your teeth."

"I have to go to work. I can't miss my train out of North Station. Don't you have to work?"

"No, the framers pushed us off until tomorrow. Come on, call in sick. We could make a snowman in that park across the street. Have a snowball fight. I bet you could kick my ass Miss Vermont. Maybe go to a museum afterwards? Come on. Please?"

She was contemplating this when he started tickling her under her arms. She immediately started laughing hysterically as they rolled around on the bed while she tried to get away from him.

"Stop. Please stop. I am really, really ticklish." She was trying to catch her breath as she kept laughing, tears rolling down her cheeks.

He was laughing that low, sexy laugh she dreamed about waking up next too. "I'm not stopping until you say yes." He started tickling her neck.

"No, No, not the neck," she gasped breathlessly. "That's the worst. I'll call, I'll call in sick."

"You promise? You're not trying to get away, are you?"

"I promise. I'm dying here, I have to call in sick." He let go of her and she lunged for her cell phone on the night table. She was lying on her stomach, scrolling her contacts then rolled on her back and looked at him. "Shh"

He mouthed the word "OK" and got up to go to the bathroom.

When he got back, she had just finished sending a text to Nick. Sometime last night when they were at the club he sent a message asking about the snowstorm. She answered him back although it was four in the morning in Dallas and she ran the risk of him waking up and calling her back. He was a heavy sleeper and might think it was four in the morning here too and call to ask why she was up at that hour. She decided to shut the phone off after she sent the message. She'd tell him she forgot to charge it when he called tonight.

He was crawling up from the bottom of the bed towards her, kissing her along the way from her toes to her neck. He stopped, looked deep into her eyes, tracing her lips with his finger and asked, "How did that go?"

"Snow day."

He laughed with his mouth closed, one of those secret, satisfied kind of laughs and they rolled over kissing, all tangled arms and legs.

* * *

There was a pale light in the room now. It was turning out to be a cloudy day and although the worst of the storm was over, snow still drifted past the window. She was in a post-coital stupor, happy and warm in the circle of his arms. He had drifted back to sleep. She pushed herself up a little bit and gazed at his sleeping face, his strong jawline and long eyelashes. Why do boys have such great eyelashes she wondered?

He had a tattoo on his left shoulder, a black outline of two hearts entwined. She frowned and wondered what that was. She traced the hearts with her finger, around and around. There was no beginning or end. He started to stir, moved his hand through her hair and looked down at her finger moving along the tattoo. "Aaah, I bet you're curious about that, huh?" His voice was really sleepy. He picked up her hand and kissed it.

"Slightly curious."

"I have to warn you. It's a sad story."

"You don't have to tell me if you don't want to."

He cleared his throat and sat up a little. "It's for my Mom and Dad. They died in a car accident my senior year in high school. An icy night the weekend after Thanksgiving."

"Oh my God, that's awful." She didn't know what to say so she just squeezed his hand. He slipped his fingers through hers and held her hand tighter.

"Yeah, it was really awful. No sugar coating that one. My sister was home from college, thank God. So I wasn't alone in the house when the cops came. My aunt and uncle live in Newburyport too, the uncle I work with, ya know?" He took a deep breath and blew it out.

"Dave's my mom's brother. He and my aunt Helen never had kids so they hung out with us all the time. They used to babysit us a lot when we were little kids. They came right over and saved us immediately. Took care of everything. My sister stayed around 'til Christmas but decided my parents would have wanted her to finish college so she went back to Amherst in late January."

"I can't even begin to imagine how you felt."

"Yeah, anyway, I lived with Dave and Helen. Finished high school, barely. I was never much of a student. My sister Ava was the brains of the family. And my parents' death sure didn't help things. Dave got me the apprenticeship. He must have had to pull some strings to get me in. My grades sucked." He laughed, a hollow sounding laugh this time.

"To make a long, sad story short, a year into the apprenticeship, Dave thought it would be a good idea to make an apartment above his garage. I think he thought I needed my own space or something. So we worked on it together. It's really cool. One big room with a horseshoe bar at the far end. There's a small kitchen at the back and a pretty good size bathroom with a whirlpool tub. You'll have to come over sometime."

"I'd love to."

He tousled her hair and gave her a kiss. "It was Dave who encouraged me to travel before I started working. We had sold my parents house so Ava and I had a small inheritance. He told me to take a little of the money and see the world. So I flew to Aussie. I wanted to surf Bondi Beach. Little did I know I'd surf Vietnam too. That's the beauty of open-ended traveling.

But now I'm back working, living above the garage and saving for the next chapter. I think when I leave for L.A. Dave has plans to turn my apartment into a man cave. He's mentioned there's plenty of room for a pool table and Ping-Pong. And of course there's the horseshoe bar."

"Where's your sister now?"

"Ava graduated from UMASS hmmm five years ago, I think? Has it been five years? Wow. Sometimes it all just seems like yesterday. Don't let anyone fool you with that closure shit. There's no such thing. You think you're okay and then some days it comes back and hits you like a ton of bricks. Grief comes and goes even seven years later." He shook his head in disbelief.

"Oh, right, Ava. Ava wanted to go to Denver. She had a job offer at a hospital out there. She's a nurse by the way. But she thought she should stay in Boston close to me. I told her no way, I was okay. She needed to go and live her own life, have some adventures. Besides it would be nice to have someone to visit in Colorado. I've been out there a bunch of times. Love the back bowls of Vail, man. And I am okay. Ninety percent of the time anyway. But enough about me. Can a guy get some coffee around here?"

* * *

She was in the kitchen making a pot of coffee. She usually mixed half Maxwell House coffee with Starbucks Sumatran. This was her idea when Nick had suggested they come up with ideas for saving money for the all important condo account. A meager contribution for sure, considering all those nights out she had when he was away on business. Thank goodness he didn't suggest a joint savings account. So this morning she just took out the Starbucks. She didn't care about the condo. To be honest, she had never cared.

He came in the kitchen wearing a white T-shirt and blue plaid boxer shorts. She thought 'God he's hot!' How can she be getting horny again? They've made love three times in less than twelve hours. A hat trick! That was more sex than she'd had in a month, another problem she'd rather not think about right now. He was carrying a book she had beside the bed in the guest room. "Have you read this?"

"Oh I love that book."

"Me too. Do you remember in the beginning when he's struggling with all that religion stuff? He wants to be a Christian, a Muslim and a Hindu?"

"Yeah that was great. I really liked that part."

"Well isn't that kind of what we were talking about last night? That's there only so many stories in the world?"

"Huh?"

"The bible, man. It's the same story as the Koran and all the other holy books. They're all different versions of the same story. And if that's true, then you can certainly write your own version of a group of friends living together somewhere and trying to make their way in the world."

She slapped her hand on the countertop and shouted, "You are so right."

"I know. I am right."

"That's it. I am going to set this story in Burlington, Vermont where I grew up. I mean there isn't much happening there but that could be the point. They all graduate from college and aren't quite ready to leave yet although opportunities are limited in Vermont. They are experiencing a kind of inertia, not ready to grow up yet, you know?"

He nodded his head. "Yeah, I'm personally familiar with that."

"Ooooh oooh. I know. I can have a character like my Dad too, a disheveled, nutty sort of cantankerous old professor. That can be a parallel story. This is great."

"There you go. You're on your way."

She kissed him as she handed him a cup of really nice, strong dark Sumatran. "Did you say you weren't a good student? 'Cus I don't see that?" She leaned back against the counter, sipping her coffee and smiling at him.

"The classroom wasn't my thing." He was looking at the boxes of cereal lined up on top of the fridge. The choices were all healthy with flax seeds and whole grains. "Do you have any Coco Puffs?"

"Coco Puffs?" She started giggling.

"Don't laugh. I like the chocolate milk it leaves in the bottom of the bowl."

They were sitting at the kitchen table, finishing their cereal. He ended up choosing one with pomegranate seeds. He didn't really like it but solved the problem by slicing two bananas into his bowl so he would have a banana with every bite.

She'd just finished telling him about her junior year in Paris and how when it was over, her friend Katie met her and they spent the months of June and July backpacking thru Switzerland, Italy, Turkey and Greece.

"That's awesome. So many places to go. Sleeping on those ferries in the Greek islands sounds great. I've got to add that to my list of places to go."

As she loaded the bowls and coffee cups into the dishwasher, she thought to herself 'this guy is a dream come true.'

DO YOU GO TO THE MOVIES?

Sophie and Ray were in the kitchen drinking coffee while Sophie was making lunches and emptying the dishwasher. "So Ray, can we start planning for this weekend? You had your golf trip and I'm glad you had fun so now let's get something done in the addition. I'm serious about selling the house this spring. The yard looks it's best when all the apple trees and lilacs are in bloom. Before everything gets wildly overgrown. You're with me, right?"

"Yeah believe me, I'm as sick of maintaining this place as you are. I'll finish the closet and the floor in the bedroom. That'll be ready when the boys come home for Thanksgiving. Then I'll move on to the bathrooms. I can definitely get those done by spring."

Sophie smiled. Instead of rushing out the door like she usually did, she optimistically kissed Ray goodbye then left for work.

Driving down the highway she looked at a stand of birch trees just over the bridge she crossed every day. This was the first time in over three years of driving this route that she had noticed them. It must have been because their leaves had fallen. Or maybe something else. Listening to the radio, she began to daydream.

* * *

In Sophie's dream, she was living in a perfect little English cottage with a thatched roof in the Cotswold's. It was on a country lane just outside of a small town with a bookstore, a pub and a bakery. A stonewall ran along the road and the front yard was a wild perennial garden. Flowers of all colors and heights were planted close together and wild roses climbed up the front of the stone house. Sophie was working at her computer by the front window, looking at the steady rain pelting the leaded glass window. Behind her a fire was blazing in a beautiful stone fireplace. She heard a knock at the door and shouted, "Come on in."

Her neighbor opened the door and peeked in. "Hey Sophie, I brought you the weekly payroll from the pub."

"Thanks Ewan. You can just put it on the kitchen table. Would you like a cup of coffee?"

"You know I don't like coffee. You're in England now dear, how about a cup of tea?"

Ewan was very handsome, about forty years old and very fit, wearing a yellow slicker and tall black rubber rain boots. "The new bartender, Seamus, told me to tell you he thinks some of the waiters are giving you duff information. They might be padding their hours, so double check the time cards."

"Thanks again Ewan."

Sophie snapped out of her daydream and saw she was passing the farm on the way into town. There were pumpkins where the sunflowers used to be. A large sign was out front and she laughed, reading it out loud, "Visit our corn maze and GET LOST."

She shook her head like she was trying to wake up. She decided she really needed to pay attention because she didn't remember getting here. The drive along the highway was a distant blur. She started to sing thinking that might help her focus on the road. Her mind drifted back to the cottage in England.

"It's a nasty day out there, isn't it?" she asked Ewan.

"Oh yeah. The weatherman had duff info too. Said it would only be overcast but the rain's really coming down. Cozy in here though." He rubbed his hands by the fire while she put a kettle on the stove to make tea.

"Yes it is. Not a bad place to work. A warm fire, a view of an English garden and the sound of rain on the window. Beats the cubicle I left behind back in the states. I used to work in a dreary windowless room thinking it was raining

outside even when it wasn't. Now I can actually see, smell and hear the rain and it's absolutely lovely." She took a break from her work and sat down next to the fire to have coffee and tea with Ewan.

Daydreaming, Sophie turned into town where there was a new detour set up today. This one led her directly through the center of town where there was a long line of traffic. She waited in front of a school where a crossing guard was waving several young kids across the street. This would normally really annoy her but instead she was still singing and daydreaming.

Sophie pulled into the parking lot. The clock on her dashboard said 8:15. Although she was fifteen minutes late she stayed in the car and listened to the end of the song. A flock of Canadian geese flew over the house across the street. A dowdy, tired looking woman, about fifteen years older than Sophie, got out of her car and locked her car door. She stopped to look in the car window, fixed her graying hair and then pulled her laptop behind her on one of those rolling stewardess suitcase carriers, shuffling off to the building they worked in.

Sophie watched her with a look of horror on her face. She said out loud "Oh my God, she looks like Ida Blankenship."

* * *

Ray was working up on the roof of a house. The front of the house was covered with a blue plastic tarp and leaves were blowing across the front lawn. He was working with three other guys and they were laying down black roofing paper. It was chilly out this morning and Ray was wearing a heavy flannel shirt with a fleece lining and black gloves with the fingertips cut off.

A little while later he stopped for lunch. He was working with another guy the same age as him who was also a good friend. His name was Brian. They usually had lunch together when they were on the same job.

"Hey Ray, what do you have for lunch?" Ray was taking a sandwich, yogurt and a banana out of his cooler. He noticed there was no drink in there. "Not sure what kind of sandwich. Sophie makes my lunch."

"Your wife makes you lunch? Lucky guy. Look at that, she even gave you a chocolate chip cookie."

"Yeah but she keeps forgetting to give me a drink lately. It's so dry without a drink."

"Here, I brought two." He handed Ray a lemon seltzer water. "How was the golf weekend?"

"Great as usual. I've been going with my buddies for fifteen years now. I won the Hawaiian shirt contest this year."

"Say what?"

"Friday night we get up to the hotel, we have drinks at the clubhouse and everyone wears an Hawaiian shirt. There's a prize for first place. This year it was a gift certificate for dinner at a restaurant. I figure Sophie and I can go some weekend. We hardly ever get out anymore, money's tight."

"You two still planning to jump ship? Move to the islands or something?"

"We're working on it. She's constantly nagging me to finish the addition but she's right, it's been too long. And I'll tell you, a day like this up on that roof." He pointed to the roof they had just come down from and shook his head. "I don't know how much more I can do it."

"You and me both my friend. Maybe I can be the handyman at your B&B."

"No, that would be my job Brian. Learn to windsurf, why don't ya? You can offer lessons to the guests. I can see you with a little surf shack down by the beach."

"Carol will never go for moving to the islands." He laughed. "So maybe I'll just come alone."

* * *

Meanwhile Sophie was standing at the printer near her cubicle. She had a stack of invoices on the table and was scanning them into the printer one at a time. She typed some info on the small keypad, hit enter and the machine then sent the scanned copy to her email. She did this thirty times while she stared at the wall as she waited for each invoice to pass through the machine. Dan passed by. She rolled her eyes at him and he shook his head.

When she finished, she went back to her desk. She opened each scanned invoice into an email. One at a time she typed something into the subject line of the email and then sent the invoice to the corporate offices to be paid. After she sent each one, she took a big date stamp and stamped the paper copy of the invoice with the date and turned it over onto another pile. She also did this thirty times.

She googled a movie theater that was on her way home, looking for a movie the actor was in. She thought it was still in the theaters. Sure enough, she found it at a theater close by but today was the last day it was playing. There was a show at four thirty. That was the time she usually left work.

Sophie opened an excel spreadsheet. She picked up a pile of checks and started entering the check number and date on the spreadsheet. An email came in from her boss Tina. *"I'm leaving at three to bring my daughter to the orthodontist."*

"No problem, see you tomorrow." Sophie replied.

She thought 'How lucky is that?' At four o'clock Sophie shut down her computer and put her coat on. She poked her head in Dan's cubicle. He was slouched in his chair, staring at his computer, smiling. He had his headphones on so she leaned over and waved to get his attention. He looked up and took his headphones off.

"I'm leaving a little early. Dentist's appointment."

He laughed. "You too? Okay. See you tomorrow." He put his headphones back on and went back to whatever he was smiling at on his computer.

* * *

About twenty minutes later, Sophie pulled into the movie theater parking lot. It was dusk and the lights in the parking lot had come on. There was one other car at this end of the lot. A bald, husky man about fifty years of age was sitting in the driver's seat, eating a sandwich.

Sophie got out of her car and walked into the theater. The lobby was empty and no one was working at the ticket booth or the concession stand. There were eight theaters, four on each side and an area with pinball machines along the back wall. Sophie called out "Is anyone here?"

She walked up and down, opening the door to each of the eight theaters and called out "Hello? Anyone in here?" Every one of the eight screens was showing the same thing, which was an ad for the concession stand. Each theater had a ticker-tape sign above the door and it was running the names of all the movies playing that day. It was impossible to tell which theater her movie was playing in. She walked up and down several more times. Now that she had escaped from work a half hour early and was here, she certainly didn't want to give up and leave.

The man from the car in the parking lot came in. She thought he might work here so she walked up to him. He looked over at her and asked, "Are they open? Anyone here to sell tickets?"

"No. I haven't seen anyone. I've been searching around."

"Maybe we can watch for free."

"I've been checking it out. I'm not sure the movie just starts. I think someone has to start the film because my movie was supposed to start ten minutes ago."

They heard a door open and looked towards the concession stand. A young man came out of a small closet behind the popcorn machine. "All right," Sophie shouted. "There is someone working here. We weren't sure you were open for business."

The young man smiled sheepishly and rubbed his eyes. He walked over to the ticket booth and sold them their tickets. The man from the car was going to another movie, a sci-fi adventure. He walked over to the concession stand and waited while Sophie bought her ticket. "Theater six," the boy told her. She walked straight back to theater six.

She chose a seat eight rows back from the screen. The lights dimmed and she watched what seemed like a half hour of previews. Finally, the theater got darker and the movie began. She was still alone in the dark theater. The Actor appeared in a car on the screen.

THE BELLE OF AMHERST

She couldn't stop thinking about him. She was sitting at her desk in her cubicle, reading an article on Emily Dickinson's poetry and thinking maybe Katie was right. Maybe she could write about her boring life. After all, Emily Dickinson was a recluse who never left her house in Amherst but look at the things she wrote.

"He touched me, so I live to know that such a day, permitted so.... And now, I'm different from before As if I breathed superior air or brushed a royal gown"

At the very least she liked the articles she was reading now. She had finished the medical advice assignment and moved on to American poetry. First it was Walt Whitman and now Emily.

"Hope is the thing with feathers, that perches in the soul, and sings the tune without the words, and never stops at all."

She hoped she would hear from him again and soon. He called Thursday after they had spent the snow day together. He just wanted to let her know the framers had pushed them off again. So he was going up to Cannon Mountain skiing for the day. Then he got a call that the work got canceled all the way to Monday so he had decided to stay through the weekend with a friend in Waterville Valley who was working as a chef at the mountain. His friend got ski passes from work and they'd both be able to ski for free. "Just wanted to call and let you know I'm thinking about you and will get in touch as soon as I get back," he said.

"I envy seas whereon he rides...I envy speechless hills that gaze upon his journey...I envy light that wakes him"

He certainly seemed to have a lot of friends. It was now another Thursday. A full week since she'd heard from him. It was early March and tomorrow was her birthday. She was getting nervous. She should have known things were too perfect. Nothing was ever that perfect.

"I dwell in possibility."

Oh well. He was busy. He was with his friend all weekend and now he must have finally started the job. He might be working late to make up for lost time? She wouldn't have been able to see him until yesterday anyway. Nick was home over the weekend. He stayed until Wednesday and was now back in Dallas for three whole weeks. There was talk he might be asked to relocate to the Dallas office. He seemed to assume she would move there with him.

"She rose to his requirement, dropped the playthings of her life/To take the honorable work of woman and wife"

She hadn't told him this yet but she had absolutely no plans to move to Dallas with him. She knew she would hate Texas and she thought this might be the logical conclusion to their relationship.

They celebrated her birthday early, on Saturday night. He brought her to a very expensive steak restaurant where just a side of broccoli cost seven dollars. She thought this was very unlike him because he also had to be thinking that was a ridiculous sum of money for a side of broccoli. He must have gotten a gift certificate from one of his clients. She wasn't sure though because she was in the ladies room when he paid the bill.

Despite that possibility, he was extremely generous but not very creative with the birthday gift. He gave her a three hundred dollar gift certificate to Lord & Taylor. She was relieved it wasn't for Talbot's and decided it was thoughtful of him to realize she would never shop there. Then she opened the second envelope he handed her. It was a gift certificate to a hair salon on Newbury Street.

"I gave myself to him.... The wealth might disappoint, Myself a poorer prove than this great purchaser suspect, The daily own of love."

"So I see. This is the total makeover package. You want me to get that more polished wardrobe and cut my hair."

"You can do whatever you want with the gift certificates. I thought it would just be a nice opportunity to treat yourself."

"Don't you think I look nice tonight?" She was wearing her favorite dress. It was strapless with a pale blue bodice and flared out to a short, puffy bottom that was white with blue dots. She thought it was flirty and the blue accentuated her eyes.

She had made two skinny braids with pieces of hair near her face and wrapped them around her head and under the loose bun at the nape of her neck. The braids looked like a headband holding back her hair except for the little curls that escaped and framed her face. She loved this look.

"I don't like your hair like that."

"Let me not mar that perfect dream"

Needless to say, the night erupted into a huge argument and she ended up sleeping in the guest room. Although it had been five days since she was in this bed, she could smell that clean soap smell of him on the sheets. She considered throwing the hair salon gift certificate away but stashed it in her desk drawer instead. She couldn't wait to go shopping at Lord & Taylor. Just wait until Nick saw what three hundred dollars could buy!

"Wild nights! Wild nights! Were I with thee"

The evening was in sharp contrast to that beautiful snow day earlier in the week. After they had finished their coffee and cereal that snowy Tuesday morning, they bundled up and headed across the street to the park. They grabbed a carrot and some Oreos for the snowman's nose and eyes. She found a piece of red ribbon for the mouth and an old scarf she never wore anymore.

They worked on the snowman for quite some time and then stepped back to admire their work. She looked over at him as he fell back into the fluffy snow and waved his arms and legs making a snow angel. She fell back too and her wings touched his.

Then the snowball fight began in earnest. They ran around the park, hiding behind trees and bushes, firing snowballs until her arm felt like it was going to fall off. He was extremely competitive but in the end she won, jumping on him and putting a snowball down his back.

Laughing she said, "That'll get you for tickling me this morning until I almost died." Looking back on it, she thought he might have thrown the fight.

They went back to the apartment and took a shower together. Now they'd made love four times in less than twelve hours. They decided to go to the ICA, the new museum out on the waterfront. She'd never been there. She and Nick had talked about going but he didn't really seem interested. Most likely he was just humoring her as he often did.

Bands of snow had been passing through, off and on all day. He thought it would be a great place to spend a snowy afternoon because the museum was a large glass building with views of the harbor. There was a special exhibit of everyday things made into sculptures. They were each displayed in a room of their own and you couldn't figure out what they were made of until you got up close. One room had white paper plates folded into honeycomb spirals that from a distance looked like coral. He loved the clear plastic cups that were stacked by the thousands and appeared to be white hills. They reminded him of skiing the moguls in Vail so he took a picture with his cell phone and sent it to his sister.

She laughed out loud in her cubicle, thinking of art made from ordinary things. It was kind of like writing about an ordinary, everyday life. She supposed anything could be interesting. It was all in how you looked at it.

What if he never calls? What if he's decided he's not interested? He probably had lots of girlfriends. After all, he was really cute and fun to be with. She was sure he had no problem meeting girls.

"Heart we will forget him! You and I tonight. You may forget the warmth he gave, I will forget the light"

She had plans to eat lunch with Dan so she walked over to his cubicle in accounting. He was talking to the woman in the cubicle next to him. Her name was Sophie and Dan said she was pretty cool for an older woman. They exchanged YouTube emails. Dan had forwarded her a really funny one from Sophie just the other day. As they walked to the cafeteria, her cell phone vibrated in her pocket. She looked at the caller ID. It was him!

"Dan, I have to take this. I'll meet you down there.... Hello?" She walked out the front door although it was freezing outside and she didn't have her coat on.

"Hey I'm really sorry I didn't call. I left my phone charger at home and by Friday the phone had died. Your number was in the phone so you know how that goes. This week has been crazy, we're working ten, eleven hour days to get this done before the sheet rockers show up."

"That's okay. I understand. No worries."

"No, I'm really sorry. I don't mean to sound like a shit, making up a bunch of excuses. I hate when people do that."

"Really it's okay. It's nice to hear from you." She was rubbing her arm and bouncing up and down to keep warm. She could see her breath.

"Can I see you this weekend? You could come up on the train after work Friday. I can make you dinner here at my man cave." He laughed at himself. "That's sounds really stupid. Anyway, you could pack some clothes, maybe spend the weekend?"

She tried to interject but he was talking kind of fast, like he was nervous. "That's pretty presumptuous, huh? It's Thursday. You probably already have plans. How about just tomorrow? Or Saturday?"

"I have no plans this weekend."

"All right! I'll meet you at the train after work. Text me when you know what time you'll be coming in."

"Sounds great. See you tomorrow." She hung up and started doing a little jig. Now this was a real birthday present! When she got down to the cafeteria, she decided to confide in

Dan. She had to tell someone and he was always confiding in her about his doubts on his impending marriage. He had those plans for the wedding in the Bahamas but he felt like he'd been dragged into it and it wasn't really what he wanted to do. She commiserated with him and often told him she wasn't quite sure how she ended up living with Nick. She often asked him, "We can't just end up in a relationship out of default, can we?"

Dan was sitting at a table by the window. She was a little breathless and very excited when she sat down. "Do you remember last week when we were running for the train in the snow? You are not going to believe what happened when I took that seat." He was amazed with her story, almost a little envious, but very supportive. He told her to have a nice time this weekend. For the rest of the afternoon, she couldn't focus on her work. She was supposed to finish the Dickinson articles by Friday and start on Langston Hughes on Monday. She would really have to focus tomorrow. How on earth was she going to do that?

"To live is so startling it leaves little time for anything else."

THE FORTY HOUR WORK WEEK

Later that night when Sophie got home from the movie, Ray was making a sandwich in the kitchen. "Hey, Sophie. How was yoga?"

"Great", she lied. She was certainly not going to tell him she snuck out of work early to go see a movie alone in an empty theater at 4:30 on a Tuesday afternoon.

"Are you going to eat something?" Ray sat down with his sandwich and a beer.

"Well I see you've taken care of yourself there. Does it ever occur to you to make dinner once in awhile?" Ray put his sandwich down and started to stand up, looking annoyed.

"Never mind. I guess it's too much to ask. I'll just heat up some leftovers. You used to be a really good cook Ray, do you remember that?"

She went to the fridge, got out a tupperware and put it in the microwave. "I work all week, forty hours plus the forty five minute commute each way. And I do this fifty weeks a year. I do all the laundry, cook the dinner, pay the bills, try to keep up with the gardens but I've lost that battle, haven't I? The gardens are an overgrown, unsightly mess.

I was also the one for years who managed the kids and all that school stuff. The permission slips, the homework, the college applications, financial aid forms. Work takes up so much of my week, how the hell am I supposed to have time for all these other things?"

"It's not like I'm not doing anything Sophie. I work all day too, come home and mow the lawn, work on the addition and fix anything and everything that breaks around here."

"I know Ray. I'm sorry. You know, the other day I was talking about this with Dan. I asked him if he knew who had come up with the forty hour work week, five days for the man and only two for yourself. Dan had no idea either so I googled it and guess who it was?'

Ray shrugged. "How the hell would I know?"

"Henry Ford. The capitalist who gave us the assembly line and the automobile. Bastard. But apparently this was an improvement. Before the labor laws were passed you could work possibly eighty hours a week. Can you imagine? You know European countries have a much better work life balance than we do?"

"So what now? Are you thinking we should get a B&B in Europe?"

"Hey we liked Spain. Maybe own a little guesthouse in one of those towns in the hills above the Mediterranean? The pueblo blancos?"

The microwave buzzed. Sophie took out her leftover meatloaf and mashed potatoes, leaned against the counter and ate right out of the tupperware. "You shouldn't do that Sophie. Those plastic containers can give you cancer if you microwave them. Something in them breaks down and leeches into your food."

"Seriously?" She sighed and got a plate out of the cupboard. She turned the tupperware upside down and dumped her dinner on the plate.

"What is that gonna do? You already microwaved it in the plastic."

"Well I'm gonna die of something, right? Although I would really prefer the good clean heart attack instead of cancer." She stood there eating quietly, thinking of her cousin Kathy who passed away four years ago from breast cancer. They had been friends all their lives. Kathy was two when her family moved into the house in back of Sophie's house. Their mothers would take them for walks into town in their strollers. Once they could walk and talk, they played together all the time. They would go down to the brook near their houses, ride bikes together and make bracelets out of embroidery floss. They went to different colleges but got together soon after graduation and moved into an apartment together in Boston. One year they left their jobs for two months and backpacked through Europe.

After they both got married, they somehow ended up moving to New Hampshire and buying homes only five miles apart from each other. Kathy could never have children and became like a second mom to Sophie's twins. The boys loved her and would often sleep over Kathy's house. She took them on treasure hunts in the woods behind her house, they went skiing and to the beach in the summer. Sophie and Kathy would drink wine after work at least once a week and discuss marriage, work and all their fond old memories of traveling and being single in Boston. They got a lot of miles out of those stories and never tired of telling them.

In her late forties, Kathy was diagnosed with stage one breast cancer. Being overly cautious, she chose to have a double mastectomy and was told they had gotten everything, no need for radiation or chemo. The reconstructive surgery was grueling and painful but when it was all over she seemed to be out of the woods so she put it behind her.

The doctors told her she needed to take Tamoxifin for a couple years. Despite her reservations and the risks she had heard about this drug, she followed the doctors' advice. Kathy and her husband Sam joined Sophie, Ray and the boys for a trip to Spain that spring. They stayed in a three bedroom condo in Marbella on the Costa del Sol. They visited the pueblo blancos, the Alhambra and Gibraltar. They had such a good time they started planning another trip and looked forward to many years of traveling together.

Two years after the breast cancer ordeal had begun, Kathy was diagnosed with uterine cancer most likely caused by the Tamoxifin. This time it was really serious. She underwent chemo and radiation. The treatment was brutal. Sophie could never quite understand how the treatment could be worse than the disease and how all these poisons could possibly make someone better. She ached watching Kathy suffer like this. She was always so brave. She continued to work and always had a smile and a positive outlook. Sophie didn't think she herself could ever be that brave and optimistic. After eight grueling months of chemo and radiation, Kathy and Sam took a trip to Italy, one of Kathy's favorite places in the whole world. Five months later the cancer came back and had spread to her liver. Seven weeks later she was gone. She remembered the morning after the day Kathy died. Waking up in her bed to sunlight streaming through the lace curtains, she felt an overwhelming sadness. Still half asleep, she couldn't remember why she felt so sad but then it dawned on her and she thought, "This is the first day without Kathy in the world and in my life."

Sophie wiped tears from her eyes and stared out the window. "I miss Kathy," she said, almost whispering.

"I know you do honey." Ray got up, put his plate in the dishwasher and kissed Sophie on the forehead. "It's okay, we all miss her." He held her for a good five minutes, stroking her hair and kissing her tear stained cheeks.

Ray took a deep breath. "I know this isn't a good time. I meant to tell you earlier. I was at the paint store and they were bugging me about my past due balance so I wrote them a check for five hundred forty dollars."

Sophie cleared her throat and wiped her eyes. "Five forty? Why so much? We can't swing that right now."

"Well that was just the balance over ninety days. I actually owe them more than that, so I wanted to clear that up. By the way, I hate to tell you this but the oil tank is low. I called for a delivery tomorrow."

"How much is that gonna be?"

"Well the minimum delivery is two hundred gallons so about five hundred twenty dollars? We need to leave a check on the door tomorrow morning before we leave for work."

"WHAT? So you never pay attention to the bills and have no idea what's in the checkbook at any given time but suddenly you take it upon yourself to pay two bills in one day totaling one thousand sixty dollars? Ray, I bring home twelve hundred bucks every other week. In one day you spent almost what it takes me two weeks to earn."

"It's not like I went out and bought new golf clubs or something. And I work too."

"I know, I know. But what about the mortgage, the car loan, the electric bill, the cell phones, the cable? Groceries! Gas! The list never ends, does it? Oh my God! How can we work five days a week all year long and still be broke? Couldn't you have called me about the paint bill and given them two hundred fifty or something?"

"Sorry. I had to do it. It's my business account. I have a professional relationship with these guys and I looked like a schmuck."

"I'm sure you're not the only one. Look we'll figure it out. Someone else will get paid late this month or maybe not at all. We'll eat hot dogs and Kraft macaroni and cheese. I'm tired. I'm going upstairs to watch TV."

Sophie put her plate in the dishwasher and went upstairs to the bedroom. Ray picked up the tupperware she left on the counter and washed it. Then he walked into the living room, got in his recliner and turned on the TV. He watched an old episode of the Sopranos and drifted off to sleep in the chair.

Sophie was lying in bed watching cable news. They were discussing the impending budget crisis. No one wanted to take the advice of Simpson-Bowles, whoever the hell that was. She wondered if there was a word for the way world events affect your personal life. When she watched the news, it all seemed so removed. But she knew it was not removed. The next day you could lose your job, your health insurance or your kids could lose their Pell grants. She'd had all these things happen to her in the past few years.

She shut the TV off and could hear a train blowing its whistle off in the distance. The sound got louder as the train got closer and eventually she could hear the loud freight engine rumbling on the tracks across the river. As she drifted off to sleep she was thinking zeitgeist? Was that the word? Not quite?

* * *

Young Sophie was in the Actor's apartment. They were discussing the meaning of the word zeitgeist.

"I think it's the spirit of the times." The Actor was making her an awesome grilled cheese sandwich. He was slicing homemade whole grain bread and a block of good cheddar cheese. He added some really nice looking summer tomatoes. He put the sandwiches on a pan and grilled them to perfection, cheese oozing over the sides. He brought her an imported beer and the sandwich. He made one for himself too.

The dream shifted to a nightclub. Young Sophie and the Actor were listening to a band. They were standing to the side of the stage and he had his arms around her. He leaned over, kissed her cheek and whispered something in her ear.

* * *

It was once again six A.M. and the alarm clock went off in the Ryan bedroom. "Is it Friday yet?"

"Sorry Sophie. It's only Thursday."

Ray rolled over and put his arm around her as Sophie moaned and pulled the pillow over her head. Ray got up, went downstairs and started the coffee. Back upstairs, Sophie stayed in bed a while longer and drifted back to sleep.

* * *

Young Sophie was lying in bed beside the Actor. Slowing she began to wake, rolling onto her side and opening her eyes. The Actor was lying on his side facing her, propped on his elbow with his head resting in his hand. He smiled at her.

"How long have you been lying there like that?" she asked.

"Just a little while. I was watching you sleep. You're so beautiful."

She blushed as he leaned towards her and kissed her. Rolling on top of her, he pulled the spaghetti straps down on her loose nightgown to reveal her breasts and started to kiss them.

* * *

She suddenly bolted awake and looked at the clock. Six thirty! "Shit." Jumping out of bed, she whimpered and put on a bathrobe that had fallen on the floor then headed to the shower.

When she got back to the bedroom she turned on the TV and started to make the bed. The anchorman on a cable news program was discussing how long into the winter the Occupy Wall Street group could stay in Zuccotti Park. It was already early November and getting cold in New York City. She shut off the TV and went downstairs. In the kitchen, she grabbed a cup of coffee.

"Hey Ray. I overslept. I'm not going to be able to make lunches today. And I'm going to yoga again tonight so do you think you could make dinner for us? Anything, even grilled cheese sandwiches would be good."

"Well I'm doing an estimate after work."

"Never mind. Forget I even asked."

"Well I could when I get home but I might be later than you. You know I have to line up work. You know things really slow down at this time of year."

"No I know, absolutely. Don't worry about it. I'll drum something up after yoga."

Sophie walked over to Ray, gave him a kiss on the cheek and left. She went out to her car. That morning it was parked in the driveway because Ray's truck was in the garage. It was a cold morning and her windows were frosted. She got in the car and turned on the defroster. The clock on the dashboard said 7:45. She sighed and rolled her eyes, turned up the radio and sipped her coffee while she waited for the window to clear.

Later that morning, Ray was at work. He was lifting large ladders off the back of his truck. The wind was whipping and all the leaves were off the trees. He set up staging on the side of a house and blew on his hands to keep them warm. He climbed up one of the ladders and stepped out on the staging at the second floor.

Meanwhile, Sophie was in her cubicle. The radio was playing softly and she was eating yogurt at her desk. She opened a tiny packet of honey and drizzled it onto the yogurt, making circular patterns. She seemed to be in a trance. Her boss Tina walked into the cubicle, all business. She put a pile of checks on Sophie's desk. "Good morning."

"Thanks" Sophie said but Tina had already moved on. She was all hustle and bustle this morning as she headed to Dan's cubicle with more paperwork. Sophie went back to eating her yogurt with a dreamy look in her eyes. She was imagining the Actor coming up behind her, leaning over, lifting her hair from her neck and kissing her.

At two o'clock, Dan and Sophie went into Tina's office for a meeting. Tina was discussing new IRS rules, something about taxes on foreign vendors and the forms they would need to acquire from these vendors. Sophie looked dazed, not really paying attention. Dan had his hands folded with his arms on his knees and he was looking between his legs, down at the floor.

Sophie had a notepad in her lap but wasn't writing anything down. Instead she was shaking her pen and making it wiggle. Once in a while she nodded and said "UmHmm." When Tina turned her attention to an incoming email for a minute, Dan looked over at Sophie and rolled his eyes.

Tina looked back at the two of them and said "I realize this is going to involve a lot more work for the both of you and it will be tricky at first. We are all going to have to put on our tax hats and learn these new procedures but we're good at that. We wear a lot of hats here in accounting. I've got to go to a meeting right now about some of this so I'll let you know what I find out."

"Sure thing" Dan said. "Okay thanks" Sophie chimed in. They both pushed their desk chairs back to their cubicles. Sophie watched as Tina walked past her cubicle and then she heard a door close. She got up and went in Dan's cubicle.

"What the fuck? We've needed help in this department for a year. And now we've got this foreign tax shit to deal with?"

Dan was slumped in his chair. "No kidding. I guess we'll be expected to work overtime for a while until they get this all figured out."

"I hate when she starts talking about that hat shit. Like it's all so interesting and different when it's all just the same shitty hat."

Dan chuckled. "Hey check this out." He turned his computer screen towards Sophie and showed her a YouTube video. It was a woman paddling on a surfboard towards some kayakers. Suddenly a whale came out of the water and filled the screen. Sophie jumped a little and shouted "Holy shit." They both laughed. Dan said, "Can you believe she didn't fall off?"

"I know. And what's with all those seagulls? Where did they come from?"

Sophie's cell phone rang. She looked at the caller ID and saw it was her sister Annie.

She looked at Dan and said, "I have to take this." She walked back to her cubicle while Dan continued to watch some other YouTube videos.

"Hey Annie. What are you calling for at this time of day? Aren't you still in school...Oh my God. Is he okay...All right, I'll tell my boss. I'll try to get there as soon as possible."

As she hung up, Tina passed by her cubicle. She followed her to her office and closed the door.

"Hey Tina my sister just called. My dad's had a heart attack."

"Oh no, is he all right?"

"I don't know much. My sister was at school. She's a teacher. She had just heard about it but apparently it happened last night or something. She didn't have a lot of details. I'm going to have to go to Providence."

"Of course, no problem. And call me later if you need to stay down there. I'll put you in for half a sick day."

Sophie thought *'Really? I have to use a sick day? I only have three sick days right now. Your dad has a heart attack and they have to nitpick about sick days. They can't give you a freebie? That's probably Henry Ford's idea too. Don't these corporations know their employees have lives? After all, didn't the Supreme Court just say that corporations are people too? Or was that Mitt Romney?'*

Out loud she said, "Thanks. I'll let you know when I have more information."

HAPPY BIRTHDAY

As the train pulled into the Newburyport station, it was dark but the parking lot was well lit. She could see him getting out of a green Taurus station wagon and walking towards the train with his hands in his pockets. He was wearing khaki work pants, a Carhartt jacket and work boots with his hair pulled back into a ponytail although numerous strands of wavy hair had escaped. She smiled and thought of Johnny Depp in the movie Chocolat.

When she got off the train, he gave her a big hug, lifting her off the ground while he kissed her. He nuzzled his nose in her hair and said "Hmm. You smell so nice. Here let me help you with that."

He put her down and took the gym bag she was carrying. She also had a backpack with more clothes in it. She had no idea how to pack for this weekend or if she was staying until Monday morning. She hoped she was staying until Monday morning. The commute to Newburyport was so quick and easy. A far cry from her daily forty minute train ride plus the subway connection to North Station. But more importantly, another night with him would be sheer bliss. She hoped. It had been almost two weeks since she'd met him and she was feeling a little nervous.

As they pulled out of the parking lot he looked over and said, "I live really close to here." He laughed but had a serious look on his face. "Hey, buckle up."

Pulling the seat belt across herself and locking it in, she finally noticed he had lost the scruffy beard. She reached over and put her hand on his clean shaven face. "Hey, where'd your beard go?"

"I was wondering if you'd notice. I was trying to trim it the other day and the razor slipped." He rubbed his chin. "What do you think?"

"Very handsome." They were sitting at a stoplight so he leaned over and kissed her. "So, how have you been? Did you miss me? I know I missed you." The light turned green.

"You were having fun skiing. I, on the other hand, was working. You did cross my mind a few times while I was reading articles on Emily Dickinson."

"Emily Dickinson reminded you of me? Wow, I've never been told that one before." He laughed and shook his head.

"Wild nights! Wild nights! Might I but moor tonight in thee!"

"Might I but moor tonight in thee? I had no idea Emily said things like that. I thought she was an old maid. Didn't she never leave her house or something like that?"

"Something like that. From what I was reading, she apparently had a very active imagination."

"Here we are." He pulled into the driveway of an old colonial home. The houses on this street were close to the road with only a small side yard between them. At the end of his driveway there was a detached garage set back from the house. A light was on in a room above the garage.

He pointed to the light and said, "That's me. Let's go inside and maybe you can show me what Emily means by might I but moor tonight in thee."

The door was to the left of the garage doors and there was a staircase inside which led up to the second floor. At the top of the stairs was an open door leading to a good size bathroom. To their right was one big room with a sectional sofa, a large screen TV, a bench press and some bookcases. At the other end of the room was a horseshoe bar with four stools. Against the wall behind the bar were bottles of booze, a full variety of bar glasses and two taps, Sam Adams and Heineken.

To the left side of the bar towards the back of the garage, the room seemed to get a little longer and tucked in this corner was a double bed, neatly made up with a southwestern textile blanket on top. She could see a doorway just past the bathroom that looked like it led to a small kitchen.

"This is it, home sweet home. Everything a guy would ever need. And those taps are for real. They are connected to kegerators in the fridge underneath the bar. But the beer I'm pouring doesn't always have what it says on the tap."

"Do you have a lot of parties here?"

"Not really. This is the place to watch the big games though. Celtics, Red Sox, Bruins, Pats. There are quite a few games I guess. My uncle and two of his friends play poker here on Thursday nights. I'm their fourth but I have yet to win any money. There's a folding card table and chairs in the garage that they bring up here."

He walked over towards the bar and put her bags on the floor at the foot of the bed. Then he walked back towards her while taking his coat off. He threw his coat on the sofa and then kissed her while sliding her coat off and dropping it on the floor behind her. He held her face in both his hands and let out a soft moan.

He pulled back and smiled. "Sorry, am I going too fast here? It's just I really did miss you. A lot. Can I get you a drink?" He walked over to the bar.

"I'd love a drink. Let's see, today is my birthday so I should have something special. Can you make a cosmopolitan?"

"No way. It's your birthday? Why didn't you tell me? I would have baked you a cake."

"Really?" She laughed and broke into a little song and dance routine, tap dancing and singing. "If I knew you were coming I'da baked a cake, baked a cake."

She was suddenly really embarrassed and covered her blushing face. She started laughing. "Wow, I don't know where that came from? That's just a little routine I learned in tap dance class when I was five years old."

"That was interesting," he chuckled. "Never heard that song before."

He brought her cosmo over and put it down on the coffee table in front of the sofa. He wrapped his arms around her and buried his face in her hair.

He started to kiss her forehead, then down along her cheek and whispered in her ear. "I was originally thinking I would cook dinner here but if it's your birthday maybe we should go out to dinner. How old are you by the way?"

"Twenty five. And dinner here sounds perfect. I don't want to go out. I'd like to stay right here."

"I was just gonna make ziti and chicken parmesan. Is that okay?"

"JUST ziti and chicken parm? That sounds really good."

"You know what, I have to run next door and get something from my aunt. I will be right back." He kissed her and ran downstairs.

She got her toothbrush from her backpack and went to the bathroom. She washed her face, brushed her teeth and made those two skinny braids she liked and wrapped them around like a headband again. She left her hair down this time though.

She got her drink from the coffee table, peeked in the kitchen and then looked through his bookcases. He had an eclectic mix of reading material. Historical nonfiction, copies of Life of Pi and To Kill a Mockingbird, a travel guide to Australia and books of poems by William Butler Yeats and Pablo Neruda. He also had a stack of children's books with Goodnight Moon on the top. She heard the door downstairs open and he came running up the stairs. He didn't seem to have gotten anything from his aunt.

"Excuse me, I've got to get out of these work clothes." He walked over to the bed, unbuttoning his shirt and taking it off. He pulled his white t-shirt over his head. She got up and followed him, coming up behind him and wrapping her arms around his waist. She kissed his lean, muscular back. Turning around, he lifted her chin and gazed into her eyes. "I couldn't stop thinking about you. It's kind of scary. You've got to know something about me. Remember when I told you I'm okay ninety percent of the time? Well the other ten percent of the time, I'm scared to death to get close to someone because I'm afraid I might lose them. I put up these walls. Or disap-pear for awhile."

"I see." She was stroking his jawline. It was really soft without the stubble there.

"It scared me how much I was thinking about you. It's kind of why I went up north because if I hadn't I might have called you every day and made a total ass of myself. Right now, all I want to do is pull you onto this bed and make love to you."

She was wearing a blue cotton sweater that she began to pull over her head. She threw it on the floor behind her. She heard him moan again as he reached around her to unsnap her bra. She reached down and unbuttoned his pants. She gently pushed him onto the bed. She untied his boots and pulled them off then slid his pants off. She never stopped looking into his blue, blue eyes as she unbuttoned her jeans and slid out of them. He reached for her and pulled her onto the bed. He twisted one of her little braids around his finger. "I like your hair like this."

* * *

They were in the small galley kitchen cooking dinner. More accurately, he was cooking dinner. She was drinking her cosmopolitan and occasionally helping. He had just added ziti to a pot of boiling water and was cooking breaded chicken in another pan. He had three bowls lined up on the counter with flour, eggs and breadcrumbs in them. She was dipping the chicken in each bowl and putting it on a platter on the stove.

He gently tapped her on the hand with a wooden spoon, laughing. "Hey it goes flour, egg then bread crumbs. I put them in order left to right. You're going backwards."

"Oops! Sorry, I wasn't paying attention. I told you I can't cook." She dipped the piece again, going back the right way this time. He raised an eyebrow and smiled, shaking his head. "That's gonna be your piece."

She stuck her tongue out at him. He grabbed her chin and kissed her while she pushed him against the fridge. They started kissing and groping each other. The pot of water started to boil over.

"Okay you're distracting the chef." He lowered the flame under the pot of ziti. "I've got it covered in here, it's almost ready. Why don't you go in the other room and pick a playlist or something on my IPod? You're the birthday girl, you shouldn't be cooking anyway." He laughed. "To be honest, you're not much help." He tapped her on the butt and lightly pushed her towards the door.

"Okay." She took a kitchen towel and snapped him in the butt with it as she was leaving the room.

He set the table and brought out a platter of ziti with chicken parmesan, a salad and garlic bread. He was searching the pockets of the long gym shorts he had changed into. "Oh right, I was wearing the other pants." He went over to the work khakis lying on the floor by his bed and got four votive candles out of his pockets. As he came back to the table, he dimmed the overhead lights in the room then centered the votive candles in a circle on the table and lit them. "Got these from my aunt."

So he did get something when he ran over there. He pulled out a chair for her, she sat down and he leaned over and kissed her neck. He poured them each a glass of Chianti and toasted. "Happy 25th birthday." He let out a long whistle. "Quarter century."

"Thanks for making dinner. This is really nice." She took a bite of chicken. "Ummmm, delish. This piece is fine."

"The piece you dipped twice? That's under here." He lifted a piece up from the platter in the middle of the table. It was over breaded and soggy looking. He winked.

During dinner, he asked her about her family and growing up in Vermont. She told him about her three older sisters and the two hundred year old farmhouse they grew up in. They had a barn, two golden retrievers and four cats, one for each girl. Her cat's name was Jennie. All the pets were females too.

"My poor Dad. We called him the crazy old professor. He was older than most other kids' dads and it's no wonder he was slightly crazy. All those hormones in the house, it must have been impossible for him. He always had a book in his hand. He would walk around the house, reading and bumping into furniture or tripping over something. I think it was his way of removing himself from the drama that was always swirling around him. But although he couldn't stand the drama, he somehow had a knack for inserting himself right into the middle of it."

"What kind of drama?"

"Teenage girl drama. It went on for years but it reached its peak around the time I was in eighth grade. The twins, Monica and Sara, were in tenth grade and Maria was a senior. It was nuts! At any given time, one of us would be in love with some boy while someone else had just had her heart broken."

"So how did your Dad deal with all these teenage boys his daughters were falling in and out of love with?"

They had finished eating and she was helping him clear the table while she continued talking. She followed him into the kitchen as he started to fill one side of the double sink with soapy water while he rinsed the plates in the other sink with the garbage disposal. He handed her a dishtowel. "Here, you can dry."

"How was he? He was awful. You'd think he would've wanted male companionship. But apparently not if the male was a teenager dating one of his daughters. He was always telling us about the dangers related to these alien creatures known as the teenage boy. How they drove too fast and always, always wanted only one thing."

"What's that?"

"Oh come on. You know. S-E-X."

"Sex? No?" He was laughing and pretended he was shocked.

"He would always say 'I know this because I was a teenage boy once.' Eww, the thought of that would make me cringe. My gray haired father with the reading glasses perched on the end of his nose? Having sex? I mean I kind of knew he had done it at least three times, right? But I preferred to pretend we were adopted or maybe the stork brought us. I would always think, why is he saying this to me?"

He was laughing. "Maybe he was trying to scare you. If I had four daughters I would probably do the same thing because he's right about teenage boys you know."

She gasped. "No? Not you?" She leaned over and kissed him. "Teenage girls want it too you know."

"I thought girls wanted a boyfriend and love and commitment."

"Not always. Maybe love. After all, girls are brought up on stories of Cinderella and Prince Charming. But commitment? I don't know about that. Based on my behavior in past relationships, I seem to run from commitment. Good solid boys with successful futures bore me. I always seemed to like the boys my Dad called Trouble. As in he would never remember their names and say things like here comes Trouble, as my date pulled in the driveway."

He furrowed his brow. "Hmmm interesting." He started to put leftovers in the fridge and put the pans in the soapy water. "Where was your mother in all of this?"

"She was always managing everything and reminding us of how she paid the bills, called the teachers and made the doctor's appointments. All the day to day stuff my dad had no clue about. She had her own decorating business too. She made slipcovers and curtains. She called them window treatments. I think because she could charge more. She was very organized and a little detached. She didn't pay attention to the minor stuff.

For instance, in tenth grade I was always wearing what my father considered to be obscenely short skirts. One night I was going out with friends in a skirt that may actually have been a tad obscene. As I was getting ready to leave, he jumped to the front door. He spread his arms like this." She leaned against the doorjamb to the kitchen and spread her arms wide. "He was blocking the door and yelling 'You are not leaving this house in that postage stamp of a skirt. Get upstairs right now and change young lady or you are grounded.'"

"Did you change?"

"Well being the youngest I had learned a lot from my sisters' mistakes. One of the biggest lessons was do not start an argument with him. I was usually really good at flying under the radar too. I ran upstairs and down the hall where there was another staircase that led to the kitchen in the back of the house. I went down those stairs and out the back door. When he saw me running down the driveway towards my friend's car he ran out the front door hollering at me 'Get back here you little whipper snapper.' I remember thinking what the hell is a whipper snapper?" She laughed. "I told you he was older, right? He would use weird expressions like that sometimes.

Anyway, my Mom followed him out and I could hear her yelling at him 'Pick your battles Bill. When will you ever learn to pick your battles? At least she hasn't come home pregnant.' And he was yelling 'Well in that skirt it's only a matter of time.' But my mother had us covered on that. We were all on the pill by sixteen whether we needed to be or not. She'd say it was for acne and my dad never suspected although not one of us had acne."

They had finished doing the dishes and she heard a song by the Cure playing out in the main room. She grabbed his hand. "I love this song. Dance with me." She was dancing backwards, holding his hand and singing her way into the other room, acting out the song as she went. At one point she sang the line "I dreamed of different ways to go"

He was laughing. "That's not the lyric. It's I dreamed of different ways to make you glow."

"Really? Hmm. I like your line better."

"Of course. Because it's right." He started spinning her around and picked her up and swung her legs to his side but they tumbled onto the sectional sofa. They were laughing and kissing and she was trying to pull his T-shirt off but he was underneath her.

"Hold on, hold on" he said while kissing her neck. "I have to run next door for a minute."

He rolled out from under her, got up and ran down stairs. She heard the storm door slam. While lying on her side thinking, "What is he getting now?" she looked at the shelf under the coffee table where there were big sheets of drawing paper with colorful illustrations. She pulled the top one out. It was a picture of a pretty little girl with curly blond hair and she was lifting up her shoe. From under the shoe another little girl was floating out. She looked like the curly blond girl but with a mischievous face. She heard the door open and she quickly put the illustration back. He shouted up the stairs, "Close your eyes."

"Okay, they're closed."

He started walking up the stairs. "Keep them closed until I tell you to open them." He put something down on the coffee table. She heard him light a match and caught a whiff of sulpher. "Okay, you can open your eyes now."

On the coffee table was a plate with six cupcakes in a circle, each with a lit candle in the center. The cupcakes had a big swirl of blue frosting on them. He started singing Happy Birthday.

"Wow, thank you." She kissed him then blew out the candles.

"When I went to get the candles, I asked my aunt to make these. I wasn't sure what you liked so I asked for chocolate. Everyone likes chocolate, right? Helen took a cake decorating class. That's why the frosting looks so good."

"This is so sweet. And you guessed right, chocolate is my favorite."

"Ummm." He was biting into a cupcake. He had a big glob of blue frosting on his lip. She licked it off.

She laughed as he reached for another cupcake. "Hey, you can have more later. Weren't we in the middle of something before you left?"

"Right." They both started taking their clothes off. He laid her back down on the couch. "You remembered to make a wish when you blew out your candles, didn't you?"

"Yes but I can't tell you what it was or it won't come true."

I THOUGHT IT WAS THE FLU

Sophie was driving in heavy traffic through Boston. She was on her way to the hospital in Providence to see her father who had a heart attack. She didn't have many details. Her sister Annie didn't know much herself when she had called. She hoped everything was okay.

As she entered the Big Dig tunnel running through the center of the city, the radio faded out and there was just the sound of static in the car. The traffic was now bumper to bumper and moving very slowly. She turned the volume down and started to daydream.

* * *

She was making the bed in a guest room at an inn nestled in the center of a town along the route from Arcos to Ronda in Spanish Andalusia. It was a pueblo blanco in one of the many villages of white stucco buildings with red roof tiles that clung to the side of a hill and had a commanding view of the Mediterranean off in the distance. There were very few cars in the town. The roads were too narrow and steep.

As she shook the sheet across the double bed, she looked out the window to a courtyard with a lemon tree in the center. Small wrought iron tables were set around the tree from which bright yellow lemons seemed to drip from the branches. Several guests were outside and Ray was serving coffee, tea and lemon cake he had made earlier that morning.

When she finished making the bed, she went into the bathroom of the guest room and began to clean the toilet, sink and tub. The floor was made of hand painted blue and yellow Spanish tiles. After cleaning the bathroom, she mopped her way out of the room.

When she finished cleaning, she went outside into the bright midday sun. She stopped to pick up the watering can by the door and watered the pots of flowers that were hanging on the side of the building at the entrance to her inn. Then she walked into town with a spring in her step to buy olives, serrano ham and manchego cheese for the happy hour she and Ray would be serving their guests later that evening.

* * *

An hour later Sophie was still driving, just entering Rhode Island. The traffic had finally broken up and she was moving along at a good speed. She got off at the first Providence exit and checked the directions she had printed. She followed them to a hospital in a working class neighborhood not far from Brown University.

* * *

The door of the hospital elevator opened and Sophie stepped out into the hallway. She walked down the hall, passing several rooms with patients in their beds. A few rooms were also occupied with nurses and visiting families.

She found her father's room. The bed next to him was empty. He was sleeping on his side with his back to her. He looked very small and thin lying there in his hospital johnny. She tiptoed back out into the hall. Once out of the room, she made a call on her cell phone. "I'm upstairs at Dad's room but he's sleeping. I didn't want to wake him. Where are you guys?... Okay, I'll be right down."

She got back on the elevator and took it down to the main lobby. From there she walked through a mostly empty cafeteria and outside to a patio. It was an unusually warm day for early November. Several people in hospital clothes were sitting outside, drinking coffee. The women were wearing the kind of hospital scrubs with baggy blue pants topped with a loose shirt that had goofy prints on them such as teddy bears or balloons.

Sophie spotted her mother and sister at one of the tables. She walked over and hugged them both. Her mom was a very tiny, frail woman with short hair that looked like she cut it herself and wide, frightened eyes. She looked disoriented. Her sister Annie was taller than Sophie and had a very casual relaxed look about her. She was wearing jeans and a sweater and was two years younger than Sophie.

"Mom, how are you doing? Are you okay?" Sophie asked.

Her Mom shook her head. "I can't believe this happened. We always thought it would be me who had the heart attack with my high blood pressure and all. I just can't get over it."

Sophie sat down and took her mother's hand. "So Annie, what are the doctors saying?"

"It looks good so far. They put two stents in yesterday and that seems to have gone well. He was laughing and joking when he came out of it. Asking the doctors when he could run a road race again."

Their Mom waved her hand at them. "Oh I don't know about that. But if he can't run again he's not going to be happy. You know how depressed he gets when he can't run." She looked perplexed. "He won't be happy about it."

Annie held her hand. "We'll cross that bridge when we get to it Mom. He'll be fine and if he can't run, he can go for long walks. Don't worry about that right now."

"He's not gonna want to go for long walks." She waved her hand, dismissing Annie's comment. "I knew something was wrong but he thought he had the flu. We got the flu shots the day before. He always thinks the shot gives him the flu."

"Then why does he get the shot?" Sophie gave Annie a be-mused look and then turned to her mother. "Well he'll get used to it Mom, not running that is, and maybe he can run again. Just not like he used to."

"Oh he definitely thought he'd never have a heart attack. He thought the running would prevent a heart attack. He was always worried about me. He thought I would have the heart attack. I can't believe this happened."

Annie got up and put her hand on her mother's shoulder. "Mom, he's going to be okay. The doctors are optimistic. Let's go up and see if he's awake."

Sophie stood up too and whispered over her mother's head to Annie, "Is she getting worse? She seems worse? She keeps repeating herself?" Annie nodded as she helped her mother up.

Sophie looked at her mother. "Why exactly did we just find out about this today when it happened yesterday?"

"He didn't want to bother anyone. You kids have lives and jobs and kids of your own."

"But Mom he had a heart attack! He's our father. And you were here all alone?"

"Well he didn't think it was a heart attack at first. He thought it was the flu. Then everything got so busy."

They walked back into the hospital and got on the elevator with an older woman and her middle-aged son. Sophie's mom looked up at them and said, "My husband had a heart attack. I can't believe this happened." She laughed nervously.

The woman and her son just nodded as the elevator door opened. Sophie held her mother's arm as they exited and helped her down the hall to her father's room. They all gave him a hug. He was sitting up with a bed tray in front of him eating oatmeal and scrambled eggs.

"Look at all this food they give you. I can't eat all this food. Oatmeal and eggs, who needs both? The oatmeal is terrible. Sophie, what are you doing here? I can't believe you drove all the way down here."

"Of course I drove down. I can't believe someone didn't call yesterday." Her father waved his hand like he was batting away a fly.

Annie put her hand on his shoulder and leaned over to hug him. "Dad I just came back to say goodbye. I've got to go home and Sophie's here to help Mom. You take it easy." She kissed him and then whispered to Sophie as she left "I'll call you."

Sophie helped her Mom to a chair and pulled another chair up to the bed, sitting down. "How are you feeling Dad? Is there any pain?"

"No not too bad. I feel pretty good considering. Just tired. When I showed up at the walk-in clinic and they told me they thought I might of had a heart attack they wanted me to go to Rhode Island hospital. I told them no way, you have to pay for parking there."

"You drove to a walk-in clinic while you were having a heart attack?"

"I thought I had the flu."

Sophie shook her head in disbelief. "But then didn't they send you here by ambulance? So why worry about the parking?"

"It's the principal of the thing. Charging for parking, the nerve of them. This hospital has just as good a cardiac unit. The nurses did tell me there was a murder a few blocks from here the other night but it's the same at the other place and these guys don't charge for parking. Don't come to visit after dark though, it's not safe at night here anymore. Did you know your mother and I lived here when you were a baby?"

"Oh really? It was this neighborhood?"

"Yeah just a couple blocks from here. The neighborhood was nice back then."

Her Mom perked up. "Remember the landlady's name was Bea and she used to babysit for us? She lived upstairs. Sophie brought her tricycle all the way up the stairs to visit her one day. I don't know how she lugged it up there. She was a little bitty thing, only three years old. She could have fallen all the way down and killed herself. Then there was the time I was hanging clothes on the line outside and locked Sophie in the apartment by accident. I had to go next door and call the fire department to get back in." She shook her head and laughed.

Sophie smiled "Yeah I remember those stories."

Her father pushed the bed tray to the side, most of the food untouched. "I had two of the nurses here in school years ago. Taught them U.S. history during the seventies. It was their junior year in high school."

"Dad, remember when I was backpacking through Europe? I met two girls in Amsterdam in line at the Heineken Brewery and we somehow figured out we were all from Rhode Island and went to the same high school. I asked them if they knew you and they said they had your history class. I sent you a postcard and told you, *Dad you're like American Express, known the world over."*

Her Dad smiled and patted her arm. "Remember all those family vacations we took?"

"Of course I do. You were the one who instilled the love of travel in all of us. The original source of never ending wanderlust and restlessness."

"We always loved D.C. Your mother and I went there on our honeymoon. Can't beat it, all those free museums and monuments."

Sophie laughed. "Like the free parking?"

"Aaagh, parking and driving were miserable in that city."

"And all those president's houses we visited, Mount Vernon, Monticello. And battlefields like Gettysburg. I remember I loved Williamsburg. What was that place in Michigan?"

"Deerfield Village."

"Yeah, yeah. I loved that too. I would pretend I was some kind of colonial girl and lived there."

Her dad laughed loudly. "Do you remember you were about fourteen and we were at Valley Forge? We were in the house Washington stayed in that awful winter when all the soldiers died from the cold. You asked the tour guide why Washington got to stay in the big house while his troops were freezing to death out in those tents."

Sophie laughed too. "Always with an opinion, that was me even at fourteen. I must have been the only teenager at my high school that had the U.S. Constitution hanging on my bedroom wall. I know when I brought it to college I was the only one in my dormitory. Everyone else had posters of rock bands and cannabis. It was one of those parchment paper things with the burnt edges to make it look old. It was rolled up like a scroll, remember? We'd get them in the gift shops of those historic places we visited."

"Huumph! I don't know what they teach these kids these days. Supreme Court deciding elections." He waved his hand at the elusive fly again.

"My favorite part of the Declaration of Independence has always been the pursuit of happiness. I had that scroll too. What other country in the history of the world guarantees their citizens the right to pursue happiness? Sure seems hard to attain these days though, doesn't it?"

"Just because they give you the right to pursue happiness, doesn't mean they guarantee you'll find it. And they sure have made it a hell of lot harder these days. You kids have it tough. Tougher then your mother and I did, that's for sure. No job security, no pensions, can't afford health care. "

Sophie's Mom interrupted them. "Let's not get all worked up here Dad. You know how you two can get."

"I'm so glad you came Sophie. Are you staying with your mother tonight?"

"Yes. And on that note, I think we should get going. You need your rest. We'll see you in the morning Dad. I love you."

"Love you too. Thanks for staying with your mother tonight."

She kissed him and then her mother came over, hugging him and rubbing his shoulder for a minute.

* * *

Sophie and her mother had just arrived at her parents' condo. Her mother was in a small kitchen off the living room where Sophie was looking through the suitcase she hastily packed earlier that afternoon. "Sophie, do you want something to eat?"

"Oh no Mom, I'm fine. I had a sandwich on the way down. I'll just have a cup of tea."

"Are you sure? That was awhile ago."

"Yeah I'm good. Come sit down. You must be exhausted."

Her mom brought two cups of tea over, put the TV on and sat down to watch the cable news show that was on. The news anchor was talking about the Republican primary field.

"That poor Mr. Obama. He is such a nice man and they are always picking on him. It's awful, he can't do anything right. It's 'cus he's black, ya know? They hate him because of that."

"You might be right about that Mom. But let's not watch this. It's so depressing. God, these candidates are a bunch of clowns. I mean seriously? This is the best they've got?" Sophie picked up the remote from the coffee table where her mother had set it down and turned the TV off.

"How are the boys?" her Mom asked.

"They're good. Jesse got a job at a coffee shop in Providence that has it's own bakery. Not far from where Sean lives. And one of Sean's roommates moved out, so Jesse moved in with him. I'm so relieved he's with Sean. It was really nice of Sean to help his brother out like this. I just hope it all works out. You and Dad will have to visit the coffee shop when Dad is feeling up to it."

"Oh we don't drink coffee. Did I tell you I met your father when I was working at the mill? He was a college boy. Just like your boys. My parents made me quit high school. I was working and going to secretarial school at night. I just said I graduated high school on the application. Back in those days they didn't check anything. When I graduated from the business school the principal said 'I found out you didn't graduate high school. How did you do that? You're graduating with honors.' But he gave me my diploma anyway. Then I got the job at the mill and met your father."

She smiled, proud of herself.

Sophie chuckled. "Doing payroll, right?" Sophie had been nodding while her mother told the story. She'd heard it many times before. Lately, her mother remembered the old stories much better than what happened just that morning. But then there were those moments of lucidness and she really did seem to be in the present.

Her mother laughed, "Right, how did you know that?"

"You told me once before."

"I don't know what I will do if something happens to your father. I'd be so lost without him."

"I know Mom. It's okay. He's going to be okay. The doctor said despite the heart attack he's in remarkable shape for a man his age. It's most likely all that running he's done and that will surely help him with his recovery. Hey, let's go to bed. You must be exhausted. You've had a hell of a two days."

"Oh Sophie I hate when you swear like that. You're looking good these days. Did you lose some weight? You were looking heavy for awhile there."

"Yeah Ma, I think I have." She rolled her eyes and thought to her self, there's the old tactlessness. She hadn't lost that, next she'd bring up Sophie's hair. "I'm doing yoga these days. Come on. I'll help you upstairs."

"The young kids are all doing yoga now. Are you letting your hair grow out? It's looking a little shaggy."

Sophie sighed. "Some mornings I don't have time to blow dry it. This morning was one of those mornings. It's been shoulder length for awhile."

"I loved those pixie cuts you had when you were a kid. You should get it cut like that. But you always wanted the long hair."

"Mom, it was the seventies and eighties. Everyone had long hair. I just wanted to be like everyone else."

Sophie took her mother's arm and helped her upstairs to her bedroom where there were two single beds.

"Are you sure you don't want to sleep in your father's bed?"

"No, no. I'll be fine on the couch. Unless you need me? But Ray says I sometimes snore and I don't want to keep you up. You know you're such a light sleeper. You really need to rest. When Dad gets home it's going to be hard at first. You need your rest."

She gave her Mom a kiss on the cheek. "Good night."

As Sophie walked down the stairs, her mother called after her. "Sophie, would you like a sleeping pill?"

"No, I'm good. I love you Mom. Good night."

Sophie covered the couch in the living room with sheets and a blanket. She settled down and tried to fall asleep, tossing and turning. She wondered why she turned down her mother's offer of a sleeping pill. She could really use one. She felt very wired and exhausted at the same time but drifted off into a restless sleep.

A little while later, the clock on the TV said two A.M. Sophie had woken up and was tossing and turning again, flipping her pillow and punching it every few minutes. She tried to relax, lying on her back in a shavasna yoga pose, arms out by her sides with her thumb and pointer finger making a circle. She was staring at the ceiling, which was made of white drop tiles with black dots. The dots seemed to make the shape of constellations like the Big Dipper. She was making a wish but she didn't know what she was wishing for. She imagined the Actor was lying on a yoga mat next to her. He reached out to her open palm and held her hand. She drifted off to sleep and started to dream.

* * *

Young Sophie was on a sofa in the Actor's apartment. He was sitting next to her working on his laptop while she was leaning back on the arm of the sofa with her feet in his lap working on her laptop.

Young Sophie leaned her head back and said, "I can't do this. My balance sheet doesn't balance. It's impossible. I'm no good at this."

The Actor looked up. He was wearing horn-rimmed glasses and looked exceptionally cute in them. "I don't know what a balance sheet is but if you explain it to me maybe I can help?"

She sat up as he put his laptop aside and they started to work together. She explained what a balance sheet was while he studied the computer screen. He pointed out a few things and she got it to balance. She put her laptop down on the coffee table, then leaned over and kissed him. He put his hand on her neck, leaned her back on the couch and kissed her throat. He lifted her shirt and stroked her breasts. She wrapped her legs around him and unbuckled his belt.

* * *

The next morning she was driving her mother back to the hospital and planning to visit with her Dad for a short time before she had to get to work. She didn't want to lose another sick day, so she'd just work late tonight.

"Hey Mom, I called Jesse and Sean last night. Jesse is working at the bakery on Wickenden Street this morning and Sean said he could meet us for coffee before he goes to work. So we're going to stop there first."

"I don't know any bakery on Wickenden Street."

"I think it's a new bakery. He's training to be a pastry chef now."

"Who is?"

"Jesse."

"Oh I thought you said the other one. What's his name?"

"Sean." Sophie crossed over the Fox Pointe Channel bridge and found a parking space not far from the bakery.

"Where are we?"

"This is Wickenden Street."

"Oh your father and I never come here."

"Yeah I suppose you never did. This is more the college neighborhood, isn't it? The boys don't live far from here. They have a nice apartment on the second floor of a two family off of Hope Street."

They walked into the bakery. It was full of young college age kids, drinking coffee and chai tea, working on laptops or reading. There was a chalkboard with various coffee and tea selections and the pastries and muffins were in a large glass case. Her mother was looking around confused.

"Mom, do you want a cup of tea? Why don't you take a seat and I'll order for us."

"Okay, that menu up there is very confusing."

"Just look in the case and see if you like something. Maybe Jesse can bring out something he made."

"I just want a blueberry muffin."

"Oh I'm sure they have that."

She got her mother settled at a little four-seater table in a corner by the window. She went back to the counter and ordered a coffee and tea. The girl behind the counter had a spiky punk haircut shaved on one side with the longer hair on the other side sweeping over to cover some of it. It was dyed jet black with midnight blue highlights that almost disappeared in certain light. She had a silver hoop nose ring and her left arm was completely covered in colorful tattoos. Sophie asked her, "Is Jesse here?"

"Yeah, he's in the back."

"I'm his mother. Could you tell him I'm here? He's expecting me. But first, could I have that blueberry muffin and I'll also have the lemon poppy seed too. Thanks."

"Oh, you're his mother. Hi, I'm Miranda. Sure thing." She rang up the order. Sophie suddenly looked worried. Miranda was being awfully friendly. As Sophie brought the drinks and muffins to the table, the girl went out back to get Jesse. She heard the little bell on the door ring as it opened and Sean walked in.

"Mom. Grandma." Sean walked over and hugged them. He was dressed in a white cotton shirt and blue khakis and wearing a very expensive looking charcoal gray wool coat. His blond hair was cut stylishly short.

"Honey, you look great. How's work?"

"Really good. It's a fun place to work. I'm going to L.A. next week for a trade show."

Out of the corner of her eye, Sophie saw Jesse come out of the kitchen in a baker's apron. His hair was in a ponytail and he had some flour on his face. He walked over to Miranda, gave her a kiss and signaled her to follow him.

"Hey Mom." He bent down and kissed Sophie then gave his grandmother a kiss. "This is my girlfriend Miranda." She smiled shyly and waved. Sophie reached out to shake hands with Miranda and said, "Yes we just met."

"Who is that girl?" Sophie whispered something in her mother's ear. "His girlfriend?" Sean covered his mouth, trying not to laugh as Jesse poked Miranda and smiled at her then gave her a big kiss.

Jesse asked, "How is Grandpa doing?"

"He's doing well. He might be able to come home in a few days."

"That's good news. Sorry I can't hang around and shoot the shit. I've got some scones in the oven. I'll call you."

"Do you have to talk like that Jesse?" Sophie nodded her head towards her mother. "Okay, it was good to see you and it was nice to meet you Miranda. Call me Jesse, we hardly hear from you. Your Dad would like to hear from you too."

After the two of them went back behind the counter, Sophie turned to Sean. "When did this happen?"

Sean shook his head. "About a week after he got here. She's actually nicer than she looks. She goes to RISD and is a pretty talented sculptress. He's moving in with her this weekend."

"What?"

"It's not really working out. The rest of us have regular jobs with Monday through Friday hours. He was waking everyone up and partying on weeknights. She lives with a group of kids over on Federal Hill. He'll be fine."

Sophie puckered her lips and let out a big breath. "I don't know what to say."

"Probably best not to say anything. When you tell Dad you don't really need to mention the tattoos and nose ring. Knowing Jesse this won't last long."

"Then where will he go?"

"He's got some other friends who go to Johnson and Wales. He's talking about taking some cooking classes so that's a good thing. I'll keep an eye on him."

"Thanks honey." She gave her son a big hug.

"I'm planning to visit Grandpa tonight and Jesse says he's coming too."

"That's sweet honey. Just make sure he doesn't bring Miranda. Your grandfather did just have a heart attack."

"I've got it covered Mom."

"At least someone does."

* * *

When they got back to the hospital, Annie was there. They visited for a short time then they left their parents alone. Annie was planning to come back later to bring her mother home.

Before the two sisters left the hospital, they decided to grab a cup of coffee in the cafeteria. They got a table by the window. The unseasonably warm temperature had come to an end. It was a blustery, gray November day with a chill in the air and it looked like rain any minute.

Sophie carefully placed her coffee on the table and leaned over to sip it. It was filled to the brim after she had added cream. "I've got a long drive back."

"Are you going to work from here Sophie?'

"Oh yeah. I only have two sick days right now. We get a half a day a month for a total of six days a year. You earn them as you go. I don't think I've ever gotten six in the bank. It's impossible."

Annie shook her head and sipped her coffee, staring out the window as the rain began.

"Hey Annie, what's up with Mom? Does she seem worse to you? With the confusion and repeating herself? Last night she was telling me the same stories she always does."

"Sorry, I meant to tell you. They heard on Monday. She went for a physical and they gave her the test."

"The Test? For Alzheimer's?

"Yes."

"She failed, didn't she?"

"Yes it looks that way. They're sending her to the clinic at R.I. Hospital for follow up."

"Oh no, parking's going to be a problem." They laughed half-heartedly.

"Shit. I'm so sorry Annie. You know you're the one who is going to bear the brunt of this especially now with Dad's heart attack. You're the one who still lives here."

"It's okay. My girls are grown."

"But still, it's going to be a lot. Wow. Now the shit begins." She shook her head. "I don't mean that the way it sounds. Not shit for us but for them. I mean this is the end of their story. Here comes the 'for better or worse'. This is what they mean by the worse. And whoever goes first, the other one will be so lost. Wow. I don't know. I just don't know. I'm so confused myself these days."

"Sophie, it's the cycle of life. Until death do us part."

Sophie's eyes were tearing up and she wiped them with the back of her hand. "They did have so many good times. Traveling around in that conversion van when Dad retired. They got to see most of Europe too. He was lucky he could retire so young. They saw their grandkids graduate from college and your oldest get married."

"Sophie, no one's died yet."

"I know, I know. I'm just a mess lately. I'm struggling with the meaning of life and what love is. How should I be spending my days? I know it shouldn't be in a cubicle forty hours a week. But how do I pay the never ending bills?" She paused for a moment, thinking of something. "Do you really believe in 'til death do us part?" Annie nodded her head yes and whispered, "Sometimes, yes." Sophie shrugged, "I'm okay. Enough of me and my existential bullshit. Hey, I better hit the road. I need at least a half day in today so I'm not working all night this week making up time." She hugged Annie.

"Next time you come down Sophie, we'll go out for a drink. Make that a few drinks."

"I'm gonna hold you to that Annie." She kissed her sister again.

THE BACHELORETTE PARTY

After some steamy lovemaking, they were lying on the couch talking about traveling. They'd eaten all the cupcakes. She was musing on their shared backpacking stories. "The more places you go and the more people you meet, the more experiences you have to write about. A writer needs experiences. That's why I need to get out of my cubicle. The world is passing me by while I sit in the same place every day. There's got to be more to life than that."

"Higgly Piggly Pop." He was licking blue frosting off his finger.

"What?" She started laughing hysterically. "You are the strangest guy." She kissed his cheek.

"Close your eyes. I have a birthday present for you."

"Again?" But she closed her eyes while he got up. She could hear him in the kitchen doing something that sounded like he was tearing a roll of aluminum foil. He was walking around and she smiled at the thought of this because she knew he was naked. She could hear him rummaging around the bookcase. "What on earth are you doing?"

"Okay, you can open your eyes. God, it's freezing in here." He grabbed a blue and green afghan from the end of the couch and laid down next to her, handing her a square, thin, flat package wrapped in aluminum foil. He pulled the afghan over them.

"I like the wrapping paper. You're very resourceful." She smiled at him and started to open the package. It was a book by Maurice Sendak called "Higgly Piggly Pop, or There's More To Life Than This."

"Wow, what is this?"

"A book."

"Obviously." She hit him on the knee with the book. "This is 'The Wild Things' author. I love that book."

"Everyone does. This is an earlier book. It's about a dog named Jennie who has everything but she is still unhappy. She decides the one thing she needs is experience. Like you. So she takes off to get some and ends up a famous actress in the Mother Goose Theater and never comes back. Let's read it. I'll start."

He took the book and she rested her chin on his shoulder as he read the first page. They alternated reading as he turned the pages. When they finished, she sat up a little.

"This is really strange and you are never going to believe this but remember I told you about the four cats. One for each girl?"

"Yes. And yours was Jennie. I picked this book for more than one reason you know. This book was meant for you."

"Wow. Well Jennie was an amazing cat. The best cat ever. She would walk me down the driveway every day and wait with me for the school bus. At the end of the day when I got home, there she would be again, sitting at the end of the driveway waiting for me. It was like she knew how to tell time. We had a neighbor who had two little babies. She would take them for a walk every morning around ten. Jennie would wait at the end of our driveway until they came by and accompany them on their walk. I always thought she did this because she was lonely while I was at school."

"I'm sure she was. Who wouldn't miss you when you were gone? I know I did." He wiggled her nose. "She truly does sound amazing."

"Like I said, the best cat ever. One time, my bus got in a little accident. Luckily no one was hurt. Some guy just bumped us from behind while we were stopped at a red light. But of course the police and ambulances had to arrive at the scene of the accident. The parents had to be called. My mother noticed we were late and she came outside. She saw Jennie pacing back and forth at the end of the driveway. She knew I was late too and when my mother came out, she started meowing at her frantically."

"Seriously? Is this a true story?"

"No word of a lie. Cross my heart and hope to die. You can ask my sisters if you ever meet them. Or my mother."

"So where is Jennie now?"

"My parents got her two months after I was born, so when she and I were thirteen, she just disappeared. Just went out one day and never came back. My mother said cats do that when they're ready to die. Being cats, they like to be alone when they die. This devastated me because Jennie was not any ordinary cat and she was only thirteen. I thought about her every night. She used to sleep in my bed with me and now I couldn't sleep thinking about where she was."

He started to stroke her hair. "I kept thinking, did an owl swoop down and get her? Or a bear? We were in Vermont after all, people had seen bears sometimes in their yards. Or maybe it was one of those awful fisher cats. And if she really did just go off and die like my mother said, where was her body? I needed to bury her and plant flowers on her grave. I hated thinking of her body out in the woods somewhere. I cried for nights." She had tears in her eyes thinking about this.

"Aaaww." He buried his lips in her hair then kissed her forehead. He whispered in her ear, "Maybe she went off somewhere to have an adventure and become a famous writer. I think she went to Hollywood and is writing screenplays."

"I like that ending much better."

"You could write it, the better ending. Write a children's book. I draw you know. I could illustrate it."

"That's a great idea. The better ending. I like that."

"I think you need to quit your job. With all these writing projects you have, you don't have much time to work."

* * *

The following Saturday morning, she was on a plane to New Orleans. Nick's sister was getting married Memorial

Day weekend and she had been asked to be one of the ten bridesmaids. Ten bridesmaids! That's insane, isn't it? Who does Nick's sister think she is? Kate Middleton?

The bachelorette party had been planned around the Mardi Gras celebration on Tuesday. The other nine bridesmaids would fly home Wednesday but from New Orleans she was going on to Dallas to visit Nick. He had bought her the ticket.

Although Nick had only been in Dallas three weeks, he had been offered a full time job with a huge promotion and a raise to match his new status. Although he didn't really want to leave Boston he said he couldn't pass up this opportunity of a lifetime. She thought he was mocking her. It felt like a dig when he said it.

He wanted her to come visit so he could show her around and look at condos with her. The plan to buy the condo had been moved up by a couple of years. With the raise and the cheaper housing costs in Dallas, he could buy it now and without her help. Clearly he'd been a lot more disciplined with the savings plan than she was. But, despite her improvidence, Nick wanted her to live with him.

She was staring out the plane window at the clouds that went as far as the eye could see. She imagined herself lying on her back, floating through the blue sky and bouncing across the tops of the clouds back to Newburyport and that comfortable bed above the garage that felt like sleeping on a cloud. It was heaven. Her thoughts strayed and she returned to the rest of last weekend and the boy she had met on the train. She had stayed in Newburyport until Monday morning.

After she told him about Jennie, he pulled the illustrations out from under the coffee table and showed her his drawings. His Aunt Helen was writing a children's book. She babysat for a family in Newburyport. They owned an import/export company and had to travel for business quite often. They had a little three year old girl named Katrina with blond curls. She had a baby brother who was four months old. She was very mischievous and got into all sorts of trouble. She would blame it all on her imaginary friend Alice. When Helen asked her about Alice she told Helen that Alice lived on the bottom of her shoe and popped out every once in a while and did naughty things.

His drawings were really good. She had already seen the one with the girl popping out of the shoe and he showed her more. He felt he was having a hard time with the imagery of Alice coming out from under the shoe but she thought they were great. He picked up a blank piece of paper and did a rough pencil sketch of a cat sitting at the end of a driveway. Tucking it in the book he just gave her he said, "For you. You better get writing."

As the stewardess came by, she snapped out of her reverie and ordered a Bloody Mary. Why not? She was using a week of vacation time for this trip so that left her only one more week for the rest of the year. Mardi Gras would be fun although she didn't really get along with Nick's sister. Olivia could be very demanding and high maintenance. She also had an entitled, elitist attitude. She was brought up as the only girl in a wealthy family and was used to getting whatever she wanted whenever she wanted it. She had no concept that other people may not be as fortunate as her.

Her mind drifted back to her birthday weekend. He had shown her around Newburyport, which was a great little New England seaport town. She loved all the shops and restaurants and the pretty little harbor. They met friends of his for dinner, two guys and a girl he had known in high school. They seemed to know all about her. It seemed like they were eager to meet her and were very happy for him so he must have been saying nice things. Later that night, when they got back to the apartment, they watched Gregory Peck and Audrey Hepburn in 'Roman Holiday'. He told her he was a big fan of old movies, which she thought was amazingly awesome.

Sunday they slept late, he made her eggs benedict for brunch and they flew a kite at the beach on Plum Island. He had brought a cooler with beers and chicken parmesan sandwiches. It was an unseasonably warm day for early March. She thought it had to be one of the most perfect days of her life thus far.

Monday morning he packed her a lunch-a ham and cheese sandwich, an apple and chocolate chip cookies-then drove her to work. When she kissed him goodbye in front of her office, she knew she was going to miss him. Even though she had to eat at her desk that afternoon to make quota on the articles due that day, she smiled when she found a note in her lunch bag. *Hope you're having a great day. Keep smiling.* She sent him a text. *Thanks for lunch and a lovely birthday weekend. I miss you already.* Her phone quickly beeped back. *Miss you too.* It was going to be a very long two weeks until she saw him again.

* * *

When she got to the airport in New Orleans, she grabbed a cab to the Ritz Carlton to meet the other bridesmaids. Many of the bridesmaids were coming in from Long Island where Nick and his sister Olivia grew up. Others were from New York City and various other places they had moved to since graduating from Sarah Lawrence with Olivia.

The cab dropped her off at the curb in front of a beautiful stately hotel with palm trees out front. A doorman opened the door for her and a bellhop took her luggage. She scrambled for small bills in her wallet so she could tip them. She hadn't thought of that! The lobby was exquisite with marble floors, chandeliers and French doors leading to a quintessential French Quarter courtyard with wrought iron tables, fountains and beautiful plantings. She had never stayed in a hotel like this before and she imagined her credit card flexing it's muscles in her pocketbook and just itching to get out and start earning interest. She was out of small bills and hoped she didn't have to tip anyone else.

At the reservations desk she received her key and a note on fancy stationary. The receptionist let her know her roommate had already checked in. She knew her name was Nan and she was one of the Long Island girls. A friend of Olivia's from Oyster Bay. They had emailed each other a couple of times. The note was from Olivia and said in very fancy script:

We are all meeting in the courtyard. Check into your room, freshen up and meet us for cocktails.

She took the elevator up to her room on the sixth floor. There were two double beds in a room with beautiful Frette linen bedding and a view looking towards Bourbon Street a block away. She quickly washed her face, brushed her teeth and tied her hair up in a loose knot on the top of her head. She was wearing a colorful print skirt she bought in Mexico. While she was living in Oregon, she and Katie had driven the Pacific coast through California and down to Rosalita Beach in Baja California. She added a loose white cotton blouse with embroidered flowers around the neckline, silver hoop earrings and five silver bracelets also purchased on that trip into Mexico.

When she got to the courtyard, she was the last to arrive. She was introduced all around and hoped she'd remember everyone's name because so many of the girls were thin, tall and had long blond hair. Nan, her roommate, had dark hair and a beautiful face but was definitely carrying several more pounds than anyone else in the wedding party.

She sat next to Nan and across from Olivia. The girl to her other side was Zoe and she had a job with Goldman Sachs in New York. Everyone was asking her questions all at once.

"So you live in Boston with Liv's brother Nick? He's so handsome."

"Yes we've been living together for almost a year and a half now."

"When are you moving to Dallas? You must miss him."

"I'm not sure if and when I'm moving to Dallas."

"What do you mean you're not sure? He's quite the catch."

"We heard this promotion and move were so sudden but what an opportunity for your future."

Was she the only one who was seeing opportunity differently? "Yes but the timing couldn't be better." She laughed nervously. What did she mean by that? She better be careful. When she was nervous she had a tendency to say stupid things. If she drank too much she could let something slip. She waited to order another cosmo.

"Where did you go to school? Oh that's right, you met Nick at Tufts."

"Where do you work? What do you do?"

"A company in the suburbs. I'm a lowly copy editor."

"Ha! Olivia said you were self deprecating. And very funny. This weekend is going to be so much fun."

"She said I was self deprecating?"

"I love your bracelets? Very bohemian. And those shoes. Are those Manolos?"

She looked down at the silver heeled sandals she had on. "I don't know what they are. I bought them at Marshall's."

"Ha! You're going to be a fun one. We heard Nick thinks you're a bit wild but that seems to turn him on. He always liked a challenge."

"Well, ladies let's get going. Is it time for the French Quarter and Pat O'Brien's?"

"Huh? He said what? I'm wild? I am really not that wild. Not at all really."

* * *

Later that evening, she was back in her room lying on her bed while Nan was changing in the bathroom. It was two in the morning. They had spent the evening at Pat O'Brien's and then walked around the French Quarter, which was full of people drinking in the streets. The sound of jazz came spilling out of the numerous open-air bars. Most of the girls were drinking hurricanes so they could accumulate a full set of the tall souvenir glasses they were served in. Dan at work had warned her about these. He said they were mostly sugar and would give you a nasty hangover so she steered clear of them and instead switched to beers. They were cheaper anyway. She knew that credit card was going to take a heavy hit this week.

A block before the hotel, Zoe dropped her bag of four hurricane glasses and broke them all. She was stumbling and very drunk, slurring her words. But four hurricanes could do that to even the most accomplished drinker. They all consoled her and said they'd go back the next night for more. She wasn't looking forward to that crowded singles tourist trap again. Hopefully they could see some awesome live music before they left.

Nan came out of the bathroom and climbed into the other bed. "Did Olivia give you the Countdown to I Do diet?"

"No. I don't think so. I got a note from her when I checked in but that was just to let me know you were all in the courtyard. What is the Countdown Diet?"

"It's like a South Beach/Atkins kind of thing. It's so we all look smashing, her word, in our bridesmaid dresses."

"You're kidding? She's putting us on a diet?"

"Well maybe you didn't get one. You're so tiny. That's why I was asking. I think I'm the only one. Maybe Amanda, I'm not sure."

"What a bitch!" She quickly slapped her hand over her mouth.

Nan laughed. "I was so glad when I heard I was rooming with you. She is a bitch. I think she only asked me to be a bridesmaid because she wanted ten and my Dad is a partner in her Dad's business. I've known her since we were babies so she was obligated to ask me. But I'm going to ruin the photos if I don't lose at least twenty pounds."

"Twenty pounds. Get the fuck out of here." She covered her mouth again. "Oops I'm sorry. I don't usually talk like that. But that's just ridiculous. She is a fucking bitch." They both started laughing hysterically. "This whole thing is ridiculous. Five days at the Ritz Carlton? The dress is already costing me three hundred dollars. When did people start doing this bachelorette party thing? I thought we just had to go to some stupid shower on a Sunday afternoon and give her some towels or sheets."

"Oh we have to do that too."

"Ugh! I hate all this stuff. I can't believe she made us wear those crowns tonight. And the matching T-shirts? Really?" She leaned over and picked up a gray T-shirt she had thrown on the end of her bed when she got back to the room. It had the word Bridesmaid written in pink script lettering across the front. She held it up to her chest then crumbled it up and tossed it towards the wastebasket at the desk. She landed the shot. She raised her arms and clapped her hands above her head. "YES!"

"Aren't you going to marry her brother? My dad said everyone seems to think so."

"No way. I am not marrying anyone. I have too many things to do. I want to quit my job and travel. I want to get serious about writing. I don't want to be someone's wife especially Nick's. And don't feel bad, Olivia only asked me to be in the wedding 'cus I'm going with Nick. And she needed those ten bridesmaids. I think there is something celestial or biblical about ten virgins or something like that. I don't know the details but I read it somewhere."

"Well that's a good thing because from what I hear my parents say, the DeLuca's are nervous about Nick settling down with you. They were stressing out about the fact that you might be moving to Dallas." Now it was Nan who slapped both hands over her mouth. "That's not true. I'm just a little drunk from those hurricanes. I shouldn't have said that."

"I'm sure it's true. I know they don't like me. Too 'bohemian', that's Mrs. DeLuca's word and I'm too opinionated. Liberal, subversive opinions. I don't have what it takes to be a corporate wife and helpmate as Mrs. D calls it. They think I have no ambition. But I do have ambition, not just the kind they are looking for. You know when people say who are THEY? As in, they say you should get a degree in business. They say this, they say that."

"Yes, I know what you mean. Who are they? No one knows."

"Of course we know who THEY are. They are the DeLucas and all the rest of the successful, powerful people who make the rules but somehow the rules don't always apply to them. The rules are meant to keep the rest of us in our places, which is working for the people who make the money and the rules. They have decided that liberal is a bad word. But who's to say what success is? If you have a different idea of success and happiness you shouldn't do what THEY tell you to do."

"Are you an anarchist? What on earth is a girl like you doing with Nick?"

"See, I tell you I'm a liberal and you ask me if I'm an anarchist. I think you've been listening to Them. And please don't tell me you listen to talk radio. But good question about Nick. I've been looking for a roommate for a few months now. But then Nick got this Dallas thing and now I've got a single apartment. Ha! That's not gonna last though. He's putting the pressure on me to move to Dallas. And you know, I really don't know why. We fight all the time nowadays and I just don't get it. Why does he want to stay with me?

Anyway, I have to tell him it's over this weekend when I get to Dallas. It's just I can't afford a place by myself and then this Dallas thing happened. That's pretty sleazy though, isn't it? I have to go on Craigslist or something. Just find someplace, anyplace. Maybe I'll move home to Vermont for a while. Or not." She laughed.

"If you break up with him this weekend, that's sure going to complicate the wedding."

"Yeah, I know. I have to think of some way to handle this tactfully. I suppose I could wait until after Memorial Day but there are..." she paused, thinking of how to put it, "other things going on. Anyway, I'm exhausted. Let's get some sleep, we have the parade and the garden tour tomorrow."

She rolled over and reached towards the light between the two beds to shut it off. She picked up her cell phone and rolled on her other side facing away from Nan. She pulled the covers over her head and sent a text message. When she left Newburyport Monday morning, he had made her promise she would let him know she had arrived safely. He seemed to be nervous about airplane travel. They were only fifteen when September 11th had happened and he seemed to still be affected by those constant images of the planes flying into the buildings.

That didn't stop him from getting on a plane though. He had flown to the other side of the globe when he went to Australia. His desire to see the world was greater than his fear of flying so he was gone this week too. He and a friend, or a buddy as he liked to call these numerous friends of his, went to Denver to see Ava. They planned to go skiing in Vail.

I made it to the Big Easy. The hotel is over the top. Partying on Bourbon Street this evening. This is going to be a long five days with the nine handmaidens and the control freak bride. My roomie is nice anyway.

A minute later her cell phone vibrated.

Hey there. I was just about to text you, I was getting worried. Just got back from dinner. Snow tonight. A foot at least. Can't wait to hit the slopes. I miss you.

The phone vibrated again. Nan mumbled sleepily "Is that Nick?'"

"No. Sorry, is it keeping you awake?"

"No it's okay. I'm fading. Who is it?"

"Just a good friend." She read the text.

Make sure to see some good jazz or zydeco while you're there. Can I call you right now?

My roommate is sleeping.

Go in the bathroom. I need to tell you something. I won't talk long.

K. Give me a sec. She got up and went to the bathroom. She closed the door, put the toilet seat cover down, took one of the ultra plush towels from the rack above and sat on it. Her phone buzzed. She whispered as softly as she could. "Hello."

"Hi. It's me."

She laughed quietly. "I know it's you." She couldn't stop laughing. She tried to compose herself. "You wanted to tell me something?"

"I didn't plan to do this over the phone but when the plane took off this morning I realized I needed to and it couldn't wait."

"Did you think your plane was going to crash?"

"Well you never know. Bad things happen."

"Right, I understand."

"Anyway, I wanted to tell you I love you."

"Already? We just met."

"Don't you believe in love at first sight?"

"I don't know. Do you?"

"I do now that I've met you. What do you mean you don't know?"

"I guess my answer would be maybe. I'm not sure. It seems unrealistic. Something made up for corny movies and fairy tales. Are you sure it isn't lust?"

"Well the sex has been amazing but no it is not just lust. Are you saying that's all it is?"

"No I didn't say that. It's just love.... that's serious. But like I said maybe it can happen."

"I guess maybe is better than no."

"I thought you said maybe meant no."

"No, that's what my mother said. I think maybe holds the possibility of yes. That's why my mother and I used to argue about it."

"Ah, I see. I wish I could kiss you right now."

"You can. Send it right now. I'm waiting."

She puckered her lips into a kiss, made a light smacking sound and blew loud enough so he could hear it. She waited while there was silence for a moment.

"Did you get it?"

"Umm. It's a long way from New Orleans to Denver. Ah, there it is. It landed under my left eye."

She laughed a little too loudly this time. "Hey I have to go to bed. It's two in the morning here."

"Hold on. I just sent you a kiss."

"I didn't catch that, send it again." She could hear him making a very loud lip smooching sound then a sound like wind blowing when you're lying in bed on a warm, breezy summer night with the windows open.

"Wow. That landed right in my ear. I love when you kiss my ears. Nice aim."

"G'night. Sweet dreams."

"Night. Carve some powder for me."

"Will do."

YOU'RE LUCKY TO HAVE
A JOB IN THIS ECONOMY

Ray was at work. He had set two ladders on the side of a very large house. A plank ran between the two ladders acting as staging. He was leaning very far to his right, stretching and hammering clapboards. A chilly wind was blowing leaves across the yard. Ray was dressed in several layers of clothing with a large insulated flannel shirt on top.

Meanwhile, Sophie was in her cubicle, typing on her keyboard. She was not the only one, the room was filled with the sound of people clicking and clacking away. One person was typing very loudly, banging the keys like they were sending someone a very angry message and taking it out on the keyboard.

Sophie was working on coding a stack of VISA card statements she was responsible for paying each month. She had twenty eight sales reps that used these cards, traveling throughout the world. She envied the hotels they stayed in and the restaurants they dined at. She googled some of the places they went as she sat in her cubicle coding each charge on the statements as either travel or meals expense. She closed her eyes and sat like that for a while. She was daydreaming.

* * *

She was swinging in a hammock strung between two palm trees by the blue Caribbean sea. She had her laptop with her and was working on her website. She and Ray ran a bed and breakfast on the island of St. John and she handled the reservations, which people often booked on the Internet. Off in the distance, she could see the town of Red Hook over on St. Thomas. The ferry was headed towards her and the little town of Cruz Bay where she lived. The only sound she could hear was the lapping of the gentle waves on the shore and an occasional songbird.

They ran the inn from December to June, returning home to New England each summer and renting a house on Cape Cod. She had finished cleaning the guest rooms before noon. Early afternoons were quiet, most of the guests were at the beach or sightseeing. She took her cell phone out of her pocket and called a friend of hers who ran a small restaurant in town. She was working a deal with him where she would refer people to his restaurant if he advertised her B&B on his website.

She thought she'd offer to take him to the golf course at the Ritz over near Red Hook for a round of eighteen holes later that week. She'd use her VISA card and take it as a business expense. She would classify it as advertising.

Suddenly she heard her boss talking to Dan in the next cubicle. She quickly sat up straighter and got back to work.

* * *

Much later that evening Sophie was at the gas station at the end of her road, pumping gas. It was dark outside, a cold night in November. The price at the pump was now $3.64. She looked up and saw Lynn pull up to the pump next to hers. Lynn got out of the car without looking around. "Hey Lynn, how are you?" Sophie shouted.

Lynn looked up. Sophie thought she looked upset and distracted. Pointing to the price of gas on the pump, she asked, "What's up with the price of this gas? I have to fill up twice a week. That sure takes a bite out of my six hundred bucks a week take home pay."

"Hey Sophie. Are you just getting home from work?"

"Yeah, I had to stay late to make up for the time I took when my Dad was in the hospital. You look upset. Is anything wrong?"

"Doug lost his job."

"WHAT? Oh Lynn. I can't believe this. He's only been there six months, right? How the hell did this happen?"

"I don't know. But I knew something was wrong when he pulled in the driveway earlier than usual tonight."

"Well come back to my house for some wine."

"I can't. I've got to get back to the house. He's so upset. He feels like he let us all down. What are we gonna do? This is the second time in a little over a year. It took him eight months to find this job."

"He didn't let you down. The American dream has let us all down." She scoffed. "How could they hire him for six months? That's nuts."

"I know. And now what does his resume look like? How does he find another job in his late forties? And we've got one kid in college, another in high school. How do we do this?"

Sophie had finished pumping gas. The total was $62.00. She walked over to Lynn and hugged her. "Jesus, what a world. Should we start an Occupy Main Street encampment in town?" They both laughed, half-heartedly.

"I couldn't even understand what he was saying. I don't really know what happened. I feel like my life is totally out of my control."

"He's just distraught. I know how he feels. When I lost my job and was unemployed for fourteen months it was a roller coaster ride. Are you sure you don't want to come over for one quick glass of wine? I have plenty. I'm making lasagna when I get back and definitely opening a bottle. I can't drink it all myself. Or maybe I could, but I shouldn't."

"You're starting a lasagna at eight at night?"

"Yeah, crazy life, huh? What are you gonna do? We'll be eating at nine if we're lucky. At least we can eat it for the rest of the week and I won't have to cook. Ray will love that. He doesn't even like lasagna."

"No, I really have to get back. I told Doug I needed to pick up milk, but I really needed wine. He's so upset, I can't leave him long."

Sophie hugged Lynn again. "Hang in there. It will work out. It always does, doesn't it?

Lynn sighed, "I know. I hope you're right. Call me tomorrow."

"I'll call while driving to work in the morning."

Sophie walked back to her car, got in and waved to Lynn as she took a left out of the gas station and drove down her street. She looked in the rearview mirror and saw Lynn pumping gas and wiping her eyes.

Later that night, Ray and Sophie were lying in bed. Ray was watching the Celtics game and Sophie was reading. She put her book down. "Doug lost his job today."

"No! Well that sucks."

"Yeah, I don't know what they're going to do. Lynn is beside herself. It's been only six months. I guess I'm lucky I have my cubicle and you've got work through the holidays. You do have work through the holidays this year, right?"

"Yeah I've got work right up to Christmas."

"God I hate the holidays. Seriously Ray, I don't know what we're all doing. Working our butts off and getting nowhere, at the mercy of some job. We give these jobs the majority of our waking time and we're treated like we're all just disposable. They call us a human resource. Am I just stupid or is there something wrong with this picture?"

"You're not stupid Sophie." He rolled towards her and gave her a kiss.

"I have my annual review tomorrow and how much you want to bet there's another raise freeze? The company's growing like crazy, we're all doing the work of two people and there's a raise freeze. But they know we're scared. They think we should be grateful we have a job."

She looked over at Ray. His eyes were closing and he'd started to doze off. She reached over and shook his shoulder. "Ray, I have really been missing Kathy lately. I was talking to her while I was driving to work today."

Ray rolled over and put his arm around her. "That's okay honey. It's hard. Grief comes and goes. It's a circle, not a straight line."

"It's been four years now. There are some days that go by and I don't even think of her then I suddenly need to talk to her and go to dial her number because I've forgotten that I've lost her. But she lost me too and all the people she loved and all the things she would have done had she not died so young. Death was her loss too."

Sophie started to cry, tears rolling down her cheeks. Ray hugged her, holding her tight.

"I have been so unhappy lately, day after day in that cubicle. I feel life is passing me by while I sit in the same place doing the same thing and living for the weekends. What kind of way is that to live? Sleep walk through five days out of seven? When I was talking to her, I realized something. I have to be happy for the both of us. I have to go on and do the things we were going to do together and didn't get the chance to do. I can't wait. I have to be happy now. Life is short. She taught me I have to live every day like it is my last. I have to remember what is important."

Ray started to stroke her hair and kiss her neck. He whispered in her ear, "I know. We're getting there. We're getting things done around here. We'll get the house on the market. We'll get you out of that cubicle and doing something you like. Something we both like. I promise."

She kissed him and wrapped her legs around him. He rolled the both of them towards the edge of the bed, shut the light off and kissed her as he rolled them back towards the center of the bed. "It's gonna be okay Sophie. I love you."

* * *

The next day, Sophie was in her cubicle, staring at her computer screen. She googled the Actor. He was filming a movie in L.A. She looked at pictures of him on the set. The very loud HVAC system stopped blowing for a minute and it got a little quieter in the room. Now she could hear the sound of people walking above her. The floor was squeaking loudly. She emailed Dan.

Do you hear that squeaking noise above us? It's like being in a cheap motel beneath an insomniac who is pacing the floor all night.

Sophie's computer made a little beep and a reminder came up. Meeting in Tina's office in fifteen minutes. She closed the screen with the Actor and left to get coffee in the cafeteria where she ran into Dan. "Annual review in ten minutes."

"Good luck. You thinking raise?" Dan laughed.

"You kidding me?"

"No shit. Hey I asked my girlfriend to move out."

"No! Hey I gotta get back up there but tell me all about it later, ok?"

She poured some cream in her coffee and hurried back to Tina's office. Grabbing a pad of paper and a pen as she passed her cubicle, she entered Tina's office and closed the door behind her. Tina looked up smiling, "So Sophie, we've had an amazing year, haven't we?"

"I'll say. We can barely keep up with all this work."

"I know. And I am hoping to get approved for more help, at least part time. But right now that's not in the budget." Tina passed an evaluation sheet across the desk to Sophie. Sophie's heart skipped a beat. Did Tina know how much she surfed the web? What if she knew about the Actor? The company did spy on people's Internet activity sometimes. This really pissed her off, as did random drug testing. Why did her generation start giving up rights instead of fighting for rights? Doesn't anyone care about the right to privacy anymore?

"I want you to know you are doing a great job and we truly appreciate it. You are a joy to work with, always smiling and willing to help. You take on extra work without being asked. You manage your time really well, have risen to new challenges and you exceed expectations."

"Thanks." Sophie started to think there had to be a raise coming next.

"Right now we have a raise freeze in effect. I am doing my best to get one for you as soon as possible. But I want you to know that you are approved for overtime if you need to complete your work."

"Well okay. Gee. Thanks." She sat there looking disappointed but then smiled. "I want to say thanks for being so easy to work with."

"Thanks Sophie. I appreciate your hard work."

Sophie returned to her desk, looked at the clock, which said 2:30, rolled her eyes and spent pretty much the rest of the afternoon googling the Actor and emailing. A friend in Rhode Island was having an ongoing conversation with her about her parents. She was also reading a long article in New York Magazine about caring for aging parents and was copying and pasting some of this info to her friend and her sister Annie. Occasionally she turned to the right computer screen and actually did some work.

An email came in from Dan. He was finally responding to her insomniac comment.

LOL

Tina walked by and said, "I have a meeting in Jodi's office."

"Okay." She could hear Dan saying, "See ya."

After the door closed, Dan hopped up and poked his head in her cubicle. He leaned against the wall. "Raise?"

"No. We've still got a raise freeze. But I can work overtime. I've been approved."

"You're shittin' me, right?"

"No I am not shitting you. Hey, so tell me what happened with your girlfriend."

"Well after we called off the wedding, living together seemed so beside the point. If we're not getting married, where are we going with this? Right?"

"Right, of course."

"I mean, I think she thought we'd work it out and get married in the end. But that's not what I'm thinking. So let's move on."

"Sure, for her sake too. I mean if she wants the whole marriage thing, it isn't fair to keep stringing her along."

"Exactly."

"So she's moving out?"

"After New Years. She's moving in with her cousin."

"How is that gonna work?"

"Awkwardly. But her cousin's place won't be ready until then and it's the holidays."

"Is she okay?"

"She's not happy but I think she knows it's the right thing. It sucks it's Christmas, you know. I feel bad it worked out this way."

"Hey, you can't just get married because you feel bad. Then it's never going to work. It sometimes doesn't work even when you think you're head over heals."

"Exactly."

Tina came back in. They both looked at her and simultaneously said "Hey." Dan went back in his cube. Sophie sent him an email.

Good luck.

Thanks.

It was finally four thirty. Sophie shut down her computer, put her coat on and walked outside into the darkness. It was pouring, the rain driving sideways as Sophie ran for the car. By the time she got behind the wheel, she was soaked. She started the engine, put the heat on and for a few minutes, watched mesmerized as the wipers went back and forth. 'This is going to be a fun drive' she thought.

Driving slowly through the rain, the lights of the other cars reflected back at her. Fog lifted off the road and swirled around like someone blowing cigarette smoke in her face. It was very difficult to see so almost everyone was driving slowly. Occasionally an SUV came flying by, spraying even more water at her windshield. She started to daydream.

* * *

Sophie was at home in her newly finished bathroom. The claw foot tub was full of bubble bath and candles were lit throughout the room. A pile of luxurious white towels were on a shelf nearby and a white hotel style bathrobe was hanging from the back of the door. Small hotel style bottles of shampoo and lotion were lined up on the windowsill above her. She was resting her head against one of those plastic pillows that stick to the side of the tub and reading a book.

FAT TUESDAY

Ash Wednesday she caught an early afternoon flight from New Orleans to Dallas. Several people on her plane had black smudges on their foreheads. Everyone else looked like they had a hangover. As a matter of fact, when she went out for her last cup of chicory coffee that morning the whole city seemed to have a hangover. The smell of stale beer was pervasive and trash littered the streets.

She was exhausted. It had been a long five days in the Big Easy. Just trying to get along with nine girls and an overly wrought bride to be was exhausting enough. Add booze and the random chunk of hash to the mix and things could get a little tense. She leaned back, closed her eyes and reviewed the past few days.

Sunday morning everyone slept late. Most of the girls were hung over from the hurricanes they drank the night before including Nan. She thought she heard her puking in the bathroom very early that morning. Good thing Dan had warned her about those.

While everyone was sleeping, she went for a run to Cafe du Monde. She got some beignets and chicory coffee and slowly walked back to the hotel through the French Quarter, taking in the sights. She fell in love with the city and it's architecture. She looked in the windows of a few voodoo shops and hoped she could get back here when they were open. She couldn't believe it when a funeral procession passed by. It was a small group, just a few family members and a jazz band playing a mournful dirge. She stood on the sidewalk watching as they somberly walked by.

Olivia had planned an extensive itinerary for the lovely handmaidens. She had begun to refer to herself and the other girls by this name. They did seem to be at the beck and call of Olivia. Nan referred to her as Bridezilla one night when they were alone in their room. She told Nan the two of them were like Cinderella and the other nine girls were like the evil step-sisters, although sometimes Zoe and Amanda were fun.

Nan and she were the only ones in a room way down the hall from the rest of the girls. Olivia said that it was due to an overbooking problem at the hotel. It was Mardi Gras after all. The other nine girls had a series of adjoining rooms which had been leading to impromptu late night get togethers. They watched Sex in the City reruns and tried different hairstyles out on each other. It had been decided that because they all had shoulder length hair or longer they would all wear the same up do with one single orchid. A team of stylists would come to the house the morning of the wedding and do their hair.

She was still upset about this diet Nan had told her about. Now they were not only going to be wearing matching three hundred dollar dresses but also they would have matching hairstyles. She thought this was creepy. Nan was just worried she wouldn't lose the weight by Memorial Day weekend. "I'll be the only one who looks out of place. Like a fat cow."

"You are not a fat cow. Stop beating yourself up. You are sexy and voluptuous. How about I cut off my hair? Nick gave me a gift certificate to a hair salon on Newbury Street."

"He did?"

"Yeah and three hundred dollars to buy clothes. He wants to mold me into the perfect woman."

"He sounds like his sister."

"Yes, he is the evil prince in this tale of the ten handmaidens. So if I can get up the nerve, I will bite into the apple or in this case use the gift certificate and like Rapunzel I will chop off my hair."

"But it was the evil witch who chopped off Rapunzel's hair and another evil queen disguised as a hag who gave Snow White the apple. Biting the apple and chopping off the hair were the traps. It's the prince in both stories who saves them."

"You're right. I'm getting things all mixed up. And as we know, in real life there is no Prince Charming to ride in on his white stead and save the day. But as you are finding out, I don't like being told I have to do something. Aren't your bridesmaids supposed to be your best friends? So you shouldn't care what they look like? And really who has ten best friends?"

"I know. I don't think everyone does it this way."

"I am eloping. If I ever get married, which is highly unlikely. Anyway if a week before the wedding you don't lose the weight, call me and I will use my gift certificate to get my hair cut short. Too short for an up do. It will be an act of rebellion and solidarity."

"You would do that? You know Olivia said that now we have come up with this idea no one is to cut their hair too short before the wedding."

"Aren't you listening? She can't tell us what to do."

"What does Nick want you to do with the gift certificate?"

"Get a sleek, sophisticated shoulder length bob. I am thinking a punk rock spiky do with pink highlights. Or should I go with blue? I just have to get up the nerve to do it or get really drunk. I have deep seated issues with haircuts. But it might be time to conquer those fears."

* * *

When she got back to the hotel that first morning after her run, there was a bevy of handmaidens in the lobby.

"There you are.

"Everyone was worried about you. Nan woke up and said you were gone."

"I went for a run. I found Cafe du Monde. The coffee here is wonderful. I love the chicory."

"What is all over your face?

She wiped her face and saw white powder on the back of her hand. "Oh that's from the beignets. They are doused in powdered sugar. You have to try them."

Olivia stepped off an elevator and clapped her hands. "Ladies, we are scheduled for the garden tour at two so let's get to Brennan's for brunch. Then we'll be taking the St. Charles trolley to the Garden District. Then back here to the spa for massages."

And so it went every day. Olivia had planned all the activities and there was no veering from the schedule. At least they didn't have to wear the T-shirts again. The only time she had to herself was when she went for a morning run and then late at night perched on the plush towels on top of the toilet, waiting for his call from Colorado.

"I saw a real N'Orleans funeral this morning. It was so awesome. You would have loved it."

"Wow, where were you when you saw it?"

"In the French Quarter, coming back from a run to get chicory coffee and beignets. I'm going to get you some coffee. You'll love it. How was the skiing?"

"Champagne powder. Awesome. Nothing like at home. We were really cruising in the back bowls."

"Nice."

"What about brunch and the garden tour?"

"Well your eggs benedict are better than Brennan's." She heard him chuckle. "The garden tour was a lot better than I expected. Such beautiful houses and courtyards. One of the girls knows someone who goes to Tulane and she took us on the tour. I was looking for that house the vampires lived in but I couldn't find it."

"There is a house with vampires?"

"There are all sorts of spooky things here. I love it. I want to go to a voodoo shop. I need to get a juju."

"What's a juju?"

"It's a little charm you can wear to keep evil spirits away."

"Can you get me one too? I can wear it when I'm flying."

Monday was parade day on their schedule. Later that evening, they had dinner and saw some jazz at Preservation Hall. They got home at a reasonable hour deciding they needed to rest up for Fat Tuesday.

"How was the skiing today?"

"Awesome but my legs are really burning. I'm used to skiing ice not snow. I always forget how deep the snow is out here. Plus I think it's the altitude. We took a hot tub earlier. The outdoor pools and tubs are really nice here at the hotel Mark's cousin works at. He slides us a pool key. It's snowing so much I think it's technically a blizzard. I got some really cool shots of Mark in the outdoor pool with this big snow hat on the top of his head. He got one of me too. It's in my phone. I'll send it to you."

"Okay. I'll send you a picture of some floats. We were at a parade today. I caught, no lie, fifty plastic bead necklaces. If I had a car I would hang some from my rearview mirror."

"Can I have some for my car?"

"Sure. Maybe I'll decorate my Christmas tree this year with them too. Where are you staying?"

"Didn't I tell you this? Mark's cousin is ski bumming out here this winter. He has a place in West Vail he rents with four other people. It's okay, leaves me money for the important stuff.... lift tickets and beer. Have you ever skied here? It's unbelievable."

"No. Kind of out of my budget."

"Well mine too. We're at the low rent end of town out past Matterhorn Circle on Gore Creek Drive. We brought our sleeping bags and we're couch surfing. I had to bring my earplugs 'cus Mark snores like a bear and I'm on the pull out sofa with him. If I catch him spooning me he's out on the deck. When are you going to see some music?"

"Well we went to Preservation Hall tonight but it was really kind of a tourist trap. I am going to lose this crowd tomorrow night and get to Tipitinas. Nan is down with this idea too. It will be mobbed because it's Fat Tuesday but so what. Maybe someone famous will hop on stage. That happens during Mardi Gras you know."

"Yeah I bet it does. How about the Ninth Ward?"

"No one wants to go there but me. They think it's too depressing and dangerous. Although the girl from Tulane offered to take us. I guess they think they'll get mugged or something. These girls don't get out of their bubble much."

"Maybe you and I will go back someday and see everything you're missing. I'd like to take one of those boats thru the bayou. What do they call those boats?"

"I think they're airboats? Does that sound right? Hey, do you promise? About traveling here someday?"

"I'd go anywhere with you. You name it, anywhere you want."

"Macchu Piccu."

"Done! That's on my list too. And Patagonia."

"Yes Patagonia too."

When she got back to bed that night, Nan was awake.

"Who are you talking to every night in the bathroom?"

"My friend Katie in Oregon. She's in grad school and she's having a tough time. The classes are really hard and she's also working plus she just broke up with her boyfriend."

"It doesn't sound like you're talking to a girlfriend. You can trust me, I won't tell anyone."

"I know that Nan. It's just, I don't know. I can't. I live with Olivia's brother."

Her phone buzzed. She opened a funny picture of him sitting in a hot tub with a pile of snow on his head. He looked sunburnt. She covered her mouth and tried to suppress a laugh.

"You're really smitten, aren't you?"

"Stop it. You're assuming things." She was talking while sending a picture of the funeral she saw the first morning.

"I noticed you said you live with him. You didn't say you're in love with Olivia's brother. Or I'm going out with Nick. He travels a lot for business, doesn't he?"

"Yes. Just about every week."

"So you're alone a lot. Plus you said you were thinking about breaking up with him this weekend. Are you in love with this guy you're talking to in the bathroom?"

Her phone buzzed. *"Do you have a picture of yourself?"*

"Hmm? What did you say?" She was scrolling through the photos in her phone and found one Nan took of her standing next to a guy in costume at one of the parades. They were in front of a float. His back was to the camera but he was looking back over his shoulder, with his hand on his hip. He was dressed in full black leather, head to toe, with holes cut out for his bare butt cheeks, assless chaps as they were commonly referred to. He had a mohawk and kohl eye makeup on.

"I'm just saying, when you're texting over there you look like someone who's in love. You can confide in me you know."

"I know. I sense that. But I have nothing to confide." She looked back down at her buzzing phone.

"Who's that? Your date for the evening?"

"Yes, he brought me to a cemetery late last night, and we sacrificed a chicken then smeared ourselves with it's blood and howled at the full moon."

"Okay be that way. I know you are talking to a guy and I'm pretty sure it's not Nick. I knew Nick in high school, we go way back you know?"

"Hey, you're still coming to Tipitinas with me tomorrow, right? Don't be mad, I have nothing to tell. Katie is my best friend since we were two years old. I just sent her that picture you took of me with that guy at the float."

"Oh my God, that was so funny. Yeah, we're going to Tipitinas. Zoe said she might join us. Well if the two A.M. boyfriend thinks that picture is funny maybe he won't mind your punk haircut."

"Will you stop it? I do not have a two A.M. boyfriend but if I did he would love me no matter what. Even if I completely shaved my head, he would love me."

"He sounds wonderful."

"He is." She winked at Nan who widened her eyes then put the pillow over her face, giggling and kicking her legs up and down.

Her phone buzzed. *"You are one crazy lady. You're scarin' me. Make sure you get me that juju. I think I am going to need it. But seriously, watch out for yourself. Tomorrow's going to be crazy. I need you to get back home safe and in one piece. I am planning to keep you up all night on Sunday."*

"I am planning to meet you at Logan in nothing but my rain coat."

"Promise? Ok you're driving me crazy. I'm taking a cold shower. Go to bed, I think you've been drinking some powerful voodoo potions."

"Good night. Check under the bed before you go to sleep tonight. There might be a vampire under there. Do you have any garlic? It scares them away."

"How do you know all these things? Are you a secret Twilight fan?"

"Every girl is."

Nan was shouting and giggling. "I knew it, I knew it. Do you have a picture? Please pretty please."

"All right. But do not breathe a word to anyone." She got up and climbed in Nan's bed while scrolling through the photos in her phone. She found one from that day at the beach on Plum Island. It was a particularly luscious one. He was wearing long boarder shorts and no shirt, jumping in the air reaching for a frisbee. You could clearly see his six-pack abs. His hair was blowing behind him and the photo really captured how blue his eyes were.

"Oh my."

"Yeah I know."

"Not a thing like Nick DeLuca."

"Not one tiny bit."

"Please tell me all about him." So as the other handmaidens planned the group wedding hairstyle down the hall, she lounged in bed and told Nan the story from the very first night on the train.

* * *

Fat Tuesday started out crazy but ended uneventfully. It started at ten in the morning in the Ritz Carlton spa with a cleansing massage for everyone. It was meant to get all the toxins out after three nights of drinking and fine dining. The massage was very nice but nothing like the ones she had been getting used to in the apartment above the garage in New-buryport. Plus it cost her one hundred twenty five dollars not including tip.

They headed to Bourbon Street around one in the after-noon. Olivia felt if they started too early, they'd never make it through the evening. They had all brought costumes to wear. She had a large white men's dress shirt that fit her like a very short dress. She paired this with sheer leggings that had one red leg and one black leg, a black beret and high heels. She added a black bow tie and ten of her beaded necklaces from the parade. She and Nan had discussed this outfit by email before they met. Nan had pretty much the same look, but with a long black tie and her stockings were all black.

Before they headed out to the mayhem on the streets, they set up a Mardi Gras shrine on the dressing table in their room. They placed a circle of beads around a votive candle made of what looked like sand crystals made into a picture of Jesus wearing a crown of thorns. Nan bought this at a voodoo shop yesterday. She scattered her juju charms around this. They put a bottle of vodka in the corner of the table and a small plastic bottle of orange juice on the other corner. An ashtray with a joint was placed strategically off center. They stood together on the bed in front of the mirror and took a picture of the shrine with their legs reflected back at them in the mirror, three black legs and one red. Nan was giggling nervously. "This is very weird. Are you sending this to Nick?"

"I don't think so."

"How about that two A.M. boyfriend of yours?"

"Shh! Remember no more talk about Mr. Two A.M." Nan made a motion like she was locking her lips.

Out on the streets of the French Quarter that afternoon, madness reigned. Men kissing men, dressed in drag. Guys wearing feathered headdresses that were two feet tall. It was amazing they could walk and balance them without falling. She snapped a picture of two men wearing naked fake boobs visibly tongue kissing. Everyone was drinking out on the streets and she had already had a couple of beers and a shot of tequila. She was wondering how Olivia ever picked this destination for her bachelorette party when her cell phone buzzed. It was Olivia, sending a text.

We are out of here, let's meet back at the Ritz' courtyard and come up with Plan B. This is so disgusting here. Maybe late dinner at the hotel?

She showed it to Nan who was talking to a group of fairly normal looking guys from Minnesota. Nan shook her head no. One of the Minnesotans seemed very interested in Nan and put his hand around her waist. He was pretty cute with a light blond brush cut that was beginning to grow out and brown eyes. She shut her cell phone off and whispered, "Let's pretend I forgot to charge it."

The guys invited them up to their hotel room for a drink. It was right on the main drag and they could watch the festivities from the wrought iron balcony. Before they went upstairs she spotted a guy in a business suit jacket, white shirt and tie. He had no pants on but he was wearing black socks and dress shoes. She stopped him and asked if she could take his picture. He posed with one knee bent, hand on hip with a big smile. She sent her first message to Nick since she arrived in the Big Easy.

I found your Halloween costume for this year's party. George Bailey goes to Mardi Gras.

Nan had texted Zoe, who wasn't ready to go back to the Ritz either and when she met up with them she had Amanda with her. They all went up to the hotel room with the boys from Minnesota where they made martinis. The guys had all the fixings including plastic martini glasses. One of the guys, whose name was Kyle, put on a pair of large orange clown pants and started filling water balloons. She sat at the table, sipping her vodka martini when she noticed a pair of plastic glasses with a large nose and mustache. She put these on as someone passed her a joint and she nonchalantly sipped her drink and took a toke of the joint. Nan snapped a picture with her camera. Everyone was very wasted and it all seemed sort of hazy and moving in slow motion.

One of the guys handed her something that looked like chocolate but when she took a bite it tasted like dirty grass. She spit it out and wiped her tongue with the sleeve of her shirt. "What's that?"

"Hash." She saw Nan take a piece too, chew it and swallow without even a grimace. Oh no. She asked Kyle for a glass of water. Someone had to keep her head and it looked like she was the most sober which wasn't saying much. He handed her a hotel glass wrapped in paper and told her to use the bathroom sink. "When you get back, meet me on the balcony."

Out on the balcony, Kyle was dropping water balloons onto the street where hundreds of people were passing. "Do you think this is a good idea?" she asked.

"I'm giving them a warning." He grabbed another balloon, lifted it high above his head and shouted, "Look out below" then dropped the balloon which splattered on the sidewalk and soaked some passersby. The common reaction was to look up and swear at him. "Fuck you asshole."

She looked back in the room and the blond with the brush cut was laying on one of the hotel beds unbuttoning Nan's shirt. Zoe was on a chair dancing and looked like she was about to start doing a strip tease. Amanda was sitting on the floor nodding off in the corner.

She decided it was time to be the Mom, not her usual role. She walked into the room and clapped her hands just like Olivia getting off the elevator the other day. "Ladies, if we're going to Tipitina's tonight, we need to sober up and get something to eat. Let's go find some red beans and rice."

It took awhile to get everyone up and out of there. As they stumbled to the elevator and rode down to the lobby, Nan hugged her. "Thank you. I am so.... so... where am I? Who was that boy?" Amanda leaned over and barfed in the elevator.

* * *

After eating a bowl of red beans and rice in a small diner, they went back to the Ritz Carlton to shower. Olivia was sipping an Irish coffee in the lobby and glared at her when they walked in, like she was the only who had been missing until midnight. "Where the hell have you girls been? I've been worried sick."

"I forgot to charge my cell phone. We're going to shower and go to Tipitina's. There's a great line up there tonight."

"That's way out of town. You are doing no such thing. It's already midnight."

"We can take a cab. I heard the music goes 'til 4 AM tonight."

She was holding onto Nan's arm and guiding her towards the elevators. Once in the room, Nan showered first. When it was her turn, she put the water on really hot and let it run over her head, through her long hair, for quite some time. She felt filthy. She remembered sitting on a curb at one point with broken beer bottles, cigarette butts and dirty water underneath her feet. Did Nan capture that on film too? She had been taking an awful lot of pictures.

When she got out of the shower, Nan was snoring. It looked like she wouldn't be seeing any decent live music this trip unless she went alone which was probably not a good idea. She was wearing a white hotel terrycloth bathrobe and had a towel wrapped around her head. She lay on the bed and turned the TV on. Roman Holiday, of all things, was playing on the classic movie channel.

Her cell phone buzzed. She thought "Wow Serendipity" and answered the call riveted to the scene when Audrey Hepburn goes to the barbershop. Did she have the nerve to do that? She would really like to piss off Olivia.

"Hey I was just thinking of you. I'm laying on my bed in a bathrobe and nothing else, watching Roman Holiday."

"Is that supposed to mean something? What's Roman Holiday?"

Oops! It was Nick. "No nothing. Just watching an old movie and tired after a kind of crazy day."

"What was that picture you sent me? I hope you're not planning on posting any pictures like that on Facebook. Which reminds me. What happened to your Facebook account? I tried to send you something the other day about some jobs in publishing here in Dallas and couldn't find you."

"Oh I closed it. I wasn't happy about the privacy issues they were having. You're calling awfully late, aren't you?"

He ignored her question. "Just as well. Stuff posted on Facebook can potentially hurt your career. You should get LinkedIn. Employers look for that, they want you to be well connected on there."

She sighed. "Yeah."

"I can't get you at the airport tomorrow. I have a five o'clock meeting. Can you take a cab?"

"Sure, no problem.'

"You have the address right?"

"Yes."

"I'll leave a key with my neighbor in 4B. She said she would be home. Just buzz her when you get there. Her name is Ashley Long."

"Sure thing."

"See you tomorrow."

"See ya." She dropped the phone on the bed. Awhile later it buzzed again. This time she checked caller ID. She picked it up and made the sound of blowing a kiss. "Hey there."

"I thought I'd be leaving a message. Why aren't you out dancing?"

"Because everyone is either passed out or puking."

"Which one are you?"

"I am watching Roman Holiday. They're riding the motor scooter through Rome right now."

"Aah, I wish I was there."

She looked over at Nan who seemed to be sleeping. She was too tired to go in the bathroom so she rolled over and whispered, "Where are you?"

"Still couch surfing in Vail but then Aspen until Friday. We're squeezing six guys in a hotel room for two nights then back to Denver. We're still meeting at Logan on Sunday, right?"

"Yes, if you're still willing to wait an hour for my flight."

"Of course I am. You'll be the girl in the raincoat right?"

"Yes."

"I'm looking forward to it."

"Hmmm." She sounded very sleepy and was almost nodding off.

"Hey I'll let you go. You sound really tired. I was just going to leave a goodnight message anyway. Go to sleep. I love you."

THANKSGIVING

Ray and Sophie were driving to Providence for Thanksgiving at Annie's house and meeting the boys there. Jesse had asked if he could bring Miranda.

They pulled up to a modest home in a suburban neighborhood not far from Narragansett Bay. Sophie's Mom and Dad were there already. Her Dad looked great and seemed to be in good spirits. Annie and her husband Jack had two daughters. Jill was twenty six and married. She was not joining them as she was at her in-laws for dinner this year. Ellie was a cute twenty one year old blonde and was home from college with her boyfriend Harry, who played lacrosse and seemed like a very nice guy. Also joining them was Evan, Sophie's older brother. He was fifty with a full head of brown tousled hair and was sporting a tan in November. Their youngest sister Kristen was here this year too. Grayson and Allie were in high school. Her husband Ted was a lawyer and they lived in Connecticut. Everyone was hugging and talking at once.

"Annie, when did you get another dog? You have two now?"

"Don't ask. Jack wanted Guster to have a friend to play with." Annie laughed.

"Oh my God. You almost have an empty nest and you saddle yourself with two dogs?"

"Dad you're looking great. How are you feeling?" Evan asked.

"So how's college Ellie?"

"How about you Allie? You're a senior now. Where are you applying to school?"

"Brown, Bates, maybe Pomona in California." Allie replied shyly.

"Wow. Good schools. You must have great grades." Ray sounded impressed.

Sophie looked over at her sister Annie. "I wonder where Sean and Jesse are. By the way, I forgot to tell you Annie, Jesse is bringing a friend. Miranda."

"No problem, there's plenty of food as you can see." Annie pointed to the food set out all over the kitchen. She was pulling a huge turkey out of the oven and letting it rest on top of the stove.

"Is this a new girlfriend?"

"Umm I don't think so. Sean said they had just met and he didn't think Jesse was serious. Just dating."

"Bringing a date to meet this crowd sounds pretty serious. Or brave." Annie laughed.

Ray walked in and rolled his eyes. "They just pulled in." She had told him about Miranda.

"It's okay Ray. Sean says she's nice and very talented."

"I'm sure. Did she do those tattoos herself?" Ray shook his head but he was smiling. "Well we all had growing pains, right? He's young."

"So is she."

"Yeah but the tattoos are permanent."

Annie looked over with a sly smile. "What is this about tattoos?" Before Annie could say anything else, Sean, Jesse and Miranda walked into the kitchen. Sean handed Annie a bouquet of daisies. "For the hostess." He gave Annie a hug. Jesse introduced Miranda to everyone while she smiled and shook hands. Miranda was wearing a short black skirt with tulle underneath, black fishnet stockings, little black boots and heavy dark eye makeup. Apropos of nothing else she had on, she had paired this outfit with a sleeveless blouse with ruffles down the front.

Sophie looked over at her Dad who was sitting next to Grayson and Allie and heard him say, "Does that blouse have only one sleeve?" Grayson laughed. "I think it's tattoos Grandpa."

Her mother chimed in. "She has tattoos. An armful. And something in her nose."

Kristen turned to Evan and said "Oh my." Evan was laughing one of his silent laughs where his mouth was closed and he didn't make a sound but his whole body rocked with laughter. Sophie was looking at Jesse who was beaming and had his arm around Miranda, whispering in her ear.

"Annie where's the wine? Ray do you want a beer?"

"Yes please."

Jesse said, "Me too Mom. And one for Miranda."

* * *

Everyone was now seated at a large dining room table passing platters of turkey, mashed potatoes, gravy and the rest of the Thanksgiving feast.

"Who wants to make the toast?"

"Evan can."

Evan stood up. "To health, happiness and good hair."

Sophie's Dad was booing. "Evan you can do better than that."

Raising their glasses they all shouted, "Here, here, Cheers."

"So Evan what are you doing now?"

"The sailing business is going really well. I just got back from the Bahamas. I sailed a couple around the islands for their honeymoon."

Jesse piped in, "That is so rad. Do you ever need a chef?"

"Sometimes. I'll call you next time I do."

"Miranda cooks too and she's an awesome photographer." Miranda looked down shyly while Jesse beamed at her.

Sophie interjected "Evan we have to get together and discuss the islands. Ray and I are still planning to run a bed and breakfast somewhere down there. Maybe you could help us with which islands are the best."

"Sure thing."

Sophie looked over at her parents. "Hey Dad, remember when you and Mom first retired. You took off in that converted van and traveled cross-country for a year? That must have been so much fun."

Her Mom had not really been paying attention to the conversations swirling around her but she looked up and said, "Oh I loved that. Something new every day."

Sophie sighed and lifted her wine glass. "Now that I can drink to. Something new every day."

* * *

Sophie had the passenger seat reclined as far back as it would go on the drive home. She kicked off her shoes. "That wasn't as bad as I thought it would be. Miranda isn't as bad as I thought either."

"She's actually okay. I was talking to her about sculpting. I think underneath all that bravado and attitude, she's a nice girl. It's just unfortunate about that tattooed sleeve." Ray laughed and shook his head. "Jesse is just taking a little longer to grow up than Sean. It's not like either of us were all grown up at twenty three. Remember?"

"Of course I do. Even though it seems so long ago. Who were those two kids? Sometimes I feel like I'm still trying to figure out how to grow up. You're right though."

"Of course I'm right." He turned and gave her an impish smile.

"You're not always right Ray. Although you think you are. But honestly, if you think about it, it's more of a puzzle where Sean came from." She laughed and pulled her seat back up. "I mean really, how did we make that kid? Mr. Startup, I'm going to own my own company by thirty. And he brings flowers for Annie. That's Sean, always so kind and polite, saying just the right thing. If he wasn't identical to his brother, I would swear the hospital gave us one of the wrong kid."

"He's more like me. Jesse is you."

"Oh really?" She raised her eyebrows, looking at him skeptically.

"Ya! I am Mr. Mellow putting up with all your moods and rantings and ravings. You're the one who's always stirring up trouble. You almost got thrown out of your book club in 2004, remember?"

"Well that's because they were all voting to re-elect George W. Bush."

"Sophie, Sophie. Always the troublemaker. Trying to change the world. How many times do I have to tell you, it doesn't work that way."

"What if Martin Luther King or Abraham Lincoln thought they couldn't change the world, huh?"

"Now you're Abe Lincoln?" He laughed then reached over and put his hand behind her neck. She leaned towards him and kissed him on the cheek.

DON'T MESS WITH TEXAS

She was waiting in Nick's apartment for him to arrive home. It was nine o'clock, the meeting had extended into dinner and drinks. He called her and told her to help herself to whatever was in the fridge. Slouched on the couch eating left over cheese pizza, she watched a movie until he came in at ten. He took his suit jacket off, loosened his tie and leaned over to kiss her on the cheek. "You look beat."

"But you are looking very dapper and professional as usual."

"Sorry, I didn't mean it that way. You just look really tired is all I was trying to say."

"Well, I am exhausted. It was a crazy five days. I don't understand how your ultra chic sister picked Mardi Gras for her party, it's really not her kind of place although the hotel and spa were beautiful." She sat up straighter and undid her ponytail, fixing it into a messy topknot. She smiled at him. "That was a pretty good pizza. How was your meeting?"

"Great. Things went well. The economy is doing really well here. Better than the rest of the country. You could definitely find a job here, no problem. If you just get your act together."

"What does that mean? Get my act together?" She shot him a look of pure disgust.

"Let's go to bed." He nodded towards the bedroom.

"Okay but I have bad news. I got my period on the plane."

"You're shitting me?"

"I know. Bummer."

"Are you going to have it the whole weekend?"

"Well it usually lasts four days."

"That only leaves Sunday and you're leaving at eight. We have to be out of here at six in the morning to make it to the airport."

"Well it's not like I planned this."

* * *

Last night he tried for some heavy petting and a blowjob but she pretended she had really bad cramps and felt awful. She thought he would force her down into his lap like he usually did but instead he just rolled over and went to sleep. She thought he could have at least spooned her, stroked her hair and whispered sweet nothings like 'I missed you so much.'

That would not have worked for him either though because she can't imagine having sex with him anymore. This felt completely different than the night she brought the Best Boy home. She couldn't imagine doing that, it would definitely feel like she was cheating on that sweet, sexy boy in Colorado. She absolutely cannot do that to him. Good thing she was fast on her feet and pretended she had her period. Today she would tell Nick everything. It was over, she just needed to tell him.

When he got up at six A.M. she joined him in the kitchen and had a cup of coffee. She told him her plans for the day while he was at work. First she was planning to visit the Sixth Floor Museum, which was the building where Oswald assassinated Kennedy. Then she wanted to take the cell phone tour of Dealey Square and see the grassy knoll. "Gee, that sounds like a fun day," Nick said very sarcastically.

"I think it will be fascinating." She laughed. "For a guy who doesn't like sarcasm, you're pretty good at it sometimes."

"Fascinating? Depressing is more like it. How's that for irony?"

"That's funny, that's what your sister said about visiting the Ninth Ward. And nothing you just said was ironic. Except for the fact that you thought it was."

"I don't understand a word you just said. What's the Ninth Ward?"

"Where Hurricane Katrina hit the hardest? Remember? The flooding was the worst there and it's still a mess."

"Now who in their right mind would want to visit that?"

"It's a part of our history. It's important to know this stuff. So history doesn't repeat itself. By the way, I've been meaning to ask you, seeing as I was in Oregon at the time, who did you vote for in 2008?"

"McCain."

Her mouth dropped open and she stared at him.

"Look I don't want to get into this with you. I have a seven thirty meeting. You'll meet me at my office at five, right? And please wear something nice. We're going to dinner with my boss. Do you need some money to buy something?"

"NO! I used part of your gift certificate at Lord & Taylor. I brought something with me."

"Good." He kissed her cheek. She felt like the wife on a 1950's sitcom she'd seen on Nick at Night. While she made the bed before she left to go sightseeing for the day, she imagined herself in a dress, high heels and pearls doing housework with a feather duster, whistling while she cleaned the house. She laughed out loud.

Later that afternoon she was getting ready for dinner with the boss. She brought a dress she thought was perfect for her temporary role as the great woman behind her successful man. It was a light blue sleeveless cotton dress with turquoise and rose flowers. The waistline was cinched above a short pleated A-line skirt and it had a scoop neckline. She had rose colored peep toe heals to match the flowers and was wearing a fake pearl necklace and earrings. She fixed her hair in a high ponytail and put on rose lipstick.

She thought if she were to marry Nick he would probably give her real pearls for her anniversary one year. It would go with the look he wanted her to cultivate. But tonight after dinner with the boss, she was planning to tell him she was not moving to Dallas. She was not sure if she would tell him she was falling in love with someone else. He didn't really need to know that. The relationship was falling apart before that night on the train.

Shortly before four thirty, he called and said to meet him at the restaurant because his afternoon meeting was running late. She called a cab. When she got to the restaurant, she got the last seat at the bar and ordered a Lemon Drop Martini, which sounded good on the drink menu, and very much in step with this retro theme she was play acting. She chatted with the bartender about the live music scene in Dallas. He told her she should get down to Austin. It sounded more like her kind of city. Thirty minutes later Nick came up behind her and kissed her cheek. "Sorry I'm late." He looked her over. "Interesting choice of dress." She thought 'is there any pleasing this guy?'

Nick's boss was in his mid-thirties and very friendly. His name was Ted and he had short brown hair slicked back off his face and green eyes. His wife joined them a short while later. She looked like a Swedish fashion model. Her name was Ana. She was wearing a tight fitting blue dress to match her eyes and had very short asymmetrically cut pale blond hair.

Ana was very cool and detached but Ted was funny and seemed to think she was very funny too. Probably because Ana said so little. The evening went as okay as an evening with the boss could go. She managed to get through it without embarrassing Nick, until the very end. Nick seemed relaxed most of the evening, as relaxed as he got especially in these work situations. But when she brought up how she worked for Obama when she was in Oregon, he gave her a slight nudge under the table and changed the subject.

But Ted had picked right up on her comment. "So don't you think Obama is not very friendly to the business community?"

"Why do you say that?"

"Well this whole Obamacare, what a mess."

"You do realize we are the only wealthy nation that doesn't insure our people, don't you?"

"Health care is not a right."

"Correct, it isn't a right. But it's the right thing to do. It's all a matter of what kind of country you want to live in. Who are we as a nation and what are our values?"

Ana smiled at her. "You should move to Sweden darling."

"Trust me I've thought about it."

Ana laughed a slow, brittle, twinkly kind of laugh. "You're very feisty. You seem to care about things very passionately. Most of us don't really pay attention to these things."

"Well that's what's wrong with this country. We stopped caring."

Nick sat up very straight. "Hey enough politics. How about those Mavericks?"

* * *

Nick was very silent on the drive back to his apartment. She decided to follow his lead and not say anything. A song came on the radio that she really liked and she turned the volume up. She started to sing along quietly. He reached over and turned it down, keeping his eyes on the road and never looking over at her. Normally, her first instinct would be to carry on with the song, singing louder. Instead she sang quietly, almost under her breath, looking out the window at the Dallas skyline.

He pulled into the parking garage of his very large, high-rise apartment building. They got out of the car in unison, closing their doors seconds apart, making a loud echoing sound in the cavernous, subterranean parking lot. Slam Bang, Slam Bang. They walked to the elevator, Nick a few steps ahead of her. As they waited for the elevator she turned and looked at him. "Why are you so pissed at me?"

"Can we wait until we're upstairs to talk about this?"

She shrugged and turned her head up to look at the arrow on the elevator slowly counting its way down to G3, the garage floor three levels below ground.

Once they got into his apartment, she kicked off her heels and headed to the bathroom. She brushed her teeth, washed off her makeup and shook out her hair. When she came out of the bathroom, he was sitting on the couch still dressed in his suit with just his tie slightly loosened. He had his laptop open next to him on the couch. He motioned to the chair across from the couch and said, "Come over here, I need to talk to you."

"Good because I need to talk to you too." She slowly walked over and sat across from him.

He cleared his throat and ran his hand across his cropped hair. He looked directly at her, very serious. "I don't know if you realize what is going on here. I am in line for some very big things with this company. I need you to be on board."

"What does that mean? Why are you accusing me of not being on board? I don't know what you're saying."

"Don't discuss your radical politics at a business dinner."

"Excuse me, but Ted asked me what I was doing in Oregon when I lived there. I simply told him I was waitressing, writing and volunteering for Obama." She shook her head and shrugged her shoulders.

"Yes and that led to a dissertation on Obamacare and your radical ideas on health care in America."

"Ted brought up health care and that was not a dissertation. Believe me, I know what a dissertation is. I read them all day at work. Obamacare is not radical. I was talking about volunteering for the man who is now president of the United States of America. What the hell is so radical about that? Please don't tell me you think he's a socialist Muslim or some nonsense like that.""

"Listen that's besides the point. It's just that you act like you're still in college or something. This is the real world now. You can't sit around and argue existential bullshit. You can't write screenplays or novels that will never sell. You have to make a living and pay the bills. This is real life god-dammit. I am trying to make a go of it here. Make some money and be a success. Stop living in a fantasy world."

She looked really hurt but he didn't notice. Write novels that will never sell? Did he just say that? "Can I speak now without being shouted at?"

"I want to show you something first."

He turned the laptop around and showed her Nan's Face-book page. Nan had posted pictures of her with the funny glasses, nose and mustache smoking a joint in the Min-nesotan's hotel room. There was also a picture of the shrine they made and another one of her with the guy in the assless chaps.

"That's not my Facebook page. I closed my account. I told you that."

"This is something that could ruin a career."

"They're not pictures of you. And they're not on my page."

"I'm just pointing this out to you."

"I was at your sister's bachelorette party, remember? Lis-ten I need to tell you something."

"Okay, I'm listening." He rubbed his scalp again.

"I'm sure you haven't noticed but I've been very unhappy for awhile now. Probably since a few months after I moved back. I hate my job, unlike yours it is not a career. Not any kind of career I want anyway. And you and I just don't seem to have that much in common anymore."

"Your job has a future and it's a good resume builder. It's time to grow up. I didn't realize you still smoked weed. How long has that been going on?"

She chose to ignore all that. "Like I was trying to say, you and I don't see things quite the same way. Your idea of the fu-ture isn't the same as mine. I think this relationship has run its course."

He loosened his tie a little more and pulled it off. He slumped back on the couch. "I agree."

She couldn't believe it was going to be this easy. How was her life suddenly turning into a fairy tale or some crazy romantic sitcom where everything goes right for the heroine? The domineering boyfriend conveniently got relocated to Texas just when Prince Charming arrived on the scene. Then completely out of character, Nick agreed to an amicable breakup. This never happened to her.

"We had a nice time Nick. We had a lot of fun. It's time now to just chase our own dreams, right?"

"Agreed."

* * *

Once they'd agreed to break up, they started getting along a lot better. She could sort of remember why she liked him in the first place. But she also realized that was exactly what it was, she had liked him. She didn't love him.

They decided it wasn't practical for her to fly home early. It would cost too much to change her flight. He was working on Friday and had to go into the office for a while on Saturday morning. She would continue to sightsee on her own, they would have dinner Saturday night and then he'd bring her to the airport Sunday morning. Once the pressure and expectations were removed, they started to get along. She insisted she be the one who slept on the couch. It was a pullout and he set up the bed for her. She continued texting her 2 A.M. boyfriend from her bed on the couch.

What is Dallas like?

Very big. Lots of skyscrapers and cowboy boots. I'm sorry I didn't get back to you last night.

It's ok.

My flight was late and we went out to dinner. I forgot to charge my phone and yes this is a shitty excuse and I too hate when people do this.

But it happens.

How's Aspen?

Great. Huge snow. Great bars.

Cute snow bunnies?
Huh?
Girls?
I've only got one girl on my mind. What about you? Find a cowboy yet?
Not my type.
Can I call you?
Sure. My friend is in the other room. I'm on the couch.

Every night she filled him in on her day. The cell phone walking tour she took of Dealey Square, her visit to the zoo. He told her more tales of his adventures on the moguls and back bowls of the Rocky Mountains. Friday was the last night she took the two A.M. phone call.

"Hey, tomorrow Mark and I are driving back to Denver and taking Ava to dinner. I probably won't call you. So we're meeting at Logan, right?"

"Right. I am arriving at Terminal C, American Flight 237, nine P.M."

"Okay I will see you at baggage claim."

"See you Sunday night."

* * *

She met Nick at his office at one on Saturday. He showed her around the very modern, sleek office he worked in with lots a chrome, steel and glass. But for all its sophistication, there were still areas with rows and rows of cubicles. However, Nick had already gotten a coveted window office. It was small but had a nice view of the city. They spent the afternoon walking around the West End Historic district. There were lots of shops and art galleries. She convinced him to have a late afternoon drink.

"Sure, why not?" He shrugged.

The cafe they chose was not that crowded at four thirty and there were plenty of seats at the bar. She pointed to two empty bar stools. "Can we sit there?"

"If you want to." he shrugged.

"So about Olivia's wedding."

"Yes, my sister's gala wedding. You're a bridesmaid."

"Yes indeed, I am." She rolled her eyes.

"Well you know, she's rented a house for the bridesmaids in East Hampton, so I assume you will be staying there. I'll be at my parents."

"Okay, that works. Are you gonna tell them we're no longer dating?"

"Probably not until that weekend. This is the kind of the thing that could put Olivia over the edge although it has nothing to do with her."

"You're right. Probably best not to say anything. Did you hear she has some girls on a diet and we all have to wear our hair the same way?"

"Jesus. Sorry about that."

"It's okay. I'll live through it."

"About the apartment."

"Oh right, I'm going to need a place to live."

"Well here's the thing. Because this move was so sudden and I have a lease through August the company agreed to pay the rent through the summer. So I wouldn't lose my deposit and I can go back if I need to. Keep my stuff there too until I find a place of my own here in Dallas. I'm thinking you could stay there until you find something. Through the summer if you need to, rent free. It's on the bank. Relocation expenses. I will need to come back in August sometime to pack up and settle things."

"Seriously? Thank you. That's very thoughtful." She looked at him like she'd just met him for the first time. "It's funny how much easier this is when we're not a couple, isn't it?"

"I was thinking the same thing."

She leaned over and kissed him. "I hope you have a happy life Nick and all your dreams come true."

"I hope you stop dreaming so much and start to find yourself. By the way, this is official right? We're no longer going out?"

"I will never stop dreaming. And yes, I would say it's official."

"So we can date other people right?"

She looked at him suspiciously. Did he know? "Yes of course."

"Because Ashley, the girl who gave you the key the first night you got here? I've been talking to her a lot lately. Seems like we're always on the elevator at the same time. I'm thinking I might ask her out."

Ah, of course! She remembered thinking when she got the key from Ashley that she looked very much like his type. Tall and blonde, she was very put together. When she answered the door, she had on a crisp white cotton blouse, perfectly ironed, paired with a thin, navy blue pencil skirt and matching blue heels.

"Sure, go for it. She seems like your type." She shook her head thinking 'am I dreaming?' then playfully punched him on the jaw.

* * *

Her flight arrived in Boston on time. She couldn't wear the raincoat onto the plane. All this heightened airport security required people to take their coats off and if that were all she was wearing it would be hard to explain. She had brought a lightweight polyester black raincoat, which could be easily rolled up and stuffed in her carryon bag.

When she got off the plane she ducked into the ladies room while she was still in the terminal. In one of the stalls, she completely undressed and put the raincoat on, stuffing her clothes and undies in her carryon bag. He was arriving at a different terminal an hour earlier than her and as she rode the escalator down to baggage claim she saw him leaning against a pole, his hands in the pockets of his ski jacket. He had a tan and the scruffy beard was back. His hair was still long but shorter than when she last saw him and it had clearly been styled. Much wavier at this length, some of his locks were even curling into ringlets especially on the top where they were shorter and had been layered. His bangs tumbled onto his forehead. He looked over, spotted her on the escalator and with a huge smile quickly walked towards her. As she hopped off the escalator, he lifted her up and gave her a big bear hug, then twirled her around, laughing. "You wore a raincoat."

"I told you I would be in a raincoat."

"I thought you were joking. I didn't think you had one with you."

"Of course I did. I've heard it's rainy in New Orleans during March." The coat had a cinch waist with a belt. There was just one button above it. He slipped his hand beneath the coat and his eyes widened. "How did you get on the plane like this?"

"I just changed upstairs after we landed."

"Let's get your bag and get out of here."

WHAT ELSE CAN POSSIBLY GO WRONG?

Sophie was in her kitchen looking out the window above the sink towards the back yard. Smiling, she watched as Ray chopped wood. On this frigidly cold night in January, he was wearing a grey hooded sweatshirt with a heavyweight blue flannel shirt over it.

The holidays had come and gone uneventfully. The boys drove up to New Hampshire for Christmas Eve and stayed for dinner the next day. Miranda didn't join them. She had gone home to Philadelphia to visit her family. Sean seemed to think the relationship was still going strong and Jesse mentioned her quite a bit over the holiday. He told them she was growing out her spiky, shaved haircut because he had asked her to. He said he liked long hair. "I think it must be love," he mused.

She saw Ray was about to say something and was sure he would ask if Jesse liked tattoos. She kicked him under the table and he looked at her, shrugging his shoulders with the 'What did I do?' look on his face.

The bedroom was actually ready and Jesse slept in there. Well almost ready, the closet was almost done. It was sheet rocked and had a pole but no shelves yet. The floor was also not done and the IKEA rug was still covering the subfloor. So really it hadn't changed that much.

Out the kitchen window, she watched as Ray tossed split logs to a growing pile of firewood in a wheelbarrow. When the wheelbarrow was full, he pushed it up the slight hill to the back door. He came in with a pile of wood in the crook of one arm and put it by the wood stove in the sitting room.

Walking into the kitchen, he opened the fridge to get a beer. Sophie was already having a glass of red wine. As Ray leaned into the fridge, she came up behind him, put her arms around his back and kissed his neck. Ray turned around with the beer in his hand. "What's up?" He leaned over and kissed Sophie's cheek.

"I was just watching you out there chopping wood, looking so happy doing one of your favorite things. You looked so sexy. You can forget everything when you're out there, can't you? Hey come upstairs with me, I want to play a song for you." Sophie took his hand and led him to the office they had at the top of the stairs. She was laughing and flirting while Ray seemed bemused. He was not quite sure what to make of this. When they got to the tiny office, Sophie pulled up YouTube on the computer and started to play a Dave Matthews Band song. "Remember this?"

"Of course. Remember when the boys were little and we'd get them to sleep in their cribs then go downstairs and make love to this song on the living room floor?"

She took his beer, put it on the desk then taking his hand she started to dance with him. He still looked perplexed but smiled and they started to dance in the small office. He placed his hand on her waist and pulled her closer. She threw her arms around his neck and sang softly into his ear. Ray took her arm from his neck, twirled her around and swung her under his arm then pulled her close again. When the song ended she chose a Dire Straits tune, turned the volume up and they began to dance again.

Ray laughed. "Remember the weekend we saw these guys in Hartford? Two back to back nights of shows? You came down with your friend Janie and met Miguel and me? The first night I forgot which parking garage I parked the car in and we walked around so long looking for it, you walked the heel right off your shoe."

"Yeah, we never found the car until the next day. We had to take a cab back to the hotel." Laughing, she gave him a big kiss then started to lead him towards the door and down the hall to their bedroom. They tumbled onto the bed and start undressing each other.

A little while later they were lying under the covers and Ray said, "Whoa. Where did that come from?"

"I don't know. You looked so cute and sexy out there at your wood pile." Ray rolled over and kissed her again.

* * *

Six A.M. Wednesday morning the alarm went off in Sophie and Ray's bedroom. Ray rolled over, shut it off and turned the light on in the very dark room.

"Please turn the light off Ray. I need a few more minutes." He got his bathrobe then shut the light off, leaving the room to go downstairs and make the morning coffee. His weekday routine.

Twenty minutes later Sophie had showered, made the bed and was coming downstairs. As she turned the corner into the living room, she saw the cellar door was open. In the kitchen the cupboard doors beneath the sink were also open. The floor had been mopped but was still wet. Ray was pouring a cup of coffee.

"What happened here?" Sophie sounded worried, knowing something had to be terribly wrong.

"I think the pipe to the leech field is clogged again. I ran the dishwasher before we went to bed last night and the drain was leaking. I'll have to rent that plumbing snake again that unclogs it."

"Shit. I knew something was wrong when I saw the cellar door open. Nothing good ever happens when the cellar door is open. What's going on down there?"

"The same thing that happened two years ago. The brown water is backing up into the basement. I'll take care of it."

"Oh Ray. This can't keep going on. It seems like every morning there's a catastrophe brewing and the bills keep piling up. You haven't had work since the week before Christmas. Six months ago when the cellar door was open, the oil burner had blown out. We're still paying for the new one, five thousand bucks later, thank you very much."

"I know, I know. But I can't discuss it now. I've gotta concentrate. How much money is in the checkbook? I'll have to rent that snake today. It's forty five dollars."

"I don't get paid until Friday and I just bought groceries. There is money in the overdraft but not much. A hundred bucks? But go ahead-use the debit card. But no more than forty five bucks, okay? Otherwise use the VISA. Oh God, that balance is so out of control. I just bought a few new clothes, guess that was a mistake." She held back tears and ran her hand through her hair. "Whatever. It doesn't matter. We have to fix this thing." She walked over to Ray and kissed him on the cheek. "Well I've gotta go, I'm going to be late. Thanks honey. I know the brunt of these catastrophes fall on your shoulders. I love you."

"Love you too."

Later that afternoon Sophie was working in her cubicle. She had an excel spreadsheet up on one screen and email on the other. She was just sitting staring at the computer when her cell phone rang. "Hey Ray. How's it going?" She listened, nodding her head with a concerned look on her face. "Oh my God, are you okay?" She nodded while she listened. "Can you drive it?" She paused, longer this time. "Well at least you're not hurt. That's what really matters. I'll see you when I get home. Be careful driving."

Sophie hung up the phone and went into Tina's office. "Hey Tina, Ray just called me and said he got in an accident. Some girl was coming out of the parking lot while he was on the road heading into Lowes. She slammed right into the side of his truck. She apparently didn't see him. She said the sun was in her eyes or something and she'd worked all night. She kept apologizing. Ray's okay but the truck is totaled. He was at Lowes because he needed some kind of pipe for the leech field, which he discovered is compromised or something like that. That snake thing I told you about this morning didn't work, the whole system is falling apart. He's trying to repair it and now this happens. It never ends."

"Oh Sophie, that's awful. But he's okay, right?"

"So he said. He saw her coming at him and gunned it to try and get ahead of her so she slammed into him just behind his door. He has the truck doors that open like this." She swung her arms open wide.

"Yeah, yeah. Right. I know what you mean."

"Well I guess he can't open them. He had to get out the passenger side."

"Thank God he's okay. That's all that really matters."

"You're right, I know. Anyway, I'll have those checks ready by the end of the day. I am working on the big request."

"Excellent. Thanks Sophie."

Later that night when Sophie pulled in the driveway, she saw Ray's truck in front of the barn. She got out of her car and walked over to the truck. It was already dark and hard to see but the light above the garage was on and she could tell the driver's side door was smashed in. Standing in the drive- way for a moment, she looked up at the night sky. Clouds were rolling in, but there were still lots of stars and she fo- cused on the brightest star in the constellation Orion.

"Star light, star bright, first star I see tonight. I wish I may, I wish I might have the wish I wish tonight... Please get me out of here, let me sell the house, let Ray and I start at the be- ginning and be happy again. And while we're at it, keep my boys safe and happy too." She turned around 180 degrees and blew a kiss at the Big Dipper. Then still looking up at the sky, she turned to the sliver of a moon and asked, "If you wish on an entire constellation is it a more powerful wish?"

She walked slowly towards the house. Ray was in the kitchen, making a vodka tonic with a splash of cranberry. So- phie walked over to him, wrapped her arms around him and rested her head on his chest. "How ya doin'?"

"I'm fine. The truck drives but I think insurance will say it's totaled. We have rental coverage so I can get something else until I find another truck. The appraiser is going to call me back. And guess what? The other driver has no insur- ance."

"Jesus. Just our luck. Live free or die in New Hampshire. What happened with the leech field?"

"Well I called around and it was gonna be at least five thousand dollars but I stopped by Jack's house down the end of the road and he offered to help. He drove his backhoe down the road and we dug a trench. Tomorrow we'll put a new tank in, run the pipe, fill the hole with stone and it'll be brand new. And guess how much he wants for doing the work? Two cases of beer and that old wood burning stove in the barn."

"You're kidding? That's awesome."

"So see, everything is working out. I get a new truck and we fix the leech field all for beer and a stove."

"Well that's one way to look at it. Another catastrophe averted."

Ray pointed to the sink. "No more putting anything down that sink. That garbage disposal shouldn't even be there."

"I don't put anything down there. Never have. Stuff gets by but not that much."

"Yeah well whatever. I'll get a better drain trap. I've got to shower." Ray gave her a kiss and headed upstairs with his drink while Sophie stayed behind in the kitchen. The cabinet doors were still open under the sink and all sorts of cleaning supplies were on the kitchen floor. She wet a sponge, sprayed some all purpose cleaner in the cabinet and wiped it out. She tossed a few things in the trash then arranged the rest of the things neatly in the cabinet.

She walked over to the stereo in the living room and put on some Springsteen because she was in the mood for some of his middle class blues and sad workingman lyrics. She got the mop and while a bucket filled with soapy water, she poured herself a glass of wine. She sang along to the music while washing the floor. Stopping by the window she stared out towards the river and could barely make out the backhoe sitting in the yard. A steady rain was falling.

When she got upstairs an hour later, she brushed her teeth then walked into the addition. She wandered into one of the unfinished bathrooms and looked around. It really was almost done, but also seemed miles from finished. The floor needed to be tiled and the plumbing wasn't hooked up. But that meant calling the plumber back and with Ray out of work they couldn't afford it right now. It had started to rain outside and it sounded very loud in the unfinished room. It seemed to be turning to sleet. She walked to the claw foot tub and ran her hand along the rim, staring off into the dark night.

When she got into bed, Ray was already snoring loudly. She was restless, tossing and turning but finally drifted off, dreaming.

* * *

She was in a house with large French doors that led out to a beautiful swimming pool. The landscaping was exquisite with tall, mature plantings of various types of palm trees and flowering shrubs. Several recliners and chairs, all covered with blue and white cushions, were placed around the pool. A stereo was playing reggae music. Off to one side was an outdoor kitchen area with a large grill and a refrigerator. The wall was covered with colorful ceramic fish and there was a center island made of light blue granite, the color of the Caribbean sea. Four tall bar chairs were placed around the island. She sensed this was her home.

TILTING AT WINDMILLS

The night she flew in from Dallas and he met her at the airport, they decided to stay at her apartment. It was a lot closer than his and he was very eager to get her out of that raincoat. During the twenty minute drive to Cleveland Circle, she told him about Nick.

"Wait a minute. I thought I was your boyfriend." He definitely seemed upset.

"You are. I think. Are we officially going out?"

"Yes. I mean, what do you think's going on here? Like what's official? Do we have to put it on Facebook or something stupid like that?" He had an edge in his voice she'd never heard before. She started to get nervous.

"Well like I said, my relationship with Nick was on its last days when I met you."

"So why didn't you just tell me then?"

"Well that first night I didn't want to complicate things. And then it got harder to tell you after I had neglected to tell you in the first place."

"Huh?" He looked annoyed and slightly confused.

"I told you. I've only seen him twice since we met. He came home that weekend before my birthday, just after I met you. And now in Dallas, where I broke up with him and slept on the couch. After all, you and I have only known each other for a month. I couldn't break up with him over the phone. I owed him more than that, so I waited until I got to Dallas and could tell him in person." She looked over at him and he seemed troubled. She reached over, placed her hand on his cheek and spoke really softly. "Nothing happened between us, I was on the couch."

He sighed. "But you're still living in his apartment."

"He's in Dallas. He said he wouldn't be back until August to settle his affairs here. It's rent free and I can save money so I can quit my job. I'll just go to Vermont the weekend he's back."

He reached over and put his hand on her thigh, rubbing it. "Or you can stay at my place."

"You're not mad at me? Because you seem mad."

"No, I am not mad at you. It's kind of stupid being jealous of what came before, don't you think? I know you didn't just start dating when you met me. And you're right about breaking up over the phone. But let's say going forward, honesty is the best policy. It's all what lies ahead of us, right? Just promise me one thing, no secrets."

"I promise." She kissed him on the cheek. "I'm sorry. I should have just told you before I left."

They weren't in the apartment for more than two minutes before he was undoing the belt on her raincoat and slipping her out of it. They made it only as far as the Pottery Barn sofa before they were all tangled up, madly groping and kissing each other. Afterwards, she was lying in his arms with her legs still wrapped around him, stroking his hair.

"I love your haircut by the way." She rubbed his beard. "And this is back. So do you change your look on a weekly basis?"

He laughed. "No. I rarely change my look. I told you, shaving the beard was an accident. It was Ava who insisted I let her cut my hair. I hadn't cut it in six months. She said if I was dating you, I needed to up my game or you'd get sick of me and my slacker ways."

"I don't think I'll ever get sick of you and you're certainly not a slacker but I do like this haircut."

He leaned over and kissed her. She moaned softly. "Hmm." She ran her hands through his hair, holding it back from his face and she gave him a long, long kiss.

"How about you? Have you always had long hair?" he asked.

"Not always. Since high school though. And I just trim it myself because I'm petrified of hairdressers. Just the smell of a hair salon gives me a panic attack. My knees get wobbly when I walk by one. My mother tortured me when I was younger, making me get awful haircuts. I don't know what her thing was with short hair, but she was the hair Nazi. I cried more tears over hair on the salon floor, I can't even tell you. It was in middle school that things got really bad. It ruined me."

"Wow, sounds like you should talk to someone about that."

"Haha! But maybe you're right."

"Okay tell me your worst hair story. And by the way, when are you giving me something you've written?"

"I'm working on that. I'll have something for you soon." She paused, contemplating for a second. "Umm haircuts, let's see, so many bad stories. I don't really talk about this to many people. Well okay, there was the violin concert. I had to take violin lessons until eighth grade. It was so not cool. It was definite grounds for being labeled a geek."

"What are you talking about? Women fiddle players are super sexy."

"Not when they're in eighth grade. Anyway there was a big concert for the whole school and my mother decided I needed a haircut for this. I cried and fought with her for days. She finally won out but told me I could tell the hairdresser what I wanted. My hair was just past my shoulders. It had seemed like it had taken forever to get it to that length after the last bad haircut. I walked in the salon, got in the chair and told the hairdresser just one inch. As I looked in the mirror, I saw my mother signal with her hand right below her ear."

"Oh shit. I can see where this is going."

"No shit. Did my mother honestly think I didn't see that? It was a floor to ceiling mirror for Christ's sake and I was looking right at her. I shouted really loud, one inch. The hairdresser said, 'It's okay honey. Calm down.' Then she takes the scissors and cuts right below my ear. I just sat in the chair

204 / SHEILA BLANCHETTE

quietly crying the rest of the time. And to add insult to injury she cut my bangs one inch long." He hugged her, squeezing her tight.

"I cried all night, wracking sobs and Jennie stayed right with me, her little motor purring all night right next to my fully exposed neck. This was two weeks before she disappeared." She let out a little sob and then hiccupped.

"Shh. Shh." He was stroking her hair and still hugging her. "This really upsets you, huh? It's okay. What happened with the violin concert?"

"I said I wasn't going. We had a big fight and of course I had to go. I was up on stage feeling like everyone was staring at me and my ugly haircut and those ridiculous bangs. I hated the way you had to hold the violin with your chin too. I thought it made me look like my fat violin teacher with the double chin. So there I was, up on the stage for all the world to see with an ugly haircut and a fat chin. All the other girls had long hair in ponytails. Eighth grade! Imagine. You're so insecure and vulnerable then. So even though I eventually forgave my mother and that was the last bad haircut, I am scarred for life."

"Wow. That's rough. Although I'd love to see a picture because I'm pretty sure you probably looked really cute."

She shook her head no and started to tell him about the wedding diet and poor Nan having to lose twenty pounds. She also told him about the same up do they were all supposed to have and the promise she made to Nan.

"So she better lose the weight because I have made a promise I can't keep."

"You know, they say you should do something that really scares you every once in awhile. Like go skydiving or something like that. Cut your hair if that's what you're scared of. Hair grows back ya know?"

"First of all I don't listen to Them. And second, what is that going to do for you, scaring the shit out of your self? That's just crazy horse shit." She tried to smile while wiping her face with the back of her hand. He furrowed his brow, looking worried. Placing his hands on her cheeks, he wiped her tears then kissed her. "Can I say something here?"

"Of course."

"Don't cut your hair if you don't really want to. You shouldn't do it because of some rash, lofty idea that you're going to teach someone a lesson, that someone being this Olivia person. Because I doubt she's going to get it. The lesson you think you'll be teaching her, that is. She won't get it, she's too self-absorbed. She doesn't sound like someone worth sticking your neck out for." He laughed. "Would that be considered a double entendre? Stick your neck out. Get it? You cut your hair short, your neck, you know?" He laughed again, trying to get her to smile.

Instead she looked at him with a puzzled expression. "I'm just trying to prove a point. And it's not fair to Nan. She told me she's been making herself puke trying to lose weight. Don't you think that's awful? She's going to end up bulimic or something."

He reached over and stroked her cheek. "Well, honey, that's her problem not yours. She could go to the gym or eat less. Why are you responsible for her? Hey, it's up to you. If you want to cut your hair, I am absolutely sure you will look awesome. I'm just trying to say, do it because you want to do it, not because you think you're going to change the mind of a self centered rich girl who won't get it."

"I don't want her to have her way. For everyone to just do what she says. She's a domineering control freak." She paused for a minute looking confused. "Did you know Jim Morrison once said some of the worst mistakes of his life were haircuts?"

He raised his eyebrows and lifted his hand up. "See what I'm saying? I think you need to put some more thought into why you would be doing this. Not that you shouldn't but you know... If you want my two cents, which I'm sure you don't, I think you'd look great. It would suit your very sassy personality. Hey, how about a back rub? You need to relax, you're getting yourself all worked up over here." He rolled her over, lifted her hair up, twisted it over her head and started giving her a massage. It was way better than the Ritz.

* * *

The next morning he got up and made her French toast and bacon before driving her to work. He made a smiley face with sliced strawberries on one of the pieces of French toast.

"Nice. French toast on Monday morning. I usually just eat something at my desk. I love the strawberry face."

"Most of your strawberries were going bad. I had to chuck them."

"Guess I should have emptied the fridge before I left."

"Well I salvaged a few. And stale bread makes better French toast."

He drove her to work, which was a much nicer commute than taking the subway to the train. They played a game her parents taught her when she was a kid. You had to find a word that began with each letter in the alphabet, in order and the first person to get to Z won. He had been stuck on Q for quite some time because she saw the Quality Inn first.

"This is harder for the driver you know. I have to keep my eyes on the road."

"Pizza. I win!"

"Pizza does not start with Z."

"Oh I forgot to tell you. X and Z are exceptions. They can be anywhere in the word, not just the beginning. I just got lucky with that Nissan Xterra."

"You're making stuff up. This game is rigged. Why isn't Q an exception too? I saw that LaQuinta Inn and you wouldn't give it to me."

"Sore loser." She laughed as they pulled up to her office and she stayed in the car awhile, kissing him.

"Hey you better go. You're gonna be late." He kissed her again.

"Ok. Thanks for the ride."

She walked up the stairs to the building she worked in and as she opened the door, she saw him waving to her. She blew him a kiss.

* * *

Walking through the rows of cubicles to her desk it seemed eerily quiet for a room full of people. Everyone was busy at their desks, eyes glued to their computer screens. The only sound was the keyboards clicking and clacking like a symphony of new age office musak lulling everyone into submission.

After settling at her desk, she opened her email and saw a message from Melody, another young girl in her department. They weren't friends outside the office but they did talk quite often. Melody had also wanted to be a writer when she graduated from college so they commiserated about their boring job and their frustration with where they were in life. She felt bad for Melody because her school loan was eight hundred dollars a month. Eight hundred dollars! And she didn't even go to Harvard. It would have to be a school like Harvard to justify that kind of loan, she thought. Didn't her parents sit her down and have the come to Jesus meeting as her Dad called it? Poor Melody, trapped for at least twenty years paying off that thing.

Coffee in the cafe? I have to tell you something that happened while you were on vacation.

OK, how about ten fifteen?

Sounds good.

At the designated time, she got up and walked over to Melody's cubicle. They went downstairs, helped themselves to the free coffee and took a seat in the far back corner of the cafeteria.

"So Melody, what's up? What happened while I was gone? It feels weird in here today, some strange kind of tension."

Melody whispered very softly, like they worked at the CIA and she was revealing top secret information. "You know Joan, the woman two cubes over from you?"

"Yeah she's really nice. She always shows me pictures of her grandkids."

"She's gone."

"What do you mean she's gone? She's been here for fifteen years."

"Sixteen. Our new boss, Lou, he decided she wasn't working fast enough and meeting quota. He gave her an evaluation three months ago and she didn't meet his goals so on Wednesday he set a meeting with her at five ten after everyone left and he fired her."

"What? How can he do that?"

"He just can. It's called an employee at will. She called Mandy at home later that night and told her all about it. She went in his office and one of the girls from HR was in there. Never a good sign. He had a list of his complaints against her, a review of her work so to speak. They went over COBRA and unemployment which apparently she will be able to collect."

"Oh, gee, that's nice of them. She's been here sixteen years. Suddenly she's too slow?" She looked incredulous.

"Then they walked her to her desk, had her take her personal belongings like the pictures of the grandkids, took her door pass away from her and escorted her out of the building."

"Oh. My. God. Done?" She waved her hand like her boyfriend's blackjack move. "Just like that?"

"Do not tell anyone I told you. Lou may call you in and tell you himself or maybe not. He told us she left due to personal reasons. But everyone knows the real story. I mean she's got friends, she's been here sixteen years. Did he think she wouldn't talk? Needless to say, morale is really low right now and everyone's scared. No one knows if someone else is next and who it will be. So we better get back to our desks, our fifteen minute break is almost up."

When she got back in her cubicle she wasn't scared, she was pissed. She googled employee at will and discovered that it was a part of American law that stated either party could break the relationship "for good cause, or bad cause, or no cause at all." As long as the company had not recognized a collective bargaining group or union.

She thought to herself, "Wow. No cause at all." She became concerned about sixty year old Joan. Where would she find a job now? And what would she do for health insurance? She was sixty, she would definitely need it. She thought she'd heard COBRA was expensive. She knew from hearing her parents' talk that Medicare wouldn't cover them until they were sixty seven or something like that. How can a sixty year old woman who just got fired find a job in this economy? She wished it had been her instead of Joan. At least she was young and could bounce back.

* * *

The following weekend, she was walking with her boyfriend across the Public Garden and then through the Boston Common. It was late March and an unseasonably early spring breeze was in the air. They were joking about global warming and the people who didn't believe it could be happening. She told him about Joan getting fired and asked him a bunch of questions about the IBEW. "Maybe I should start a union at work."

"Ah honey, that's not gonna work. Unions are a dying breed. A lot of big construction jobs won't even hire union workers anymore. You'll just get fired. Companies like yours don't have unions and most people won't be interested in fighting along with you."

"Baaa! They're all sheep. Just wait until they sit on the same side of the desk Joan did, your boss and someone from HR on the other side. No one on your side defending your rights. Anyone who thinks HR is on the side of the employee is crazy. Yeah they'll get you an ergonomic chair if you need one but they won't go to bat for you when you're getting fired for no cause at all."

"I know. You don't have to tell me. People fought for unions for years, coal miners and railroad workers. But ever since Reagan busted the air traffic controllers in the eighties, it's been down hill ever since. Unions are seen as the bad guys. You should hear my Uncle Dave on this subject. He's a union steward and it pisses him off."

"I should have gotten fired. I'm not that good at my job and she probably needs her job more than me."

He laughed softly. "Ha. You've only been there over a year. You're probably making less money than her for the same work, cheaper to keep you on. It's all about profits and the bottom line. What you need to do is get out of this job and just start writing." He stopped and turned to her, putting his hand on her cheek and kissing her. "You're not paying rent right now."

"No but I have a school loan." She sighed. "I didn't even get a raise at my annual review. Raise freeze they said although the company's growing and increasing profit. Someone's getting a raise! I just don't know. I'll stay until the lease is up. I'm really saving money now without the rent."

"You can pay your loan waitressing part time, can't you?" They were coming out of the Common onto Tremont Street near the Park Street T-station. He pointed down the street. "Hey have you ever been in this graveyard up here near the Park Street church?"

"No. Isn't Sam Adams or someone like that buried there?"

"Yeah, he is and John Hancock too. But guess who else? I'll give you one hint, the person has nothing to do with the Revolutionary War. She was a writer."

"Ok let me think." She stopped on the sidewalk outside the gate to the cemetery and tapped her chin with her pointer finger. "It can't be our friend Emily Dickinson because she's gotta be in Amherst."

"No, it's not Emily."

"Louisa May Alcott?"

"Who's she?"

"Little Women? My sisters and I loved that book. You know, the four sisters?"

"I didn't read that one."

She laughed. "I'll let that go, it's okay... I'm not gonna get this. Who is it?"

"Mother Goose."

"No way. Get outta here. She's not real."

"Oh yes she is. She was married to Mr. Goose and took care of his ten kids then had ten kids of her own."

"Are you pulling my leg? Seriously?"

He opened the gate. "Come on in. I'll show you."

As they walked around and looked at the gravestones, she shook her head. "What do you think some of these guys would think about America today?" She scoffed.

"Face it, this country's a mess. But it's like your crazy thing with this Olivia chick. You can't really change people's minds. Most people have their minds made up. Focus on what you can achieve, like leaving your job and writing. That's something you can control."

"Humbug. Do you think Sam Adams and Thomas Jefferson thought that?"

"I think you're a starry eyed romantic with unrealistic ideas about other people but that's one of the things I love about you. You're idealism and conviction. That and a million other things." He stepped in front of her, wrapped his arms around her waist and leaned over to kiss her.

* * *

The rest of March and April flew by in a happy haze. They spent weekends together either in Boston or Newburyport. He did most of the cooking at both places although he was teaching her some recipes. "I can't believe you don't even know how to make scrambled eggs. What do you eat when I'm not around?"

"Cereal, cheese and crackers, salad. I told you my mother never let us cook. It was all about keeping the kitchen clean, not actually cooking in the kitchen. My mother was a decorator building her nest. She didn't like to cook. Besides you're so good at cooking." She wrapped her arms around his waist and hugged him.

"Oh okay, butter me up and get out of doing the cooking. In that case you're on permanent KP duty. You must know how to keep the kitchen clean, right?"

They did lots of things with his friends and sometimes hers, like going to concerts and small music clubs. They would stay at her place the nights they were in the city although he was still uncomfortable with the fact that she had lived there with Nick and some of his things were still around. He seemed to prefer Newburyport on weekends and she didn't mind. Once she called in sick to take a three day weekend at his friend's place in Waterville Valley for some spring skiing. Although she didn't beat him down the mountain at Cannon they were pretty evenly matched on the slopes. Other weekends they took long hikes around the area, cross country skied at a beautiful state park on the Merrimack River not far from his house or visited small towns across the border in New Hampshire and Maine. Sometimes they were just happy staying home, eating the delicious meals he cooked for her and watching movies. She soon found out he really preferred movies like The Godfather, Good Fellas and Pulp Fiction. But if she really wanted to watch a chick flick or classic film, he was easy going enough to oblige and most of the time he stayed awake until the end. For her part, she did keep the kitchen clean and she was also back to writing the story based on her time in Portland, now set in Burlington. He was very good with constructive criticism and positive reinforcement.

One Wednesday in late April he was working near her office and called to meet her for lunch. They had a picnic in a park. She was fighting a cold and her head was all stuffed up. She sounded awful. "You should tell your boss you need to go home. Take the afternoon off and go to bed."

"I only have two sick days right now which I want to use for long weekends this summer. Besides, I'm already here."

He called her later that night around seven. She was very groggy and feverish and couldn't remember what she said to him. At eight fifteen, she heard her doorbell ringing but thought she was dreaming. It buzzed three more times before she got up. Dragging herself to the intercom by the front door, she pressed the button and rasped "Ya?" She barely got the word out before she started coughing and hacking.

"It's me. Let me in, it's pouring out here."

"Who?"

"The doctor. Come on, are you okay? Buzz me in." When he got upstairs his hair was dripping wet from the rain and he was soaked. He was carrying a few grocery bags. She was standing in the living room in an old college T-shirt and undies, shivering.

"Okay, come on." He put the bags down on the coffee table and got her to her room where he found a bathrobe and some cotton p-j pants, which he helped her into and then put her back into bed. "What are you taking for this?"

"I took the last cold pill early this morning before I went to work. I was going to get more stuff on my way home but felt awful and it had started to rain. I barely made it here." She closed her eyes.

"Okay I've got a bag full of stuff." He left the room for a minute and came back with cough medicine, a glass of water and gave her two pills. He put his hand on her forehead. "You're really hot. Do you have a thermometer?"

"No."

"Damn! I knew I should have got one. Well, let's see if this stuff works."

She didn't remember falling right back to sleep. Around midnight she woke up feeling slightly better but very weak and thirsty. She could hear the TV out in the living room. As she walked past the sofa, she saw him dozing in front of the Celtics game, which was in double overtime. He stirred and opened his eyes. "Hey you're up. I just checked on you a half hour ago and you were sound asleep. How are you feeling?"

She started coughing. "A little better. I was just thirsty."

"You don't sound better. Do you want some ginger ale or something? Sit down, I'll get you some."

"I'm kind of hungry too."

He made her chicken noodle soup with saltines he had also brought with him in his grocery bags. "This is what my mom always made me when I was sick." Then he put her back to bed and climbed in next to her. "Now you're gonna get sick too." She whispered weakly.

"I'll be okay." He kissed her forehead. "You're a lot cooler, I think your fever broke."

The next morning he insisted she take a sick day. He had to leave for work but checked on her throughout the day and came back later that evening. He never did catch her cold.

By May their relationship had become very comfortable, but not comfortable in a boring way at all. Not in the least. She still got excited every time he picked her up at the train station in Newburyport or pulled up to her apartment in Boston. The sex was still amazing and they still had a hat trick at least once a week. They had yet to have an argument that escalated into a fight, which was a little scary to think about. How could that possibly be?

It was now May and Katie was moving in with her. Nick thought it was a good idea when she asked him if it was okay. Katie had finished graduate school in early May and had a summer internship at the state house in Boston. Meanwhile she would be looking for a permanent job in healthcare public policy work, which would most likely bring her to D.C. Nick's lease would be up by then so maybe they could both move to DC?

"You aren't going to leave your new boyfriend are you? He sounds so nice," Katie smiled.

"But he's moving to L.A. in September." She looked really sad.

"I'm guessing he's going to ask you to come with him. If he does, will you go?"

"I don't know. I'm just coming off a bad domestic partnership. Maybe I'm only good at beginnings. The day to day routine doesn't seem to work for me."

"I don't think that's true. Nick just wasn't the one. This guy could definitely be the one. You won't know until you try. When do I get to meet him?" They were boxing up some of Nick's clothes that he had left behind and getting ready to ship it to Dallas. Katie was taking Nick's room because she had settled in the guest room.

"He's picking me up at the bus station after the wedding Memorial Day weekend. Are you here that weekend?"

"I'll make sure I'm back on Monday. I'm dying to meet him. Hey, what are you going to do with your furniture in September?"

"Well my sister Monica is getting married in late June so she's going to take my parents stuff."

"Oh that's right, the summer weddings. I forgot there were two."

"I didn't, although my sister's isn't costing me nearly as much. I was back in New York for that bridal shower last weekend. Another bus ticket, a gift for the bride and I had to pitch in for favors and food. This wedding is costing me a shit load of money I don't have."

"Memorial Day is in two weeks right? How is that gonna go?"

"I don't know. I've been talking to Nan. She's actually gained five pounds. And I told you about that promise."

"Well you don't have to do it."

"I don't want Nan to be the only outcast bridesmaid. Olivia will probably have her standing behind everyone just to hide her. It's the principal of the thing. She can't just be a total bossy bitch just because she's getting married. I mean we're all spending a ton of money to be in her stupid wedding and she's telling us to lose weight and how to wear our hair? Honestly? Besides, Nan is nice. She doesn't deserve this. This is not what weddings are supposed to be about, right?"

"Yeah, you're right but you'd really be going the extra distance to prove your point. It would be very quixotic of you. Hey, if you decide to do it, I'm here for you. I'll come with you."

"Thanks. I'll keep you posted." She twisted her hair into a messy topknot and looked at herself in the mirror over the Pottery Barn sofa.

ICE STORM

It was 7:15 in the morning and Sophie was running late. Ray called to her from upstairs in the office. "Hey Sophie. I'm trying to print this bill and I can't get the printer to work."

"Oh God." She stomped upstairs thinking when would he ever learn basic computer skills. No matter how many times she showed him how to save a document or send an email, he always forgot. When she got upstairs, he was sitting at the desk with his reading glasses on. She had to smile because he looked cute in those glasses. "Okay get up and let me do this. It's faster and I'm late."

"You don't have to get all pissed," he complained. She tried to print but nothing happened. She stood up, looked behind the printer to make sure everything was connected then looked at the wall outlet and saw the printer was unplugged. She held up the electrical plug, waved it at Ray and plugged it in. The printer began to make noises and then spit out a printed bill. "See, that wasn't that hard," Ray laughed.

"Apparently it was for you," Sophie replied, sounding really irritated.

"Hey I'd like to see you sheet rock a room."

Sophie sighed. "Oh Ray. I'm sorry. I'm just so unhappy."

"No shit. Why don't you just quit your job?"

"Oh and lose insurance and my paycheck. That will just create more problems. Which will lead to more unhappiness. I don't know who said money doesn't buy happiness but they were wrong."

"Find another job then."

"Easier said than done. I am having a mid-life crisis in case you haven't noticed. Seriously, you don't know the half of it." Sophie chuckled, then paused. She put her head down, covered her eyes and shook her head, then looked up again.

"Anyway, two nights ago I was reading a journal I kept when you and I broke up and I went cross country with Kathy. Here I was leaving because I was mad at you and then I'm writing in my journal, pining for you the whole trip. I was writing things like I love Ray so much, I miss Ray so much."

"Really?"

"I can't even remember feeling that way. How on earth did we get here? Arguing all the time. We've lost the love. I'm not that girl anymore. But maybe I am? She's inside me somewhere just screaming to get out. She keeps me up at night." She laughed.

"Sophie. I know you're unhappy. I hear about it every day."

"That's just it. You say it like you're aggravated. Why can't you hold me, give me a hug, tell me everything is okay? You used to do that. Bring me flowers, make me dinner once in awhile. Instead you ask me to fix the printer when you know I'm running late."

"Sorry, I didn't mean to put you out. I know all this. You hate your job, you hate this house. You tell me this every day. I'm doing the best I can. I'm trying to finish the addition."

"I know, I know. And the leech field crapped out. There's wood to chop, snow to plow."

"I'm as frustrated as you, believe me. I can't manage this house either. But if we run off and go somewhere and then don't like it, how do we come back? We won't be able to afford it."

"We can't afford it now. Maybe we'll succeed where we're going. Maybe we'll make enough money to come back here in the summer, rent a place on the Cape, go to the beach, golf! Did you ever think of that? Maybe I'm a lunatic but I have to try. I can't keep living like this, the two of us working every day and getting nowhere. Just once I want to order the lobster."

"You're right, you're right. And that was my line by the way, ordering the lobster. You stole it."

"Then show me. Get this house ready to sell, let me help you. I think you're scared Ray."

"I'm not scared. I hitchhiked to Colorado when I was seventeen. I lived in New Zealand for a year when I was twenty two."

"Yeah but we're not seventeen anymore. Are we still the people we were when we were seventeen? Remember when we first got married? You were going to fix up old houses and sell them? Two young kids in love with big plans. I'd like to think I am that same girl with the world ahead of her, ready to make all her dreams come true. But the future is shrinking. And I'm still living in the first house we bought! And it's not finished! We have to do it now." Sophie started to cry as she walked towards Ray and rested her head on his chest. He put his arms around her and hugged her. They stayed like that for a minute or two. Sophie laughed softly. "Now I'm really late. I've got to go."

"Careful. It's supposed to snow."

"What? How come I didn't hear about this? How much?"

"Six inches. Just take it slow. You should leave work early. It's supposed to be heaviest during rush hour."

She groaned. "Well I can't do that. I'm going to be late so I'll have to make up the time by staying late. And I have that month end deadline. It's always month end, quarter end, year end, over and over. If I don't get out of here, it'll be the end of my life. Accounting is like the slow march of death. The work just marks the passage of time from one month end to one quarter end to one year end. Every year the work's the same, it never changes. And your life marches on." She made a sobbing sound.

"Hang in there Sophie. Don't lose it on me. Okay? I love you. See you tonight. Drive slow." Ray hugged her tight and kissed her. "I love you too Ray," she said, still sobbing quietly.

As Sophie pulled out of the driveway at eight o'clock, light snowflakes were floating through the air.

* * *

Sophie was in her cubicle looking up at the clock on the wall. Four o'clock. She walked to Tina's office and looked out her window. Tina was gone for the day, having left early because of the approaching storm. The snow was coming down very heavy, thick large flakes that stuck to the pavement and the cars. There were several inches out there and the road had not been plowed.

She returned to her cubicle and checked the weather on her computer. She saw the time period four to seven p.m. outlined in red. WINTER STORM ADVISORY was across the screen in bold, red letters. She entered St. John, U.S. Virgin Islands. She saw it was eighty-two degrees and sunny.

Sophie and Dan were the only ones left but Dan took the train so he didn't have to worry about driving. She poked her head in his cubicle. "I'm leaving Dan. I don't give a shit if I didn't make my eight hours. It's getting really bad out there."

"You know I won't say anything."

"Thanks. You always cover for me. I owe you big time."

"No problem. Drive safe."

She took her laptop with her. It might be difficult getting in tomorrow morning so at least she could get something done from home and not lose more hours. When she got outside, it was dark and visibility was poor. The sidewalk to the upper parking lot hadn't been shoveled. Sophie walked slowly thru the deepening snow, the wind blowing hard crystal flakes that stung her face.

When she got to her car, she opened the door and put her things on the passenger seat. Leaning over towards the driver's side, she put the key in the ignition, started the car and pushed the defrost button. She started searching for the window scraper to clean the car. She slammed the front door, opened the back door, pushed the front seat forward and looked underneath. She slammed the back door shut. Walking around to the other side of the car, she did the same thing, crawling in over the back seat, hunting around, picking up things that were back there like a beach blanket and thinking 'Yeah I still need that!' She slammed that door shut.

As she walked around the front of the car she slid her hand across the windows, clearing some snow. It was still light and fluffy but not for long. The snow pelting her face was getting icier. Her hands were cold. She put them together, bringing them to her mouth and blowing on them to warm them. Back at the passenger side again, she opened the front door and grabbed some gloves she had on the floor. The radio was blasting from the car and the front window was slowly de-frosting. She pushed the button for rear defrost and closed the door. Rummaging around in the trunk, she found another beach blanket, an umbrella and finally the window scraper. When she finally got the car clean, she hopped inside, buck-led up and gripped the steering wheel, staring out at the swirling snow and muttering, "Eighty two degrees in St. John."

Pulling out of the parking lot, she drove very slowly down the unplowed streets. People were cleaning their cars and slipping along the sidewalks. The train came through town and she waited at the crossing. On the road past the farm, she saw they still had their "Christmas at the Farm" sign up. Bales of hay were wrapped in white plastic and stacked to look like snowmen with stick arms and top hats. Some houses on the road still had Christmas lights and those blow up Santa's and wise men that deflate on the lawn during the day. She wondered how they worked.

The wipers were on high but the snow was already piling up along the edges of the window and freezing on the wipers. The snow was getting wetter and heavier. Sophie made it to the highway where traffic was moving very slowly, bumper to bumper. The road was down to two lanes with the occa-sional SUV blowing by in the third lane. A few cars were off the road in the median, mostly rolled over SUV's and a tow truck's lights were flashing up ahead. Holding the steering wheel tightly with both hands, Sophie inched along.

* * *

When she finally pulled in to the driveway two hours later, she saw Ray working on the snow blower. He waved her into the garage. She got out of the car and walked over to him. "Is the snow blower broken?"

"I hope not. I think it's just a loose belt. I've got to get the driveway cleaned up. It's turning to ice and it'll be a mess by morning. I should've got this thing tuned up in the fall."

"Okay, right." She was aggravated but decided not to say anything else.

"Keep the fires going in there. We could lose power."

After Sophie entered the house, she went over to the wood stove in the sitting area and put a couple of logs on the fire. The wood box was now empty. She checked the stove in the living room and added more logs to that fire too, also emptying that wood box. She went back outside and checked the wheelbarrow by the door. There were an armful of logs in there so she brought them in the house. As she went back out again, she saw Ray had gotten the snow blower going and was plowing the driveway. As the snow shot out of the top of the blower, it stuck to the side of the barn. She watched him for a while, smiling. Then she took the wheelbarrow down to the woodpile out back. The light in the garage guided her part of the way but by the time she got to the woodpile she was in the dark.

She filled the wheelbarrow with wood, had a difficult time turning it around in the deep snow then finally pushed it up the slight hill back to the house. She got stuck a few times and really had to push to keep it going. She looked out towards the driveway again and saw Ray was also struggling with the snow blower, pushing it through the heavy snow. Sophie grabbed an armful of wood and went inside.

By 9:30 that night Sophie was watching the news in the living room. They were talking about a winter storm advisory for the rest of the evening. The weather girl was saying things like "downed limbs, widespread power outages." A little later, they were discussing another Republican debate. The candidates had been asked who didn't believe in global warming. Most of them had raised their hands!

Ray finally came in from plowing, knocking his boots by the door and getting out of his coat and snow pants. "Good job keeping the fires going. It's nice and warm in here." He stoked the wood stoves then got a plate out of the oven Sophie had put there earlier and a beer out of the fridge.

"God I hope I don't have work tomorrow." She poured herself a glass of wine from the bottle on the table.

"This could be a bad storm."

"I know. I'm watching the news. It looks bad." They were in bed by ten thirty, both exhausted.

* * *

Sophie was dreaming. She wasn't young in this dream, she was herself as she was right now. She was in the backyard in a blinding snowstorm. It was late afternoon and very quiet, the falling snow muffling all sound. Struggling with a wheelbarrow full of wood, she looked across the yard and barely made out a young man coming towards her. He waved. He was wearing a blue pea coat. He waved again as he came closer. It was the Actor.

"My car is stuck in the snow at the end of your property over there." He pointed towards the river. "Can I use your phone? I can't seem to get any reception on my cell phone."

"The power's out. You can come inside, my cell phone was working a half hour ago."

"Thanks. Can I help you with that?"

Sophie laughed. "Yes. Thanks."

The Actor took the wheelbarrow and pushed it up the hill to the back door. Both of them grabbed an armful of wood and he followed her inside. There was a stockpot on top of the wood stove in the sitting area. Some candles were lit throughout the room. Sophie took her coat off. "My husband went to Vermont to work this week. I did reach him a half hour ago by cell phone and it's a lot worse there but it's headed our way." She walked to the kitchen counter and picked up her phone. "Take your coat off and warm up by the stove. Do you think you need a tow truck?"

"Yeah." He smiled sheepishly at her. "I live in L.A. I don't drive in the snow much anymore. Just stupid, backing up into a snow bank and getting stuck like that."

"Well it's practically white out conditions. Even an old Yankee could get stuck in this weather."

She opened a kitchen cabinet by the phone and took out the yellow pages. She flipped through, looking for tow trucks.

"Something smells delicious, are you cooking on the wood stove?"

"Beef stew. When the power went out I figured I could cook something on the stove. Never tried it before. We could have some while we wait for the tow truck. It could be a while, I imagine it's a busy night for a tow truck driver." She found a number, tried to dial and waited. "Nothing. I don't have a connection. Maybe the cable lines are down too."

The Actor was sitting on the couch. He'd taken his coat off and was now pulling off his boots. He stuck out his arm to shake hands with Sophie. "My name is Ryan."

"I know who you are." She shook his hand. "Sophie."

"Oh. You know who I am?"

"What? Do you think I always let strange men in my house during blinding blizzards? I'm just wondering how you ended up in my backyard?"

"Long story. Could I have some of that stew? It smells great."

"Sure. I just opened a bottle of wine. Would you like some?"

The snow and ice were pelting against the window and the wind began to make a howling, whistling sound as it blew around the eaves of the house. There was a loud noise from outside, like a rifle shot. Sophie rolled over in her sleep, still dreaming.

In her dream it was dark now in the Ryan house. The sitting room was lit only by candlelight. The Actor and Sophie were sitting on the rug in front of the wood stove. The Actor leaned over, took a log from the wood box and put it on the stove. He left the doors open and reached for a screen that fit in the stove opening. The fire from the stove illuminated the room a little more. He leaned back towards Sophie, put his hand on her cheek and kissed her.

She pulled away and looked into his eyes. She seemed to be hesitating but then she put her hand on the back of his head, gently pulling him towards her and kissed him longingly. He laid her back down on the rug and began to undress her. He pulled off her shirt, unbuttoned his pants and slid out of them. He kissed her again and they began to make love on the rug in front of the fire. The storm was still howling outside and the sound of snapping tree limbs could be heard in the yard.

"I think I know who you really are," she said with an aching sound in her voice. "Where have you been? It's been so long. Once upon a time you told me you loved me and in return I loved you as if you were the boy I'd always dreamed of. I hitched my wagon to your star and I do not want to regret that. But that was once upon time, wasn't it? We were so young and carefree. That seems such a long, long time ago."

The sound of branches snapping was getting louder. A large thud reverberated through the bedroom and woke Sophie from her dream. The house was dark. The alarm clock was off, the power had gone out. Sophie was lying on her back listening to a plow go by and watching the blinking yellow lights travel across the room. She could hear the beep, beep of the backup lights as the plow reached the end of the road and turned around. The lights came back across the room. She continued to lie there, eyes open. A train in the distance was blowing its horn loudly. When it passed on the tracks just across the river, the house rumbled. A really loud snapping branch could be heard then a thud on the roof this time. Sophie shouted and Ray woke up. "Did you hear that?"

"Wow. It's the ice on the trees snapping the branches."

"Should we go downstairs? Something just hit the roof. What if it comes crashing thru?"

"That won't happen." Another loud snap was heard.

"Your new truck is in the driveway. I hope a tree doesn't fall on it."

"It won't. I moved it near the barn."

"How can you say that? My van was there when the tree landed on it during that lightening storm two years ago and totaled it."

"Yeah, so that tree is gone. And lightening doesn't strike twice."

"That's not true."

Ray rolled over towards Sophie, reached for her and pulled her close. He kissed her and Sophie put her arms around him. Ray pulled her nightgown over her head then took his T-shirt and boxers off. They kissed then began to make love. There was a loud crack and they heard several more branches fall. Ice pelted against the window.

AZURE HAIR SALON AND SPA

Nan called on Saturday before Memorial Day weekend to say she hadn't lost any weight and was still carrying two additional pounds in addition to the twenty she was supposed to lose. "It was just too stressful. It made me eat more thinking about it. Food has always been my crutch."

"It's okay. It's ridiculous she is making you feel this way."

"You don't have to do this. This is my own fault."

"Nothing is your fault. It's Olivia. I'll see you Thursday, late afternoon. I'm taking a bus to Manhattan then the train. Nick is picking me up and he'll bring me to the bridesmaids house. We're roommates again and we most likely have the Cinderella room in the attic or the basement."

Nan laughed. "Okay, I'll see you. Don't do anything crazy on my account."

She got the gift certificate out of the desk drawer where she threw it back on the last day of February. When she called the salon, they gave her a hard time at first. They were apparently a very busy place and styled the hair of several women on the local news channels. "Oh wait a minute. If you can make a six P.M. on Wednesday I can get you in with Andre. He had a cancellation. He is our best, most in demand stylist."

"Sounds good." Nothing but the best for me she thought as her heart skipped a beat. Katie had insisted on accompanying her. Drag her in to the salon by her hair would be more like it.

Andre seemed very nice and extremely sympathetic to her anxiety. He loved, loved, loved doing makeovers. He spoke with a heavy accent and told them he was from the Czech Republic. They would have a consult first to make sure she got exactly the cut she wanted. Her hands were shaking when she took out the photo she printed from the Internet. It was a beautiful model with a short pixie. It was definitely not as radical and edgy as some other photos she found. She decided she could not cut her hair and go extreme all in one day so choppy, spiky and short was edgy enough for her. She wished she were as beautiful as the model.

Andre explained he could achieve this look with a chisel. He showed it to her. It looked like a box cutter. It was the latest hair cutting tool from a stylist in Australia he informed her. He was going to cut the hair all over her head to two centimeters. "Oh my God, how many inches is that?"

"Roughly an inch, but with the chisel it's choppy and has a lot of texture. It's standard *peexie* length." She couldn't help giggling over his accent. It must have been nerves because what he said was more scary than funny. "Does it have to be that short?"

"To look like this, yes." He pointed to the picture she gave him and the way the model had it styled all spiky and mussed up. "Hers is definitely two centimeters."

"That doesn't look like less than an inch."

"The top is a little longer. Don't worry about it."

"Don't worry about it? Easy for you to say."

"I am going to be dropping the chisel at a forty five degree angle," he swung his arm with his elbow "working my way all around the head. It gives a soft, spiky, uneven look. You will look nice with this cut. It suits your face."

"Katie can you open the wine?"

"Sure and don't forget I have those Captain Morgan nips in my pocketbook." Katie reached in her bag and rummaged around for the rum.

"Oh right. Can I have one now?" She cleared her throat.

Katie handed her the nip bottle and she swigged it down in one gulp. Then Katie turned to Andre, "So is her hair going to really look like this? I know sometimes you bring a photo but your hair is a different texture and it just doesn't end up looking like you wanted it too." She was so glad Katie was here. Katie got her haircut every six weeks and had numerous styles over the years. For her it was like buying a new pair of shoes or a dress. Right now it was cut in a short bob. Nick would have liked it.

Andre was running his hands through her hair, lifting it up and letting the hair fall down her back. "Her hair is perfect for this. It should look just like *peeksure*."

She laughed again, "Am I going to be able to style this myself?"

"Definitely, it is, how you say, low maintain? I'll show you what to do."

"Okay, let's do this." They headed over to the chair. Her knees were wobbling and her heart was pounding. She thought she might faint. Andre snapped the black cape he was holding like he was a toreador at a bullfight and wrapped it around her neck. He lifted her long hair out of the cape. "Okay, first because you are donating locks to love, we're going to make a pony tail and cut off ten American inches which is requirement." He got some coated elastics out of a drawer, pulled her hair into a pony tail with one elastic at the top and two more further down to hold all the hair in place. He took out a ruler and measured the ponytail. "Little over ten inches. Perfect." He grabbed some very large scissors and made a clip, clip motion with them, smiling devilishly. "Are you ready?"

She squeaked out a yes and closed her eyes. She felt her stomach muscles contract and her knees bounced up. Katie got up and held her hand. Andre was sawing through her thick hair and it seemed to take forever. She felt loose pieces of hair fall towards her face, brushing her chin. When it was over, her head felt lighter. Her eyes were still shut and she was squeezing back tears. Katie placed another nip bottle in her hand. She unscrewed the top with her eyes closed then opened them. As she swigged the rum, her eyes popped when she saw a girl in the mirror with a choppy chin length bob. "Oh my God."

Andre handed her the ten inch ponytail and gave her a plastic bag to put it in. "Some little girl with cancer is going to get a very nice wig. You have beautiful hair." Her eyes welled up but she did a pretty good job of keeping back the tears. "You can change your mind and stick with the bob. I can just clean it up."

"No. I got this far. Let's do it." It reminded her too much of the violin concert haircut.

He brought her to the sink, washed her jagged bob and put a towel loosely over her head. When they got back to the chair, he vigorously rubbed her head with the towel then combed her hair. "This cut requires little to no combing just fluffing."

She gulped and sipped some wine while trying to think about something nice. Like sex in the bathtub the next time she was in Newburyport. But instead she started to think about how itchy her throat was and Katie was worried she might be getting a nervous rash so she got a wet towel and wiped the front of her neck for her while trying to calm her down. "Breathe. Just breathe."

For the rest of the haircut, Andre never used the scissors. He sectioned her hair then just kept slicing with the chisel, eyeballing the length to two centimeters (she had to get a guy who used the metric system!) working around her entire head. When he got to the top and front he asked her to bend forward a little. He kept parting her hair, chiseling then parting it again. The haircut took fourteen minutes. She wanted to reach to the hair in back and touch it but she was petrified.

When he was done, he slipped his fingers through her hair, checking her entire scalp to make sure the length was the same throughout. It appeared he did a good job because he didn't cut anymore. Thank God, she thought. He pulled little pieces in front of her ears and fussed with them. She saw a pile of hair in her lap and wondered how could there be so much there after she already lost ten inches? She shook the cape and knocked the hair to the floor so she didn't have to look at it anymore. Her hair was shorter than it had ever been even after those horrid haircuts her mother made her get. It was very messy right then and spiky.

She looked over at Katie and said, "What the hell did I just do? Spitefulness is a terrible thing. If I ever make myself the heroine of one of my novels I guess I will have to deal with this character flaw. Oh God, everyone told me this was rash and stupidly impulsive."

Katie was smiling at her. "You look really awesome. I love it." She was whimpering so Katie jumped up and hugged her. "I wish you knew how really pretty you look."

"I'm scared he's going to hate this. Talk about cut your hair to spite your face. And he told me that you know. He pretty much said what you did, it was a crazy, quixotic idea."

"Nick? Don't we want him to hate it?"

"It's Olivia I'm mad at. Not Nick, well yeah him too for wanting to change me into someone I'm not but I meant..." She sobbed and shook her head no.

"Oh, right. Don't worry, from what you've told me honey, he loves you very much. So! When do I get to meet this guy? I know you told me."

"Monday night after the wedding. He's picking me up at the bus station and we're coming back to the apartment." She pulled a two centimeter piece straight up on top of her head. "If he wants to come back with me. Look at this. I am having serious flashbacks but my mother never even made me get my hair cut this short."

"You still have money on that Lord & Taylor card right?"

"Yeah. Two hundred dollars."

"Okay we are getting you the sexiest backless dress in the store for the rehearsal dinner. You are going to look so hot and awesome. Stilettos too. Clothes for the whole weekend."

"I love you Katie. I could never have done this without you."

Andre got the blow dryer. "Just watch how easy this is, anyone can do this. If you choose to air dry it sometimes, just run your hands thru it every once in awhile." He turned the dryer on and started massaging her head with his other hand, working his fingers through her hair and sometimes squeezing the hair and rubbing with his fingertips like he was scratching her entire scalp. Then he took the palm of his hand and rubbed it all over her head like you would rub a cat's belly. The whole process felt really, really good. Then he started rubbing with his fingertips again and pulling her hair up. When he was done, he fussed with the short bangs, pulling a few short pieces down over her forehead. He got the pieces in front of each ear to lay exactly the way he wanted. There were slightly longer pieces in the back that were just below her ears. He curled these up with his fingers. Her hair was spiky but soft looking and the little curls in the back peeked out from behind her ears.

She left the salon, slightly tipsy and very light headed. It was styled exactly like the photo. She actually liked it. But she was sure she'd never get it to look like this again.

BETTER TO LIGHT A CANDLE
THAN CURSE THE DARKNESS

—Old Chinese Proverb

Sophie woke up in bed alone. Light was streaming in the window and she had no idea what time it was as the power was out. She breathed a huge sigh of relief that the storm was over. She could see her breath as she exhaled. She got out of bed, put on her bathrobe and slippers and walked downstairs. Ray was in the sitting room, sleeping on the sofa by the wood stove. "Hey Ray? How long have you been down here?"

"I don't know, the power's out. Probably four. I wanted to keep the stoves going. It's really cold out now and the pipes could freeze. I've got some bad news."

"Do I want to hear it? As you always say, do we have to start every day like this?"

"I went out to get more wood and checked the driveway. That loud noise we heard while making love? A tree landed on the cab of my truck."

"Oh my God, your new truck. How bad is it?'

"Just the back cab, looks like nothing else is damaged. Insurance will replace it."

Sophie started to cry. "Yeah but we have a deductible."

"I don't need a cab on the bed. I'll just get it removed. It's more a pain in the ass sometimes with the ladders."

She walked over to Ray, sat down next to him on the couch and put her head on his chest. He put his arms around her and stroked her hair. She muttered into his chest. "I can't take it anymore. Do you think somewhere on a sunny island in the Caribbean people wake up to sunshine and happiness every day?"

"Not when there's a hurricane."

Sophie laughed but it sounded like crying. "Okay so weather can't be controlled. But what if most days you had a job you actually enjoyed and your bills weren't more than you make. Most days were sunny and warm. Admit it, weather affects your mood."

"Well we know it affects your mood. But it has been a bad year, hasn't it?"

"It seems like just a year to you? We've been here twenty five years Ray. It's just been one thing after another. They said the house was haunted and I think they were right."

"Well let's just get through this storm. Then we'll see. I mean I agree. I need a change too. The boys are finally off on their own and I'm tired of this old house too."

"Well I called the weather hot line at work and electricity is out down there too, so they're closed for the day. That's good news."

"Snow day! All right. See things are looking up. We'll be okay."

Sophie put her arms around Ray and they sat like that for a moment. "It was good when we were first married wasn't it Ray? In the beginning?"

"It's still good Sophie. We're just in a rough patch."

She kissed him. "My eternal optimist."

Later that evening Ray and Sophie were sitting by the wood stove playing scrabble and eating sandwiches. "This is fun. Like time has stopped for a while. But I sure hope the power comes back tomorrow. I imagine this will get old quickly. Especially with the well and no water." She looked over to the sink where there was a pile of dirty dishes.

"So you're definitely going to Lynn's tonight?"

"Well I have work tomorrow, I checked and power is up there. Lynn has a generator and I need a shower. You should come. It'll be warmer."

"It's fine here. I have to keep the fires going, we can't have the pipes freezing."

Sophie left a little later for Lynn's house, driving through the dark streets of town where most of the power was still out. There were very few cars on the road and she used her high beams the entire way even while driving through the center of town, which had an eerie, deserted feeling about it. She imagined some kind of nuclear disaster had happened and she was the sole survivor looking for companionship.

* * *

The next day she did make it to work. Forty five minutes south of her house things weren't quite so bad and everything was pretty much back to normal. The day passed uneventfully. She did have an interesting conversation with Dan though. Somehow the subject of doing something other than accounting came up when Dan randomly said, "My friends and I are writing a screenplay."

"Dan, get out of here. I'm writing a screenplay. That is so weird."

"Yeah, really. Where are you at with it?"

"I'm half way through but I haven't had much time lately. I do have a beginning, a middle and end. Just have to find the time to get it down on paper. And you?"

"We're halfway through. One of my friends does most of the writing and we meet on Tuesday nights to read it out loud and critique it."

"That's a really good idea."

"We know a guy in L.A. we can show it to when it's ready."

"This is so strange. We sit in cubicles next to each other working in accounting and we're both writing screenplays. What does that tell you? I think it tells you cubicles lead to madness or creativity."

He laughed loudly, "Or both. Hey, if I get mine sold first, you can send me yours and I'll give it to this guy." They were still laughing when Tina returned from a meeting. They quickly went back to their desks and got to work.

* * *

She had been unable to reach Ray all day. His phone must have died and without electricity he wouldn't be able to charge it. She pulled into the driveway of her house and saw his truck with the crushed back cab. When she walked in the house Ray was loading the wood stove. She gave him a kiss on the cheek while noticing there was a stockpot on the wood stove. "Hmm. It smells good in here."

"I've got beef stew cooking on the wood stove. I figured I would use up the stuff in the fridge before it goes bad."

"Really? Wow." She laughed. "That's," she paused thinking of the dream she had the other night, "a good idea." She hugged Ray and gave him a long kiss.

"Power's still out. You going back to Lynn's? You should stay for dinner. I'll open a bottle of wine. Romantic candlelight dinner, you and me?"

"Okay. I'll just get a flashlight and go upstairs. Get a few things for tomorrow. I'll be right back." She grabbed a flashlight from the table and walked through the dark house then up the stairs, following the beam of the light. When she got to the bedroom she hunted around in the dark closet, pulled open some drawers and packed a few things in a suitcase. Back downstairs Ray had placed a few candles on a footstool in front of the fire. He had set out two bowls of stew and two glasses of wine and he was sitting on the rug. "It's warmer here by the stove."

"Very romantic." She sat next to Ray on the rug and smiled shyly at him. He was loading a small wooden handmade pipe. He lit it, took a toke and passed it to Sophie.

"Careful. Go easy." Sophie took a big hit, held it then started coughing. "I told you to go easy."

"I wasn't getting anything." She laughed while still coughing then took a sip of wine. They ate quietly for a while, both lost in their own thoughts.

"Do you remember the first present you ever gave me Ray?"

"Of course I do, it was a Christmas tree."

"Right. You pulled up to my apartment in the old VW bug you had with a Christmas tree tied to the roof. The tree looked bigger than the car."

"You always knew when I was coming. The muffler was so loud. Despite all the noise in the city you knew the sound of my car."

"I looked out the window and saw the tree and ran out to the sidewalk. It was starting to snow. We decorated it with a box of tinsel and plastic necklaces I had. We made a popcorn garland too. Did we have anything else?"

"I don't remember. Didn't we use a sparkly mitten for the star on top? I do remember you later got poison ivy. I cut the tree down myself in the woods near my house and there must have been poison ivy in the tree."

"Oh my God that's right. I forgot that part of the story. Was that an omen?" She laughed.

Ray laughed too. "Whatta ya mean?"

"I don't know. There was going to be good with the bad. For better or worse. Like the fairy tale, watch out for the troll under the bridge." Sophie smiled at Ray and touched his cheek.

Ray shrugged. "It hasn't been all bad."

"No it hasn't." She ran her hand through his hair and gazed into his eyes. "Then it was Valentine's Day remember? You came into my office with a dozen red roses. You got off the elevator and that crazy lady I worked with, Leslie I think her name was, said 'Look it's the Human Valentine'. You used to be so romantic Ray. Where is that guy? Where'd that girl go for that matter? I don't think she was so cranky and pessimistic way back when."

Ray shook his head. "They got married and bought a really old house that needed tons of work and lots of money. They never had money but they had energy, at first anyway. But then they had kids who became teenagers who needed to go to college and they had to work more and more just to make ends meet. They got older and now they not only don't have money, they don't have energy. But they do still take vacations, they have their health, they have their friends."

"God we used have so much fun. We met dancing in a bar Ray! Remember all the concerts we went to? The two month cross country trip? We hiked the Grand Canyon! You won money in Vegas! When the boys were young, we had the weekends on the Cape and the year you worked in Nantucket. We like to have fun. Whatever made us think we could settle down in a three hundred year old house that constantly needed work?"

"I admit the upkeep was more than I ever expected. It never ends, there's always something."

Sophie sighed. "I always said I was happiest in hotel rooms and other people's vacation homes." She laughed at herself. "I love those little bottles of shampoo and hand lotion. But I thought we could make this work, live a middle class life in a funky old house. Fix it up, have dinner parties with friends. And we do that. But the work never ends and there is never, ever enough money."

They sat quietly, looking at the fire. Ray threw a couple more logs in the stove. "I'm so sorry Ray. I think you handle all of this better than me. I know I'm cranky and bitchy most days. It's just I didn't imagine my life being like this, being such a struggle. Every year I think it's going to get better. I won't need to use the credit card this Christmas or I'll pay the real estate taxes on time or I'll have some extra money to save. But I can't ever get across the bridge, the troll gets me every time."

Ray wrapped his arm around her. "I still love you. You know that, don't you? I know I don't tell you often enough. I am doing the best I can. I've started buying into your crazy dream of selling the house and taking the money to buy a bed and breakfast in the islands. It's going to be hard work but we're used to that. And it'll be our business, in a beautiful place. I think it might just work."

"Seriously? You're on board? Because sometimes I don't think you are."

"This past year has convinced me. So maybe it doesn't work but we can't keep doing what we're doing. We're digging a deeper hole here. I'm definitely on board. As long as the B&B wasn't built in the eighteenth century!" He laughed. "If we close the place in the summer and come back to New England for six to eight weeks a year, I'll go."

"Done. That would be awesome." She kissed him as she pushed the footstool aside. They made love in front of the fire and she forgot about going to Lynn's and spent the night with Ray in front of the wood burning stove. When they woke up the next morning, they heard the clicking of the baseboard heat. The power was back on.

She left her apartment at seven Thursday morning to catch a Greyhound bus departing at eight thirty for Manhattan. She showered but didn't wash her hair as it had just been washed last night. She was afraid she wouldn't be able to get it to look as good as Andre had. She just ran her hands through it, spiking it up and it looked fine.

She slept most of the way to the Port Authority bus station. She planned to walk the eight blocks from Penn Station to the Long Island Railroad, detouring over to Times Square because she had never been there. Nick was meeting her at the Jamaica train station in Queens. He was flying into JFK and renting a car.

The wedding was taking place in East Hampton. Nick's grandfather had a large home on the ocean where the reception was being held. Another large house about a mile from there, closer to the center of town, had been rented for the bridesmaids and groomsmen. Although some of the bridal party had their dates staying with them, Nick was staying at his grandfather's with Olivia and his parents. He had already told his family they were no longer an item. He said they took the news in stride. She was sure they did.

She got to Jamaica a little after three thirty in the afternoon. Nick had texted her earlier and said his flight was late and he wouldn't be there until four thirty. She came out of the train station under an overpass where buses and cabs were pulling in. She was wearing a coral sundress with ribbons of shiny, small gold sequins encircling the dress every few inches. It was cinched at the waist, sleeveless and just above her knees. She had matching gold sandals with one inch heels, gold hoop earrings and bangle bracelets. She had paid particular attention to her wardrobe this morning knowing her hair would cause quite a sensation so she wanted to at least be wearing something eye catching.

Looking around for a place to eat, she saw a large Fried Chicken sign across the street. Dragging her suitcase with the wheels behind her and carrying her dress bag over her shoulder, she came out from under the overpass and into the bright warm sun. People of all colors and nationalities were passing along the street.

She ordered chicken fingers, cole slaw and a coke and took a seat at the counter that ran along the window. Seeing her reflection staring back at her, she couldn't believe she was that girl with the short spiky hair. She looked down as her cell phone buzzed, moving along the counter. It was Nick. "Hey we made up time in the air. I've got the car and I'm on my way to get you. I should only be about fifteen minutes."

"Okay. I'm across from the train station at the corner of Sutphin and Archer. It's a fried chicken place. I was starving. I'll be out at the corner when you get here."

"You went wandering out of the train station? That isn't a safe neighborhood you know."

"It's the middle of the day. It seems fine. The chicken fingers are delicious."

"Some things never change with you. Have you ever heard of drive by shootings? Fifteen minutes, be out there waiting. I'm in a red convertible Chrysler LeBaron, top down. You need to hop right in, I'm not hanging around there."

"Yes sir." She hung up and finished her chicken. Twenty minutes later she saw him coming out from the underpass and he wasn't alone. Ashley Long was in the front seat with him, a silk Hermes scarf tied around her blond hair and movie star rhinestone sunglasses on. She was also wearing a crisply ironed sleeveless linen blouse.

She knew he was not going to recognize her so she stepped to the curb and started jumping up and down, waving madly at him. He pulled right up and slammed on the breaks, looking at her incredulously. As she threw her bags in the back seat and climbed in, he shouted at her. "What the hell did you do to your hair?"

"I finally used the gift certificate you gave me for my birthday. Do you like it?" She was trying for an air of bravado but she wasn't quite sure she was successfully pulling it off.

"Jesus Christ, it's short. Does Olivia know about this?"

"No. Am I supposed to tell her when I get my hair cut?"

"Yes, before the wedding you are."

"Oh right. Shoot, I forgot about that." She laughed. Ashley turned around and put out her hand. "Remember me? Ashley Long. I met you when you arrived in Dallas a couple of months ago."

"Of course. You live in 4B. You had a key to Nick's apartment." She shook her hand.

"I love your hair cut. Don't mind Nick, he doesn't seem to take to change well. You look stunning and very chic. The dress and sandals are great too."

"Thanks."

Nick pulled out into traffic and took off towards the highway. The drive to East Hampton was over two hours and with the top down conversation was difficult as Nick was driving fast and it was hard to hear them in the front seat with the wind blowing. Although she could feel her hair blowing slightly in the wind it was short enough that it was not going to get too messed up. Good thing, because she didn't have a Hermes scarf. It might look even better slightly more tousled and wind blown. She was getting very anxious about confronting Olivia. She put on her IPod headphones and pulled her sunglasses down from the top of her head. Stretching her legs across the back seat and leaning against her bags, she sent a text message on her cell phone.

Checked out Times Square. Amazing! Will send you a pic. Had some really good fried chicken for lunch in Jamaica waiting for my ride. Nick brought a date. A girl who lives in his building.

Jamaica? Thought the wedding was in NY. He brought a date? That's kinda rude.

Not that Jamaica, mon. The one in Queens.

OH. We need to add Jamaica to our travel list. You know how I love Bob Marley. Would love to hear reggae in Jamaica. I hear jerk chicken is really good too. Maybe we'll sail the whole Caribbean. Chillin' every day if ya know what I mean.

Definitely. I know I'd love the islands. I'm comfortably stretched out in the back seat of a convertible right now with the top down for the two hour drive to the Hamptons, listening to my IPod and ignoring the lovebirds in the front seat.

Sorry. You should have brought me as your date! I hope you're wearing your seat belt.

Yes. She put her phone down and fished the seat belt out from under her suitcase. It made it more difficult to stretch her legs across the seat so she put the shoulder strap behind her. He didn't have to know about that. He was such a nag about the seat belts. But understandably so, she thought.

Hang in there. Did Nan lose twenty pounds or did you cut your hair?

You'll have to wait 'til Monday to find out.

No fair. Send pictures. From her perch in the back seat, she took a picture of Ashley leaning over to put her hand on Nick's cheek. She sent it to him. Then she sent a picture of One Times Square with the ball that dropped every New Years Eve.

Long weekend ahead, huh? She looks uptight. Can't hold a candle to you sweetie. Whatever you look like right now. Picture please. Love you. XXOO BTW, nice pic of NYC.

Luv U 2.

Are you OK? Did you go thru with this crazy plan of yours? You're not traumatized or anything are you?

She took a picture of her feet in the gold sandals with the coral pedicure she got the other day and sent it.

Nice. Very tropical. Higher please. You know I will love it cus I love you. Just want to make sure you're OK. I've been worried about you. You seemed very edgy when I left you Monday morning.

I'm fine. Sorry, that's all you get. I am not doing this on cell phone pic. See you Monday. Je t'adore. xxoo

That's OK. I understand. ???? Hey was that French? No comprende senorita.

I adore you.

Sweet. P.S. Don't take shit from anyone this weekend. You are beautiful.

Merci beaucoup. Or muchos gracias for you.

* * *

The drive out to the Hamptons was really nice. Once they got past the suburbs and out to the south fork, it was one cute, picture perfect town after another. However, the traffic was bumper to bumper even on Thursday night. Most people must have wanted to get an early start on the holiday weekend. Although it would have been easier to talk now that they were crawling through traffic, Nick and Ashley were deep in conversation in the front seat, laughing and flirting, occasionally kissing. She eavesdropped for a while but they were talking about their jobs and she found it boring so she put her IPod back on and grabbed a journal out of her purse. She was working on the story about Jennie. He was getting way ahead of her with the illustrations and he told her he needed more copy.

East Hampton was even prettier than the previous towns they had driven through. A picture perfect all-American seaside town with a green in the center and white clapboard houses. They pulled up to the sidewalk of a large white house set behind a hedge. Between the hedges, there was a white gate with an arbor covered in pink roses. "Here you are my dear, this is where you are staying."

"Aren't you coming in?"

"No we're going straight to Granddad's." Why was he talking in this snotty, patrician tone of voice, she wondered. Granddad? My dear?

"I see Olivia's car is here, so I'm going to let you handle that situation on your own. Tell her I said hi."

Ashley pouted at him. "Oh Nico, we should go in with her. I haven't met your sister yet."

Nico?

"You won't want to meet her right now," he said, smiling at Ashley.

She ran her hand through her hair, fluffing it up after the windy drive. She reached in her purse and put some lip gloss on. Grabbing her suitcase and dress bag, she straightened her shoulders. She felt very much like Maria in The Sound of Music when she arrived at the von Trapp's house.

"Well thanks for picking me up. I guess I will see you at the beach party tonight." She opened the gate, marched through the arbor and whistled thinking "I have confidence, yes I have confidence. No I do not. But I will pretend I do."

She stepped onto a beautiful wrap around porch with white wicker furniture and hanging baskets filled with pink and white flowers. Peering into the wooden screen door, she could hear lots of people laughing and talking so she just opened it and let herself in. She put her bags down by a large umbrella stand and called out "Hello?" Nan came running from the kitchen. She was in a very loose muumuu type sundress, most likely trying to disguise her weight. She thought maybe she should have worn a hat to hide her hair. "Oh my God, you did it. I love you." Nan gave her a giant hug. 'You look smashing as Olivia would say. Turn around and let me see."

She spun around really quickly, feeling very self conscious. "Where's Olivia?"

"In the kitchen. We're having Sangrias and mojitos. I bet you need a drink."

"Shit yeah. I just drove almost three hours with Nick and his new girlfriend."

"I heard she was coming. How rude, huh?"

"You heard?" She sighed and rolled her eyes. "Tact was never one of his strong points." As she entered the kitchen, Olivia looked up and let out a scream. "Oh. My. God. What the hell did you do to your hair?"

Everyone turned to look at her. She felt her face turning beet red and she immediately reached for her hair, running her hand through it. She tried not to cry but could feel her eyes tearing up. Next to Olivia stood a guy about five foot seven with dark black hair and green eyes behind black horn rimmed glasses. He was not heavy but not thin either, just average and clearly not very athletic. She thought there was something soft about him and his hands were very small and slightly feminine looking. But she loved it when he gave Olivia a very nasty look and walked towards her with his hand out.

"Hi, I'm Henry. I believe I am the usher you are paired with this weekend. It's very nice to meet you, you are much lovelier in person than pictures I've seen you tagged in on Facebook." His handshake was very limp but he looked directly and confidently into her eyes. "Nice to meet you Henry."

"Can I get you a drink?"

"I would love a mojito. And is there any Captain Morgan?"

* * *

The rest of the evening went a little better than it had started. Henry became her protector and self designated knight in shining armor. She and Nan went up to their room to change for the beach party, which was a hot and stuffy, small maid's room in the attic with a tiny fan that didn't help much. "Well Nan, it looks like we did get the Cinderella room again. At least it not's the Harry Potter room. I saw one of those stairway closets when I came in through the front hall."

Nan filled her in on Henry's background. "Very, very eligible bachelor. Graduated from MIT, living in New York now. Invented something or other, I'm not sure what but it has to do with medical equipment. A millionaire by the age of thirty."

"He's thirty? He looks twenty."

"Yeah and most of the girls think he's too short."

"Doesn't the million bucks trump the height with this crowd?'

"You are so funny. Trust me this house is full of well off men tonight, a lot of them taller than Henry. Olivia's fiancé Liam hangs with the crème de la crème of Wall Street."

"Well Henry seems nice."

"Hey are you still seeing Mr. 2 A.M?"

She smiled. "Yes."

"Are things still good?'

"Very good. I believe in spite of myself I have fallen in love."

There was a party that night on the beach at 'Grandad' DeLuca's house. Volleyball nets were set up and a lobster bake was getting under way when they arrived. Henry gave her, Nan and Amanda a ride there in his Jaguar XK convertible. She loved the color, racing blue.

Tiki torches and picnic tables were also set up on the beach and a country music band was playing. Although she'd always been a little too short to play volleyball competitively she gave it her best try. Henry was very attentive all evening, getting her lobster and always making sure her drink was full.

When they got back to the house later that evening, a few of them stayed up late playing charades and she and Henry were partners. He was extremely impressed when she did a dead on impersonation of Charlie Chaplain and she was amazed at his ability to figure out other people's horrible attempts at acting out the different movies they were assigned. They won the game easily. Later that night in the nanny's room, Nan started teasing her about Henry. "I think he really likes you."

"No he doesn't. He's just polite and he seems to have impeccable manners. I think he was appalled at Olivia's reaction when I first arrived."

"No, he's usually very shy. He likes you. Isn't your boyfriend an electrician or something?"

"Yes, he's an electrician. What does that have to do with anything?"

"Nothing. But Henry is a millionaire."

"Yes, you keep telling me that."

"Just saying. You need to think ahead."

"Ahead to what?"

"Your future. So will you be getting calls at 2 A.M. again?"

"No, he's going out to the Isles of Shoals with his uncle this weekend. Fishing for striped bass. No phone service out there off the coast of New Hampshire."

"Well we better get to sleep. Olivia has scheduled those emergency appointments for us with the seamstress to let out my dress and the hairdresser to figure out what to do with your hair so you fit in with the rest of us."

"I can't wait," she said, her voice dripping with sarcasm. "But I don't think I'll ever fit in and honestly I don't want to." She punched her pillow, rolled over and quickly fell asleep. She was beginning to think Nan wasn't worth a foot of hair. What the hell was that electrician comment about?

* * *

Friday started early for her and Nan, at eight A.M. The rest of the house was still asleep but the wayward bridesmaids needed consultations. Nan had a fitting with the seamstress who let out her dress. She had a consultation with the hair stylist who would try to make her hair compliment the other girls. The chosen hairstyle was two small braids in the front wrapped around the head underneath a loose, low bun. One of her favorite ways to wear her hair when it was long. An orchid would be tucked into the bun in back.

For the first time since Wednesday night, she felt like really balling her eyes out but she wouldn't give Olivia the satisfaction. She'd really begun to think Katie and her boyfriend had been right. This was another one of her stupid, quixotic, impulsive moves and she would bear the consequences for quite some time. It would take forever to grow this haircut out. Why was she supporting a girl who didn't have enough willpower to lose weight and was looking for a rich husband?

They decided on a leather headband that matched her hair color and looked like a braid. It wrapped around her head and an orchid would be clipped along the side of the headband behind her ear. She thought it looked okay. Tomorrow the stylist said she would comb her hair down flat but she was planning on messing it up after the stylist left.

A manicurist came and gave everyone French manicures and pedicures. She had just had a pedicure and liked the coral but admitted it wouldn't really match their short navy blue bridesmaids dresses with one bare shoulder and silk navy blue rosettes along the neckline. She could possibly wear it again, which her mother would tell her would be the practical thing after spending three hundred dollars.

They spent the afternoon at the beach. The caterers and the tent company were up on the lawn handling the final preparations for tomorrow. Henry set his towel next to hers and brought her a beer. "So what do you do for work?"

"A very boring job in editing. I would rather be the writer who has an editor."

"I know someone at the Times. Maybe I could get you an interview."

"Really? You could?""

"Yeah, they work in the Style section but it's a start. You look like someone who would work in the style section." She laughed loud and raucously, although she was wearing a stylish bikini she loved. The neon pink tie-dye bandeau top matched the very skimpy bottom and showed off all that running she'd been doing lately. Plus the lifting she occasionally did in Newburyport on her boyfriend's bench press. "Ha. I have never been told that before. But that would be an awesome start. Give me your email Henry and I'll send you my resume."

Later that night, the rehearsal dinner was at a very fashionable restaurant in town where Jay-Z, Beyonce and Steven Spielberg had been known to dine. She and Katie had picked out what she thought was a very stunning dress for the evening.

She had been receiving numerous emails from Olivia and her maid of honor, Brooke, regarding what to wear to this event. They would send photos from various websites with notes like:

We just love this summer sundress matched with the accessories attached.

Pastels are our very favorite this Memorial Day weekend.

We think sexy little heels complement this very flattering dress.

They spoke in a voice of authority like they were the arbiters of fashion and everyone would want to follow their amazing sense of style and fashion.

She and Katie had chosen a periwinkle blue dress that fit tightly and showed off her figure perfectly, making her eyes pop as Andre would say. It looked very conservative from the front with a scoop neck and long sleeves. But it was very tight fitted and short. The back plunged to her waist and had tiny gold chains across her back. With this she chose to wear black ankle boots with two inch stiletto heels. She really spiked her hair up that night and wore a smoky eye makeup she had learned how to do watching YouTube. Olivia didn't speak to her all evening but Liam, Olivia's fiancé, asked her to dance. "I had no idea you could look quite like this. You always seemed so apple pie, girl next door like."

"Well you never know, do you? Can't judge a book by its cover, right?" She laughed.

Henry was enamored with her and followed her around all evening making sure her drink was always full (she thought to herself "Is he trying to get me drunk?") and getting her hors d'oeuvres ("At least he's feeding me."). Nick was completely occupied with Ashley most of the evening but did come up to her just before everyone was leaving. "I wanted to let you know you look quite amazing this evening. Sorry for my initial reaction when I picked you up. I just knew Olivia would have a fit."

"Thanks."

"No! I mean really amazing." He leaned over and kissed her on the cheek and then turned and walked back to Ashley who smiled approvingly at him. She must have sent 'Nico' over here to say that, she thought. She and Nan discussed the evening later that night. "I am positive Henry has a thing for you."

"It appears that way."

"You should give him a chance. He's a nice guy and filthy rich."

"Does it matter to you that I have a boyfriend and I told you I'm in love?"

"I'm just saying. You never know. Check him out."

"I hear what you're saying. Honestly, I do. But what is it with chemistry? Why do you have it or you don't? I mean Henry has been nothing but chivalrous all weekend and he's very smart. But talking to him is like pulling teeth. There are always these awkward pauses."

"If you don't want him, I would love to date him. A quiet husband would be nice. Goes off to work, does his own thing and lets you spend the money, join the country club. Provides you with a nice, secure life. You know? But it's you he's interested in."

"No I don't know. Wow, Nan! In New Orleans I did not get the impression that was what you were looking for."

"Well it's just as easy to fall in love with a rich boy as a poor one."

"Yes someone else told me that too." She laughed. "Like falling in love is as easy as buying a pair of shoes, right? You just pick and choose based on their portfolio or something?"

"Well, what are you looking for?"

"What am I looking for? True love. Someone who is my best friend, who loves me as I am. Someone I have fun with and who listens to me and shares my dreams. Security is not one of my dreams. I'm not saying that's a sensible thing but who dreams sensible dreams?"

The wedding day dawned with a beautiful sunrise. She went for a three mile run to the next town, Amagansett, where there was a large farmer's market. She thought she might have seen Gwyneth Paltrow but the guy she was with didn't look like Chris Martin so she wasn't sure. But she was going to tell people at work it was her anyway. Outside on the lawn, she found a table and sat down to have her iced coffee and a scone. A few minutes later Henry sat down across from her.

"Well fancy meeting you here." He smiled shyly. He was wearing Nantucket Red Bermuda shorts and a white polo shirt with expensive looking huarache sandals. He looked very fresh and clean. She on the other hand felt all sweaty in her old Grateful Dead tie dyed T-shirt and gym shorts. Running her hand self consciously through her hair, she sipped on the straw in her iced coffee while looking up at him, slightly bemused. "Hey, what are you doing here?"

"I live on the Upper West Side and I'm a daily patron of Zabar's. They sell their bread and pastry here because Eli Zabar lives near here. So when I'm in the Hamptons, I always stop by."

"Ahh. I see. Well the coffee and scones are delicious."

"You should come to New York sometime. I could show you around. I live near the Museum of Natural History and I have a view of Central Park."

Ignoring the invitation, she said, "That must be nice, being near the park. I hardly know New York."

"Didn't you go out with Nick for several years?"

"Yes, but he didn't like the city, back then." She laughed. "We only went in once or twice. But apparently now he loves the city." She sipped her coffee, so the conversation quickly died. He unfolded his New York Times and started reading. She finished her scone and when he offered her a ride back to the house, she accepted because the bridesmaids would be getting ready in two hours and she needed to take a shower. There would probably be a wait for the bathrooms but she was planning to take a shower outside. She loved beach houses with outdoor showers.

* * *

The ceremony took place in a beautiful old stone church. With ten bridesmaids, three flower girls and two ring bearers the procession was quite long. They played two different wedding marches. Before getting back to the reception at the house by the ocean, they had almost two hours of pictures taken at a park and then more photos down on the beach. She could see the other guests milling about on the lawn above them, drinking cocktails and mingling. She desperately wanted some of those hors d'oeuvres the waitresses were passing around. She was starving, she hadn't eaten a thing since that scone several hours ago. Henry caught her rubbing her jaw and making funny stretching faces with her mouth. He waved at her and laughed. She covered her mouth and laughed too.

"I didn't know anyone was looking. My mouth is tired from smiling. I feel like I'm at prom. First there was the picture taking at a friend's house, always the friend with the biggest house and nicest backyard. Then the Grand March and then the long line for the formal pictures, which my date and I blew off. We snuck out to get high."

"You did?" He seemed shocked, truly shocked not pretend shocked.

"I just wanted to start dancing and eating, you know? Let's get on with the prom. I mean what were we taking pictures of? An event we never got to because we were taking pictures all evening? Apparently it's all about the dress. Like today, right?"

The tent was decorated with long tables covered in white linen table cloths, tall hurricane lamps with white candles and vases filled with pink ranunculus, white roses and babies breath. There was a swing band and everyone danced until midnight at which time she thought she would turn into a chambermaid and have to return to her room in the attic.

Earlier in the evening, when Olivia threw her bouquet, she saw it coming straight for her. If she hadn't put her hands up to catch it, it would have hit her in the face. Her immediate reaction was to toss it over her shoulder where a gaggle of girls lunged for it and Ashley came up the winner of the coveted prize. She saw Nick at the bar shaking his head in horror and she wasn't sure if that was because she tossed the bouquet like it was poison ivy or because Ashley caught it.

As the night was winding down, she was exhausted from trying to make conversation with Henry. She really wanted to be alone, or honestly, just go to bed. But somehow, she found herself hiding over where the older family members were congregated. Sitting at a table with Nick's mother and a friend of hers from her tennis club, she sipped on a sour tasting cocktail called an old fashioned while eavesdropping on Mrs. DeLuca who was discussing Olivia's community service in the Bronx.

"It is so important to have charitable work on your resume and it was such a good lesson for her. She learned just how hard it is for some kids who don't have the advantages she does. And you know what she told me when she got back from New Orleans? That now when she stays in hotels, she always makes sure to leave a nice tip for the chambermaids because she realizes others are not as well off as she is and have to work hard for a living."

She thought she should check under her pillow when she got back to her room and see if Olivia had left a tip there, kind of like the tooth fairy. A small contribution towards the cost of the dress, for those bridesmaids who were not as well off, worked hard for a living and couldn't really afford three hundred dollar dresses they would wear only once.

* * *

Sunday there was a brunch for the wedding party and family members. Olivia and Liam had left for their honeymoon on Ibiza off the coast of Spain. The rest of the day was spent shopping in town. She bought her boyfriend a 'Surf Ditch Plains' T-shirt. He had gotten very excited about the chicory coffee and juju she brought him from New Orleans. He had bought her a Ski Aspen sweatshirt when he was in Colorado and some really cool Oakley sunglasses he said he found on sale but nonetheless they looked very expensive. She had gotten numerous compliments on them this weekend. He liked to exchange souvenirs. Maybe it was the sentiment of I missed you while I was gone? He always wore his father's watch on his left wrist but now alongside it he also wore the small silver heart shaped juju attached to a leather rope.

She was wandering through the tony, expensive shops of East Hampton with Nan and five other bridesmaids. They were in a very hip clothing shop where the other girls were trying on lots of cute things. The sales ladies were very solicitous, bringing the girls different sizes and keeping the growing pile of items they were going to purchase at the register until they were finished shopping. They probably worked on commission and realized they had hit the jackpot this afternoon with this crowd. She pretended she was looking for something she just couldn't find, not wanting to admit it was the price tags that were holding her back. How did the other girls do it? She worked forty hours a week, fifty weeks a year and couldn't afford a pair of socks in this store. Why was that? Her school loan wasn't unmanageable, she wasn't paying rent anymore, and she didn't own a car.

She felt terribly lonely and suddenly had the sensation of an empty pit in the bottom of her stomach, a familiar feeling from her childhood. She used to try to describe it to her mother when she would get it the night before the first day of school or other scary times like that. She used to call it her Hansel and Gretel bellyache. It was the scary, anxious feeling of being lost and all alone. Of not being able to find her way home. She went outside to wait for the other girls to finish shopping and sat on a bench along Main Street. Tilting her head back to feel the warm sun on her face, she closed her eyes and thought about being home tomorrow. But she wasn't thinking about her apartment in Boston or any specific place at all. She was imagining just herself wrapped in the arms of her boyfriend.

Nick was supposed to bring her to the train station in Jamaica on his way to the airport but Henry offered to take her all the way to the city and drop her right at Port Authority where she would catch the bus to Boston. Driving back across Long Island, they talked about college and work. As usual, she had the burden of keeping the conversation going. "Did you like the wedding?" she asked.

"It was nice. I've been to so many of these society weddings lately. Seems like most of my friends are of that age when marriage seems to be the thing to do."

"Are you getting to be of that age?"

"Me? No. I don't think I'll ever marry. Too set in my ways. I like my solitude a little too much. How about you? Do you see yourself getting married?"

"I don't know. I don't really think about it. I'm only twenty five. But if I ever do, it certainly won't be a big wedding like that. I wonder how much a wedding like that costs?"

"I heard Liam say it was close to eighty thousand dollars with all the other events like the lobster bake and rehearsal dinner and the house they rented for us."

She shouted "Eighty Thousand Dollars? You're shitting me? That's two years of college. For one day?"

He laughed to himself and smiled over at her like she was some rare kind of flower or bird and he wasn't quite sure how she happened to be in his car. "Well if you have the money, why not?"

"Oh, I could think of many reasons why not. It seems so, umm... so extravagant? Wasteful? I don't know. You could use the money to buy a house or pay off your school loans. Do you think people feel if they spend lots of money and have a big wedding it will buy them happily ever after?"

"Possibly. Besides, I don't think Olivia has school loans." He smiled at her.

"But a big, expensive wedding doesn't guarantee happiness. And then what?"

"An even more expensive divorce a few years later?"

"Haha. Yeah, probably. I think it would be much more romantic to elope. If and that's a big if, I ever decide to get married. All I know is between the trip to New Orleans, a trip to New York for a shower, this weekend and the dress, I have spent close to two thousand dollars and if you knew what I made you would understand that is like eighty thousand dollars to me. I could think of better ways to spend that much money. And I can guarantee you I will never see Olivia DeLuca again. She'll probably drop me as her Facebook friend after the first year."

As they pulled up to the bus station, he said, "Make sure to send me your resume. You could make more money at the Times." She had his email and told him she would definitely send it. She did have to plan for the possibility she might be single again in the fall if she wasn't moving to L.A. Was she ready to move to L.A.? She thought maybe she was. But the New York Times sounded very exciting. Why was she so confused?

A RASPY OLD HEN

It was now late March at the Ryan house. The alarm went off at six A.M. as it always did on weekdays. Sophie had just gotten out of the shower and when she looked through the old window into the addition she could see signs of progress. The room was sheet rocked. She smiled.

While was making the bed, she looked up to see a TV commercial for President Obama. It was a clip from his State of the Union speech. Sophie sat down on the bed for a minute, nodding her head in agreement as she listened to the ad. *"We can either settle for a country where a shrinking number of people do really well, while a growing number of Americans barely get by, or we can restore an economy where everyone gets a fair shot."*

A short while later, as she was driving to work, she rode past the farm into town. The sun was shining directly into her eyes, making it difficult to see the white plastic sheets that were covering parts of the fields. Sprinklers were spraying water in V-shaped arcs and little rainbows could be seen through the spray. She felt hopeful for the first time in a long time.

Ray was going up north tonight to ski at Cannon Mountain tomorrow. It would probably be one of the last good ski days of the season. There had been several inches of snow in the mountains last night and it was 'Buy One Get One Free Wednesday' so he was meeting his friend Miguel there. Miguel the master of distraction. But, Ray deserved a day off. He had been working hard.

After another long, boring day she faked another dentist appointment. She thought everyone must think she had really bad teeth. She called Lynn on her way home. "Are you up for a wine emergency?"

"Always. I am picking Sarah up from track but I won't be long. Just let yourself in, you know where the wine is. I'll be right behind you."

When she got to Lynn's front door she knocked and as usual opened the door while knocking and let herself in. "Hello? Lynn? Are you home?"

Doug called from upstairs. "Sophie? She should be back in ten minutes."

Doug came to the top of the stairs. He was dressed in camouflage pants and a matching jacket. He leaned over the railing. "Looking for a wine emergency? Aren't you a little early today? It's only four?"

"Ya. Bad day. Bad week. I left early, fictitious dentist appointment. Couldn't take another minute in the cube. How are you doing? Any luck with the job hunt?"

"A few leads, nothing definite. Hey I'm going out back. Turkey watching. Help yourself to some wine if you want, you know where it is. Lynn should be back soon."

"Huh? Turkey watching?"

"Ya. I have a blind out back. Early evening is the time they come out, just before dusk. I'm luring them in with cracked corn. I saw thirty last night."

"Get out! Can I join you?"

Doug made a skeptical face and looked at Sophie. She was wearing a dark gray pea coat and black pants. "Well they might not spot you in the blind, your clothes are dark enough. Sure, come on. We're losing daylight."

"Cool. Next time I'll be sure to wear my camo." On their way outside, Doug grabbed a few strange looking things on a table by the doors and put them in his coat pocket. It was so cold outside they could both see their breath. "What's that stuff you grabbed?' Sophie asked him.

"Turkey calls." Doug picked up a ten pound bag of cracked corn on the deck and they walked towards the woods at the edge of the back yard. He spread some cracked corn on a large, flat rock, also scattered some on the ground and returned the bag to the deck. They walked towards a group of pine trees that formed a copse. Inside it looked like a cave with openings where they could see into the woods out back. There were additional cut pine branches lying vertically around the trees. Inside was a blue cooler large enough for two people to sit closely. Doug opened it. "Beer?"

"Thanks." They opened their beers and sat on the cooler. Sophie whispered because she thought she should. "Now what?" Doug whispered back. "We call them in." He reached into his pocket and took out a rectangular box shaped turkey call. He continued to whisper. "We'll try this one first."

Sophie read the print on the top of the box and laughed loudly. "Raspy Old Hen? Haha. God I think most days Ray would say that's me." Doug put his finger to his mouth, shushing her. He grasped the base with his left hand and the lid with his right. He pulled the lid across the box in short strokes and it made a loud, piercing sound. He did this sev-eral times. Sophie watched, drinking her beer.

"That was the turkey yelp. Toms yelp. You can make a clucking noise too. That's the hens." He started to make shorter, sharper strokes and the box clucked. He did this for a minute.

"What else ya got in that pocket?' Doug took out a small slate circle and a dowel. He held the dowel like a pen and drew it across the slate. It made a more high pitched yelping sound than the box caller, like fingernails on a blackboard. Sophie covered her ears.

Doug suddenly sat up at attention. "Shhh." He pointed to-wards the woods. Three turkeys were walking along a path towards the rock with the cracked corn. A little further behind them followed an entire flock of about thirty turkeys. Doug and Sophie watched raptly as the turkeys wandered around, eating corn and pecking at the ground. A few minutes later some of the turkeys seemed to startle and a few of the Toms fanned their tail feathers. Sophie and Doug were spellbound, totally engrossed as the turkeys scattered quickly back into the woods.

Lynn shouted from the back of the house. "Hey are you guys out there?"

Doug shouted back, slightly annoyed. "Yeah. You scared the turkeys away."

"Is Sophie out there? I saw her car in the driveway."

Sophie shouted back. "Yeah, I'm here. I'll be there in a minute." She turned to Doug. "That was so cool." They stood up from the cooler, took out another beer each and sat back down. "How about when they puffed up like that? That was so amazing Doug. Thanks for letting me join you."

"Those are the Toms, the males. The peacocks of New Hampshire."

"I don't know about that. They are some ugly bird. Except when they fan their tails." They drank their beers, contemplating their surroundings and the spectacle they had just witnessed.

"Hey I forgot to show you this one." He took another turkey call out of his pocket. This one was a plastic spiral, like a piece of vacuum hose with a wooden handle. He stood up, lifted it above his head, then shook it, rhythmically moving it down to his waist and lifting it again like a tambourine. He was rocking with the rhythm of the warbling sound with his eyes were closed.

Sophie laughed. "Sorry. You look like some kind of Indian shaman. Ya know something Doug? You are so relaxed when you are unemployed. Not as tense and edgy, just a completely different person. This is weird but I think unemployment agrees with you. Even Ray commented on it. He couldn't believe how different you were at the UNH hockey game last weekend. He said you even had a second beer and stayed 'til the end of the game, no rushing to the parking lot to beat the traffic."

"Guess I'm getting used to it. It's the third time in my career I've been laid off. Corporate buyout with jobs shipped overseas, downsizing and now some office politics type of bullshit."

"Yeah, what exactly happened with that?"

"Never mind, too ridiculous to even talk about. But this time around I have a decent nest egg. Almost thirty years of working and I managed to save something for myself. Not as much as I would have liked but enough to ride this out until I find something. If we're careful."

"Well there's that at least. You're lucky. Ray and I have nothing, just that stupid old house of ours. Neither one of us ever had the kind of job with profit sharing, stock splits, bonuses or whatever it takes to really save money. Just working for every penny we make and spending it paying the bills faster than we can make it."

"I mean I've gotta keep working but I think I'm done with corporate life. The nine to five rat race and the two weeks vacation. Every time I get a job I'm back to two weeks. Shit that's not enough time to relax, fish, do the things I enjoy."

Sophie laughed. "Watch turkeys." Doug nodded in agreement and took a long sip from his beer. "I feel your pain Doug. I'm in the same boat. I think the French have it right, six weeks vacation. Remind me again why we hate the French? Life is too short. We all know that. Look at my friend Kathy, she never got to spend her 401K." She paused to take a sip of her beer. "There comes a point in your life when time is more valuable than money. And I'm thinking that point should come sooner than later because you just never know." She stopped and gazed off into the distance. "Half the shit we spend our money on, we don't even need."

"I've been looking into buying a franchise. A wild bird store. Selling bird feed, turkey calls, bird houses, you know the other outdoor hobby stuff too."

Sophie chuckled. "Seriously? Can't you buy a lot of that stuff at Wal-Mart? I mean that's going to be your competition, right? Do you think in this economy people will shop at a high end bird store?"

Doug looked back at her dejectedly. "Well, I shop there and I'm unemployed."

"No, no I didn't mean it that way. I think it's a good idea. Always better to be the boss, work for yourself. You work for the man, you come home with empty pockets. It's something you obviously love." She swept her hand around the turkey blind. "And you know what they say, do what you love and the money will follow."

"Who are they? I've always wondered that."

Sophie laughed. "Me too. Most of the time I don't listen to them. But in this case, they might be right. Hey it's no crazier than Ray and me running a bed and breakfast in the islands, right? Buy another house we need to maintain and try to make a living doing it? Most people think we're nuts."

"Yeah I mean of course I'll check out all of the expenses, get a business plan. I just don't think I can go back to the corporate grind. I've been kicked around one too many times. And you're right. I am more relaxed. Speaking of which." He reached into his pocket and pulled out something that looked like a cell phone. "Want a coupla hits?"

"What is that?"

"It's called a vaporizer. Doesn't smell when you smoke it and..." He put it to his ear like he was talking on a cell phone. "Just in case the teenagers walk in the room or something." He reached in his pocket, pulled out a baggie and loaded the vaporizer. He lit it, took a hit and handed it to Sophie. She took a hit too and passed it back to him. They continued to pass it back and forth while they were talking.

"Your pockets are like Mary Poppins' bag." She chuckled. "You should go for this bird store. I like the idea."

"Yeah. Ya know Ray was talking about your plans at the hockey game. I think you've convinced him it's the way to go. He was telling me about that roofing job he was doing awhile back. I don't know how he does it. Manual labor in the freezing cold, up on a roof at his age. It's not like he's twenty anymore." Doug shook his head.

"Tell me about it." She paused, took a long hit off the vaporizer and stared off into the woods, sipping her beer. "So he really seemed like he was with me on this?"

"Sounded that way to me."

Lynn called from the house. "Sophie where are you? Come in and have some wine."

"Oh, that's right. I came here for a wine emergency. But before I go, I have to ask you something. Do turkeys fly?"

"Domesticated ones don't but these wild turkeys do."

"How come I never see them flying?"

"They only go about a quarter mile at a time and not very high. They perch in trees and that's when they fly, to their perch. They feed on the ground, so that's why everyone thinks they don't fly."

"I see. So they make low, short flights. Do you ever dream of flying Doug?"

"No, can't say I have."

"Wow that's too bad. Flying dreams are exhilarating. You feel awesome when you wake up from one. I used to dream them all the time. I'd fly high like a bird. But when I got older I started flying like a turkey. I wouldn't even say it was flying. I'd just be walking down a sidewalk or something and my feet would take off from the ground and I'd float for about a quarter of a mile. Then I'd take another long step and float off again. Those were cool but not as nice as really flying."

"What do you think that dream means?"

"I googled it. It's a symbol for rising above something in your life that is troubling you, holding you down and making you unhappy. I haven't even had a low flying turkey dream in quite some time. I guess no longer having those dreams explains my unhappiness. I feel stuck, like I can't rise above my problems. I've lost control over my destiny."

"I wish I dreamed more. Maybe I do dream but I never remember them."

"Well I better go inside and see Lynn. Thanks for the turkeys, that was very cool." She raised her beer bottle and tapping Doug's bottle said "To turkeys and trade winds."

* * *

Later that night she dreamt she was on the Isle of Capri, off the coast of Italy. She was on the deck of a bed and breakfast she and Kathy had stayed at many years ago when they backpacked through Europe. She had washed some of her jeans in the bathtub and was hanging them off the back of some deck chairs to dry as she gazed out at the Tyrrhenian Sea. She could just glimpse the Faraglioni, the three large rocks just off the coast in the Bay of Naples. Suddenly Kathy walked out onto the deck.

"My God, where have you been? You never come to me in my dreams and I've wanted you to visit so badly. There is so much I need to talk to you about. Ray and I are struggling. Things are so hard. This house is killing us and since you passed away I lost my job and now have this job in a cubicle that is driving me mad."

Kathy sat down next to her. "I forgot we washed these jeans in the tub here. Remember we filled the tub with soapy water, climbed in barefoot and stomped on them like we were crushing grapes. They were filthy."

"That's because we were sitting on that muddy hill in Munich during Oktoberfest wishing on stars and watching fireworks with that guy from Australia."

Kathy laughed. "Right. I forgot about that too."

"I remember it all. Why did you leave so soon? We were supposed to end up in a nursing home together when we were ninety, smuggling wine into our room and telling each other our backpacking through Europe stories. And all the other stories over the years that we had shared."

"What is it you need Sophie?"

"I need your advice and wisdom. I miss your wisdom."

"Do you remember what I told you about love? That your husband can't be everything to you. That's why you need your friends and your sisters. Because there are just some things only women understand."

"Yes but you were my friend and like a sister to me and now you're gone."

"You still have friends Sophie. And Ray is your friend, he always has been. You're just going through a rough patch. Things have been hard and some of it is due to circumstances beyond your control. But hang in there. Remember what he told you when you eloped? That he would always try to do his best. He has tried. He reminded you of that a while ago. Remember the ice storm and the dinner by the wood stove?"

"You were there?" she asked Kathy. "I'm always with you Sophie." Looking back towards the Bay of Naples for a second Sophie then she turned to say something else to Kathy, but she was gone.

SUMMER WEDDINGS PART TWO
A BACKYARD WEDDING

The bus from New York pulled into South Station in Boston at four P.M. He had called her when she was traveling through Connecticut somewhere and said he had caught lots of striped bass and would like to cook Katie and her dinner tonight. When she texted Katie, she said she would be home by six thirty. She couldn't wait for the two of them to meet each other.

She tried to look at her reflection in the scratched, dirty bus window. Did she really look that awful or was it the window? She fluffed up her hair, which had gotten flat from resting her head against her backpack while she slept. She pulled out a small mirror and some makeup and touched up her eyes then rummaged through her bag and found some rosy lip gloss. Oh well.

As she walked out onto Atlantic Avenue, she saw his car along the sidewalk just a little way down the road. Her heart started to pound and her legs were wobbly as she approached the Taurus. Her stomach felt queasy. She could see his seat was reclined way back and he looked like he might be sleeping. Multi-colored Mardi Gras beads were hanging from his rearview mirror. When she got to the car, the windows were open so she leaned in the passenger side and quietly said, "Hey. Are you asleep?" She thought her voice sounded shaky.

He moaned softly and stretched his arms out then rubbed his face. He turned towards her and bumped his knee on the steering wheel. "Ooooww." Rubbing his knee, he squinted with a puzzled look on his face. As he leaned over the passenger seat, he broke into a huge smile. "Why it's you." He made a funny face, like he was doing a double take. "Or is it?"

"Were you expecting someone else? And do you really know the lines to every movie you've ever seen?" She smiled shyly.

"Only the ones I've watched a few times. I'm really better with the mafia movie dialogue. It's just I was asleep and when I woke up I thought I was Gregory Peck waiting outside a bus station in Rome and Audrey Hepburn had popped her head in my car."

"What do you think?" She was still a little nervous, not knowing what he really thought of her haircut.

Trying to sound more like Peck, he said, "I like it," then he paused for dramatic effect. "A lot!"

"Stop it," she laughed. "Honestly?"

He chuckled and reached over to the door handle, pulled it and pushed the door open. "Get in here, gorgeous. I need to smother you with kisses." She opened the door, passed him her bags, which he tossed in the back seat and hopped in the car. He wrapped his arms around her, kissed her and slid his hand up her neck, running his fingers through the hair at her nape. "Turn around, I've gotta get a look at this." She shook her head and distracted him by kissing him some more. "You survived the weekend I see. You'll have to tell me all about it."

"I missed you so, so much. I was so lonely without you."

"I missed you too." He was kissing her neck and running his hands through her short hair. "God, you're adorable. Hey, can I hear you say that French thing you texted me?"

She whispered in his ear, "Je t'adore" as a car honked its horn. He continued to kiss her for a few minutes more, burying his face in her neck, inhaling her very essence as she buried her face in his soft, thick hair that smelled like springtime. He slowly moved his hand up her skirt, pulled her panties down then slipped his fingers inside her, stroking her as she rocked back and forth. Then he slowly sat up, ignoring the irate driver waiting for his parking space. Smiling contentedly, he put the car in drive and merged into the traffic passing by.

When they got upstairs to her apartment, it was only five o'clock. He put the cooler of fish on the kitchen counter and wrapped his arms around her waist. "An hour and a half 'til Katie gets back. Are you thinking what I'm thinking? Because I really need to see you with your clothes off."

"Well then, let's not waste any time. Come with me." She took his hand and led him to her room.

* * *

The three of them had a great time making dinner. He grilled the fish and she made a salad of baby spinach, sliced pears, cranberries, walnuts and goat cheese. "See, I'm learning to cook. I invented this salad myself."

He laughed and rolled his eyes. "I don't think making salad counts as cooking. Although this salad is award winning, restaurant quality. The best salad I personally have ever had."

Katie contributed a batch of homemade chocolate chip cookies. He and Katie seemed to hit it off right away and she told him all sorts of funny stories of their childhood in Vermont, like the time they ran away after one of the bad haircuts with only a grocery bag of Oreo cookies. They lasted a couple of hours hiding out behind Katie's garage and when the Oreo's were gone, they decided to go back home. No one had come looking for them.

"Also, there were some boys near our house who had a tree house and we were constantly sneaking up there when we knew they were at baseball practice."

"My sister Ava and her friends would do that too. They'd bring dolls up there and play house. I would get my mother's Lysol and wash the place like it was contaminated or something. We made Keep Out signs and NO Girls Allowed but it didn't work." He told them a story about the time he tried to protect the entire neighborhood from a huge underground hornet's nest. He dropped a giant rock on it but the bees escaped before the rock landed and he got gang stung. His mother had to take him to the emergency room "You should have seen me. I was so swollen, I looked like a deformed monster."

After dinner they all took a walk because it was hot in the apartment. When they passed CVS, he noticed fans were on sale and bought three more for their apartment. When they got back he set up all the fans for cross ventilation, some blowing into the apartment and others blowing out. It felt like air conditioning.

"This is awesome." Katie gave him a big hug. "I knew I was going to like you."

"Same here. We have a lot in common and most importantly, we both love this girl." He grabbed her hand, pulled her close and kissed her. "She blushes very easily, doesn't she? Do you remember when I met you on the train that night? When you tapped me on the knee while I was singing out loud, making a fool of myself?"

"I didn't think you noticed that. I had been running for the train so I was hoping my cheeks were already flushed." She blushed even more and her face felt warm as he kissed her again. He whispered in her ear, "You also had some kind of magical, sensual look on your face when I knew what the undertoad was." She looked up at him with wide eyes, incredulous.

Katie made a giant bowl of popcorn and they all settled in to watch To Catch a Thief with Cary Grant and Grace Kelly. Katie liked old movies even more than she did. During the scene when they were riding along the Riviera, Katie pointed out this was close to where Princess Grace died in a car crash. "Princess Diana died in a car crash too. Tragic princesses."

She realized she had never told Katie about his parents. She turned to look at him sitting in the middle of the two girls, with the bowl of popcorn in his lap. He seemed to know what she was thinking and put his arm around her. "There are no real life fairy tales. No one's immune to tragedy, right? It's okay."

Katie looked over at them. "Am I missing something?"

"My parents died in a car crash when I was eighteen."

"Oh my God, I'm so sorry. I didn't know that."

"It's okay, how would you know that?" He passed her the bowl of popcorn. Later that night they made love again and as she lay in his arms afterwards she mentioned her sister Monica's wedding.

"Another wedding? And you're a bridesmaid again?"

"Yeah, lucky me. Although this wedding will be different. Still stressful but different stress. Just the usual family stress. Would you like to come as my date?"

"Are you kidding? I'd love to come. I can't believe you waited this long to invite me."

"I thought you'd be bored. It's in three weeks in Vermont, in the backyard of the house I grew up in. My older sister Maria and her husband Josh bought the house when my parents moved to Florida."

"Bored? No way, this is exciting. I get to see the driveway where Jennie kept vigil. The secret back stairway you ducked out of in the obscene mini skirt. Hey, do I need a suit? Because I'll have to buy one."

"No, it's a casual wedding. A nice shirt and khakis will suffice. Katie is coming too. Maybe we could all drive to Vermont together?"

"Definitely. I'm in."

* * *

He slept over Wednesday night before the wedding and they left early Thursday morning, driving in his car. "Buckled up ladies?" he asked as he buckled himself into the driver's seat. Everyone was very competitive with the car games. They started with the alphabet game because as she pointed out there would be more businesses and road signs closer to the city. He said, "I'll play only if you also make the letter Q an exception." Laughing she said that was okay. She won again anyway despite the change in rules. He turned around to the back seat and told Katie, "I should have warned you that game is rigged in her favor. She seems to always win."

Katie laughed. "It's because she's never driving and she rides shot gun. It's harder for the driver or from the back seat. She's positioned to win."

He nodded in total agreement and gave Katie a thumbs up while she just ignored the two of them. Katie suggested a game called I'm going to the beach. You had to name something you were bringing to the beach and then the next person had to add something and list all the things that came before. "I'm going to the beach and bringing a beach towel, flip flops, a book etc." She won that game too. He suggested twenty questions which Katie won.

"Okay, no more games."

"You're just a sore loser." She leaned over and kissed his cheek.

"Am not. I mean I don't like to lose, but I'm not sore about it. Well, maybe a little." He laughed then turned up the volume on the radio and started singing. When Beyonce's 'Halo' came on, she and Katie knew all the words and sang along with great feeling and passion. When the song was over, he put his fingers in his mouth and gave one of those loud, piercing whistles you hear at concerts sometimes. "That was awesome. A truly spiritual experience."

Katie piped up from the back seat. "Hey, has she told you about the time she tried to start a union at a factory she worked at one summer?"

His eyes lit up and he looked at her with a smile. "So you're already a union organizer. You were asking me all those questions the other day but it sounds like you already know what you're doing."

"I wasn't starting a union. I just called the Massachusetts State Labor Board."

"Ok, this I have to hear."

She sighed and looked in the back seat. "Thanks Katie."

Katie just laughed. "He's a card carrying member of the International Brotherhood of Electrical Workers, right? He'll like this story." He looked in the rearview mirror, smiled and winked at Katie.

"Oh all right. So, the summer after my freshman year in college the only job I could find was on an assembly line. I was renting a house on Cape Cod with friends from school and desperately needed a job to pay rent or I'd have to spend the rest of the summer back in Vermont. It was a packaging company for pens and pencils. You know the packages of pens you see hanging on those pegboard racks in stores? The front is clear and you can see the pens under a plastic covering which is glued to a cardboard backing?"

"Yeah I know what you mean."

"Well okay, I was on the line for the multi-colored pen packages. There were four of us, two on each side of the conveyor belt with a box of red, green, blue or black pens. You picked up a handful at a time and the plastic covering would come down the line and you'd drop one pen in each covering then it would go through a machine which glued the cardboard backing on. We would do this eight hours a day. Eight very long hours."

"Holy shit, how do you find these jobs? I was a lifeguard in the summertime."

"I'm just lucky I guess. There was a lady I always worked on the same line with who taped a little sheet of paper onto the side of the belt with the metric system conversions on it. We were trying to learn that to help pass the time."

Katie looked puzzled. "So how come when Andre said two centimeters, you didn't know the equivalent in inches?"

She laughed. "Because I didn't stay long enough to master it. Anyway, one day the shipment of pens hadn't arrived and they rang the bell ten minutes after we got there. They usually only rang the bell for breaks and lunch. We all went in the cafeteria and they told us to punch out and we would be paid for fifteen minutes. They were rounding up they said, like they were doing us some kind of favor."

"That's bogus. They can't do that. Isn't there a minimum amount of time you need to be paid for?"

Katie clapped her hands and laughed. "Bingo. See, he knows this stuff too."

"Yup, if you show up to work in most states you have to be paid for a minimum amount of time. I had taken a labor law class freshman year and learned about the minimum show up law. So I got the number for the state labor board and they told me it was three hours in Massachusetts. When the boss saw a group of us still standing around the cafeteria, he came over and asked what was going on. I told him I had called the labor board and they were required to pay us three hours for showing up."

He was laughing and shaking his head. "You go girl. Awesome. What happened?"

"We all got paid for three hours but I got laid off. For simply knowing my rights. I mean they said it was due to a shortage of work but no one else got laid off. You know I forgot all about that Katie. I was just like Joan at work, an employee at will. They were always speeding up the belt too. Once we got good at a certain speed, they'd make it go slightly faster."

He laughed again. "Like Lucy and Ethel in the chocolate factory?"

"Yes, exactly. It's like where I work now, you edit a certain amount of papers, and get good at it then you have to do more. Shit, it's 21st century factory work. I went to college for this? Anyway, it all worked out. I got a job waitressing at a fried seafood joint near the beach and made a lot more money."

He looked over at her, smiled and shook his head. "What did I tell you? Waitressing and writing. When are you gonna listen to me?"

She smiled back at him and stroked his cheek with the back of her hand. "Hey, I'm hungry and I've gotta pee. Montpelier's the next exit." They stopped for a bathroom break and some nourishment. The culinary school had a bakery and they loaded up on scones, muffins, cookies and iced coffees to go. When they got back to the car he handed her the keys. "You take it into Burlington. I've got my guitar in the trunk, I can play us some tunes if you want?"

Katie jumped up and clapped. "Yes. Let's do that." She drove, with Katie riding shotgun and their serenading minstrel in the back seat. He played a lot of Jack Johnson and also knew Catch the Wind and Blackbird. The girls sang along to a fairly decent rendition of John Mayer's Heart of Life. Whether he agreed or not, he had a nice voice. She turned around and asked him, ""Has anyone ever mentioned you sound like Eddie Vedder?" He scoffed, "Absolutely not. He's amazing."

When they dropped Katie off at her parents' house they all got out of the car and hugged . "That was the best drive home to Burlington I have ever had. See you two at the wedding."

* * *

They were upstairs in her old bedroom on the third floor, getting ready for a BBQ at her aunt's house. Her parents were staying there. He had met all her sisters but her parents arrived late that day from Florida so he hadn't met them yet. He had really hit it off with Maria's husband Josh who had enlisted him to help set up for the wedding and do all the wiring and lighting. The ceremony was taking place outside in the yard. The weather was looking spectacular for Saturday although a tent was being set up just in case. Dinner would be served in the yard while the music and dancing would take place in the barn later in the evening.

She was stressing about seeing her parents. "What exactly is it you're upset about?" he asked her.

"My mother is going to make a big deal about my hair." She started to mimic her mother with an all knowing, superior tone in her voice. "I knew you would realize short hair looked better on you. It was just a matter of time. Ugh. I just don't want to hear it. If she only knew the torture she put me through. And please don't get involved in any long conversations with my father. He will try to trick you into revealing too much."

"Too much of what?"

"I don't know, something he can use against you."

"I think you're being paranoid." She was sitting on the end of the bed wearing the dress she wore with Nick the night he gave her the gift certificates. The one with the puffy bottom and the blue polka dots. He was unpacking his clothes. He bought a beautiful light blue short-sleeved shirt for the wedding, made of some kind of brushed silk material that was really, really soft. It was going to look awesome with his eyes. He seemed to be taking this all very seriously as he also bought a new pair of khakis, shaved his scruffy beard and got his hair cut again. This time he went to a salon and it was still slightly long, collar length, but more layered and much shorter in the front, with curls just brushing his ears. It was a head full of thick, tousled, wavy soft curls and she loved it.

"Chill, okay? It can't be that bad. They're your parents."

"Exactly."

He sat down next to her and took her hand. He sweetly kissed her and stroked her hair. "You look really pretty. What can I do for you?"

She shrugged. "Nothing, it's just me."

"We're in your childhood bedroom. How about something really naughty? I can see you're the rebellious type."

"Huh?" He laid her back down on the bed and ran his arm up her leg. The strapless silver sandals she was wearing dropped to the floor. He lifted her a little bit and moved her up the bed then tugged at her panties.

"Hey, we have to be at my aunt's in twenty minutes."

"We'll be fashionably late." He kissed her again, more intensely this time. "Ok I'm going under."

"What?" He lifted the puffy skirt on her dress and his head disappeared underneath. "What are you doing?"... "Oh my." She felt his tongue probing her and she let out a long, low moan.

When they did arrive fashionably late to her aunt's, a full forty five minutes late, her mother made an immediate bee-line for her. "Where have you been, you're late. Your sisters told me you cut your hair. You look so nice. And you must be the new boyfriend." Her mother gave him a big hug. "Don't you think she looks nice with her hair short?"

She just stood there holding his hand, which he kept squeezing. She smiled a dreamy, silly sort of smile. He wrapped his arm around her waist and said to her mother, "I think she's gorgeous anyway she wears her hair." He had a dopey smile on his face too.

* * *

The day of the wedding was a perfect summer day, sunny and warm but not too hot. The weekend was going really well. Her sister Monica had kept her plans very low key. The rehearsal dinner had been at a local Italian restaurant where they had always gone for special occasions like graduations and birthdays. The food was served family style.

Everyone seemed to love him. Maria told her he and Josh were becoming fast friends along with Mike, Monica's fi-ance. Sara said he was like the brother they never had and their Dad seemed to really like him too. "You're kidding?" She wasn't sure what to make of this news. Her boyfriends were always picked for shock value, like Jared. She dated him her senior year and went to the prom with him, where she didn't have formal pictures taken because they had hid out by the dumpsters getting high. He had about twenty tat-toos, always dressed in black leather including for the prom and wore black ear stretchers. He rode a motorcycle, angering her father beyond belief. Every night she left the house that year he sat up listening to sirens in the distance and pacing the floor. He was so relieved when she left for college that fall. She felt bad about that now.

On the opposite end of the spectrum was Nick but she knew her father wouldn't like him either. After all, her Dad had staged protests on campus when Bush decided to invade Iraq. He made signs saying "No War for Oil". He hated Dick Cheney with a passion. Every Wednesday night, peace vigils were held in the center of town and he was a regular participant. She knew he had influenced many of her own opinions. Liberal politics were the religion in her house growing up. Do Unto Others, There but for the Grace of God and To Whom Much has Been Given Much Will be Expected took on a secular, political twist. Despite the changing political times, her father was a product of the sixties and never gave up his ideals. Therefore, Nick with his capitalist goals and lust for earning lots of money was as anathema as Jared in her father's book.

Her mother had discovered he had a great eye for colors so she enlisted him as her head assistant wedding planner. She was calling him her Best Boy! He worked all afternoon stringing little white lights around the trees in the yard and hanging them from the rafters of the barn. The morning of the wedding, he was up at the crack of dawn, getting the yard ready. Bales of hay were being stacked like benches and covered with colorful old quilts. Seating arrangements were set in conversational groupings around the yard. The barn had been full of old furniture her mother sold at consignment shops and these were all carried out to the yard or arranged along the barn walls-rocking chairs, wicker furniture, Adirondack chairs, antique benches. Old crates were used as coffee tables. The center of the barn was to be the dance floor and a stage was set up at the far end.

Long tables for eating dinner were lined up to the side of the yard and covered with more quilts and antique linens. She and her sisters were filling mason jars with wildflowers and small jelly jars with votive candles floating in colored water. At the edge of the yard wind chimes were strung in the trees and a few hammocks hung between some of the tall pines. He came up with the idea of putting the beer and wine on ice in an old claw foot bathtub. He pointed out that as the ice melted, it would just drip out the old drain. Her mother practically swooned.

The wedding was at five. She was going to get ready with her sisters and he wanted to take a quick nap so he could dance all night. He was very pumped about the fact the music was a local reggae band. "I love your family."

"You seem to be a big hit." She stopped him at the bottom of the stairs and as he leaned on the banister the knob at the top of the newel post came off in his hand.

"Hey, look at that." He tried doing his best Jimmy Stewart impersonation. "This is a very interesting situation. Apparently your family had a wonderful life living here." He smiled a huge smile, the one she fell for that night on the train.

She leaned over to kiss him, smiling and laughing, "I love you. You really are the best boy I've ever met."

* * *

About a half hour before the ceremony, she was stressing out over her hairpiece. It was a beautiful band of silk flowers, just three soft roses with green leaves on a twisted hemp rope that tied around their heads. It matched the silk rose colored, knee length dresses they were wearing. The problem was, there was a big knot in the back and everyone was wearing the knot under their long hair where no one would notice. Except her knot, which was resting on top of her short hair. She was trying not to freak out. As the youngest girl, she was always accused of being the crybaby in the family although she thought this was so untrue. Her mother took charge. "All right, I know who can fix this. I'll get the Best Boy."

"No Mom. He doesn't want to come in here. And stop calling him the Best Boy. You make him sound like he's five years old," she complained, sounding very cranky. Her mother bustled out of the room. "Agggh!" she groaned, falling back down on the bed in her sister's master bedroom where they were getting dressed and a photographer was recording this pre-wedding activity for posterity. When he came back to the room full of girls with her mother, he smiled sheepishly and sat down next to her.

"Come on, sit up. What's the matter?" She sat up and pointed to the big knot on the back of her head. "This looks stupid." He took it off and examined if for a minute. Her sisters were just standing there watching and the photographer snapped a photo of them on the bed.

He looked up at the photographer and put his hand up like he was fending off paparazzi. He laughed. "No photos, please. Can someone get me some scissors?" Her mother ran off to find some. He patiently started to untwist the hemp while everyone watched raptly. When he got the ends to one strand, he tied it off and cut the excess with the scissors her mother handed him, like she was a nurse in an operating room. He tied it back on her head and covered the now tiny knot with her short hairs. Her sisters started clapping.

"If anyone has any necklaces that are tangled up I can fix those too. I fixed three of them for my sister when I was in Colorado." He gave her a kiss and left the room.

Her sister Sara laughed and said, "Who was that man?"

Her mother said, "I love that man."

She plopped back down on the bed and groaned.

* * *

The wedding was a huge success. The bride and groom danced to One Love and everyone joined them. He requested 'Mellow Mood' because he had decided this was 'their song'. Grills were set up beyond the long tables and steak and swordfish kabobs were served along with various salads friends and family had made. A huge cheese selection was placed on three old Singer sewing machines set in a row with pots of flowers on the foot pedals underneath. Again she caught the bouquet. Again her first instinct was to toss it but when she saw him sitting next to her father smiling, she just blushed, curtsied and kept it.

They left for Newburyport late Sunday afternoon after he helped clean up the yard. Katie had decided to stay and visit with friends for a few days. She didn't have to work until Wednesday and would take the bus back to Boston. As they drove out of Burlington, he looked over at her. "I don't know why you don't like weddings. That was awesome. I had a great time, thanks for inviting me."

"It was nice. They just don't seem very romantic, making a big spectacle of things. What does it have to do with two people in love? I would rather run off and elope instead of shout out to the whole world, hey look at us, we're in love and getting married and spending lots of money so you all know. It's a huge cottage industry of florists and caterers and dresses and tuxedo rentals. It's big business."

"I don't think you're sister's wedding was like that. You're sounding jaded."

"You're right. It really didn't even cost my parents that much money."

"See, I'm right."

"Don't get cocky, you aren't always right."

"Are you tired? You seem really cranky."

"Hey, I noticed you were sitting with my dad during all that toasting and cake cutting and bouquet throwing rigama-role. What were you two talking about?"

"Some very interesting things."

"Really? Like what?"

"Well, he told me to ask you about Jared?"

She sat up straighter. "He didn't? Oh my God, I can't be-lieve him." Slouching back down in her seat again she put her bare feet on the dashboard and sulked. "I am not talking to you about Jared. That is ancient history."

"Are you wearing your seat belt?" She glared at him. "You don't have to tell me about Jared. Your dad kind of told me some of it. Ear stretchers? Really?" He laughed. She tried not to smile but couldn't help herself. "I was eighteen. What else did he tell you?"

"Hmm. He told me the principal called you into his office because you were on some list of top ten IQ's in your senior class? He thought you should be making high honors and was encouraging you to try harder. But it backfired because you intentionally got all C's your last semester. But fortunately, you had already gotten a scholarship."

"What a blabber mouth. I told you to watch out for him. And weren't you the one who also wouldn't take advanced math classes?"

"Yeah that's why I understand you. He was saying this stuff not me." He reached over and tousled her hair. "By the way, you said it would be me he would be interrogating."

"Guess I was wrong about that. See I can admit when I'm wrong."

"He did say some really nice things too. I think you're his favorite, he said you're the most like him."

"WHAT? No way. I am not like him."

"He said you were a restless soul. You would never be content. Sometimes you wanted the conventional things in life but when you got them you felt trapped and bored and had to move on. You were always seeking something new. Thinking life would be better somewhere else. And he knew this because he was your father and he was like that too. He said the man who caught you was going to have to like adventure and change. He would need to be spontaneous and very patient."

"Why on earth was he telling you this stuff?"

"Because he likes me. But he told me not to tell you that. Because that would most likely backfire on me, like the principal." He laughed. "A very interesting thing he said was YOU were Trouble."

"I was Trouble?" She looked at him incredulously.

"Yes you. Not the boys you were bringing home. He said you had a tendency to shoot yourself in the foot. Rebel even when it was not in your best interest. But he really wants you to quit your job and write. He thinks your job is bad for your spirit. He said you should waitress part time so you can write and when I said I had told you the same thing he slapped me on the back and said 'you hang in there son, you might just be the best thing that's ever happened to her' but I wasn't supposed to tell you that either."

"Then why are you telling me?"

"Because I think he's right and he might just know you better than you know yourself. He is your Dad after all."

BE BRAVE

Early June was always the nicest time of year in the Ryan yard. Lilacs and apple trees were in bloom and their scent perfumed the air. Sophie was outside raking and spreading bark mulch. Some of the gardens needed professional help but the peonies and rose campion were abundant enough that they covered the weeds that would overpower the gardens by July. She tried to do some weeding too and Lynn was there helping. Lynn would garden anywhere, any time because she loved it so much and she was just an amazing friend. Ray leaned out the upstairs window in the addition. "Sophie, could you come up and give me a hand?"

She put down her rake and met him in the unfinished master bathroom off their bedroom. "I just need a hand getting this piece of sheetrock on the ceiling. It's going to be really tricky over the shower enclosure here. It's a tight space and a tough angle."

"Okay just tell me what to do."

Ray explained what he wanted from her, showing her a long piece of wood with a triangle at the end which would hold the sheetrock against the ceiling once it was in place. He demonstrated how he wanted her to use it. Sophie stood behind Ray while he maneuvered the heavy piece of sheet rock into the corner and above the shower unit. She held the back end, while getting pressed against the wall as Ray lifted it to the ceiling and tucked it into place. Then she grabbed the triangle bar and slid it carefully along the sheetrock until it was wedged against the ceiling. Ray got the nail gun, climbed on a stepladder and nailed the sheetrock into place. "Nice job."

"That was heavy." She shook her arms while Ray gave her a kiss.

The following weekend Sophie and Lynn were painting the doors on the deck. A radio was playing loudly and they sang along to some of the songs. Lynn stepped back to look at the door she was working on. "We're really making progress here. What can we paint next?"

"We've got the door and entranceway over near the garage. The rest of the house Ray did last year and it's still looking pretty good, don't ya think?"

"Yeah it's looking great. So when does it go on the market?"

Ray poked his head out the window upstairs. "When I'm done."

Sophie shouted back at him. "Early July dear, whether you're done or not." She turned and whispered to Lynn. "If he doesn't have a deadline this will drag out forever. I wanted it on the market in early June when the yard looked awesome. Look at the lilacs, they're already past peak."

"And the market is good right now, things have been improving and interest rates are still low. You've got to move now."

Ray shouted, "I can hear you two out there."

Sophie shouted back. "Get back to work up there and stop eavesdropping." She looked back at Lynn. "He's golfing at three with Miguel. The master of distraction. They went fishing for striped bass last Monday on the Cape."

"Is there any male past time Ray doesn't like?"

"Not that I know of and friends who'll do it with him? It would take more than two hands to list them all." Ray poked his head out the window once again. "Have we earned a lunch break yet?"

"Yes we have. I'll make it."

"And a cold brewski please."

"Well Lynn, in that case, we get wine with lunch. I've got a bottle of wine chilling in the fridge."

"Better days are coming Sophie."

"I'm actually beginning to think they might be."

* * *

Later that week, Sophie was at work emailing her old college boyfriend. Somehow he had found her work email. She couldn't remember if it was their alumni website when she was unemployed and networking or if it was through LinkedIn. Anyway, they corresponded every once in awhile.

She broke up with him a year after college. She wasn't ready to settle down although they had dated all through college. She spent the rest of her twenties traveling, including a backpacking trip through Europe with Kathy. She bounced around various accounting jobs and took a year off to waitress and ski bum in Vail. She traveled cross country twice, once with Ray. She always made just enough money for the next adventure. She thought that might explain why she was stuck in a cubicle this late in her so-called career. Ted was a nice guy but much more settled than her. He was making quite a name for himself in the engineering field and also wrote music and played in a band on the weekends.

They were having an ongoing conversation about writing. He had told her he still cherished the letters she sent him in college and that he always thought she was a great writer. He had recently found those letters in the basement of his house in upstate New York. He told her he would give them to her and that they still had the faint scent of L'air du Temps. She forgot she wore perfume. She didn't wear perfume anymore and she found it hard to believe she not only wore it back then but also had a signature scent. Maybe she should start wearing it again she mused. That afternoon an email came in from him.

Obama is really an amateur. I can't think of anything he has done in almost four years to help the economy. I thought he was a unifier not a divider. Would you agree?

Oh that's right she thought, we're also having a political discussion. Maybe that was another reason she broke up with him? She couldn't remember now but marriage was hard enough. If she were married to a Republican it would certainly be a house divided. But maybe money wouldn't be a source of so many arguments? When she got overwhelmed with the bills, she often said to her friends she should have married a Republican. She went to a business college for goodness sake, how did she not marry a CEO or hedge fund guy?

No I do not agree. Ask the people in Michigan and Ohio who work for the auto industry what Obama has done about jobs.

Hey Ted. I am going to be upstate next weekend. We are having a girl's weekend at Lynn's fishing cabin again. Maybe I can get the letters?

Two years ago, she and her friends had been in the Adirondacks on another girls' weekend and they had walked into a bar he was playing at. When he saw her, he was singing a cover of Neil Young's 'Rockin' in the Free World'. As she walked in, he immediately recognized her despite the fact her hair was now blond and she had gained a few pounds. He changed the lyrics to "Sophie O'Neill is rockin' in New York tonight". Her girlfriends where hootin' and laughing all weekend about this. She attributed it to the fact that women in their forties will look for romance anywhere they can find it even when it doesn't exist. He gave her a couple of his CD's that night and she was mentioned in two of the songs he wrote about his college days. Imagine that she thought, immortalized in song.

Gee I can't give up those letters yet. They have inspired me to write a new album titled Letters. I'm only half way through pouring over the letters. There are sooooo many good stories and songs in your words. It's funny how inspiration comes to us...

I can't believe you are going to use my copy! Hey I am going to need royalties on that you know. BTW my screenplay is now a novel.

That's so cool! I thought you told me that all copy is up for grabs????? Even the great writers like you steal wherever they find a good hook.

Give me a hook, it's mine after all.

The story/song is evolving. Maybe after I read the letters I should destroy them and let the sweetness of the memories linger.

Don't you dare.

Let the sweetness linger? Funny, she doesn't remember their relationship quite that way. What she remembered was heartache and too much time spent in the wrong relationship. She regreted she stayed with it so long. It should have ended two years earlier than it did.

Later that evening she stopped by the farmers market in town. Ray was golfing after work with Miguel. It was still early in the growing season for fruit and vegetables in New Hampshire. Nothing like farmers markets she had visited in Santa Monica and Napa. But there was locally raised beef and poultry available along with soaps, honey, some early lettuce, alpaca wool and a Middle Eastern vendor selling tabbouleh and baba ganoush.

"Can I try your tabbouleh? My roommate in college was Lebanese and her mother would send huge tubs of homemade tabbouleh every few weeks. I have yet to find anything that tastes that good in the supermarket."

The young man selling his products was dark and handsome, around thirty years old and extremely flirtatious. "You will love this. It will bring back memories of your youth." He put some on a pita cracker and handed it to her. "Ummm. You're right. I feel twenty one again. I'll take some." As he packaged it for her in a plastic container he said "You don't look a day over thirty." She laughed. "You're a very good salesman. Your tabbouleh is delicious."

Next she stopped at a tent where a woman with loose, wavy gray hair flowing to her waist was selling goat cheese. She looked like a gypsy with her Birkenstocks, extremely large hoop earrings and the tattered hem of her Indian print skirt brushing the ground. She had varieties of cheese set out along with a basket of crackers. Sophie tried the first one. "This is excellent. You make these here in New Hampshire?"

"Yes, just down the road in Kingston." She reached out to shake Sophie's hand. "My name is Sally Kingston." She handed her a card. Sophie looked at the card and laughed. "Sally Kingston from Kingston, New Hampshire?"

"Yes. You're thinking coincidence, right?"

"Sure."

"More like serendipity. I had been working as a microbiologist for a drug company and living in Haverhill, Massachusetts. I didn't like my job very much, too much stress and I disagreed with some of the policies of the company. I was just extremely unhappy."

Sophie was nodding as the woman looked directly into her eyes, the window to her soul.

"One Sunday afternoon my husband and I took a drive through the countryside as we often did on Sundays. We ended up in Kingston on Haverhill Road and saw a farm for sale."

"A farm in Kingston on Haverhill Road?"

"Yes. That was five years ago. We bought the farm and some goats, left our jobs at the age of fifty and started making cheese. I sell it at the farmers markets around here and to several local restaurants in the area. I also travel to Brooklyn once a week to the large market they have there on Saturdays and several of the farm to table restaurants in New York also buy my cheese."

"Wow. It must be hard work though? Getting up early, milking the goats, making the cheese?"

"Nothing's too hard when you're doing what you love. We didn't think about it, we just did it. We had no fear."

"I work in accounting, in a cubicle. I hate my job too. I have a dream of running a bed and breakfast in the islands. I'm going to be fifty this year too."

"Life is short dear."

"I know that. I lost my best, life long friend to breast cancer four years ago. Life is very short."

"It's never too late to find yourself. Follow your dream. Would you like some advice?"

"I would love some advice." Sophie was hanging on her every word.

"Be brave."

THE COMPANY PICNIC

One night after work, Dave and Helen picked her up at the Newburyport train station. There was a large surfing competition at Hampton Beach. It had started earlier this afternoon and she really wished she could have escaped work but she'd get to see the tail end of it at least.

She loved his aunt and uncle. They invited them to dinner quite often especially now that it was summer and they were grilling in the backyard. Helen offered to read her screenplay and had been extremely helpful, writing notes in the margins and offering advice. Dave was in Desert Storm and had very strong opinions on the current wars they were involved in. He thought if there was a draft people would think twice before voting for hawks and there would be far less war. "People who haven't seen war shouldn't decide to send other people's children off to fight."

He loved discussing politics with her, probably because she agreed with him on most everything. She thought her father and he would get along great. He thought she was very well informed. "Most kids your age don't pay attention to any of this. Don't even vote for Christ's sake. I hope they learned after this election that their vote does matter. They can change the future." Tonight he was very excited about the surfing competition. "Wait'll you see that nephew of mine surfing," he boasted to her.

"I've seen him a few times but the surf wasn't great. He tried to teach me but I was a disaster. It's not quite like skiing although he kept saying it was."

"Tonight's gonna be great. That storm the other day really kicked up the surf."

Helen had brought sandwiches and Dave had packed a cooler of beers and ginger ale. They spread a blanket close to the water and Dave spotted him right away. "There he is, on the blue board." He was cresting a wave and spinning around. " Aaaah, nice three sixty."

He was amazing out there on his board. Early in the evening, he rode low on the board catching a beautiful ride in the hollow pocket of a very large wave while it was breaking just over his head. Everyone on the beach started cheering. Dave told her he tubed it. The ultimate reward of surfing. "The waves don't usually get big enough in these parts but that was a decent one. I told you it was going to be a good night."

A couple of hours later, the sun fell lower in the sky, the wind shifted and the waves died down. And the hot dog on the beach that day walked out of the water carrying his board, shook his wet hair and ran towards the blanket where she was sitting and gave her a big kiss.

* * *

Katie got a job offer in D.C. It started in the fall. She was happy for Katie but a little depressed about this as it had been a great summer living together. "So I could come with you. I could look for a job down there."

"Hasn't he asked you to go to L.A. yet?"

"He hasn't talked about L.A. much."

"Well you need to talk to him. Maybe he isn't going anymore. He might not want to leave you."

"I'm pretty sure he's still planning to go."

"Well then, come right out and ask him. What are you afraid of?"

"That's he's going to leave without me."

"I don't see how that's possible."

"Or if he asks me to go maybe I'll get cold feet and say no."

"Now why the hell would you do that?"

"Because according to my father I have a tendency to shoot myself in the foot. And I'm afraid of commitment."

"Well you need to get over that. You moved in with Nick, didn't you?"

"Yeah and it didn't work out. I think in retrospect, I moved in for the wrong reasons. I don't think it was real love. This feels like the real thing but how do I trust myself? Besides, nothing lasts forever. Just the thought of forever is pretty scary."

"You are crazy. I think you need a shrink. Forever is not scary, it's what we're all looking for, isn't it?"

"Yeah but two out of three marriages end in divorce. I'd rather go out on a high note."

"No you wouldn't and you know it. Stop it. Do you remember that nursing home I waitressed at in high school? When I used to wear those batik headbands all the time?"

"Oh right, you were headband girl."

"Very funny. Did I ever tell you about the old couple I waited on every night? The husband was almost entirely deaf but he had a little box thing that looked like an IPod and his wife could shout in it when she wanted to tell him something. She would usually order dinner for him because she knew what he liked but once in awhile she would shout out the special to him."

"That's cute."

"Most of the time they just sat there in comfortable silence. One night I was given a different station and she was very upset. The hostess told me she had asked for me to come to her table. She really liked me and always complemented me on my earrings and headbands. When I got to the table she pointed to her hair. She had made a headband like mine but hers was a chiffon type of material with red roses. She was so proud of it. Her husband smiled over at her with such a look of love on his face and reached out and held her hand."

"Hmmm. That's a really sweet story. What are you telling me?"

"Sometimes love lasts forever but you will never know unless you try. Talk to him about L.A."

* * *

The day of the annual company picnic was a spectacularly beautiful day without a cloud in the sky. The office closed at noon and everyone would be going to a beach that was only a few miles away. Dan had driven to work that day and offered her a ride.

The tents and barbeques were set up on a grassy hill above a small beach. A gentle breeze was blowing. The weatherman called this a top ten day. People were sitting in groups on the grassy hillside eating lobsters and drinking beers. She was sitting with Dan and a few other people she knew. Dan had wandered over to the group from accounting sitting right next to them. She only knew the woman Sophie who sat in the cubicle next to Dan. She was always very friendly and she often bumped into her in the ladies room. She sensed Sophie wasn't happy in a cubicle either as she always said things like "Thank God it's Friday" or "Is it Friday yet?"

Suddenly, she heard people shouting, "Stop." She looked up and saw a white van backing down the hill into a group of people. At first she didn't understand what she was looking at. People were shouting and jumping up. The van just kept backing down the hill in what seemed like slow motion. Why was someone backing into a group of people? Wasn't the driver looking in the rearview mirror? Paper plates, napkins, and lobsters were flying through the air and scattering across the lawn as people ran from the oncoming van. A few people actually ran towards the van and managed to stop it, placing a rock under the tire to keep it from rolling anymore. She was only a few yards away from all of this. She looked at the people standing around her and everyone looked like they were in a state of shock. Some people were crying.

When the van had finally been stopped, it was apparent some people had been hit. She saw feet sticking out from underneath. People either began running and screaming, stood their stunned or made calls on their cell phones. She stood there stunned. It didn't take long though for someone of authority to ask everyone to go down the hill to the beach. There was only one dirt road into the spot they were picnicking at so they didn't want people leaving yet and blocking access for the emergency vehicles already on their way.

She grabbed her beach bag and her beer, wondering if it was inappropriate for her to finish the full beer she had just gotten but desperately wanted anyway. Everyone started walking down the sandy path to the beach. She saw Dan and grabbed his arm. "Oh my God. I can't believe this."

"No shit. My head is really fucked up right now. I'm thinking about my Dad. This is so fucked up."

Down on the beach people were milling around in groups, stunned and mostly quiet. A few families were there who were unrelated to the company picnic. Sailboats were bobbing on their moorings and the sun was sparkling on the water. A perfect summer day.

She finished her beer quickly and started to panic about the people she loved, her family and her boyfriend. She wasn't sure why she was worried about everyone. They were most likely going about their day. But weren't they all just going about their day? She suddenly felt an overwhelming urge to call her boyfriend although she had no idea how she would articulate what just happened. She didn't want to alarm him. She knew how he was about sudden tragedies and random catastrophes. Airplanes that flew into tall skyscrapers on beautiful days like today, high school students in trench coats shooting classmates. The phone call at two in the morning, the police at your door on an icy night.

She walked down the beach along the water's edge, away from her co-workers. It seemed so strange to being sharing this event with so many people she barely knew. And the ones she did know, she didn't know that well. Except Dan, who seemed to be dealing with his own turmoil off at the other end of the beach. It seemed so odd that she spent so many hours in a day with these people but couldn't talk to anyone right now. She walked in the water up to her knees. She was wearing a short sundress. The hem was getting wet as the gentle waves lapped her legs. She dialed his number.

"Hey aren't you at the picnic?"

"Yes but something awful has happened. I'm okay. I just..."

"What happened? Are you sure you're okay? You don't sound okay?" He started to sound really nervous.

"Yes, yes I'm okay. I shouldn't have called you and got you all alarmed. I'm sorry. There was an accident and some people got hit by a van. I think some of them are not okay." She started crying.

"Honey what are you talking about? Aren't you at the beach? Who got hit by a van?"

"I don't know. I don't know how or why it happened. We were sitting on a hill, eating lobsters and this van just started rolling down the hill."

"Where are you right now?"

"On the beach. We're waiting for the ambulances to come." She heard something and looked up to see a helicopter heading towards them. "Oh my God, I think one of those medical choppers is coming. Yes it's definitely a med flight and it's landing here."

His voice was getting louder and very panicky. "Where are you right now?"

"I'm on the beach standing in the water. I'm okay, the accident happened on the hill above us."

"Jesus."

"Listen we can't leave yet. I came with Dan and as soon as we can leave I'm going to get the train. I'll call you."

"Call me the second you're on your way. I'll come and get you. You're sure you're okay?"

"Yes. Are you okay?"

"Why wouldn't I be okay?"

"I don't know. Why isn't everyone okay? I love you." She suddenly felt an uncontrollable urge to go swimming. She wanted to plunge into the cool Atlantic, feel the water wrap around her and float on her back. She hadn't worn her bathing suit. But she did have new Victoria's Secret lingerie on. The undies were the kind that looked like short shorts and the bra looked like a bikini top. They were solid red and unlike most days her panties matched the bra because they were brand new. She thought they could definitely pass as a bathing suit.

She walked out of the water, put her cell phone in her beach bag and pulled her dress over her head. Then she turned and ran into the water, passing that woman Sophie who was standing in the water up to her ankles, staring off into the distance. She dove into a small wave and as she came up she flipped onto her back and floated, looking up at the blue, blue sky. With her ears underwater, everything sounded muffled and far away including a second helicopter passing overhead. The water felt so cool as it enveloped her, just like when she was lying in bed in the circle of his arms. She closed her eyes and bobbed along with the rhythm of the sea. She decided right then and there she was going to quit her job and go to L.A. When he picked her up at the train, she was telling him she was going with him.

* * *

When the train pulled into Newburyport, she saw him pacing back and forth on the sidewalk. She got up quickly, hopped off the train and ran to him. He wrapped his arms around her and hugged her very tightly. She started sobbing. "It's okay. It's okay. Come on, let's get you home." On the short drive back to his place, she tried to explain again what happened.

When they got upstairs he suggested he fill the bathtub. As she eased into the warm water, she realized every muscle in her body ached. He climbed in after her and turned the jets on. She leaned back and closed her eyes while they sat there quietly for a few minutes. She finally felt safe. "Hey, I need to talk to you." His voice sounded raspy and deep.

She opened her eyes. "About what?"

"L.A. I realize I've been kind of slacking. I'm confused. I'm not sure if you're ready to come with me and make that kind of commitment right now so I've considered not going. Just give you more time, ya know? But my friend Nate has been talking to some people he knows and he says he can definitely get me a job. But I need to get out there soon, the opportunity is now. It's something I've always wanted to do and I have to give it a shot. I want you to come with me."

"Oh my God. So do you think I won't come with you?"

"You seem to have some serious commitment issues. Maybe you need more time. You were talking about that job in New York. Then you started talking about moving to D.C. with Katie."

"Oh that. I sent my resume but I still haven't heard anything. Apparently my job isn't that great a resume builder like Nick told me it would be. Not for cool, exciting jobs at the New York Times anyway. And Katie says I can't come to D.C. with her. I have to ask you about L.A."

He chuckled, "I love that Katie. You need to listen to her more often." Stretching his leg across the tub, he poked her with his foot. "Listen, if you come you can write you know. You don't have to work. Writing will be your work. And Nate knows agents who read screenplays. I've talked to him about you. I have a place lined up to live in. It's a big house in Venice. Some rich dude's dad bought if for him and Nate is really good friends with him. Nate and his girlfriend live there and the rich dude and his girlfriend and two other guys. He doesn't charge a lot for rent 'cus his dad owns the place. It's got a pool. Nate says he would be cool with you staying with me. I already talked to him about it. I can pay the rent 'cus I was gonna be paying it anyway." He was talking fast, selling her on something he didn't realize she had already decided she wanted.

She floated over to him and put her finger on his lips. "Shhh. Slow down." She floated onto his lap and wrapped her legs around him. He took a deep breath and exhaled. "I went swimming after I called you and while I was floating out there I decided when I got here I was going to insist you take me with you to L.A."

"You were?" he said with a grin. Smiling she replied, "Yes. Life is short. Sometimes frighteningly short. It could all end on a beautiful, ordinary day. So I really need to make every day count. I need to be happy. You make me very happy." She kissed him then whispered in his ear, "Besides I need to find my cat."

Grinning, he said, "Oh, right. Jennie."

A DAY JUST LIKE TODAY

Sophie was mad at Ray. It was Saturday and he was golf-ing again while she and Lynn were painting the master bath-room. There was still a lot of work to do. The floor needed tiling and then the old bathroom needed to be ripped out and turned into a small laundry room and walk-in closet.

"This is so typical of him. He gets a burst of energy then his attention span wanders and he's off with Miguel and two other buddies of his golfing again. This is the second week-end in a row. It's now July and the house is still not on the market."

Lynn stopped painting and put her hands on her hips. "Hey we're just about finished here. I say we goof off too and go to the beach. It's a beautiful day."

"I say you're right. I have some cheese and crackers and a bottle of wine. We'll stop and get some lunch. Have a picnic. Let's go."

On the way to the beach, they stopped at a local Mexican place and got taco salads. They managed to find a parking spot close to the beach access and spread their blanket back near a sand dune. The tide was getting higher and beach real estate was shrinking fast. Sophie opened the wine and they ate their salads while discussing their kids and work. Lynn had found a part time job while Doug was consulting but they still didn't have health coverage.

"Well the Supreme Court did the right thing anyway so maybe those insurance exchanges will kick in sometime in the not too distant future. God, I've based so many decisions on getting health care instead of finding work I like. Making horrible career choices like working in a cubicle doing bor-ing, repetitive work just to insure my family." Sophie sighed and shook her head. "So Lynn, does this mean we have to like Justice Roberts now?""

"NO! And wait until 2014? I don't think we can afford insurance on our own until then."

"Well maybe I'll sell my house by then." Sophie knew she sounded slightly bitter. They sat quietly for a few minutes, looking out towards some surfers on the water. A group of teenagers were playing frisbee near by. Suddenly a frisbee whizzed towards them and hit Lynn in the calf. A very cute blond and bronzed eighteen year old boy ran up and said "Sorry ma'am."

"Did he just call you ma'am?"

"He did."

"Oh my God. I hate that. We're invisible women now. I'm looking at that kid thinking he's hot and he thinks I'm just some old lady. He doesn't even really see us. Not that there's anything worth looking at."

"Hey speak for yourself."

Sophie laughed. "You think you're hot, don't you? Because some guy said you look like Annette Benning."

"I am hot, I'm a movie star."

"What a day, huh? You know it was a day just like today almost a year ago that the accident happened at my company picnic."

"Oh my God, that's right. I can't believe you witnessed something like that."

"I know. It still haunts me. It was shortly after that I started writing."

"How's that coming along?"

"I'm almost done. Actually would you want to read it? It's no longer a screenplay, it's a novel."

"Really? Sure, what's it about?"

"The picnic. I remember suddenly seeing this van backing down the hill into a crowd of people picnicking. I kept asking myself what the hell is it doing? Doesn't the driver know people are sitting there? I couldn't get out of my mind the image of those white paper plates and red lobsters flying up in the air as people scattered across the lawn. It wasn't until a few days later we found out the driver had lost control. When the van finally did come to a stop, those feet sticking out from under it were such a frightening, sickening sight. I don't remember seeing people getting hit, maybe I blocked that out. But, knowing people were under there..." She shook her head and took a deep breath.

"Oh my God, how awful."

"It was such a beautiful, ordinary day then suddenly something so random and violent happened and someone lost their life. Imagine going to a company picnic and then in an instant, it turns into the last thing you ever do."

"That's the story?"

"Well, it's about a lot more than that. After it happened and they made us all go down on the beach, I was so confused and distraught. It was such a hard thing to process. Here I am standing at the water's edge on a picture perfect day unable to understand what I was feeling or what had just happened. I didn't really want to talk to anyone. I saw Dan briefly and he was really upset. I'm close to my boss but she wasn't at the picnic. Here I was surrounded by these people I spent more hours in a week with than my husband and kids and I had no one to talk to. So I just stood there looking at the sun glistening on the water and a few sailboats bobbing up and down. I really wanted to go swimming but I didn't bring a bathing suit. No way was I wearing a bathing suit at a company picnic. I may be invisible but that would sure get me noticed." Lynn laughed quietly and filled their cups with more wine.

"Suddenly a young girl who was a friend of Dan's ran by and dove into the water. I had seen her earlier, crying to someone on her cell phone. I envied her youth and her ability to strip down and I desperately wanted to go swimming too. I wanted to feel the embrace of the cool water. I needed that quiet, muffled sound you hear when you're floating because I had just seen a medical helicopter fly overhead. I knew something really bad had happened back up on the hill."

"What was her name?"

"I have no idea. A few weeks later Dan told me she quit her job and left for L.A. with some boy she had fallen in love with. Oh by the way, did I tell you Dan is leaving for L.A. in September?"

"No." Lynn laughed. "Did he sell his screenplay?"

"Not yet but he had been out there visiting friends and met a girl." She laughed. "One of Ray's favorite movie lines, 'I have to see about a girl.' Or something like that. Anyway, after that wine emergency about a month later, I watched Blue Valentine when I got home and started having all those dreams."

"Right. God I wish I was having those dreams."

"They are good." She laughed. "The girl who was swimming looked so much like a fairy or a nymph. She used to have long hair but she'd chopped it all off. She was like a mermaid floating out there. Like that fairy tale, Undine?"

"I don't know that one."

"Undine was a water nymph who had to marry an imperfect human to gain a soul. Anyway, I started to write this fairy tale about her. I made an entire life for her and the wonderful boy she fell in love with. The story began to take shape while I was driving everyday on my long commute to work. It would unfold like a movie in my mind. Which is why it started as a screenplay.

I remembered a time in Europe when Kathy and I were backpacking. We were on a train sitting with a couple from Ireland, a young boy and his girlfriend. The boy was quite a storyteller. We were in Spain somewhere, in the Pyrenees I think. We kept going into these tunnels carved through the mountains. No lights were on in the train so as we passed through the long tunnels we would sit there in total darkness. The boy was smoking a cigarette and he used his hands a lot when he was talking. All you could see was the light at the tip of his cigarette moving and swirling as he continued to tell his stories in the dark. They were just tales of his everyday life but they were fascinating. It was the first time I realized anyone's life could be interesting if you told the story right, even the boring parts.

Then I started having those dreams after I watched that movie. I would wake from them in the middle of the night and lie in bed listening to the three A.M. train rumbling by. I've always loved the sound of a train, it reminds me of back-packing. For me it is the sound of adventure and romance. Sometimes the whistle blows, as the train gets closer to my house. That's the sound of sadness and regret.

Every day I drive to work, I cross the railroad tracks before the parking lot. Some days I have to stop at the railroad crossing and wait for the train to pass. I park next to the train station. I dream of getting on a train and taking off some-where on an adventure instead of going to work in my cubi-cle. So as I wrote the story of the girl who looked like a water nymph, her fairy tale began on a train. But something annoy-ing happened while I was writing. Bits and pieces of Ray and I kept creeping into the story. The boy lived in an apartment above a garage like Ray when he first moved to New Hamp-shire, he worked in the building trades, and he had lots of friends and skied and surfed. She had very strong political views and hated working in a cubicle. She wanted to be a writer."

"Ray surfs?"

"No!" She laughed. "It's not entirely the Ray and Sophie story but it's similar. Better. They do have lots of things in common. I realized I was doing a rewrite of my life. It be-came clear to me I still carried the young girl I was inside me. She's with me always. She is inside of this fifty year old body and some days she's just screaming to get out. In my mind, I am still her. It was just yesterday that I was twenty five." She laughed. "When I see myself, I am wearing a bikini."

"The girl who went swimming reminded you of yourself."

"I guess. I think what I was trying to do was love my im-perfect husband by writing a story about him as a perfect boy. Very weird. But the strange thing is now I am in love with that boy and I'm starting to get along with Ray again. But then he keeps messing things up. All the hurt and hardships and fights over the years keep getting in the way. The years have created a distance I am not sure we can breach."

"Yeah I know what you mean. After years of marriage you pick up some bad habits and it's hard to break those patterns."

"Yeah bad habits. You're right Lynn." Sophie laughed. "It's easy to know when you've fallen in love. But it's not always so obvious when you fall out of love, is it? Is there a specific moment when it happens or is it a slow erosion made up of so many little hurts? You know what Ray said when I finally told him the next morning about the picnic? He asked what they were serving that day and I told him lobster, grilled chicken or a veggie burger. He said 'can you imagine if you saw the van coming and understood that in an instant you would be gone. And what if you'd ordered the veggie burger and your last thought was I should have ordered the lobster?'"

"Oh my God, he said that?"

"Well I know exactly what he meant. It was his usual live for the day mentality. The same mentality I have. The reason I fell in love with him was his sense of humor and his eternal optimism. He has such curiosity and a sense of adventure. I wouldn't want to die thinking I should have bought that inn in the islands, I should have traveled more, I shouldn't have spent so many days in a cubicle doing something I really didn't like. I don't want to die at my desk like Ida Blankenship. I always want to order the lobster."

"Yeah I guess I see what he meant."

"By writing this story I have been trying to forgive myself for the imperfect life I've lived and rewrite some of the choices I made. Try to learn to live with my regrets. Witnessing that accident made me realize that while I am still alive there should be no regrets, just opportunities to do better and be happier. All I want is one more beginning before I get too old. When everything is new and exciting and possible. I need to take chances again. Age shouldn't hold me back. It should make me bolder. And I'd like to do this with Ray but I don't know. I just feel if we can get out of this house and start somewhere new we could get that romance back. That feeling you have when you first fall in love. Before your first fight as Linda said. We could get to know each other again away from the bills and the hassles and the heartache."

"How does this story end?"

"I don't know. I'm still working my way to the end. I want a happy ending. That's what I realized I was doing. I wanted a better ending to that movie I watched the night the dreams began. I was writing myself out of the life I was living by starting at the beginning again and trying to get to a better, happier ending."

"Do you know Doug never proposed to me?"

"Ray never proposed to me either. No wonder you and I are such good friends. Ray and I were living together and just decided to elope."

"Us too. I always wanted a romantic proposal. You know, the guy gets down on one knee and says will you marry me?"

"Me too. You know what, I'll write one for us. After all, if I can write myself a happy ending, it's going to need a romantic proposal."

LET'S GO BACK TO THE BEGINNING

At a tall round table by a window in a cafe in Sedona, Arizona, she sat reading a book while sipping on a Sangria and nibbling at the free chips and salsa the waitress brought over. They had been on the road for four weeks, headed to L.A. and every day had been better than the one before. They spent a weekend in Denver with Ava and then she joined them for a week hiking in Vail and Aspen. It was obvious Ava and her brother were really close and she thought she might feel like a third wheel. But just like her aunt and uncle back in Newburyport, Ava was so happy to see her brother so obviously in love she fell in love with her too. While driving back to Denver, they all began to make plans to meet in Utah or Tahoe for a ski trip in the winter.

From Denver, they stopped in Colorado Springs to visit the Garden of the Gods on their way to Taos and Santa Fe. And from there it was on to the Grand Canyon where they met Mark in the national park cafeteria. They took two days to hike to the bottom of the Canyon. The first night they camped on the Kaibab Plateau and the second night by the banks of the Colorado River.

Four days later her legs were still really sore but she would never forget the morning they started to hike back out of the canyon. They broke camp while it was still dark. As the sun started to rise they were hiking along a trail lined with cactus, some blooming with little white flowers. The pink and pale blue of the sky against the red canyon rock was breathtaking. Except for the sound of their boots scuffling on the dry red dirt and their steady breathing, as the ascent got steeper, it was quiet all around them.

She was out in front of the two guys when suddenly a deer jumped across the trail, almost knocking her over. They all stopped and stood still as the deer hopped to the side of the trail then turned and looked back at them for several minutes in the early morning light. No one moved for a camera for fear the deer would startle. They all agreed later it was just a photograph they would always hold in their memory.

They dropped Mark off in Flagstaff to visit an old girl-friend who was going to college there. She invited them to stay for the night and it was so nice to sleep in a bed. Other than the weekend in Denver at Ava's, they had been camping the entire trip. Their plan was to spend one more night in Se-dona then go back to Flagstaff to get Mark. He was rejoining them for the trip to Vegas where he would stay a few days then fly home to Boston. It was still uncertain if his old girl-friend would join them for this leg of the trip. They hadn't heard how that was going.

Everyone was looking forward to staying at the Bellagio hotel. She planned to spend all her time in the pool or the hot tub. Then it was on to L.A. where he had an interview with a studio's electrical unit. He didn't want her to look for a job right away. He still insisted he wanted her to devote her time to writing and really give it a shot. He said he had things cov-ered financially.

* * *

That morning they split up. He was getting the oil changed in the car and she was running errands in town, getting neces-sities at the drug store and doing laundry. They planned to meet here at this cafe at two thirty but it was now three o'clock. Hopefully, there was nothing wrong with the Taurus. It sure had logged a lot of miles.

She looked up and saw a really handsome young guy walk in the door. He had brown hair that was cropped short on the sides and in the back. The top was just an inch longer, with no real part, just tousled and mussed up with a short cowlick sticking up in the back. He had incredibly blue eyes that twin-kled like the first star in the night sky. The star she always tried to wish on. He looked over at her and smiled the biggest, most charming smile that had ever been directed at her. He looked like a movie star. He walked over to her and rested his arm on the tall table. "Do I know you?" he asked flirtatiously.

"I don't think so. You don't look familiar," she teased.

"Hmm. You look like someone I met almost a year ago on a train headed into Boston one night. But maybe not, she had much longer hair. But she looked an awful lot like you. Can I sit down? Maybe we could get to know each other?"

"I don't know about that. I'm waiting for someone who I happen to be hopelessly in love with."

"Hopeless? That doesn't sound good." He paused, like he was thinking what to say next. "Hey, you know I just met a guy at the barber shop down the street. He told me he was supposed to meet a girl in this very cafe who he is madly in love with. I have reason to believe from the description he gave me and what you have just told me, that you are that girl."

"Really? Hopeless and mad, they sound like quite a pair. Did he have long, curly hair?" He had only a few wavy curls on the top of his head and she was feeling very bad about this but she didn't want him to know because he still looked very handsome.

He laughed while trying to keep a straight face. "He did when he came in but I don't think he does anymore. After all, he was walking into a barbershop and he mentioned something about an important interview he had in L.A. Anyway, get this. When he heard I was headed over here, he said he was running late and he had to go on ahead without her. So he asked me to deliver her a message and a small package."

He was wearing a light blue T-shirt that matched his eyes and khaki knee length cargo shorts with lots of pockets. The pockets on the side had buttons and the pockets in the front had a zipper. He put his left leg up on the rung of her chair.

"He has been carrying this very valuable package with him for four weeks now. The package has something in it that belonged to his mother and he would like this girl to have it now. He asked me to put it in my pocket with the zipper for safekeeping. He gave me strict instructions to give it to this girl as soon as I got to the cafe." She looked at him with a puzzled, apprehensive face.

"Go ahead. Look in the pocket."

"Are you sure you have the right girl?"

"I am absolutely certain you are the right girl."

"Okay. What was the message that goes with the package?" Her hand was shaking a little as she tried to pull the zipper. He put his hand over hers and helped her slide it open.

"After you receive the package, you are to go to the Bellagio in Las Vegas on Saturday and meet him on the sidewalk in front of the fountains. He said you might want to purchase a white dress for this rendezvous but he also said you didn't have to if you didn't want to. He did say you had some strong opinions on this subject. I'm not sure what he was talking about but he said he wanted to make sure he was getting everything right regarding the arrangements for this rendezvous. Again because you have some very strong opinions regarding this subject."

She started to shake with laughter but managed to control it. He winked at her.

"A car is going to meet you there and take you out to the desert where there is a small open air chapel carved from red rocks. You'll arrive just before sunset, just before the stars come out. The desert sky should be a pretty amazing backdrop for this auspicious occasion, all sunset, stars and moon glow." He looked down at her hand still resting on his thigh. "Reach inside the pocket."

As she slipped her hand into the pocket, she could feel a small velvet box. She pulled it out of his pocket and placed it on the table in front of her.

"Aren't you going to open it?"

"I'm not sure I'm ready to open it. I'm only twenty five and I don't know if I believe in happily ever after. I'm very happy the way things are right now and I just don't know if I want things to change. If I get married at twenty five that's a lot of ever after ahead of us. Real life begins awfully early."

"Things change every day. There are no guarantees anything will stay the same." He ran his hand through her hair which she had decided to keep short for now because he sincerely seemed to like it this way and didn't seem to be saying it just to make her feel better, which was something he was apt to do. "Every day is real life, the only one you get. Trust your heart. Be brave."

"Is that you talking or did he tell you to say that? Because he might have anticipated I would be hesitating over this."

"That was me talking but I am sure he would say the same thing. He did mention you could sometimes be difficult. But he also said nothing would change regarding your immediate plans. You will still move into the big house in Venice and you are to start writing full time when you get to L.A. He wants you to treat your writing like a full time job. Oh and the haircut's just for the interview. He said to remind you, hair grows back. He said you might be upset about this, yes?" She shook her head no. He laughed nervously. "Okay. So where was I? Umm, it's just that he loves you very, very much and he wants a commitment from you."

She laughed and looked down at the box. "Oh is that what he wants?" She spun the box around a few times. He put his hand over hers to stop her. "Honey, look at me." She looked up at him. "What are you afraid of?"

"That this feeling we have now of hopeless, mad love will not last. That twenty five years from now, maybe after several rough patches along the road, our love will die and the passion will fade. I'm afraid the idea of happily ever after is really a hopeless romantic fairy tale and only people who are mad believe in it."

"Well I can't guarantee what will happen. But I promise to do my best, every day. And maybe I am mad but I know I will love you twenty five years from now."

"Am I meeting him at the Bellagio this Saturday? Two days from now?"

"Yes exactly two days from now. Saturday at three P.M. It's all been arranged, he's taken care of everything. Katie and Mark will be in the limo when it picks you up at the Bellagio fountains and they will go out to the desert with you."

"Katie is coming?" He nodded his head and she smiled. He picked up the box, opened it and took out a beautiful diamond ring. He bent down on one knee and took her left hand. "Will you marry me?"

"Yes. I will marry you. Of course I will marry you. Was there ever any doubt?" He slid the ring on her finger.

"I thought for a minute there you might say maybe but I was counting on the possibility of yes."

"Of course it's yes. You're the best boy I've ever met." Suddenly she smiled at him playfully, with a mischievous look in her eyes. She pretended she was confused. "How am I getting to the Bellagio if he's already gone on ahead?"

He chuckled quietly, and then winked. "For the rest of your journey, wherever we go, you will be traveling with me. I promise to take good care of you. I will always love you." He stood up, wrapped his arms around her and they kissed. A very long, passionate kiss.

* * *

Two days later, very late that night, as he carried her in her white dress across the threshold of their honeymoon suite at the Bellagio, he stopped for a minute to ask her something. "Did you see that first star out there in the desert when we arrived?"

"Yes."

"You didn't forget to make a wish did you?"

"Of course not. But I can't tell you what it was or it won't come true. Did you make a wish?"

"Of course, you know I did." He kicked the door shut behind him and carried her to their king size bed.

HAPPILY EVER AFTER?

The weekend after she and Lynn were at the beach, Ray worked both days finishing the tile floor in the bathroom. He told Sophie he had scheduled the plumber to come on Tuesday to finish the final hookup and they would be able to use the bathroom.

"Awesome. I called the realtor and she's coming next weekend. Although you haven't finished the master bathroom and the floor in the bedroom, she says we need to get the listing online now. The real estate market is a lot better and summer is the time to sell."

"Okay, I'm ready. I've been looking at B&B's on line. And places in Florida. We could hang there, find work and be closer to the islands to look for something. Houses are so cheap in Florida, we could buy a place cash and rent it if we move."

"I sent our resumes to that guy in St. John who was looking for a couple to run his inn."

"That might not be a bad idea. Run someone else's place, see if we like it."

"My thoughts exactly." She walked over and kissed Ray.

He stroked her cheek. "Honey, we're gonna do it. Better days are coming. We will get you out of that cubicle."

* * *

Tuesday night, Sophie took her daily route home from work. It was hot in her car when she got out of work so she rolled down the windows and turned the air conditioning on. She put the volume up really loud on the radio and sang along. Passing the farm, she saw the corn was getting high. Later that evening when she arrived home, Ray was on the deck having a cocktail.

"Hey Soph, you want a drink? This raspberry lemonade you bought is great with vodka."

"Sure." She plopped down on a chair and gazed out at the river. They would really miss this river. Ray even more than she as he had gotten into ice fishing over the last few winters. But maybe an ocean view was in their future? Or at least a short walk or bike ride to the beach?

Ray came back out to the deck and handed her a tall drink. "Here you go. I'm going to grill that striped bass Miguel and I caught the other night after work."

"Thanks. Hey do you think you should move that ice shack behind the shed out of here before the house goes on the market this week?"

"Nah, why? It's a selling point. Maybe the next guy who lives here will get into ice fishing too."

"Well it's kind of unsightly. It's called a shack for a reason." She laughed.

"I'll put it in the barn. It comes with the house."

"Okay, okay."

Ray pulled a chair close to Sophie's and squinted towards the river. "It's going to be a beautiful sunset. I'm going to miss this place but twenty five years is a long time and a lot of sweat equity. It's time to cash in that equity and start the next chapter."

Sophie raised her glass and clinked his. "I'll drink to that. To the next chapter." Ray smiled at her and winked. "Look Ray, the first star."

"Make a wish. I will too." They both looked up at the sky then Sophie stood up and found another star above the roof of the house. "Right there Ray, blow a kiss."

He stood up too and looked at the second star and blew a kiss. "Shh, no telling. We want it to come true." Then he kissed her. "Another kiss for good measure."

After dinner, Ray went upstairs while she cleaned the kitchen. She loved grilling. It made cleanup so much easier. She smiled when she thought 'where we're going we can grill all year'.

Ray came up behind her while she was standing at the sink and wrapped his arms around her. "Hey you haven't asked about the bathroom?"

She shut the water off and wiped her hands on a dishtowel. Turning to him she said, "How did it go with the plumber?"

"Come on upstairs and see."

When they walked into their brand new bathroom, it was lit only by candlelight. The claw foot tub was filled with bubbles and a bottle of champagne with two flutes was set on a small table next to the tub. Ray's IPod was playing Dave Matthews.

"Oh Ray, this is beautiful. You really do nice work."

"I think we should use the tub every night until we leave."

"Absolutely." A live version of the song was playing and the saxophone sounded very sexy. She and Ray had seen Dave Matthews a dozen times and had actually heard them play this song numerous times, exactly like this. Ray knew it was her all time favorite.

They submerged themselves in the bubbles then reached over and picked up the champagne flutes. Ray smiled at her and toasted. "To you and me." Sophie smiled back at him. "You and me."

* * *

A week later, Sophie pulled in the driveway past the For Sale sign and smiled. Several people were calling the realtor asking about the property and an open house was scheduled for Sunday.

She was exhausted. She had been cleaning every night after work, getting the house ready for prospective buyers. Tonight she had worked late then stopped at Lynn's for a drink. Ray was golfing. They would certainly miss their friends and family when they left but the plan was to work nine months of the year and spend summers back in New England after a few years of saving. Savings, wow, could there possibly be enough money that they would actually save some of it? It didn't matter, they were moving on, moving forward.

It had been a beautiful, hot summer so far but she hadn't had any days off since the Fourth of July. She'd used all of her two weeks vacation time for the year and was earning only six hours a month, live time as they called it in HR. It would take her another seven months to earn a week off. She chuckled to herself and thought who cares? This could all be changing soon. She thought of the woman she met at the farmers market that told her to be brave. Was she brave enough to make her dreams come true? Could she and Ray really start over? No fear she told herself, be brave.

Sophie walked past the very clean rooms on the first floor. The furniture had been rearranged and a lot of the extraneous knick-knacks and unnecessary things had been removed. Lynn had helped her stage the rooms, as she called it. She shut the lights off as she passed through the house and climbed the stairs. She was so tired she didn't even stop in the bathroom to brush her teeth. She just plopped down on her bed and closed her eyes, falling asleep minutes after her head hit the pillow.

* * *

The dream began in black and white, which was unusual as Sophie always dreamt in color. As if through the lens of a camera, she watched herself sleeping on the bed. The camera panned out and left the bedroom, traveling down the stairs. It was dark in the hallway with only the pale light of a full moon lighting the way. It passed through the living room and as it turned towards the room with the farmer's table, the door to the outside magically swung open.

It was daylight outside but everything was still black and white. Sophie could see herself inside her car, backing out of the garage. She watched the car pull out of the driveway, onto her street then out onto the highway. She had now lost sight of the Hyundai. The view in the dream had moved further out. It was like she was viewing everything from a low flying plane. The highway was beneath her and she was following her usual route to work.

At the farm she passed every workday, a burst of color appeared beneath her. Everything was still black and white except for bright yellow sunflowers swaying in the breeze. The picture was speeding up and quickly passed over the town she worked in and the building where her cubicle was. From this distance above it all, she could see the Atlantic Ocean was not far from her office.

Sophie felt like a bird flying above the ocean. The water was a steely shade of blue gray and white caps appeared here and there. A seagull flew close by her side. Things started to speed up. She passed cities in the distance, a boardwalk with a ferris wheel that had bright red seats that were the only pop of color in a black and white film unreeling before her mind's eye. She sped past beaches with long stretches of sand.

Suddenly the water turned a beautiful cerulean shade of blue. She felt closer to the earth, her bird's eye view was zooming in. She was skimming along a beautiful tropical beach when everything burst into full color. Green palm trees lined the beach where brilliantly blue water gently lapped the powdery white sand beach. The water was so clean and clear she could see colorful fish swimming in the shallow water. Multi-colored rowboats bobbed on the sea.

It seemed to her she was walking the beach now, looking out ahead at a little shack lined with colorful wind surfing boards and sails. Red and yellow bougainvillea was in bloom. She entered a shady area a few yards back from the water's edge. There was a tiki hut and behind the bar she saw Ray in a multi-colored Hawaiian shirt, shaking a silver cocktail mixer and talking to a couple sitting at the bar. His eyes were an amazing shade of blue and they twinkled like the first star in the night sky. He smiled and winked at her. She blew him a kiss but kept going.

Walking through gardens with dozens of flowers in bloom, she approached a white gingerbread house. A sign swayed in the breeze, The First Star Inn. She climbed the stairs leading to a wrap around porch furnished with white wicker furniture, colorful cushions and hanging baskets with bright red flowers. Approaching the screen door, she peeked in and then opened it. Sheer white curtains gently billowed and waved as a tropical breeze blew through the front room. She saw herself behind a desk near the window. She was wearing a coral sundress and had a white flower tucked behind her ear. She was smiling.

"Hello, welcome to the islands. Do you have a reservation?"

THE END

About the Author

Sheila Blanchette grew up in Warwick, RI and attended Pilgrim High School. After graduating from Bentley University, she bounced around in various accounting jobs for almost thirty years until she found her voice and began to write. Currently she is living in New Hampshire with her husband Rich and pursuing her dreams. She still wishes on stars.

Visit her blog: sheilablanchette.wordpress.com
Twitter: @sheilablanchett

Email: sheilablanchettetheauthor@gmail.com

Sheila is currently working on the sequel to "The Reverse Commute". Check in on her blog for that publication date, and sample chapters.

Made in the USA
Charleston, SC
03 December 2012